Will C. Wood

Sabbath Essays

papers and addresses presented at the Massachusetts Sabbath conventions, at

Boston and Springfield

Will C. Wood

Sabbath Essays
papers and addresses presented at the Massachusetts Sabbath conventions, at Boston and Springfield

ISBN/EAN: 9783337369446

Printed in Europe, USA, Canada, Australia, Japan

Cover: Foto ©Andreas Hilbeck / pixelio.de

More available books at **www.hansebooks.com**

SABBATH ESSAYS:

Papers and Addresses

PRESENTED AT THE MASSACHUSETTS SABBATH
CONVENTIONS, AT BOSTON AND
SPRINGFIELD,

OCTOBER, 1879.

EDITED BY

REV. WILL C. WOOD.

BOSTON:
CONGREGATIONAL PUBLISHING SOCIETY,
CONGREGATIONAL HOUSE,
BEACON STREET.

ELECTROTYPED BY C. J. PETERS AND SON,
73 FEDERAL STREET, BOSTON.

PREFACE.

THIS book seeks to embody in the most readable form for the general public the material portions of the essays and addresses presented at the Massachusetts Sabbath Conventions; and also, as far as practicable, to be a memorial of the conventions. Some matter has necessarily been omitted; transpositions in the order of the papers have been made; the historical account of the conventions has been set at the end of the book; and, of the less formal evening addresses, excerpts only have been given of the most suggestive facts and sentiments.

These essays were intended to present and maintain — with generous latitude allowable to independence of thought — the views enunciated in the "Statement of Principles." In their totality, and, in the main, in the separate papers, they are representative of the conventions. We publish them, leaving each writer and speaker responsible for his own utterances.

The papers of Rev. Drs. Mallalieu and Alden, omitted in delivery, are given in these pages. President Woolsey's address, read at St. Louis a few days after our conventions, is substituted for the paper which — to his regret and ours — Judge William Strong of the United-States Supreme Court was at the last moment prevented from preparing. Rev. President Seelye's opening address at Springfield he did not revise for publication. Excerpts from Rev. A. A. Wright's address, "Church Members and the Sabbath," are withheld at his request.

3

A full account of the addresses and of the conventions will be found in the historical statement at the close of the volume.

The conventions will have gained one of their principal objects, should their fruit prove a volume of permanent value and power.

TABLE OF CONTENTS.

ESSAYS.

I.—RATIONALE OF THE SABBATH.

FIRST: THE SABBATH IN NATURE.

SECOND: THE SABBATH IN THE WORD OF GOD.

v

SABBATH ESSAYS.

OPENING ADDRESS.

BY REV. ALEXANDER McKENZIE, D.D., OF CAMBRIDGE, MASS.

Mr. President and Brethren, — There is but One who by right and by the gracious declaration of his goodness to men is entitled to open a sabbath convention; and he is the One who opened the sabbath, who gave the day to man, and who alone can prescribe the reason and the method of its observance. We have done well, then, at the outset, to wait with listening ears and with obedient hearts at the throne and mercy-seat of God, to hear what he will say; not that we may sit in judgment upon it, nor consider the question of heeding and obeying, but only that we may know it and do it. If we are God's servants, the followers of Christ, our one acknowledged duty is to do the will which he has declared to us.

> "Ours not to reason why;
> Ours but to do and " — *live.*

We have committed ourselves and our doings here to the will of Him who by the right of righteousness bears rule over us. In obedience to him we have liberty and delight. To the freemen of the Lord his statutes are

1

songs. In asserting his law, and bidding men obey it, we are filling the air again with the glad sound which rang out a hundred years ago in the "portentous text" written on the bell which declared our independence, — "Proclaim liberty throughout all the land, unto all the inhabitants thereof." The truest use of independence is in loyalty to the King eternal. We cannot now make all the land loyal to his will ; but we can declare the duty and honor of loyalty while we assert in many ways that the sabbath is the Lord's day.

This Convention is worthily called ; and it answers its end if, while it fails to secure this year or for many years the right observance of the sabbath, it makes, in the name of freemen and loyal men, a declaration that the sabbath *ought* to be kept ; and that, so far as we can have it so, pledging "our lives, our fortunes, and our sacred honor," the sabbath *shall be* kept.

It is a day, from first to last, of gladness. There is no minor tone in the true idea of the sabbath. There is not a sad, desponding note, not a feeling of bondage, not a sense of oppression, not an added burden, in any true thought of the day of the Lord. It is a day of liberty, a day of gladness, a day of help. So is it in the beginning : man's first day in the world was the sabbath day ; he opened his eyes which never had looked out upon the wonders and beauties of nature, and he beheld all things good, — the brilliant flowers, the majestic trees, the spreading fields ; the song of the birds he heard, and he breathed the pure inspiriting air. All was good to him ; and he saw what we some day shall see, when man's handiwork is undone, when our misdoing is displaced by the return of God's first doing, in that glad time when nature shall again be in sympathy with men, when redemption shall be complete. Then, as the redeemed of the Lord go up to Mount Zion with songs and everlasting joy upon their heads, the mountains and the hills shall again break forth before them into singing, and all the trees of the field shall clap their hands.

This first thought of the sabbath was a thought of delight. The other thought which crowns the sabbath, which brings it closer to men, and with a different meaning, is still a thought of gladness and hope. The grandest day, the gladdest day, man ever saw, was like the first day man ever saw, — the day of the Lord. It may not have been the same day of the week; that is of small account: it was the Lord's day, chosen of him and honored of him, when there came in that new creation wrought out by Him by whom all things were made, and without whom nothing was made that was made; that new creation, the new heaven and the new earth, and the new men, wherein forevermore dwelleth righteousness.

Now, taking these two thoughts which give the meaning to the sabbath day, — first, that God gave it to man at the beginning of things, at the creation of the world; second, that he renewed the gift, and brought it closer to man, in the reformation of the world, and the redemption of men, — then we have the first thought, which ought to be the middle thought and last thought in all our consideration of the sabbath, that it is ordained as a day of joy and hope and triumph for man. It is in this way that it is represented uniformly in the Holy Scriptures, from the time of God's rest when, in the majesty of his Deity, having made all things, he paused in the work of his creation, that his divine heart might enjoy his glorious and cunning handiwork, to that day when God's word was uttered amid the thunders and the lightnings of Mount Sinai, telling every wearied man, that, for one-seventh of his time, he was released from the law of labor; telling every servant, that, for one-seventh of his time, he need not be servant; telling the wearied cattle within the gates, that, for one-seventh of their time, they might have the benison of that rest which God took to himself when he made the world. In all the sovereignty, strength, law, and justice of Sinai, there is this thought of helpfulness and quietness. It is, in effect, the loving father saying to his weary child, the tender master to his tired servant, the good-hearted man to his tired cattle, My child, my servant, my horse, you and I, by God's will, may rest.

Passing from that to the further declaration of the sabbath day as read to us this morning, we find still the thought of deliverance and assistance. They who keep it are exalted; those who revere it as the Lord's day, and call it honorable in their lives, — what happens to them? Not that life becomes more wearisome, not that added burdens are given to those already burdened enough, not that they bow down under the yoke, and become the weary footmen trudging the dreary and tiresome paths of the world. They who keep the sabbath, they shall *ride*, — poor men, feeble men, tired men, they shall ride. No chariot may be theirs, no horses may be theirs: they shall ride; not along the swampy places, not through the byways of the world, not over its craggy hills or through its barren valleys; they who keep the sabbath shall ride, and not be weary; they shall "ride upon the high places of the earth!"

This, brethren, is the thought of the sabbath in Holy Scripture, — rest, relief, gladness; a time when man, released from his common work, may turn to his higher work and diviner thoughts, and, in the rest which God gives, commune with Him who himself rested on the sabbath day.

If we pass from Holy Scripture to human history, it is quite the same. History is the varied account of man's varied deeds; yet always the sabbath comes in pleasantly. It runs along with the idea of plenty and peace and quiet,

—good order, good laws, good kings, large harvests, peace with neighbors, and peace within the gates. It is among these benefactions of the best days of human history that the sabbath has its place.

If we turn to expressions of the feelings of good men, — the best expressions, more eloquent than their lives, more eloquent than our dull prose, — if we take the songs which boldly and without restraint utter the feelings of men, it is still the thought of gladness which rests upon the sabbath. No wailing in all our hymns over the sabbath day; no deploring tone. "Welcome, sweet day of rest," "delightful morn," "auspicious morn," "festal morn." It is the earnest of the everlasting day which is to crown man's highest aspirations: so have the poets sung for us the day of the Lord.

If we take it in our own experience, it is equally the thought of gladness. We go back to the innocence of our homes, to the security of our boyhood, and recall our release from study, our best attire brought forth for the best of days, and the sacred memories, more delightful possibly as memories than in the reality of them, of the time when with our father and mother we went up to the house of God, and sat to listen to the word of God. May that man be pitied who remembers the childhood which he had with a God-fearing father and mother in a sabbath-keeping home, but whose heart does not grow tender and tearful at the sanctified memory!

If we take it again as connected more especially with the history of our own country, it is a day of honor and advantage. To my mind, as I look over what our fathers have done, there is no time which seems more significant of all their purpose and the character of the men than that last sabbath which is recorded of our Pilgrim Fathers before their feet had trodden the soil of Plymouth. They had been a month on the coast, running up and down the

curving shores of Cape Cod, if so be they might find the
land and the spot of promise. Week after week passed by.
At last one Friday afternoon they deemed they drew near
a certain country. They found an uncertain country.
Presently their pilot told them he did not know where they
were. Their mast was broken in three pieces; their rudder
was broken; their sails were destroyed; they lay almost
at the mercy of the fierce winds, and the snow and the
sleet were driving mercilessly upon them. As that Friday night's sun went down, they reached the unknown
shore. In the morning they found they had come upon
an island. It was Saturday. God had shown them his
favor: the sun was shining upon them; they were not far
from the shore they sought. But they could not reach
the shore, and establish themselves there, within the brief
hours that remained after the closing of the storm and
before the dawning of the Lord's Day, or the coming of
the night which brought in the Lord's Day. There they
stopped, so near what was to be their new home, yet, in
their thought and by their piety, so far from the land.
Saturday and Sunday they spent on Clark's Island. It
seems to me that the staying on Clark's Island is a greater
event than the landing on Plymouth Rock. They must
needs land at some Plymouth: they had crossed the seas
to stay. To land and stop there, meant repose for them,
the end of painful wandering. Their declaration of principles had been made: they were exiles and pilgrims, and
it was the indulgence of their fondest desires to step on
Plymouth Rock. But they staid on Clark's Island because
they loved God, and reverenced his law. They had not
come in that wintry time, in mid-December, to lose a day
of waiting hard by the place where they were to abide.
They declared more emphatically than on Plymouth Rock
that they were here in the name and for the sake of Him
who had said, "Remember the sabbath day to keep it

holy." With that commandment in their minds, and the habit of their life upon them, they could not, would not, sail over the narrow intervening water, and build themselves houses on Sunday, when they could endure the cold and privation of the island upon which they had been cast. That persistence and that principle, the lingering there because the next day was the sabbath, — I think is grander and more heroic than the comparatively tame act of stepping their foot upon the shore they had crossed the sea to find. If I were to build a monument to the Pilgrims, one which should generously represent the character of the men, it should be on Clark's Island; where now, indeed, their daring and piety are commemorated in the living rock, inscribed by hands which delight to do them honor.

Brethren, I have said that the sabbath is a day of gladness; yet I am not unaware that it is with some degree of depression and misgiving, and because, perhaps, of misgiving and depression, that we have come together. But, for every thing that may dishearten us, there are more things which may encourage us. If there be nothing more than this, that in these busy days, and from their places of work, so many have turned aside to bear the testimony of their presence to the reality and worth of the sabbath day, — that is something to be thankful for. We say that the sabbath is broken. We mourn that its holy hours are profaned. To what extent are these things true? Are the stores open on the sabbath? No; save with here and there an exception too rare to escape notice. Schools are closed on the sabbath. In few places is there a library open on the sabbath. I believe this Puritan city is the only one in New England which has the distinction of opening a museum upon the Lord's Day. Are our railroad-trains run upon the sabbath? Not as upon other days. Men turn from their stores and offices. Wandering through the business part of Boston or New York, you might almost think you were treading the streets of Pompeii. The churches everywhere are open, and the sabbath bells break delightfully the silence of the sabbath morn with their call to worship and their testimony to the reality and authority of the day of worship. With too much to lament and to remedy, there is far more for which we should be thankful. The day remains, and holds its place of honor. Let us not forget the engines which are still, the shuttered windows and barred doors, the treasures of art and literature which are deserted for the eternal riches of righteousness and truth.

The light of the Lord's Day is spreading. Even now, upon the Continent of Europe there are earnest efforts to restore to the sabbath the sacredness which it once possessed. "In Germany, in Switzerland, and in France," it is said, "there are already organizations and thoughtful men who are seeking to banish the Continental Sunday." The large and successful efforts to introduce our Sunday school among the children of the Old World favor the true recognition and proper observance of the Lord's Day. Tidings have come from Japan, that the sacred day of that land is changed to the first day of the week, the Lord's Day. To all this at a distance let us add the greatly increased attention given to the sabbath by Christian people in our own land, and the new efforts to preserve and promote its sacred observance, and we have abundant reason to take courage with thankfulness, while we address ourselves to the work to which now we are called.

There are two lines of thought which we need to carry out in all our consideration of this subject. The first is the thought of obligation. Whether we like it or not, whether we can demonstrate the practicability and the reward of it or not, men *ought* to keep holy the sabbath day. Unless I misread these times, there is no thought which

men need more to hear and feel, whether in their private
lives or in their church and social relations, than that of
obligation. The old word *ought*, suggesting something
which I owe, and therefore must pay, needs to be enforced.
We have dwelt so much upon the blessedness of being
God's children, upon the sweet peace and reward of being
the followers of Christ, that I am afraid we have lost sight
of the fact, that, whether it be pleasant or not, we ought
to be Christians ; whether we can see the gain of it or
not, we ought to be Christians. It is obligation, first :
to be a Christian is of great advantage in all respects ;
let us never fail to be thankful for that : but I think
sometimes that the very gain is a disadvantage. It seems
sometimes a disadvantage, that every thing which God
wants us to do, it is for our good and pleasure to do. I
have almost wished, that, in the wide will of God, there
might be something asked of us which it would hurt us
to do ; that we might be asked to give up something
which it would be better to keep. We never are ; we
never are asked to do any thing when we should not gain
by the doing ; we are never asked to go anywhere where
we shall not be richer and better. It is well : it marks
the great kindness and beneficence of God ; but it is a
perilous condition to be in, because we may come to think
that the great intention of religion is to make us happy ;
but it is not : that the great reason why men should
come to Jesus is because they will have peace ; but it is
not : that the great reason why men should turn away
from their sins is that they may get to heaven ; but it is
not. The great reason why I should love God is because
I *ought* to love God ; the great reason why I should come
to Christ, the Saviour, is because I *ought* to come to him ;
the great reason why I should follow him in loving obedience is because I *ought* to follow him ; and the great
reason why I should try to get to heaven, and succeed in

the effort, is because I *ought* to get to heaven. I hope
we shall not dwell simply upon the advantage of keeping
the sabbath, and content ourselves with showing that it is
better for the laboring-man, and for the horse and the
engine, and that it contributes to the peace and good
order of society ; but that we shall take the more mascu-
line thought, and say we will keep the sabbath because
we *ought* to keep it. "Thus saith the Lord, Remember
the sabbath day to keep it holy."

The other thought, closely allied with that which I have
already suggested, is of the exceeding advantage of keeping the sabbath day. It was made not by man, but for
man ; made to help him ; made to be strength for his
weakness, and light for his darkness; made to give him
new encouragement, and therefore new accomplishment,
in the work of life. When our Lord found the day so oppressive that it was in many respects a burden instead of
a help, he took off the burdens, and left the day. I wonder we so often fail to see that our Lord's reformation of
the sabbath must have this meaning, that he would have
the sabbath preserved. Men say sometimes that Christ
did away with it. It was a very singular method of doing
away with it. It would be strange conduct for a man
with a ruined house, to put it in repair the day before he
pulls it down. It would be strange dealing for a man
with a ship which has outlasted its usefulness, to put the
sails upon it the day before he would break it up. Yet
men say that our Lord repaired the sabbath, took off its
burdens, and restored its true spirit, the day before — nay,
the same day, that he sought to abolish it. When I hear
our Lord say that a man may upon the sabbath rub the
barley-ears in his hands because he is hungry ; may do
works of charity which can be done only upon that day, —
I say this is the witness that he who thus reforms and
restores the day, restores and reforms it because he means

to have it last. It still is to be kept and enjoyed. The redemption of the sabbath was a part of his gracious work, whereby he would make every man's life richer, every soul stronger, and bring the spirit which is man into more close and loving intercourse with the Spirit who is God. The Good Shepherd gave his life for the sheep. He gave gifts to men. It is for our good to accept his gifts, and to obey his commands. Let this be remembered and repeated while we are here and when we have gone back to our work.

How shall we keep the Lord's Day, that we may honor it and receive its benefit? It should be kept in a manner appropriate to its nature and design. It celebrates the resurrection of our Lord and our Redeemer. Evidently, therefore, in the observance of the day, his resurrection should have the central place. It should be sacred, and it should be delightful. The day should begin early, and be greeted with holy song. In its sacred leisure we should prolong our communion with our Lord. We should worship him together in our homes, and go up to his house in company. We should extend the blessings of his salvation to those who have them not, that they may rejoice with us, that "now is Christ risen from the dead." The heart which is absorbed in the love of him will find the fitting method to please him.

Our Puritan fathers, so often regarded as cold and stern men, knew the joy of the Lord's Day. Their observance took its character in part, and very properly, from the circumstances in which they stood. A smoother time might have shown them softer men. We owe our liberties to their firmness and strength. The nature of the men entered into the nature of their sabbath. Yet they had their tender and gentle thoughts towards lovely things; and they came with devout and warm hearts to the remembrance of the sabbath day.

That sturdy Puritan Thomas Shepard, whose "ortho-dox and soul-flourishing ministry" was on the farther side of the Charles, has left us his thoughts, the result of his elaborate studies upon the sabbath, in a treatise well worth reading, still as fresh and interesting, perhaps, as any thing that English scholarship has given us upon the sabbath. He has described the day in the gentlest and most affec-tionate terms. Hear him : "We are to abstain from all servile work, not so much in regard of the bare abstinence from work, but that, having no work of our own to mind or do, we might be wholly taken up with God's work, being wholly taken off from our own that he may speak with us, and reveal himself more fully and familiarly to us (as friends do when they get alone), having called and carried us out of the noise and crowd of all worldly occasions and things. . . . Upon every sabbath we should be in a holy manner drowned in the cares and thoughts and affections of the things of God. . . . Such is the overflowing and abundant love of a blessed God, that it will have some special times of special fellowship and sweetest mutual embracings. . . . Herein God's great love appears to weary, sinful, restless man ; all the treasures of his most rich and precious love are set open."

Such was this Puritan's idea of the sabbath. It was a day when God and man could meet ; when man, released from his usual work, could have special leisure to sit down with God, and converse with him. "Sweetest mutual embracings," as if the heavenly Father threw his arms around his obedient child, and welcomed him to hours of holy intercourse ; as if he said, "Now rest, my son ; your week is ended, and its work all done : let us enjoy my day together, and talk of the Christ whom I gave to the world, whom you have received, in whose redemption and resurrection I and you rejoice."

How shall the day be restored to its own place in the

lives of men ? Laws will do something in its behalf ; our influence in the community will do more. But the sabbath must rise, like other spiritual institutions, by the rise of the spiritual thought that is beneath them. It is not very strange that the sabbath is not well kept. It is only a secondary part in that great fact that the world does not care very much for Christ. There is not the longing of the heart to see him or to honor him. You recall the first Lord's Day, when Christ brought in the new creation and the new commemoration. He came forth from the sepulchre, and it was his coming into the world over again. There is a gentle sadness in that single clause of the Evangelist, "There was no room for them in the inn." We do not blame those who were before him at the inn ; yet it always seems unfit that for him there should have been no room in the inn. There is a darker time than that. He lived three and thirty years in the world. He went away for three days ; he said that he should return ; and he came back into a world that had nobody to receive him. Not a man of all the men he had blessed, not a mother of all the mothers whose children he had cradled in his arms, met him with songs when he returned. Oh ! it is sadder than the coming to Bethlehem ; and one of the saddest things in all the Gospel is that a few of those to whom he had promised to return at last came to meet him, not with their songs, but with funeral ointments in their hands. Why this absence ? Why this unfitting welcome ? They loved him. They had not heard, or they had not remembered, how he spake unto them when he was yet in Galilee. It must be in the remembrance of him and of his teaching, that we honor and serve him. To receive the sabbath from his hands, is to receive it aright. To keep it in the true remembrance of him, is to keep it aright.

It must be by the love of him that we come to love his day. It must be in the obedience of him that we come to obey that precept which is from the beginning unto the end, that the sabbath day is to be kept holy, — here, in this one day out of the seven ; there, in that day which is seven days out of the seven, the day which never wanes to night, where every heart is consecrated to the living Christ, who died and rose again.

THE SACREDNESS OF THE SABBATH, ESSENTIAL AND ETERNAL.[1]

BY REV. JOSEPH T. DURYEA, D.D., OF BOSTON.

MY own view of the sacredness of the sabbath rests back upon what was essential and eternal in the primitive precept. God does not arbitrarily ordain and enact. He is always at one with himself: whatever he does receives into it his intelligence, his love, and his righteousness. If he has ever done any thing, it was because he saw a worthy end, and devised appropriate means of accomplishing the end; and both the end and the means were consonant with love and justice. Whenever the time comes that the end shall cease to be desirable, and the means suitable, then the ordinance may be revoked, the institution may come to its term. These remarks are pointed toward the common notion in some minds, that the law of the sabbath has been revoked. I simply ask, Why?

This brings us back to the primitive promulgation of the statute. God commanded that men should rest on the seventh day from their labors; but why? In the first place, because they needed rest; and, in the next place, rest would afford leisure for occupation not inconsistent with rest. We have found from an observance of this day a physical benefit: where it has not been observed, we have discovered a physical injury. We have gained by the observance of this day a sphere and opportunity for the life of the soul: where it has not been observed,

---

[1] This address really preceded the previous address, as it was delivered in connection with the preliminary prayer and Bible-reading led by Dr. Duryea, which occupied the early hour before the organization of the conventions.

we have found there has been a dwarfing and corruption of the life of the soul. God therefore instituted the sabbath at the beginning because it was needful for man. In meeting that need he demonstrated his love; in laying down the rule which sets forth the means by which the need may be met and fulfilled, he has manifested his righteousness. Does the need no longer exist? Is not the rest needful to the body yet? Is not the opportunity needful to the soul still? If, then, the ends are still to be gained, and the means are suitable to the ends, the statute holds by virtue of the essential and eternal in its propriety. God does not wilfully enact laws: he declares that to be good which he first sees to be good; he declares that to be right which he first perceives to be right. Not even the will of God is the fountain of authority, but the nature of God, by means of which spontaneously God's will is as it is. It is his nature to love; and he will seek the best for his creatures, and in his ordaining wisdom he will give the rule that goes straight to the end; and that is right, and the spirit that accepts and obeys it is righteous.

Now the argument comes rolling up like the surges of the sea, and thunders *a fortiori.* If Adam and Eve in the garden, without necessity of toil, without raiment to be wrought, or food to be prepared, or work to be done for others, under a genial clime exposing their flesh to the sun and the air, lying down under the trees of the garden, and opening their mouths to catch the falling fruit, needed to rest, surely the men of this age need to rest. And if they whose days were all sabbath days needed to take one that should be a sabbatism in the midst of an unending sabbath, surely we, who get not even a little hurried sabbath each morning after breakfast for short reading and for prayers, need one day wholly set apart and consecrated for the rest of the body and the restful activity of the soul.

Do these men tell us that we are no longer tired at the end of the sixth day? Do these men tell us that we have lived the life divine so perfectly through all the hours of the six days, that we do not need to come to a pause, and have special time for the development and exercise of this life God-ward and man-ward? Certainly not. The question then comes back, Why did God institute the sabbath at the first? Are the grounds on which his wisdom raised its foundations undermined and displaced? Because he did it once, and the reason still abides for the doing of it, there cannot have been an abrogation. It is true, we need to go back to the terms of the law, and see precisely what he did ordain, — namely, that men should rest. He knew very well, however, that the mind cannot come to a pause; that it must be active, and that the rest of the body should be simply an opportunity for a new form of mental exercise; that thoughts would come of themselves, if men did not seek them; and, having provided the Truth to enlighten us and the Spirit to inspire us in all our judgments, he left to us spontaneously to develop that form of action that, on the one hand, would be in harmony with our rest, and, on the other, in agreement with his boundless and ceaseless activity of whom Jesus said, "My Father worketh hitherto, and I work."

In coming before the world, therefore, we lay down the authority of the statute as pressing men to the obligation of resting: we leave to the conscience and heart of the individual the form of activity which he will substitute for the common activities of life. We do not propose to prescribe to him that he shall do what we do; for we do not enact hypocrisy, neither does God. It is marvellous that not one word is ever said concerning the manner in which Jesus kept the sabbath day. It is true, now and then we get a glimpse of him in the temple, and once in a while in the synagogue; but during all those three long years, and those months of his passion, how did he observe the sabbath? The Evangelists are silent. God in his wisdom has pressed authority upon us, and put us under the stress of obligation just where he knows we can obey the letter without the sacrifice of the spirit. Whenever his law goes deep enough to touch the spirit, he leaves us to the work of the Holy Ghost and the spontaneousness of the spiritual life within us.

A great many superstitions have grown up amongst us, and a great many fallacies run in many minds because we have not discriminated here. It is supposed by many that we must keep the sabbath by going to church, that there must be a certain number of services in certain forms, and that, if these shall ever cease, there will be a breaking of the sabbath.

The secular newspapers, which understand well how to instruct us in our duties, tell us whenever they see a closed church in the summer, whenever they discover a silent pulpit, whenever they learn of the absence of a minister, that the sabbath has ceased. Has Christ told us to worship, and worship only, in that house made with hands? Has Christ taught us to preach in such a place and on such a structure as this on which I stand, in carrying out the great commission, " Go ye into all the world, and preach the gospel to every creature " ? By no means. Rather, the house we erect is simply a school in which we prepare for the constant worship of the soul under the ever-abiding presence of Him who seeketh worshippers to worship him in spirit and in truth. Teaching in this place is simply the fulfilment of that paideutic office which is to make others competent to go forth, and, in social converse and close fellowship, teach the truth as it is in Jesus. We have narrowed the sphere of our Christian life, and we have limited the power of the Christian institute of preaching, by supposing that we must build a house, erect a throne for a man, ring a bell, and throw the responsibility upon the world to come to him and get the gospel of the grace of God. The commission is, "Go, and, as ye go, preach," —preach not to assemblies that come to get the gospel, but ring the gospel in willing or unwilling ears until every creature on the globe shall hear and enjoy the sound. And so very much of the criticism of those who judge us falls short, and very much of their estimate of the power of Christianity is entirely too low, for it is from the reverberation of the continuous echo of the gospel that you are to know how far the gospel goes. And, when you tell me that we have not preached the gospel to every creature in this land, I tell you that you are not free from the inspiration of him who is called the "father of lies."

There is not a man, woman, or child, on this continent, that does not know Christmas Day and the meaning of it. Yea, in great portions of this land, there is not a man, woman, or child, who does not know Good Friday and what it means. The incarnation and the crucifixion stand out from the firmament of modern thought like the sun in the daytime and the moon in the night, and only the wilfully blind can fail to see it. Yea, I believe there is truth enough in the darkest mind, in even these great cities which are surrendered to heathenism, if the Spirit only will give it light and power, to quicken in men a saving faith and living love in God our Saviour.

So then, on the one hand, holding to the spirit and shearing down to the letter as close as we may in order not to engender hypocrisy, let us stand firm for the sabbath. It seems to me, that, as I remember my childhood days, the sabbath was the brightest and the sweetest, and of all the times most sacred. The sun rose with purer light, the atmosphere breathed more gently, flowers showed their colors more brightly, and odors in the air were sweeter. It seemed as if the earth with man did feel the breath of God's love, and for a little while was wooed from sin and drawn to peace.   I have stood on the wharf when the steamboat came back on Sunday night, and have seen tired and sweltering mothers, irritated and intoxicated men, and little children dragged by the arm across the pavement; and I have said, "Is this the infidel's way of giving rest, communion with nature, and spontaneous religiousness, to the people?   Give me the sabbath of my father, my mother, my good old pastor, and my sabbath-school teacher!   Let me go hushed from the house of God, with the music ringing in my soul and the benediction warm upon my heart, to the pillow where in holy restfulness and peace I say, —

> ' Now I lay me down to sleep,
> I pray thee, Lord, my soul to keep.' "

ESSAYS.

I.

RATIONALE OF THE SABBATH.

FIRST:

THE SABBATH IN NATURE.

THE NATURAL LAW OF WEEKLY REST.

BY REV. W. W. ATTERBURY, SECRETARY OF THE NEW-YORK SABBATH
COMMITTEE.

Is there a natural law of weekly rest? and, if so, what are its bearings upon other points of the Sunday question?

It is not proposed in this brief paper to attempt to collate all the facts at hand, but to indicate their general character and the conclusions to which they seem fairly to point.

I. Is there a natural law of weekly rest?

1. The very fact of the wide-spread and long-continued observance of a weekly rest-day supplies presumptive evidence, to say the least, in favor of a law of our nature underlying this observance. No principle is better understood in historical investigations than this, — that the institutions of a people are not imposed upon them suddenly and by outward force, but are the natural outgrowth of the character and conditions of that people. Institutions which are common to several peoples or nations grow out of characters and conditions common to them all. The more widely and persistently any institution prevails, the stronger is the presumption that it grows out

25

of and expresses some want of our common humanity; in other words, that it embodies a natural law.

Now, the weekly rest-day is emphatically such an institution as could not have been widely imposed and long maintained by mere outward force or arbitrary law. It involves so costly and constant a sacrifice, so abrupt and complete an interruption of the ordinary habits of life, that, if thus arbitrarily imposed, it could not have maintained its place against the currents of every-day life, against the pressure of those wants and desires the gratification of which it suspends for so large a proportion of time.

But such an institution has existed from the earliest history of our race. From time whereof the memory of man, and history and mythology, run not to the contrary, the division of time into the week of seven days has been the almost universal law. It prevailed among peoples far removed from each other, and remote as well as near to the Asiatic centre whence the nations of men radiated; among Persians, Chaldæans, Egyptians, Hindoos, the ancient Chinese on the farthermost east, and the Scandinavians on the north-west. In most of these instances, it is certain that the week revolved upon a day of rest; and as religious rest-days, *dies feriati*, are found all through history marking the divisions of the year, it is altogether probable, that, wherever the division by weeks existed, it was marked originally by the observance of rest-days.[1]

---

[1] The Chaldæan cuneiform inscriptions prove that the weekly sabbath was observed not only by the Assyrians and Babylonians, but by the earlier primitive inhabitants of Chaldæa (at and before the times of Terah and Abraham), and was believed to have been ordained at the creation. (*Transactions of Soc. of Bib. Archæology*, vol. v., p. 427 *sq.; Academy*, vol. vi., p. 554; Sayce, *Babylonian Literature*, p. 55, &c.)

Wilkinson (*Manners and Customs of Ancient Egyptians*) shows that the week of seven days existed in the earliest times in Egypt, though afterwards superseded by the decade.

Professor Ernst Curtlus, the eminent German Hellenist, says, "The alternation of working and resting days appeared, even to the ancients, as something so primeval in

Be this as it may, the weekly rest-day has held its place, not only among the Jews through the long ages of their checkered history, but, for many centuries past, among existing nations, Christian and Mohammedan. And just as nations have advanced in civilization from barbarism, as men have come to know themselves and their wants better, the institution has taken stronger root. The most significant step onward in the march of civilization, known to modern history, that of Japan, was marked by her public and formal adoption of the weekly rest-day.

Do not these facts point with a strong presumption to a fundamental law of human nature of which this observance is an expression?[1]

2. We come to the *direct* proof of the natural law of weekly rest.

This presents itself in the form, first, of what may be called empirical testimony, — the facts of experience and observation on the part of those who are not scientific, — and then, of the more strictly scientific evidence, the facts and generalizations of professional physiologists who have made the matter a special study.

Testimony of both kinds has accumulated surprisingly within a few years past.

Laboring men of all classes, men who control large industries, philanthropists, political economists, concur in attesting the fact, that, as a rule, the nightly rest does not entirely restore the energies expended in ordinary daily labor, — that a supplementary rest is needed of about one day in seven, to maintain men in the state of highest

its origin, so indispensable, and so closely connected with religion, that they perceived in it, not an innovation of human cleverness, but a divine ordinance: as Plato says, 'Out of pity for the wretched life of mortals, the Deity had arranged days of festal recreation and refreshment.'" (*Alterthum und Gegenwart*, Berlin, 1875, p. 148.)

[1] "Antiquity has bequeathed the sabbath to modern nations ; and the fact that this institution has subsisted in spite of the changes which have taken place in the domain of politics and religion, testifies to its intrinsic value, and to its absolute necessity." — HAEGLER, *Der Sonntag, vom Standpunkte der Gesundheitspflege*, &c.

efficiency. Men are found, in the long-run, to accomplish more by working six days and resting one day in the week, than by working without such rest. The same is found to be true of animals, when working under the control of man, and not moving and resting according to the promptings of instinct as in their natural state. It is worthy of remark, that this testimony is given most explicitly by many who deny the religious obligation and uses of the sabbath, or who look at the matter wholly on its physical and secular side. Take, for instance, the very striking testimony of the radical atheist, yet acute philosopher, Pierre Proudhon, in the elaborate essay in which he sets forth the hygienic as well as the political, domestic, and moral ends of the Mosaic sabbath, and seeks to show its accordance with the fundamental principles of man and society. Take such testimony as that of the eminent French political economist, Michel Chevalier, when he says, "Let us observe Sunday in the name of hygiene, if not in the name of religion."

A few years since, the locomotive engineers of the New-York Central and Hudson River Railways, in a petition asking to be relieved from Sunday labor, said, —

"This never-ending toil ruins our health, and prematurely makes us feel worn out, like old men. Give us the sabbath for rest after our week of laborious duties, and we pledge you that, with a system invigorated by a season of repose, with a brain eased and cleared by hours of relaxation, we can go to work with more energy, more mental and physical force, and can and will accomplish more work, and do it better, if possible, in six days than we can now do in seven."[1]

As to the proportion of rest to labor which is fixed by this law of nature, William von Humboldt confirms his own testimony by his personal observation of the results

---

[1] Numerous testimonies to the same effect are given in the documents of the New York Sabbath Committee; the opinions of many prominent railway-managers of this country are cited in Doc. 35, Sunday Railroad Work.

of the experiment in France, at the close of the last century. He says, —

. . . "However it may seem to lie, and in one respect really may lie, within the power of the will to shorten or lengthen the usual period of labor, still I am satisfied that the six days are the really true, fit, and adequate measure of time for work, whether as respects the physical strength of man, or his perseverance in a uniform occupapation. There is also something human in the arrangement by which those animals which assist man in his work enjoy rest along with him. To lengthen beyond the proper measure the periods of returning repose, would be as inhuman as it would be foolish. An example of this occurred within my own experience. When I was in Paris during the time of the Revolution, it happened, that, without regard to the divine institution, this appointment was made to give way to the dry, wretched decimal system. Every tenth day was directed to be observed as the Sunday, and all ordinary business went on for nine days in succession. When it became distinctly evident that this was far too much, many kept holiday on the Sunday also, as far as the police-laws allowed; and so arose, on the other hand, too much leisure. In this way one always oscillates between the two extremes, so soon as one leaves the regular and ordained middle path." . . .—*Letters,* &c., vol. i., p. 207.

There is next a rapidly accumulating mass of evidence from what may be regarded as higher sources, — the declarations of medical men and physiologists.

Such is the well-known testimony of Dr. John Richard Farre, in 1832, before a committee of the House of Commons, composed of Sir Andrew Agnew, Mr. Fowell Buxton, Sir Robert Peel, Lord Morpeth, Sir Thomas Baring, &c. : —

. . . "As a day of rest, I view it as a day of compensation for the inadequate restorative power of the body under *continued* labor and excitement. . . . But, although the night apparently equalizes the circulation well, yet it does not sufficiently restore its balance for the attainment of a *long* life. . . . I consider, therefore, that, in the bountiful provision of Providence for the preservation of human life, the sabbatical appointment is not, as it has been sometimes theologically viewed, simply a precept partaking of the nature of a political institution, but that it is to be numbered amongst the natural duties, if the preservation of life be admitted to be a duty, and the premature destruction of it a suicidal act. This is said simply as a physician, and without reference at all to the theological question." . . .

In 1853 a petition was presented to the British Parliament, signed by six hundred and forty-one medical men of London, which contained the following: "Your petitioners, from their acquaintance with the laboring classes, and with the laws which regulate the human economy, are convinced that a seventh day of rest, instituted by God, and coeval with the existence of man, is essential to the bodily health and mental vigor of men in every station in life."

Similar testimony has been given by numerous eminent physicians, medical societies, and other experts, within a few years past, in terms not unfrequently as explicit as the statement of Dr. Willard Parker of New York: "The sabbath must be observed as a day of rest. This I do not state as an opinion, but knowing that it has its foundation upon a law in man's nature as fixed as that he must take food, or die."

There is also evidence of a more purely scientific character. Stimulated by the interest which the Sunday question has awakened recently in Europe, quite a number of physiologists have made the relations of work and rest to hygiene a subject of special study. By a careful analysis of the chief organs and functions of man, and the effects upon them of exercise and rest, variously proportioned in men of different avocations, the evidence is reached of a natural law of weekly rest. The lines of investigation and illustration pursued by these writers differ somewhat, but the conclusions arrived at are identical.

Ochsenbein (*Die Heiligung des Sonntags in hygienischer Hinsicht, von General Ulrich Ochsenbein*, Nidau, 1876) finds the physiological value of the Sunday rest in the restoration of the equilibrium of the various elements of the body destroyed by weekly labor, and the recovery of the elasticity of nervous and muscular force lost in the same way. This can be most perfectly secured by the most nearly perfect rest of body, mind, and spirit, the emotions, passions, &c. By means of rest we supply a deficiency of oxygen, and by means of albuminous food supply a loss of flesh and fat, and thus at the same time restore the power of tension (*Spannkraft*) of the muscles. Laborers, who with hard labor join a poor diet deficient in nitrogen, instinctively crave on Sundays better food, and choose a piece of meat, or other food containing nitrogen. Various tables are presented showing the result of experiments with men under different circumstances of labor, rest, and food, confirming his views. The physiological effects of a neglect of the Sunday rest are a general emaciation of body, loss of nervous and muscular elasticity, the retardation of the various vegetative functions of the system, and a general discomfort; the chyle loses its due proportion of fluid and solid constituents, while on the whole the fibrous tissues increase, and the adipose and mineral elements (e.g., lime in the bone) diminish; the blood becomes more watery, the pulse slower and weaker, the secretions impeded, and digestion and other processes impaired; and the system is predisposed to disease, and an easy prey to epidemics.

The author holds that the frequency of the periodic rest is not precisely determinable on purely physiological and hygienic grounds. The precise seventh-day proportion he would rest on historical, social, economical, as well as religious grounds. To the objection that the Chinese and Japanese, comprising so large a part of the human family, are very industrious, yet have no regularly recurring rest-day, he replies, that the Sunday rest has become by so long observance a second nature to the more highly civilized and more finely organized western nations, and that the former have numerous holidays by which the need of bodily rest is in a measure met.

Another treatise which discusses the question also from a purely scientific standpoint is by Dr. Paul Niemeyer, professor of hygiene in the University of Leipsic (*Le Repos Dominical, au point de vue hygiénique,* Paris, 1876). In his introduction he says, "If the author of this work does not deceive himself, he has exhibited for the first time the medical reasons which demonstrate the necessity of the Sunday rest in a manner as certain as other reasons demonstrate the necessity of disinfection in case of an epidemic, or vaccination in case of smallpox."

It is impossible to give, in the brief space at our command, any satisfactory summary of this interesting discussion of Niemeyer's. He makes a careful and minute analysis of the organic movement of the human body and its various effects, and the compensating and restorative effects of rest and change, the sum total of which he describes as the restoration of the natural elasticity, physical and moral.[1] In respect to the proportion of rest to labor, he refers to the Mosaic legislation, and to the significance which Pythagoras attached to the number seven in the human functions. He goes on to say that "a medical philosopher, Cabanis, has established theoretically a like significance for medical tests; and modern medicine has found by very exact methods that the fluctuations of the heat of the body, that criterion of good or bad health, move in a cycle of seven days. Proudhon himself, who practised neither religion nor medicine, arrived at the

---

[1] A curious and interesting analogy is found in a law of fatigue and refreshment in iron and other metals, as announced by Professor Egleston of the Columbia College School of Mines, New York, at a late meeting of the American Institute of Mining Engineers at Montreal. His investigations show, as he claims, that iron, &c., subjected to force or heat (as in machinery, railways, &c.), undergoes a change of deterioration, from which it recovers by rest. He does not affirm any ascertained proportion between the amounts or periods of service and recovery.

same result, when he said, 'Shorten the week by a single day, and the labor bears too small a proportion to the rest; lengthen the week to the same extent, and labor becomes excessive. Establish every three days a half-day of rest, and you increase by a fraction the loss of time, while in severing the natural unity of the day you break the numerical harmony of things. Accord, on the other hand, forty-eight hours of rest after twelve consecutive days of toil, you kill the man with inertia after having exhausted him with fatigue.'" Niemeyer then shows that his own investigations lead him to the same proportion. He sums up his argument by saying, "If religion calls the seventh day 'the day of the Lord,' the hygienist, for the reasons I have exhibited, will call Sunday 'the day of man.'"

Dr. Haegler of Bale (*Der Sonntag, vom Standpunkte der Gesundheitspflege,* etc.) follows a somewhat similar course of argument and illustration, and shows how the conditions of our modern civilization make this law of weekly rest the more imperious. Noting the intimate relation of the soul and the body, he emphasizes the importance to the bodily health of the normal development of the sensibility, the imagination, the will; on which development the Sunday rest exerts a marked effect. He uses with effect the evidence of this law which the superior vitality of the Jewish race furnishes.[1] By the following simple diagram he exhibits the expenditure and partial recovery of the forces in the ordinary daily labor and nightly rest, and

---

[1] Richardson in his work, Diseases of Modern Life, gives data which prove conclusively the remarkable superior vitality of the Jews. He says that, "from some cause or causes, this race presents an endurance against disease that does not belong to other portions of the civilized communities among whom its members dwell." The average life of the Jews, according to the German statistics cited by him, is eight or ten years longer than that of their non-Jewish neighbors. Richardson ascribes this to the greater "soberness of life," the better physical conditions of the Jews; but the physical condition of the Jews is not in any such proportion superior to that of the non-Jewish races of Europe, except as connected with their characteristically strict observance of the sabbath.

the need and effect of the supplementary rest of Sunday,
to maintain them at the level of highest efficiency.

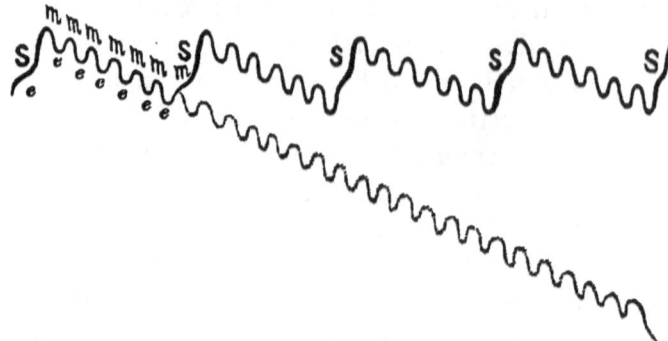

EXPLANATION. — *m*, morning; *e*, evening; S, Sunday. Beginning on Monday morning,
each downward stroke marks the daily expenditure of energy, and the upward stroke the
nightly recovery, which does not rise quite to the height of the previous morning; so that there
is a gradual decline during the week, which only the prolonged rest of Sunday repairs. The
dotted line shows the continuous decline of the forces when they are not renewed by the weekly
rest.

Our attention has been confined, thus far, to the physical and mental nature of man. But man has also a spiritual nature. It is subject to natural law ; or, rather,
whatever is a natural law for man must respect as well his
spiritual being, must be adapted to his needs and conditions as such. The evidence in this direction, of the
natural law of weekly rest, is given abundantly by the
religious history of man. Indeed, there are few who profess to pay any regard to the wants of their spiritual
natures, who are not ready to set their own hands to the
testimony of one who was regarded as holding lax views
of the sabbath, — the late F. W. Robertson of Brighton,
— when he said, —

. . . " I am more and more sure by experience that the reason for
the observance of the sabbath lies deep in the everlasting necessities
of human nature, and that, as long as man is man, the blessedness of
keeping it not as a day of rest only, but as a day of spiritual rest, will
never be annulled. . . .

" For the sabbath was made for man. God made it for men in a
certain spiritual state, because they needed it. The need, therefore,

is deeply hidden in human nature. He who can dispense with it must be holy and spiritual indeed. And he who, still unholy and unspiritual, would yet dispense with it, is a man who would fain be wiser than his Maker. We, Christians as we are, still need the law, both in its restraints, and in its aids to our weakness. . . .

" I certainly do feel by experience the eternal obligation, because of the eternal necessity, of the sabbath. The soul withers without it: it thrives in proportion to the fidelity of its observance." — *Life*, Boston, 1865, vol. i. p. 248 ; *Serm.*, 2d series, p. 205.

The argument has been presented in the form of a syllogism, by Professor E. H. Plumptre, thus : —

"What the Christian society has accepted everywhere, and in all ages (obviously eccentric departures from the rule excepted), may legitimately be regarded as essential to the Christian life ;

" The religious observance of the Lord's Day has been so recognized :

"Therefore the religious observance of the Lord's Day may legitimately be regarded as essential to the Christian life." — *Contemporary Review*, vol. i. p. 168.

Montalembert presented the argument in yet briefer form : " There is no religion without worship, and there is no worship without the sabbath."

There is another branch of inquiry, — the evidence of a natural law of rest for man in society, the family, the community, the state, — into which our limits will not permit us to enter.

II. Having thus indicated the evidence in favor of a natural law of weekly rest, furnished by experience and science, we come to the second inquiry proposed, viz., the bearings of this law upon other points of the Sunday question. As these points are each separately discussed in other papers, let us merely glance at that view of each which is given from the standpoint of a recognized natural law.

1. If the weekly rest is a natural law, it is a natural *right ;* and the state should secure to each citizen, so far as practicable, its enjoyment.

2. If the weekly rest is a natural law, then its observance is a moral duty, and not merely a positive ordinance. Whately defines positive ordinances to be those
which become duties because they are commanded, and
moral precepts those which are commanded because they
are right in themselves. Now, if there is a natural law
of weekly rest, obedience to it is right; and, because it is
right, it is commanded. The distinction between the
fourth and other commands of the Decalogue, that it is
positive while they are moral, ceases as soon as the natural law of weekly rest is ascertained.

3. The recognition of this natural law of weekly rest
constitutes a common ground for the different theories in
respect to the sabbath, or Lord's Day, which divide the
Christian Church. On the one hand, there is widely held
in the Church, what has been called, for convenience, the
Continental view, — that the sabbath of the Old Testament
and the Lord's Day of the Christian Church are two distinct institutions; that the former was matter of explicit
law, a law binding on the Jews alone; that the latter is
not matter of law, but of privilege only, or, if of law, it is
only a law of the Church, like other church festivals. On
the other hand, what has been called the *Anglo-American*
view holds the sabbath and the Lord's Day to be substantially one, the basis of law under the former not being
lost but strengthened, while at the same time it is transfigured, by the brighter light and blessedness of the latter.
Now, the advocates of the Continental theory, who exclude
so jealously the thought of a divine command from their
conception of the Lord's Day, do, almost without exception, acknowledge it as founded on a natural law of
weekly rest. But, if God has made man such that he
needs the weekly rest, it is God's will surely that man
observe that rest. And does not the ascertained will of
God constitute divine law? Have we not, then, in the

natural law of weekly rest, a divine law, vested, like all other of God's laws, with divine authority and obligation? The sabbath of the Decalogue, the Lord's Day of the Christian Church, each is an embodiment of this law. Are they not, then, one in substance as in authority?

4. The recognition of this natural law of weekly rest has an *a priori* bearing upon our understanding of God's word. All the other great laws of our nature — obedience to parents, chastity, &c. — find each its counterpart in the written Word. Each is there explicitly enjoined, with a "Thus saith the Lord: Thou shalt; Thou shalt not." Now, with the knowledge which we have of this natural law of weekly rest, should we not expect to find in the Bible an explicit recognition of it, as of the other great laws of our nature? We open the sacred volume; and there on its very first pages, after the account of man's creation and the establishment of the family, comes the declaration, "Thus the heaven and the earth were finished, and all the host of them, and on the seventh day God ended his work which he had made: and he rested on the seventh day from all his work which he had made. And God blessed the seventh day, and sanctified it, because that in it he had rested from all his work which God created and made." Is this recorded here, proleptically, out of its historical place, and with relation to the Jews alone, to give divine indorsement to a ceremonial and municipal Jewish institution? Or is it not, rather, just what it appears to be, and what in some form we should have expected, — a divine recognition of this great law which God had already imposed on the nature of man, of the whole race, sanctioning it in some sense by his own example, and, by making it a memorial of himself as the great Creator, lifting it above the sphere of a merely physical law, and making its observance a spiritual sacrament as well?

And this law of weekly rest remains unrepealed, unchanged, when, for reasons of a moral expediency, under the New Testament, it is reckoned no longer as the last, but as the first, day of the week; and when, in addition to its spiritual sanction as a memorial of the creation, it bears a yet higher significance as a memorial of the new creation, the redemption of man.

5. Our knowledge of the natural law of weekly rest has a bearing upon the question as to how the law of the sabbath or Lord's Day is to be kept, — upon the *casuistry* of the Sunday question.

The law, so far as stated in the Bible, is very brief in terms: — Six days thou shalt labor, one day thou shalt rest. The Jews, who perhaps knew little of any natural law in the matter, were guided in the practical application of the command by sundry specific rules. How, under the gospel and in the absence of specific rules, shall the command be understood and applied? Our Lord, when this question of the mode of sabbath observance came before him, asserted the truth, "The sabbath is made for man," — for man's benefit and use, — clearly implying that man needed it, that it is adapted to man's wants. In other words, he affirmed the natural law of the sabbath. So he teaches us how we are to obey the command. Keep it in such a way as best to secure the benign ends for which it was given, — rest and refreshment for the body and the soul, under those limitations of necessity and mercy which apply to all ordinances made for man.

In closing this brief and necessarily incomplete discussion of the natural law of weekly rest, it should be remembered that the obligation to obey any revealed law of God does not depend on our understanding of the reasons for it; and that any light which comes to us, as to the natural grounds of a command, while it makes our obedience the more intelligent, should make it none the less implicit.

PHYSICAL, INTELLECTUAL, AND ECONOMIC ADVANTAGES OF THE SABBATH.

BY REV. JOSEPH COOK, OF BOSTON.

(Read by Rev. Professor J. W. Churchill, of Andover Theological Seminary.)

INFIDEL France, during her Revolution, while opposing Christianity with merciless hatred, and abolishing the Christian calendar, yet made provision for a periodic day of rest, and enforced its observance by law. An enactment of 17 Thermidor, An. VI., required the public offices, schools, workshops, and stores to be closed, and prohibited sales, except of eatables and medicines, and public labor, except in the country during seedtime and harvest. This action of a secularized anti-Christian republic is a sufficient reply to any who think Sunday laws are demanded only by the Christian prejudices of modern civilized nations. The French legislation required rest for the population on only one day in ten, but it recognized emphatically the great natural law of periodicity in its application to labor and repose. The black, far-flapping Gehenna-wings of the French Revolution, flying through history as a bat through a parlor at night, and putting out the candles, left the taper of a legalized day of rest still shining.

It is now two hundred years since Great Britain placed on her statute-books a law providing that "no tradesman, artificer, workman, laborer, or other person whatsoever, shall do or exercise any worldly labor, business, or work of their ordinary callings, upon the Lord's Day or any part thereof, works of necessity and charity only excepted." This is the language of an enactment of the 29th of

Charles II., 1678. It is yet the basis of British and American Sunday laws. The physical and economic advantages of a weekly day of rest support it as a civil institution among eighty millions of English-speaking people, embracing the two most free, wealthy, industrious, and powerful nations of the globe.

It is fifteen hundred years since Constantine put into execution the law which brought an unwonted hush one day in seven to all industry in the Roman dominion. Ten centuries from the time when Christianity closed her chief political struggles, the United States — a republic built chiefly by Christianity, and governing more square miles than Cæsar ever ruled over — calls peace to the industries of her continental domain one day in seven, and sends nine millions of her population — one in five — to a World's Fair, and shuts its doors every Sunday.

What are the great industrial and economic advantages of a weekly day of rest, which have preserved Sunday as a civil institution, under the law of the survival of the fittest, through all the changes and turmoil since Constantine?

At the Dublin meeting of the British Association for the Advancement of Science, on the 4th of September, 1857, Mr. Bianconi, to whom Ireland is greatly indebted for establishing and maintaining its system of public cars, presented in a scientific paper the results of his extensive experience. "I found," he said, "that I could work a horse with more advantage eight miles a day for six days, than six miles a day for seven days; and therefore I discovered that by *not* working on Sunday I made a saving of twelve per cent." This mathematical statement of the commercial value of piety extorted a laugh from the men of science; but the application of arithmetic to the solution of the problem of the right arrangement of work and rest for man and beast is neither ridiculous nor unimportant.

Suppose that an operative in a mill, a farmer at his plough, a clerk behind his counter, and a student at his desk, are taken as representatives of society at large, and given their choice either to work ten hours a day for six days of the week, and rest the seventh day, or to work eight and a half hours a day for seven days, and have no rest-day. In the former case they would work sixty hours a week, and in the latter slightly less; but I venture to affirm that each of the four would choose the former alternative, and be justified by experience in doing so. When a man must work sixty hours a week, what are the reasons which make it wise for him to labor for six days and do all his work, and rest the seventh, rather than to divide the labor equally between the seven days?

1. Monotony in toil is not broken up when the seventh day must contain as much labor as either of the preceding six days.

2. Without the breaking-up of the monotony of labor, there can be no adequate rest.

3. Without adequate rest, the pace and speed of labor soon slacken.

4. Lashed forward monotonously, without proper rest in their work, the brain and body fall into disease.

5. Productive power is therefore, by unalterable natural law, dependent for its highest efficiency on periodic rest of such length and frequency as will break up the monotony of toil, and maintain the physical and mental elasticity of the laborer.

It is very significant, that while sixty hours of labor may not be too much for body or brain, if performed on six days of the week, and followed by a day of rest, the same number of hours of labor, if distributed equally through the seven days, may ruin both body and brain. It is chiefly this physiological and arithmetical fact which has preserved Sunday as a civil institution since Constantine.

Coleridge said that God gives civilization, in its Sundays, fifty-two springs a year.

In Switzerland, recent legislation grants to all railroad employees and government officials the concession of at least one Sunday in every three.

Two drovers start from Ohio together for Philadelphia. One drives Sundays, and the other does not. The latter passes the former, and is two days ahead in the market.

After a Continental Sunday comes a Continental blue Monday. It is very common in France and Germany and even in England, among the lower class of operatives, for Monday to be an idle day, on account of the necessity of obtaining recuperation after the dissipations of Sunday. Let us have the Parisian or Continental Sunday, and our trades will have the Continental unproductive Monday. "Operatives are perfectly right," said John Stuart Mill, "in thinking that, if all worked on Sunday, seven days' work would be given for six days' wages." Manufacturers abroad often affirm that American operatives can well demand higher prices than the Continental, because they are not incapacitated for work on Monday by the necessity of getting rid of the effects of Sunday's dissipation.

In portions of California, however, the days of the week yet are, Tuesday, Wednesday, Thursday, Friday, Saturday, Picnic Day, Blue Monday. It is simply a question of the distribution of hours of labor and rest, whether a man works sixty hours a week, and has a jaded, unproductive Monday, or the same number of hours, and has an elastic Monday. This is the large magic of periodicity, the industrial sorcery of mere arithmetical distribution of hours. The law by which these results are effected is written in the very constitution of man, and will not soon be repealed, nor even modified, by either capitalists or trades-unions.

Safe popular freedom consists of four things, and cannot be compounded out of any three of the four, — the diffusion of liberty, the diffusion of intelligence, the diffusion of property when it is earned, and of the opportunity to earn it, and the diffusion of conscientiousness. In the latter work the Church is the chief agent, and her most important instrumentality is the Sunday. Goldwin Smith very justly says that it is the freedom of religion and the educating power of Sundays which explain the average prosperity of America.

There can be no diffusion of conscientiousness adequate to protect society from danger under universal suffrage, unless a day is set apart for the periodical moral and religious instruction of the masses. Sunday laws are justified in a republic by the right of self-preservation. The Sunday is the only adequate teacher of political sanity. It is the poor man's day of rest. The enemy of laws providing opportunity for the religious instruction and the physical rest of society is the enemy of the working masses. Among the enemies of the masses, therefore, are to be reckoned railroads that break Sunday laws; Sunday theatres and public amusements; the opponents of the laws for closing rumshops on Sundays; immigrants who favor the Parisian Sunday; churches, Romish or Protestant, that turn half of Sunday into a holiday; and secularists who would abolish all Sunday laws.

Working-men desire to build co-operation up into a palace for the protection of themselves and their children, and God speed their effort to defend their own! But how can co-operation succeed without the large confidence of man in man? And how can that come without the moral culture given by the right use of Sundays? Co-operation and the allied schemes for the benefit of labor fail in a majority of cases, because men are not honest. How are men to be made honest without a time set apart for moral and religious culture? *The population which habitually neglects the pulpit, or its equivalent, one day in seven, can ultimately be led by charlatans, and will be.* Give America, from sea to sea, the Parisian Sunday, and in two hundred years all our greatest cities will be politically under the heels of the feather-heads, the roughs, the sneaks, and the money-gripes. Abolish Sunday and the social health it fosters, and in less than a century the conflict between capital and labor would issue here in petroleum fire-bottles. Capital in our great municipalities is fleeced now to the skin. Does it wish such political disorder to spring up as shall cut it through the cellular integument to the quick? If it does, let capital abolish Sunday.

I am no fanatic, I hope, as to Sunday; but I look abroad over the map of popular freedom in the world, and it does not seem to me accidental that Switzerland, Scotland, England, and the United States, the countries which best observe Sunday, constitute almost the entire map of safe popular government.

Hallam says that European despotic rulers have cultivated, as Charles II. did in the day of the "Book of Sports," a love of pastime on Sundays, in order that the people might be more quiet under political distresses. "A holiday sabbath is the ally of despotism." Wherever either the Romish or the Parisian Sunday has prevailed for generations, it has made the lives of peasant populations a prolonged childhood.

An important distinction exists between Sunday observance as a *religious* ordinance and as a *civil* institution. American courts, while enforcing the Sunday laws, disclaim interference with religion. They base these laws on various secular grounds, among which are the right of all classes to rest, so far as practicable, on one day in seven; the right to undisturbed worship on the day set apart for this purpose by the great majority of the people; the decent respect which should be paid to the institutions of the people; the value to the state of the weekly rest-day, as a means of that popular intelligence and morality on which free institutions depend for their maintenance.

The Supreme Court of New York, in sustaining one of the Sunday laws, says, "The act complained of here compels no religious observance, and offences against it are punishable not as sins against God, but as injurious to and having a malignant influence on society. It rests upon the same foundation as a multitude of other laws upon our statute-book, — such as those against gambling, lotteries, keeping disorderly houses, polygamy, horse-racing."

The action of the State as to Sunday laws proceeds upon the principle that the liberty of rest for each depends on a law of rest for all.

A peculiar Christian law, you say, justifies Sunday observance in this country. A peculiar Christian law justifies monogamy; and we have lately had a decision, from the Supreme Court itself, that polygamy can be opposed under the law of this nation. Monogamy is a distinctively Christian institution; and if, according to the highest authority known to our courts, we have a right to oppose polygamy, and uphold monogamy, we are in that doing something as distinctively Christian as we are when we uphold fair, tolerant Sunday laws. If you attack the latter, I point you to our judicial decision as to the former, and tell you that the United States are, after all, based politically upon the foundations not of the French, but of American, republicanism. Not Mirabeau, not the leaders of the reign of terror, are our prophets in America; but Washington and Adams and Madison, and the men who so founded New England upon moral training that property can be safely diffused here.

Lift an archipelago above the sea, and it is no longer a set of separate islands, but a single mass of firm land.

Lift the warring interests of classes out of the sea of
selfishness, and the solidity of society is secured. In
Mrs. Stowe's " Poganuc People," class prejudices fade out
of New England towns only during a religious revival. I
have seen factory proprietors, managers, and operatives
sitting side by side on the floor in the same aisle in an
overcrowded church, and singing psalms from the same
book, when a few weeks previously they had been almost
ready to draw knives, and use them on each other's
throats.

When our fathers on Clark's Island, on the Massachusetts coast, rested on their first sabbath day, they were setting an example which the industrial, economic, intellectual, and political, as well as the religious experience, of
civilized nations for ten centuries had shown to be a wise
one ; and this verdict of history has now been confirmed
by two and a half centuries more of experience on our
own soil. It is to experience that the friends of the
sabbath as a _civil_ institution may confidently make their
appeal.

Many men now alive have slept in houses with unbolted
doors in the country-side of New England fifty years ago.
If we wish to restore to public and private life that sweet
security, and to industrial life that peace, which filled New
England when she had a sabbath worthy of the name, we
must imitate the hallowed Sundays of our fathers. I look
back to the moonlight dropping through the open doors of
New England country homes in the midnights of fifty
or eighty years ago, and find in that unsuspicious radiance,
and in the religious culture, the united citizenship, the
theocratic brotherhood, which lay beneath it, the pillar
of fire, and the only pillar of fire, that can lead us out of
communism and socialism and the political dangers of
universal suffrage.

THE SABBATH A NECESSITY TO ALL FORMS OF SOCIAL REGENERATION.

BY REV. J. O. PECK, D.D., OF BROOKLYN, N.Y.

In the dark days of 1863, Dr. Robert J. Breckenridge of Kentucky wrote a patriotic letter to the Hon. Robert C. Winthrop of Massachusetts, dated June 25, bearing this pregnant passage: "In past years I have spoken freely in disapprobation of much that has been felt as an evil influence from New England, as it appeared to me. But I never doubted — and now less than ever — that the roots of whatever produces freedom, equality, and high civilization are more deeply set in New England than in any other equal population on the face of the earth."

This generous and merited compliment — if still merited — imposes upon New England, and upon Massachusetts as the informing genius of New England, the heroic responsibility of making on her soil the Thermopylæ and Spartan defence of the Christian sabbath, which is one of the chief sources of her freedom, equality, and high civilization, and of resisting the infidel hordes which would break through her sacred gates, and trample under their vandal feet the welfare, the social order, the morality, the religion, and the prophetic hopes of man. And the Massachusetts sabbath conventions are the sign and pledge that New England is aroused and armed, and sworn to defend the sacred pass against the ruthless invaders, with a zeal and moral heroism kindled at the altar-fires of her early defence of civil liberty in a Christian state, and her later devotion to the overthrow of slavery and intemperance. She is in line of battle *again* with the moral forces of the universe; and she is marching *again* to victory under the banner and leadership of the Lord of hosts. The conscience of Christian public sentiment has been quickened in many directions, and will soon take the field in full strength. The encroachments upon and desecrations of the Christian sabbath have shown us too tardily that the Philistines are upon us. The Sunday excursions by rail and steamboat, the revelry and riot of beer-gardens, the godless sacred concerts on Sunday evenings, the indefensible camp-meeting trains on Sunday, indicate the breaches in the wall, summon us to their repair, and to the defence of the citadel of the Christian sabbath.

But the discrete phase of the sabbath question assigned me — "the sabbath a necessity to all forms of social regeneration" — demands a few

DEFINITIONS.

1. *Society* is the union of many individuals in a common interest.

2. *Regeneration* is the act of forming into a new and better state.

3. *Social Regeneration* is the remoulding of society into a better state.

4. *The Sabbath* is a weekly holy-day, divinely instituted, consecrated to physical and intellectual rest and to religious devotion.

5. *The Civil Sunday* is a police regulation of the state for the preservation of social order, public morals, and civic welfare. The state cannot enforce the religious observance of the sabbath; but it can prohibit the desecration of the civil Sunday by disquiet, disorder, dissipation, and demoralizing influences that undermine the peace and prosperity and protection of society.

ORIGIN OF THE SABBATH.

The sabbath — a weekly uniform day of rest and religious observance — was instituted of God in Eden, and hallowed by his blessing. It is pre-eminently a religious institution. Holiness is the essential atmosphere of the day. It is God's benediction, not bondage, on the world. Next to the family, it is the oldest institution established of God for the good of man. It is fundamental, imperative, and perpetual, like the marriage relation, — the two great unchanged and unchangeable institutions saved to man from the ruin of Paradise. The necessity of the sabbath continues parallel with the necessity of the family. The one can no more be abrogated without involving the moral disorder, degeneracy, and degradation of society, than the other. The sabbath was made *for* man in the same high sense that the family was made for man. It is a colossal institution, wide as humanity, perpetual as time, and deeply rooted in the constitution of man's nature, like the sunless pillars of the mountains in the heart of the earth, so that the body, brain, and soul of man are penetrated by the law of the sabbath to that degree that to uproot the day of rest would tear up society by the roots.

It is as truly a law of man's nature as it is a religious institution, and is enjoined upon man's observance because it is a natural law of his highest welfare. I say it reverently, that God himself could not abolish the weekly day of rest without violence to man's physical, intellectual, and moral needs. Every weary body and tired brain and uncomforted soul, harnessed in the everlasting, unresting treadmill of work and wear and waste, for three hundred and sixty-five days per year, would rightfully protest against the injustice and cruelty of abolishing the day of rest, which is as necessary to man as the night is for sleep.

NEVER ABROGATED.

And this sabbath which God made for man at Eden has never been abrogated nor modified in substance, and never can be annulled unless man's original, constitutional nature and needs are changed. It is a necessity of man and society to-day as much as in the beginning.

We find this sabbath in existence before the giving of the Decalogue; since, some weeks preceding that, the Israelites were prohibited gathering manna on the sabbath day. That it was unmentioned during the lives of the patriarchs, no more argues its non-existence than the fact that it is unmentioned in the books of Joshua, Judges, First and Second Samuel, proves its non-existence after we *know* it was in the Decalogue and Jewish ceremonial law.

RE-AFFIRMED AT SINAI.

It was simply re-established at Sinai in awful solemnity not by Moses but by Jehovah; not on parchment as transient, but lithographed by the finger of God in stone in token of everlastingness; not in the civil or ceremonial law of the Jews that should pass away, but in the moral law of the Decalogue which is for all men and all ages, one jot or tittle of which, Christ declared, should never pass away. The exceptional manner in which it is ordained, "*Remember* the sabbath day to keep it holy," proves it an *existing* institute, and points back to its primeval institution. But by the finger of God it was raised into equal authority and permanence with the rest of the Ten Commandments. It is inserted in the middle of the great moral code which is in force to-day; and it would seem strange that the three preceding and six succeeding commandments are binding to the end of time, while the fourth is abolished as no longer obligatory. The Fourth Commandment is as binding to-day as the sixth or seventh.

No man can put his finger on the chapter or verse which abrogates the sabbath — a weekly holy-day — as a part of the moral law perpetually obligatory on all men.

THE CHRISTIAN SABBATH.

Christ as the "lord of the sabbath" took this rest-day with him into the sepulchre, and divested it of Jewish ritualism, tradition, and burdensomeness. It rose with him in the resurrection on the first day, unchanged in substance or obligation ; was sanctified by the descent of the Holy Ghost at Pentecost ; was regenerated and Christianized, and adopted into the new dispensation ; was commemorative of the redemption finished, as the original sabbath was of creation finished ; and was to be observed to the end of the world in the plenary sanctity and obligation of the Fourth Commandment, but upon the first day of the week by the same divine authority that instituted it in the beginning. The sabbath therefore, old as Eden, unchangeable as the moral law of the Decalogue, re-instituted on the first day with all the moral force it had on the seventh, by the same divine and apostolic authority which established the Christian dispensation, is so woven into the texture of Christianity, — indeed, is such an integral and essential constituent of the Christian system, — that to weaken the sabbath is to weaken Christianity ; to disannul the sabbath is to disannul Christianity ; and to overthrow the sabbath altogether, is altogether to overthrow the possibility of the progress and triumph of the Christian religion. The sabbath is the lungs by which it breathes. Destroy *it*, and Christianity dies of consumption. To my thought the logic is irresistible : —

1. Christianity is necessary to social regeneration.

2. The sabbath is necessary to the progress of Christianity.

3. Therefore the sabbath is necessary to all forms of social regeneration.

It was because of this stark necessity that Christ perpetuated the sabbath, and explained the reason therefor, in words which, though often perverted, are the strongest possible ground for the preservation of the day and its holy observance : " *The sabbath was made for man.*"

If Jehovah *made* the sabbath for man, it was because of some great necessity. Man is the end in view, the sabbath the means to his welfare. It is a divine provision to meet his highest good, by the same infinite wisdom and love that provide food for his body, air for his lungs, light for his eye, beauty for his taste, truth for his mind, and atonement for his sins. It was *made* for man as a moral, religious, and immortal being. He always was, is now, and ever will be, such a being to the last generation ; and hence the sabbath was, is now, and ever will be, a necessity to the end of time. It was made for all men and all time. Christ declares it "was made for MAN," — not for the Jew and Mosaic dispensation, but for the *whole race* and for *all* dispensations. The Jewish sabbath is gone ; but the Christian sabbath is here in full force, struck at and invaded by many, but intrenched in the nature and needs of man, in the moral law of God, in the necessity of Christianity, and in the best interests of society ; and here it will remain by the fiat of God, and by the fidelity of those men whose hearts and heads God inspires. Society, which is but the aggregation of individuals, can only be regenerated by the same influences and moral forces which elevate the individual. What is necessary for the moral transformation of the individual man is necessary to society.

A REST-DAY.

I. The sabbath as a rest-day is necessary to the highest good of man and society. The demand for one day of rest in seven is imperative for the welfare of man. Those do the most work, and best work, with the most comfort, who rest on the sabbath. There is not an exception to this rule, in mental or physical labor, the world over. Manufacturers see that goods made on Monday, after a day of rest, are superior to those made in weariness Saturday. Merchants in London, New York, and Boston, have testified that those men have prospered best, who have observed Sunday. Six hundred and forty London physicians petitioned Parliament for the enforcement of the rest of the sabbath, or the health of the city could not be preserved. It was found, during our war for the life of the nation, that those great manufactories which stopped on the sabbath turned out more and better war-material, with greater profit, than those which worked the whole seven days. Mr. Bagnall, the great iron-merchant, declared that he found by experience that he manufactured more iron, and made larger profits, after he ceased work on the sabbath, than when he employed the seven days of each week. God puts a premium upon the day of rest. Fifty-two sabbaths in the year count on the right side of the balance-sheet. The sabbath is better health, longer life, greater wealth, more equally distributed, larger self-respect, kinder humanity, and juster application of the Golden Rule. All these factors are necessary to social regeneration. The celebrated Count Montalembert says that the superiority of the lower classes of England to those of other nations, that the extraordinary wealth and supreme maritime power of England, "are clear proofs of the blessing of God bestowed upon this nation for its distinguished sabbath observance."

THE SABBATH A MORAL DIKE.

That portion of our country which has presented the highest social condition is New England, where the sabbath has been most sacredly observed as a holy-day of

rest.   And any decadence of the type of society here has
been preceded by a disregard of the sabbath day.   Better
far that we return to the Puritan sabbath with all its rigors
and severity, than that we plunge into the slough of the
unrestful, revelrous, immoral, Continental sabbath !   Unless we want American society to become the counterpart
of European society in volcanic unrest, in social incendiarism, in immoral corruptness, and in irreligious feculence,
we must dike society with the rest and hallowedness of
the sabbath, against the inundations of foreign and domestic degeneracy.   The sabbath is the Gibraltar of social
security.   Break down the sabbath, and you break down
the levees that prevent a Mississippi flood of evils from
devastating the peace and prosperity of society.   The
workingman who assists in lowering or desecrating the
day of rest is forging the chain of conscienceless rapacity
with which in the future he may be hopelessly bound.
And the employer who through carelessness or cupidity
winks at its violation is breaking the great moral bond
that holds his employees to serve him in honesty and
fidelity.   Nay, he has sapped the moral foundation upon
which his permanent prosperity rests.

A startling statistic of the destructive tendency of sabbath disregard, in a body of men the most necessary to
the peace and security of society of any class in the community, is found in the official records of the London
police.   Of the 5,000 policemen of that city, in one year,
921 were dismissed, 523 were suspended, and 2,492 were
fined for misdemeanors ; leaving only 1,066 of the 5,000,
who were faithful to their trust.   Now, if the moral depression of disregard of the sabbath be so fearful on the class
most indispensable to civic good order, what must be its
degenerating influence upon those who violate the day of
rest without excuse or palliation ?

A DARK PICTURE.

Abolish the day of rest in imagination, and look on the picture. The shops all open, the stores all active, the manufactories all driving, the banks all busy, the mills all running, and the business thoroughfares all crowded and pushing. Tired men and weary women, unrested by a sabbath, dragging themselves to their ceaseless grinding work, and little children sighing under their unremitting tasks. Possibly a gasp at pleasure in the afternoon, and a visit to some stifling, demoralizing place of amusement at night. Everywhere weariness, disheartenment, feverishness, — conditions inviting to dissipation and debauchery. Tell me if out of such a state of things social regeneration be possible or even thinkable? Such is the actual condition of society, just so far forth as the Christian sabbath is lowered or disregarded. Upon this putting of the case we predicate an unanswerable argument for a sabbath of rest as a necessity to social regeneration.

A RELIGIOUS DAY.

II. The sabbath is necessary to social regeneration as a religious day. The command to keep the sabbath day *holy* is not an arbitrary command, but an injunction grounded in man's moral needs. Separating the day from all Jewish ritualism, all Puritanic severity, all extremes of fasting or feasting, gloom or gala-day, asceticism or dissipation, let us indicate its rational religious observance.

Man, as a religious being, owes one day in seven to religious devotion and the worship of God. The Christian observance of the day as a holy-day (1) prohibits all labor not required by necessity or mercy. This is true of physical and mental labor, and is grounded in man's constitution, as previously argued. (2) It prohibits all amusement and recreation violative of keeping the day *holy*.

Any abuse of the sabbath to godless amusement and dissipation is more injurious to the *moral* tone of society than the perversion of the day to secular business.

To keep the sabbath holy as a religious day, requires the employment of a part of the time (1) in specific acts of private religious duty. Among these may be emphasized, the study of the Bible, prayer, and devout meditation. (2) In family religion. The word of God puts prayerless families and heathenism in the same category (Jer. x. 25). (3) In the public worship of God. In regenerate society God is adored and worshipped and supplicated. In degenerate society he is forgotten, despised, and blasphemed.

When the sabbath is kept holy in private, family, and public worship, it fulfils the felicitous words of good Philip Henry, "If this is not heaven upon earth, surely it is the road to a heaven above." Such a Christian sabbath is necessary to social regeneration. In countries where this most perfectly obtains, like England, Scotland, and New England, society is found in its highest moral tone. In countries where the sabbath is most profaned, like France, Spain, Italy, and Bavaria, society is most grossly immoral. Cause and effect are unmistakably clear in these facts.

A MORAL FORCE.

Social regeneration cannot be divorced from the highest moral forces. The regeneration of society is a moral act of moral causes. The sabbath is one of the chief moral forces operating on society. Therefore the sabbath is a necessary factor in the regeneration of society.

An eminent judge of the United States Supreme Court forcibly said, "Where there is no Christian sabbath there is no Christian morality; and without this free government cannot long be maintained."

Blackstone, whose competence to form a judicial opinion

in the premises, is undisputed, covers the relation of the sabbath to social regeneration in these emphatic words : "The keeping one day in seven holy, as a time of relaxation and refreshment, as well as for public worship, is of admirable service to the state, considered merely as a civil institution. It humanizes, by the help of conversation and society, the manners of the lower classes, which would otherwise degenerate into a sordid ferocity and savage self-ishness of spirit ; it enables the industrious workingman to pursue his occupation in the ensuing week with health and cheerfulness ; it imprints on the minds of the people that sense of their duty to God so necessary to make them good citizens, but which yet would be worn out and de-faced by an unremitted continuance of labor, without any stated times of recalling them to the worship of their Maker."

HARD FACTS.

The operation of the Golden Rule without which, in its approximate exercise, there can be no regenerate society, demands the sabbath to enforce and re-enforce its recipro-cal duties. And only so far forth as men love their neigh-bors as themselves, does society give evidence of moral regeneration. Now, wherever society desecrates the sab-bath by labor or amusement, the moral and regenerating forces are always below mediocrity. Pick out the hamlets or cities, or wards of cities, where there are the lowest moral conditions, and there just in proportion the sabbath is desecrated and ignored. Contrariwise, select the most elevated, moral hamlets, cities, and wards of cities, and there the sabbath is most sacredly observed. Morality and sabbath-keeping walk hand in hand in inseparable affinity. God has joined them in eternal wedlock, and accursed be the hand that would put them asunder! Go to Mexico, South America, and Europe, where the sabbath is profaned by ordinary labor, elections, beer-gardens, Tivolis, open dancing, theatres, bull-fights, and universal carousal, and there morality is at its lowest degree among civilized nations. Immorality, degradation, and debauchery are dissolving the foundations of society. Man sinks his honor, woman her purity, and childhood its innocence. Poverty, ignorance, disorder, and crime blight and curse society. A standing army alone prevents a suppressed Pandemonium breaking forth in its horrible ghastly atrocities. The blood-curdling horrors of the French Revolution sample the dreadful state of society wherever the sabbath is abolished and religion dethroned. One such example is enough to send a shudder of horror through ten thousand years to come! And there is no middle ground on this question, between keeping the sabbath holy unto God, and its utter licentiousness. Compromise is treason. Surrender is cowardice. To fight for the right is heroism. Compromise with slavery, or intemperance, or infidelity, or any moral wrong, never benefited mankind. It is odious in the sight of God, and entails a blistering curse on society. We shall never regenerate society, divorced from the moral and religious plan of Jehovah. And the sooner we wheel into line under his banner, and march in defence of the Christian sabbath, the better evidence we shall give of our faith, and of our intelligent zeal to regenerate society.

HOLY-DAY, OR HOLIDAY.

Another argument for the preservation of the sabbath is furnished in the character of the substitute for the sacred day. If it is not sacredly observed as a holy-day, it becomes a godless holiday. That means an archangel fallen and become a fiend. It is a settled fact that men will not work seven days in the week regularly. Nature compels a halt. They must rest. How shall they use the rest-day? If not as the Christian sabbath, holy unto God, then as a carnal, irreligious day. I hesitate not to affirm that the Sunday of Paris and Venice and Madrid, and the Sunday which the enemies of the Christian sabbath would force on America, is the *wickedest day of the week*. While the Christian sabbath is the great instrument of social regeneration, the godless Sunday that is crowding out God's holy-day is a tremendous engine of social degeneration. When men do not sacredly keep the day they sacrilegiously abuse it. Hence, relaxed from the restraints of the toil of the week, they make Sunday a carnival of sin and crime. More oaths hiss in the ear of God on his holy-day, more drinking and drunkenness keep up the orgies of hell, more foul immoralities rot into society, more revelry and carousal and fighting debase mankind, more crime riots, and more murders redden the earth with blood on Sunday, where the sabbath is disregarded, than in any other day, not to say all the days, of the week. Strike the Fourth Commandment out of the Decalogue, and men will trample every other command under their feet. It is the key-stone in the arch of the Christian religion. If we allow men to strike that down, the whole fabric of Christianity will become a heap of ruins. For without the sabbath, religion will disappear, and with that will perish the hope of social regeneration. This is no idle statement that

CHRISTIANITY SURVIVES OR PERISHES

with the Christian sabbath. The Continental sabbath is proof of this. The decided profanation of the day there is attended by a hollow farce of religion. In Italy, Spain, and France, but few *men* attend the churches. Vital piety among them is the exception. The women are more under the sway of the priesthood. Pure morals, the proof of genuine piety, are deplorably lacking in both sexes. The sabbath is not a religious day; and Christianity there is but the shadow, or echo rather, of a religion born at Pentecost. Society degenerates as Christianity is corrupted, and Christianity is vitiated as the sabbath is perverted. I repeat it, the Christian religion and the Christian sabbath stand or fall together; and the regeneration or degeneration of society follows, as the holy-day survives or perishes. The positive side of this argument is no less effective.

At least nine-tenths of all the Christian work of America is done on the sabbath. Overthrow the sabbath, and you strike down all work in our hospitals and prisons. Overthrow the sabbath, and you overturn a million family-altars with their conserving mighty influence on the homes. Overthrow the sabbath, and you paralyze at a stroke seventy-five thousand Sunday schools, stop the work of eight hundred thousand officers and teachers, and orphan seven million of the youth of our land of their chief religious instruction. You turn these lambs loose among wolves. Overthrow the sabbath, and you dry up the fountain of the great charities of society. Overthrow the sabbath, and you silence sixty thousand pulpits, the tremendous artillery which God has planted to bombard the fortresses of wickedness and immorality; you silence sixty thousand trumpets calling sinners to repentance, and inspiring the hosts of Israel in gospelling the world for Christ. Overthrow the sabbath, and you poison the fountains of public and private virtue; you break down the banks which protect society in its morals, and bring in an inundation of drunkenness, licentiousness, and irreligion. Overthrow the sabbath, and you undermine the moral foundations of all that makes society peaceful, prosperous, and virtuous. Is not the sabbath, therefore, the stark necessity of social regeneration? With the sabbath gone, there is no hope for society. We must, we will, defend the charter of our hopes.

A BLOW AT RELIGION.

It is the old battle against Christianity renewed. The enemy hardly conceal their ultimate purpose. Their objective point in overthrowing the Christian sabbath is the inevitable destruction of evangelical religion itself. Some avow this, — all are contributing to this end. Purposely or blindly they are sapping and mining the cross of Christ.

The two hundred thousand saloons and beer-gardens of the land, that clamor for the overthrow of the sabbath; the liberal leagues, that demand the abolition of the sabbath so that every man may do as he pleases on the Lord's Day, and that insist upon the privilege of spreading broadcast the vilest obscene literature; the free-lovers, that hate the marriage-laws; the free-thinkers, that hiss at our holy religion; the Ingersolls, that spit their venom on the Bible that they may pocket twenty thousand dollars a year of blasphemous money; the communists, that would wrap our cities in conflagration while they riot and pillage; and the more respectable liberalists who are mere camp-sutlers to the bolder legions of the army of sabbath-vandals, — are the common enemies of the Christian sabbath, the Christian church, and the Christian religion. And in this they are the enemies of social regeneration. The sabbath-lovers are the loyalists to God and humanity, like the Union army fighting for the life of the nation, and the starry symbol of our national glory.

NO SURRENDER.

With the whole of the Lord's Day we must stand or fall. In the West — notably Chicago — there is a pusillanimous spirit to compromise on a part of the sabbath. That is treason. If the day is at all holy time, it is *all* holy time. Compromise to-day of half the sabbath means the capture of the whole to-morrow. Half a sabbath is scarcely worth fighting for. "A half-loaf of good may seem superficially better than none at all; but a loaf, one-half of which is mixed with arsenic, is worse than going hungry." It is cowardly to sit in sackcloth and ashes before the enemies of the sabbath. The war-drums of the foe are beating, their bugles are sounding a charge. They are marching upon us. Nay, they have already assaulted the citadel of the sacred day. "We must fight! I repeat it, sir, we must fight." But the only way we can defend the citadel is to fight for the *whole* of it. "Hold the fort!" are our Divine orders. Would that the answer from all Christians and good citizens might reverberate in thunder-tones over the land, and echo to the throne of God, "By thy grace we will!"

A FOREIGN WAR.

We are trying to maintain this Christian nation which our fathers founded and bequeathed to us. We welcome all transatlantic comers who propose to assimilate with us as American citizens, and to perpetuate our Christian republican institutions unimpaired. But, if Europeans propose to Europeanize America, we intend to meet them with the counter declaration, that America proposes to Americanize Europeans. It is the height of impudence for men who have here found asylum from their home wrongs and hardships, before they get the brogue off their tongues to strike at our most sacred institutions. Liberty here does not guarantee license.

American asylum to foreigners does not mean social incendiarism and sabbatic disorder. If they do not admire our sabbath and Christian institutions; if they prefer a Continental sabbath of unrestricted license, a go-as-you-please sabbath, they are welcome to enjoy it — by re-crossing the Atlantic — as soon as they choose, and that too with our warmest benedictions! But if they stay here they must cease the attempt to rob us of the holy sabbath. The claim that Sunday laws are an interference with the personal liberty of a portion of our citizens is fallacious. Insisting that the Fourth Commandment is a part of the moral law of God, and as necessary to the moral welfare of society as the sixth, or seventh, or eighth, it follows that Sunday laws are no more an infringement of personal liberty than the State laws against murder, adultery, and stealing. And the only classes which inveigh against Sunday laws and the laws of social order are those who lust for the license to break the laws of God and society. And against all such men and their schemes we must educate and tone up the public conscience. The Christian sabbath is a tree of life. It shelters our civil and religious liberties. Its branches are loaded with peace, purity, prosperity, temperance, health, morality, and religion. Its leaves are for the healing of the nation. It was God's good gift to our fathers. The heritage of their children smiles beneath its dews of life. We will never submit to see the axe laid at its root. Blending the tones of expostulation and authority, the voice of America cries, —

> "Woodman ! spare that tree !
> Touch not a single bough !
> In youth it sheltered me,
> And I'll protect it now !"

THE SABBATH AND THE FAMILY.

BY REV. HENRY M. KING, D.D., OF BOSTON.

In "The Princeton Review" for September, 1879, there is a valuable article by Rev. Dr. Schaff upon "The Progress of Christianity in the United States of America." The author having quoted the profound remark of De Tocqueville, that "Despotism may govern without faith, but liberty cannot," continues: "God's Church, God's Book, and God's Day are the three pillars of American society. Without them it must go the way of all flesh, and God will raise up some other nation or continent to carry on his designs; but with them it will continue to prosper notwithstanding all hinderances from without and within." This statement is worthy of emphatic and perpetual repetition, yet the figure may be chargeable with incompleteness. Four pillars instead of three are needed to bear up steadily and securely the great weight of a pure social system, so that no corner shall be without its adequate support; and that fourth pillar is the family, which is also a divine institution, older than the others, and inseparably connected with them, appointed to minister untold earthly blessing to man, and to be preserved as the type of all heavenly good.

It is often said that there is an interdependence and correlation of Christian doctrines, that the system of revealed truth is a unit, that one doctrine rightly apprehended suggests and demands the others, so that some theological Cuvier could, from any part of this harmonious system, reconstruct the whole. It is not unreasonable to suppose that this is true, and that the doctrines of

Christianity in this divine scheme of grace are put for each other's defence and support.

It is no less reasonable to suppose that the institutions of religion are interdependent and correlated, that they not only give their united strength to the support and advancement of the gospel of Christ, and the elevation of social life, but that they depend upon and support each other. The strength of each is imparted to all. The neglect of one is followed by damage and disaster to all. They are strands of a beautiful cord, links of a perfect chain, parts of a divine whole. God's Word would lose half its power, were there no church in which its truths are enshrined and illustrated, and no day sacredly set apart for the acquisition of its heavenly knowledge, and no family with its parental authority and responsibility and its filial trust and obedience, in which may be inculcated an early reverence and tender regard for divine things. God's Church lives and thrives only as it is nourished by a divine and authoritative revelation, and receives the support of a day regularly consecrated to its service and worship, and is held in sacred and loving connection with the home, which is its type and image. The Lord's Day will not long maintain its existence, unless its observance is seen to be based not simply upon the physical and temporal needs of men, but upon the divine authority of the Word of God, and unless there is the church which shall sacredly and conscientiously keep it, and the family which shall hail its holy hours with delight, and gather from their sunshine spiritual health and beauty. So the family, which as we find it in Christian lands is one of their fairest and most fragrant flowers, would fade and decay, without God's Word to give it life, and God's Church to overshadow and protect it, and God's Day to sanctify and sweeten it. If one strand is snapped, the cord is by so much weakened. If one link is broken, the strength of

the chain is gone. These are the four mutually supporting and all-sufficient pillars, on which rest the purity,
peace, and perpetuity of American society.

History tells us what changes the introduction of Christianity, with its beneficent institutions and its teachings of
love and equality, produced in the social and domestic life
of the heathen world. Family! How wonderful is the
transformation which Christianity has wrought in the
meaning of that word! *Familia*, the old heathen Latin
word, denoted simply a retinue of slaves, bound together
by no affection or natural ties, but only by a cruel, despotic will and slavish fear. But Christianity has filled it
with a meaning expressive of the most tender relations
and the most sacred emotions. It breathed upon the marriage relation and the domestic life; and where before was
the miasmatic bog of an unspeakable corruption, there
appeared a garden of virtue and holy affection. It elevated and ennobled the position and life of woman; it
developed the sense of parental responsibility; it threw
off the chains of gross passion and political expediency,
and wove instead the strong, unchafing bands of domestic
love and fidelity; out of the coarse and uncomely mate-
rials which it everywhere found, it constructed the purity
and the comeliness of the Christian home. Schmidt [1] thus
describes the condition of woman and the nature of
the marriage relation in heathen society: "Woman was
treated all her life as a minor: if married, the husband
was her tutor or master, as the law defined it." "According to the opinion of philosophers and legislators,
marriage was not a union of hearts: it was only a union
formed in the interests of the State to perpetuate it. It
had no moral importance to the persons contracting it.
It was only a political institution designed to give citizens

[1] Essai historique sur la Société civile dans le Monde Romain, et sur sa Transformation par le Christianisme, pp. 28, 206.

to the country." Against these prevalent views Christianity brought to bear the full force of its higher and more spiritual teachings, viz., that "marriage with one wife, instituted by God himself when he created the first pair, . . . is a union of souls . . . designed to glorify God and to last beyond this life. It is a mystery, for it is the type of the union of Jesus Christ with his Church. Thus sanctified it becomes a school of virtues and of duties between the married, for their own education, as for that of their children, unto life eternal. Each home, each family, ought to be an image of the Church; for, where two or three are gathered together in the name of Jesus Christ, he is present in the midst of them." When and where these teachings have prevailed, the Christian home, with its hallowed life and its divine mission, has become a realized fact, on which the Church has built its largest hopes of ultimate triumph, and in which society finds its securest basis ; "the corner-stone of the temple, and the foundation-stone of the city."

Says Canon Farrar: "For families in which, like sheltered flowers, spring up all that is purest and sweetest in human lives ; for marriage exalted to an almost sacramental dignity ; for all that circle of heavenly blessings which result from a common self-sacrifice ; for that beautiful unison of noble manhood, stainless womanhood, joyous infancy, and uncontaminated youth ; in one word, for all that there is of divinity and sweetness in the one word *Home:* for this — to an extent which we can hardly realize — we are indebted to Christianity alone." [1]

Now, then, what Christianity has founded and established as part indeed of its own organic life, Christianity by the combined force of its teachings and its institutions must preserve, if it is to be preserved at all. Here again history has its impressive lessons for us. In the dark days

[1] Witness of History to Christ, p. 183.

of the French Revolution, "the shabbiest page of human annals" as Carlyle calls it, when "Catholicism was burned out, and Reason-worship guillotined," when God and his word were blasphemously ignored, and religion and its holy rites and institutions were trampled in the dust, when the Lord's Day was blotted out of the calendar, and a tenth day of rest was substituted without divine sanction of sacredness, then it was found that the destruction was most complete, that the very safeguards of domestic virtue and peace had been overthrown, and that the home, that inner sanctuary of purity and holy affection, that school of good morals and of refinement, that shrine of whatever is tenderest in sympathy, noblest in self-sacrifice, and most sacred in joy, was involved in the common ruin.

Says Gilfillan,[1] "The National Convention enacted a law permitting divorce, of which there were registered, within about a year and a half, twenty thousand cases ; and within three months, five hundred and sixty-two cases, or one to every three marriages, in Paris alone. Well might the Abbé Gregoire exclaim, 'This law will soon ruin the nation.'" Moreover it is said that at that time, in the general and wicked repudiation of parental obligations, "infancy was committed to the tender mercies of State nurseries, in which nine out of ten children died."[2] A contemporaneous French writer acknowledged, "The domestic virtues are extinct." "Domestic crimes, parricides, the murder of husbands by their wives, and wives by their husbands, are almost as common as larcenies were wont to be."[3] And subsequently when an attempt was made in that country to save the Lord's Day from its prevalent profanation, a member of the French Institute wrote : "Whenever a nation fails to keep this commandment [respecting the Sabbath], Christianity ceases to exist.

---

1 The Sabbath, p. 232.   2 Beecher's Perils of Atheism, p. 86.
3 Boyle Lectures for 1821, by Harness, vol. ii. p. 110.

There would then be an end to domestic life, to family ties; and civilization would soon be succeeded by barbarism."[1]   In Spain, where the Sabbath as a holy day is virtually abolished and is given over to amusements, — the theatre and the bull-fight, — the record of licentiousness and infanticide is no less dark and repulsive.   Wherever in nominally Christian countries the Lord's Day has been neglected and profaned, the family has deteriorated ; while, on the other hand, the better observance of the Christian Sabbath, as seen in certain periods of English and Scottish history and in the annals of Puritan New England, has been uniformly attended by a marked prevalence of domestic virtue and a distinguishing purity of social life.

History repeats itself in its worse as well as in its better aspects.   The secularization of the Sabbath, which is one form of the abandonment of religion and of forgetfulness of God, will inevitably result in expelling the sanctity from the home-life, in letting down the standard of domestic morals, in opening into the family the flood-gate of worldliness and crime, and will imperil the very existence of that which, with our schools and our churches, has been our strength and our boast, — the influence of the Christian homes of New England.   The Sabbath stands as the guardian and protector of the family, with its hallowed associations and its blessed trusts, the faithful watchman who returns upon his regular beat to insure the safety of the home, and to cry "All is well."   The family, no less than the Church of Christ, needs the Sabbath to purify and sweeten the tone of its daily life, to cultivate and strengthen those domestic virtues and graces without which the home is but an empty name, and to give time for the recognition and fulfilment of those higher religious duties and obligations, in the absence of which the home fails to accomplish its divine mission as an educator and

1 See The Sabbath, by Gilfillan, p. 231.

heavenly type. He who attempts to undermine the Sabbath, as a holy day to be religiously observed, lays his hand sacrilegiously upon the altar of home. He who cries, "Down with the Sabbath," cries with the same blasphemous breath, "Down with the family!"

On some beautiful autumn Sunday, when the great wheels of busy life are silent, when the air is filled with a soft inspiration, and the blue heavens look down in loving benediction, and every tree and bush looks as if it stood upon the mount of transfiguration, it may be mere sentiment to say then, that Nature has on its Sunday dress. Nature always preaches, always worships, always is clad in Sunday robe, to him who does not look upon it with worldly eyes and secularize it with his worldly heart. To him who does, the first day of the week can be no different from the other six, and has no added glory for the blind and the unspiritual man, whose only confession must be, —

"E'en Sunday shines no Sabbath day to me."

But it is no mere sentiment, when the family, one day in seven, brushes off the dust of the toil of life, and lays aside its working garb, and, with clean and restful hands, dons its better suit, to say it has on its Sunday dress. This may be the least benefit of the Sabbath to the home. But whatever breaks in upon the dull monotony of life, brings unwonted order, cleanliness, and brightness to the dwelling, rescues its inmates for a little time from the common manual drudgery on which they depend for daily bread, breathes a spirit of rest within the walls, lifts off the load of care, attires the family in the best it has, as if in anticipation of some honored guest, compels the body to quiet, and stimulates the mind to activity, — whatever does all this cannot but elevate and bless the life of the home. The miner who toils day after day in the dark caverns of the earth, unvisited by the glad, health-giving sunlight, and surrounded by the dust and echoings of his own blows, comes up at length from his pit to breathe the pure air of heaven, exchanges his soiled garments for those that have gathered none of the cavern's dust, wipes the grime from his dusky face, and finds himself a man, — more than the spade and pick whose companion he has been. Sunday is the rest-day, the breathing-spell of the family, when it is lifted up from dusty contact with material things, and in a purer air and a brighter sunlight feels the pulsations of a higher and more spiritual life. May the time never come when the Sabbath shall cease to shed even this external beauty on the humblest home, developing its finer tastes, interrupting its low earthly care, and smoothing out its wrinkles, clothing it in Sunday hues and brightness, and bringing it into contact with the good thoughts of good men! The outward re-acts upon the inward; and the Sunday attire may be the ascension-robe of the mind, in which it rises to a truer self-respect, a higher aspiration, and a nobler purpose. A Sunday which has only this external observance, as a day of rest, order, and beauty, will inevitably impart a healthful and beneficial influence to the home-life.

But it does more than this. It furnishes needed opportunity for the cultivation and strengthening of the natural affections, those ties which bind together parents and children in a common life, which unite the different members with different personalities and wills into the unit of the family, which harmonize all wishes and temperaments, all idiosyncrasies and tastes, into the one significant, magnetic word, "home."

> "In every clime the magnet of man's soul,
>   Touched by remembrance, vibrates to that pole."

Another has said, "The rust of the world would soon

corrode the chain of domestic sympathy and love, were it not burnished at these frequent intervals of holy rest." There is no good affection so natural and spontaneous that it does not need cultivation and care, times when, untouched by the absorbing, chilling, separating cares and occupations of life, it shall grow and strengthen under the genial influences of rest and freedom. We live in a time when to large classes of our fellow-citizens the demands of business are most exacting. Daylight summons them from home to tasks which with almost no intermission stretch themselves into the evening and even into the night. The family board is hurriedly visited, and too often deserted. The social life of the home, in which parents and children meet in affectionate converse, and all minister to the common joy, may be for days wholly neglected; and the home, to some members of the family, becomes little more than a sleeping-place for a weary body and a troubled mind.

Grahame's familiar lines tell only half the truth:—

> "Hail, Sabbath! thee I hail, the poor man's day!
> On other days the man of toil is doomed
> To eat his joyless bread, lonely: the ground
> Both seat and board; screened from the winter's cold,
> And summer's heat, by neighboring hedge or tree;
> But on this day, embosomed in his home,
> He shares the frugal meal with those he loves."

Sunday is more than the poor man's day. It is the rich man's day as well, who too often finds that increasing wealth and business bring increasing care, and make fresh demands upon his already exhausted time and strength, and, while checking more and more the expression of the natural affections and the cultivation of the domestic virtues, at length take complete possession of the man, and monopolize him. The words of that eminent Dissenting clergyman in England, Mr. Dale, whose name is known and whose influence is felt on both sides of the Atlantic, find an equal application in our country, and are worthy to be repeated. Speaking of the Sunday he says:[1] "It is also a check on that feverish and insane devotion to secular business which is one of the most serious perils to the moral life of our own country. There are too many people in England [and in America also], on whose grave-stones the French epitaph might be written, 'He was born a man, and died a grocer.' Apart altogether from the higher relationships of man, it is for the interest of the nation that tradesmen, manufacturers, and merchants should find the doors of their shops, their works, and their counting-houses locked and barred against them during one day in seven, and that for twenty-four hours they should be emancipated, by a compulsory law, from the bondage which they love too well, and should be compelled to spend their time with their children and friends." By the advent. of the Sabbath, and the compulsory absence from business which it brings, man is made to feel that he is more than a mere provider of food and raiment, that it is not the fruits of his labor and the accumulations of his industry alone that make the home, — not the dwelling, however well-furnished and elegant, but it is something which the mason, the carpenter, the decorator, cannot give, — which, indeed, no wealth can purchase : it is the presence of warm sympathy, sweet affection, a life that lives in loving hearts, increases by communion, and gains strength as it is lavished, that will gild the commonest roof and make amends for the absence of many a luxury, — indeed, which all luxury cannot bring, — and without which the splendid mansion is but a splendid mausoleum, where lies buried all that is noblest and best in human hearts. The rest-day of the week comes with its divine breath to quicken into new life the domestic affections, to gather into closer fellowship

[1] The Ten Commandments, pp. 117, 118.

the family, so that its unity shall be lovingly felt and manifested, to bind all hearts together in conjugal and parental love and filial confidence, and to seal anew and anew a union which, begun on earth, should look for · its perfect consummation in heaven.

And this leads to the consideration of the highest benefit of the Sabbath to the family, — the opportunity it furnishes and the ever-repeated invitation it gives for the introduction and maintenance of the religious element in the home-life, without which that life is fatally incomplete. We look upon the Sabbath not simply as a rest-day, but as a holy day, a divine institution, a day set apart by God for religious purposes, for worship, for prayer, praise, and the study of God's word. We look upon the family also as a divine institution, in which God is to be honored, his laws revered, and his praises sung, and designed to be in some sense the nursery and the earthly miniature of heaven. It is the religious element that gives to each its highest dignity and value. Take away this, and the Sunday is robbed of its peculiar glory, and the family fails of its divine mission. Every family, like that of Joseph and Mary, ought to be a "holy family," in which the child Jesus is a welcome and abiding guest. It is only when the affectional nature, which is the basis of the home-life, is moved towards God and divine things, and into the love of the home there comes a higher love, heaven-born and holy, purifying, strengthening, and encompassing all, that the family, exalted above all merely earthly and temporal interests, assumes its true office and relations, and becomes a spiritual body, a school and type of heaven. In patriarchal times the father of the family was prophet, to impart the knowledge of God and his will; and priest, to lead the worship at the sacred altar of home; and king who as God's representative should rule in his little domain with wise and gentle authority, whose throne, whose

law, whose sceptre, should be love. Under the dispensation of Christ and his spirit, the true home is to possess a
thoroughly religious character and spirit. Husbands are
to love their wives even as Christ also loved the Church,
and gave himself for it. Wives are to submit themselves
unto their husbands as unto the Lord; parents are to
bring up their children in the nurture and admonition of
the Lord; children are to obey their parents in the Lord;
servants are to render obedience in singleness of heart as
unto Christ. The whole family is to be under the control
of that love which is the essence of religion, and which will
manifest itself in self-surrender, the sacrifice of personal
preference, mutual submission, and all kind offices. In the
implantation and cultivation of this spirit, in securing and
preserving this beautiful Christian ideal of the home, the
Sabbath holds a most important position, and exerts an
incalculable influence. By its sacred purposes and its
quiet, hallowed influences, by its larger and uninterrupted
opportunities for religious instruction and the delightful
worship of home, it interrupts the hurry and bustle of the
week, beats back the encroachments of worldliness, brings
God and truth and heaven near to the heart and life, pours
fresh sweetness, purity, and gladness into the home, and
converts it more and more into the very sanctuary of God.
During its peaceful hours, solemn parental obligations can
be more completely met, the precious truths· of revelation
can be more systematically unfolded and applied, the rest,
the joy, the worship of heaven, can be more vividly and
touchingly portrayed, and all hearts be led to anticipate
the home, the Sabbath, the rest, and the worship of another world.

> "Then kneeling down, to heaven's eternal King
> The saint, the father, and the husband prays;
> Hope springs triumphant on exulting wing
> That thus they all shall meet in future days,

> There ever bask in uncreated rays,
> No more to sigh, nor shed the bitter tear,
> Together hymning their Creator's praise
> In such society yet still more dear,
> While circling time moves round in an eternal sphere."

In the old cemetery at Nuremberg, on the monument which marks the grave of Albrecht Dürer is carved the word "*Emigravit*," indicative of his faith in the future life. God's word represents this life as a pilgrim-life. The Sabbath is the wayside spring at whose pure waters the emigrant family tarries and drinks as it seeks its other home. The Sabbath is the furnace-glow which melts all hearts into one common life, and separates the dross of selfishness and worldly impurity. The Sabbath is the great open eye of the Pantheon, which ever looks upward towards the heavens, and through which there fall into the home the very sunlight of God's love, and the refreshing rains of his grace. The Sabbath is the strong dike which God has built to protect domestic purity and peace against the rising waves of corrupt socialism and infidelity. The Sabbath is the pearly gate of the earthly type of the celestial city, open to all good influences that minister to the spiritual life of the home ; but "into which there shall in no wise enter any thing that defileth, neither whatsoever worketh abomination, or maketh a lie." In the words of another: "The Sabbath has attached to home a worth and an interest which can be derived from no other source, . . . and stands second to none of the agencies through which are shed upon us the holy and happy influences of Him in whom all the families of the earth are blessed."

I have not time to indicate, further than I have already indicated, how the hours of the Sabbath should be employed in the family. Physical rest should be joined with delightful spiritual activity, serious thoughtfulness with holy gladness, mutual love and helpfulness with heavenward aspiration and desire, confiding communion and fellowship with the appropriate recognition of God in prayer and praise and the learning of his will. The Sunday school should not be made a substitute for the home in any such way as to allow the primary and untransferable responsibility of parents to be laid upon it. Nor should the home be made the substitute for the sanctuary which God has ordained, and where his "honor dwelleth." For "the Lord loveth the gates of Zion more than all the dwellings of Jacob." Let the Sabbath bring to the home all holy and pleasant attractions: let it drive away all clouds of sorrow and worldly care; let it be a day of grateful joy and richest blessing, a day so calm, so bright, so good, that every family shall hail it with a song of irrepressible delight.

> " Sweet morn, whose light from far beyond the sun
> Breaks with a brightness earth-clouds cannot dim —
> We hail its coming with a holy hymn
> Of gratitude for six days' duties done,
> Of supplication for a week begun —
> To God upborne, whose countless blessings brim
> Life's chalice till they overflow its rim,
> And shame all wealth our wit and toil have won.
> 'Safely,' we sing, and dangers thick recall,
> That through another week our way beset,
> 'Safely' his loving hand has brought us yet —
> One of our weeks, but pattern of them all.
> 'Tis more our soul's sweet zeal than body's rest,
> That makes this day 'of all the week the best.' "

THE RELIGIOUS CHARACTER AND USES OF THE SABBATH.

BY REV. A. J. GORDON, D.D., OF BOSTON.

WHATEVER in the universe is great is God's work. We reason rightly, therefore, whether we say that the sabbath is God's work because it is great, or the sabbath is great because it is God's work. Either proposition can be easily defended. I say, "the sabbath, *God's work.*" I do not forget that it is a rest rather than a work, — that it represents God's cessation from labor, rather than the fruit of his labor. But, as the silence of the wise man is more majestic than the utmost speech of the ignorant, so God's rest is a greater piece of workmanship than any thing which the toil and skill and patience of man have ever wrought.

And yet who has not found it necessary sometimes to fortify the saying of Christ, "*The sabbath was made for man,*" with the qualification, "But the sabbath *was not made by man*"? So many reason, that, because it was made for man, he may outgrow it, as the youth outgrows the swaddling-clothes of infancy. This is what we hear constantly said; and with the assertion comes the inevitable charge, that in defending the sabbath and maintaining its restraints, we are trying to force men back into their ritual baby-clothes, and to impose upon them ceremonial constraints which they have long since outgrown; so that virtually man is seeking to remake for his fellow, what God once made for him, but which he has outgrown.

Well, in meeting this statement, that we have outgrown the sabbath, let us see what of truth there is in it. For there is truth. Man does outgrow his infant-dress. And since Christ has come, and brought the Church into larger development and maturer spiritual age, she has outgrown and cast off the *ritual* sabbath with its cumbersome rites and burdensome ceremonies. If any would bind back upon the church or the world these Levitical burdens, or any fragment of them, he is clearly rebuked by the New Testament, which says, "Let no man therefore judge you in meat or drink, or in respect of an *holy day, or of the new moon or of the sabbath days.*" Beyond all question we are done with these things, since we are not under law, but under grace. But, following the figure with which we started, while men outgrow their clothes, they never outgrow their skin. Clothes are external, and can be put on or off. Skin is internal, as well as external. It is a part of the body, knit up with its nerves and blood-vessels and vital tissues, and woven so into the fabric of the system, as well as upon it, that man would die without it. So the law of the sabbath is wrought into man's native constitution. What was graven on the tables of stone, had long before been graven on the tables of man's flesh and blood. The commandment, "Remember the sabbath day," is written in every muscle and sinew of the human frame; and he who despises Moses's law will sooner or later be arrested by a law in his own members, rising up to inflict its penalties of lassitude and pain and bodily exhaustion. Yes, men might outgrow the Jewish sabbath when the Jewish dispensation came to an end. They may, for aught I know, outgrow the Christian sabbath when the Christian dispensation shall come to an end; but *the sabbath* older than Jew or Christian, the sabbath that enjoins one-seventh of a man's time for rest and worship, can only be outgrown when the race has perished. That law is wrought into nature, not written without it. Like the figures on the potter's vessel, which are first stamped into the

plastic clay, and then baked in by fire, so that they can
only be erased by breaking the vessel itself; so the sabbatic law and requirements were stamped into man's natural constitution, and educated upon him by long discipline,
and can only be effaced when He who made the nations
shall "break them with a rod of iron, and dash them in
pieces as a potter's vessel." This principle, the sabbath
as old as creation, it seems to me, settles the controverted
questions about the change from the Jewish to the Christian sabbath. It is simply a change of dress and habit,
not of the thing itself. The primeval sabbath took on the
Hebrew vestments, if I may say so, when the Hebrew
religion prevailed; when this passed away, and the Christian economy came in, it took on the Christian garb.
The change of day was both fitting and inevitable, as the
great idea of redemption rest took the place in men's
minds which the creation rest had held before. But there
has been no change in the sabbath law and principle. The
day comes just as often, brings the same boon, summons
to the same release from care and the same communion
with God.

I spoke a moment ago of the greatness of the sabbath.
It is well for us to grasp something of its magnitude and
glory, preparatory to discussing its religious character
and uses. What majestic tree is this with roots so vast and
far-reaching, that they are found running back into Eden,
and with branches so wide and outstretching, that the whole
millennial age lies under their shadow? This is no mere
figure of speech, but a fact so literal that to him who
grasps it, the violent assailant of the sabbath seems as
puny as a man trying to level with his fist one of Yo-
semite's mighty pines. We, indeed, who are seeking to
uphold this institution to-day, are but birds defending the
nests which we have built among its branches, and in
which we have laid our young. The tree needs no defence

from us. Trace the law and development of that wonder-ful sabbatic system in the Jewish economy, — a system which was evidently designed to educate men in a great septenary idea. In the Hebrew calendar there was the seventh day pointing onward to the seventh week, the seventh week to the seventh month, the seventh month to the seventh year, the seventh year to the seventh year of years, which introduced the Jubilee; each sabbatic period thus conducting to a larger, and all seeming de-signed to carry the thoughts on to some final era of blessed fruition and release, as the successive barrels of a telescope conduct the vision onward to a star.

Turn now to the New Testament, and read that these sabbaths are "a shadow of things to come," and that "there remaineth therefore a *sabbatismos* — a sabbath-keeping — for the people of God;" that rest-day for a weary world, when at last a happy release shall be granted her from her weekday toil and pain. In the light of such sublime teaching as this, what do we seem to be doing who are trying to defend the sabbath? Are we fighting for a fragment of antiquated Jewish ritual? Are we seeking to impose some sacred day of our church calendar upon men? Nay! we are only asking that the spoiler may not be allowed to tear down the way-marks to the millennium; that he be not permitted to obliterate the guide-posts which direct our toiling and tired humanity to the golden age of its redemption.

What are the religious character and uses of the sab-bath?

The day looks ever in two directions, towards God and towards man. In the one direction it calls for worship: in the other it invites to rest. "*Hallow ye the sabbath day*," — that is the call to worship. "*The sabbath was made for man*," — that is the gift of rest. Thus the sab-bath is both divine and human; given to minister to God's glory and man's refreshment; seeking to awaken in man a filial regard for God as his Creator, while it declares God's regard for man as his dependent creature. Let us consider it now in these several relations.

First, then, as related to God, the sabbath is appointed for worship. And worship, we must remember, has to do primarily and chiefly with God and not with man. It is an act of acknowledgment addressed immediately to the Most High. Praise, which contemplates and adores the person of God; thanksgiving, which sets forth our admiration for the attributes and works of God; confession, which acknowledges the violated claims of God, — all these acts are of the nature of worship. It is that which the soul renders to God, not that which it receives from him ; and hence is first and highest in importance.

Now, if it is necessary that God's people should have rest in order that they may worship fitly, it is first of all necessary *that God should be at rest in order to be worshipped.* For the essence of worship is communion, — the sharing of a common state or condition. The ship which is embosomed in the ocean can only rest when the ocean rests; and so the soul which is in communion with God can only rest as it enters into God's rest. Here, then, is where we find the first warrant for sabbath-keeping : " Remember the sabbath day to keep it holy. . . . For in six days the Lord made heaven and earth, the sea, and all that in them is, and rested the seventh day ; *wherefore* the Lord blessed the sabbath day, and hallowed it " (Exod. xxii. 8, 11). When the great series of creative acts had been completed, all material laws established, and every independent form of life originated, then Jehovah rested, and creation gave place to holy contemplation and delight : " And God saw every thing that he had made, and behold it was very good." It is the almighty repose, not less majestic than the almighty energy, — the satisfaction of the infinitely perfect One in a work in which no single flaw or imperfection is to be found. And does it seem strange, that, immediately after God had entered on his rest, he should summon the sons of men, whom he had created, to share it with him, and to enter into his lofty delight over the glory and perfection of his works? When an artist has wrought some transcendent work, and, after years of thought and toil, has laid the finishing touch upon the canvas, is not his first impulse to invite his friends to gaze upon his work, to enter into communion with his thoughts, and to share with him in his delight over his achievement? So God summons man to share with him his lofty joy over his completed work. And, just as we might expect, much of the worship of the patriarchs and prophets consisted in admiration of the material creations of Jehovah, and of praise to him as their framer and fashioner. How much of the Book of Job sounds like a lofty " *Te Deum* " of the elements ! — the morning stars singing together while the sons of God shout for joy. How much of the Psalms, that hymnal of Hebrew worship, has its praise set to the music of nature, — the sun and moon and stars, the winds and waves and waters! The first rest, then, was the creation rest ; and the first worship was worship of the Creator, and communion with him in his contemplation of his finished work.

But Jehovah's primeval rest is disturbed by man's sin. So, in the incarnation, God is seen working once more in the great undertaking of redemption. In the toiling life of the Son of God, in his sacrificial death and burial, we see his work progressing and ending. On the third day Christ rises from the dead. Once more God rests from his labors. The first day of the week becomes henceforth the Christian sabbath, because on that day the Lord Jesus entered into the redemption rest, even as the Father on the seventh day had entered into the creation rest.

Very plainly is this set forth in the Epistle to the Hebrews : "*For he that is entered into his rest, he also ceased from his own works as God did from his*" (iv. 10). That is, just as God rested after the toil of creation, Christ rested after the toil of redemption. The story is exactly parallel in both Testaments. "Thus the heavens and the earth were *finished*," says Genesis as it describes creation's Friday night. "*It is finished*," says Jesus as on redemption's Friday night he bowed his head, and gave up the ghost. "*And God rested the seventh day from all his work which he had made*," says Genesis. "*He also hath ceased from his own works as God did from his*," says the Epistle to the Hebrews.

And now, just as God invited man to share his rest at creation, so the Son of God takes us into the joy of his redemption rest. "For we which have believed do enter into rest," says the Epistle to the Hebrews.

Hence the Lord's Day takes its place at once in the calendar of the new creation as the Christian's sabbath. His worship commemorates redemption now completed. On this day the Lord's Supper begins its touching rehearsal of the "sufferings of Christ, and the glory which should follow." Christ, having purged our sins, is seated at the right hand of God ; we that believe are seated with him in the heavenly places. All the symbols and services of the Lord's Day tell of this rest in the finished work of Christ. The song of the Lamb now employs men's tongues, and they rejoice and are glad in the day which he has made.

Thus we see that the sabbath is essentially one under different manifestations. As God is one, and yet reveals himself as the Father and the Son and the Spirit, — each person in the Trinity having his successive dispensation in the world, — so the one sabbath manifests itself in successive revelations. As Ebrard beautifully says, "The seventh day was the sabbath of God the Father; the first day is the sabbath of God the Son; and, with the future setting-up of a new heaven and a new earth, the sabbath of the Holy Ghost will begin." The first sabbath marked the finishing of creation; the second, the finishing of redemption; and the third will mark the finishing of regeneration.

Now, the one thing which characterizes the sabbath always and everywhere is worship. This duty is laid upon us by our relations to God as our Creator and Redeemer. This fact cannot be too strongly insisted on. Man's worship is a part of God's vested rights in a world which he created and redeemed; and on the sabbath day the gates of praise are opened, and we are required and commanded to enter in, and pay this sacred tribute. "Praise is comely," says the Psalmist; but that is not all: praise *belongeth* unto the Most High. George Herbert says quaintly,—

> " The Sundays of man's life,
>   Threaded together on Time's string,
>   Make bracelets to adorn the wife
>   Of the eternal glorious King."

We may admit that it is *fitting* that we should deck the King of glory with these sacred ornaments; but that is not the whole question. It is, whether we may withhold them, whether we may pawn these jewels from heaven's casket for some cheap amusement, or loan them to the Devil to increase our working-time at God's expense. That is the sin of the world to-day. The Devil's pawnshop is full of the Lord's goods. It is not enough that he should put his trade-mark on God's property, and get men to render worship which is spurious and hypocritical. No, he sets himself up as a receiver of stolen goods, and persuades even Christians to barter away their rest-days for the privilege of doing his work in pleasure-seeking or

Sunday labor. Oh, what trades men will make with God's capital! We owe to God a revenue of worship, and are guilty of moral fraud if we withhold it.

But it is evident also, that rest on man's part is absolutely essential to true worship; for worship is the reflection of God. Its aim is to conform us to the image of God by meditation on his character and communion with his person. Contact and communion always tend to beget likeness. When two persons talk much together, their words are as swift-flying shuttles, weaving their thoughts into the fabric of a common life. When two persons love each other, their interchange of affection tends to mutual conformity of character. When one admires another, and contemplates his excellences, he inevitably becomes assimilated to him in disposition and life and conduct.

So pre-eminently in our relations to God. Communion with him begets likeness to him. And this is the great end of worship, — conformity to God. So we are summoned to contemplate the Almighty, and to reflect upon his greatness and glory. But we must rest in order to do this. It is only the still and tranquil lake that can mirror the sun. No true reflection, but only broken rays, can be caught by the turbulent and troubled waves. Therefore, in order that we may remember our Creator, God says to us, "Remember the sabbath day to keep it holy." Let the troubled sea of earth's toil and tumult become a calm, that God, who has been driven from men's thoughts, may be seen and adored, and his faded image be once more mirrored in the heart.

This is where God's claim asserts itself most powerfully. Unless we are willing to shut him out of our lives, and not to have him in all our thoughts, it is a principle of simple justice that we should give him an opportunity to be heard; that we should wipe the week-day's dust from the soul's object-glass, and let the image of God shine upon it.

What deep significance there is in the words of the Almighty, "*Be still*, and know that I am God"! as though he could only be known in the hush and stillness of the soul. "*Speech is silver, silence is gold*," says the proverb. Eminently so is it in our relations to God; for silence is receptive. It is the soul's waiting and teachable attitude; it is the upturned ear which says, "Speak, Lord, for thy servant heareth;" it is the submitted heart which says, "Lord, what wilt thou have me to do?" How greatly in this age, when the currency of speech is so inflated, do we need to learn the value of this gold of silence! How vastly important, in the intense activities of this nineteenth century, that we should learn that hardest lesson of "masterly inactivity" on the appointed days of rest! Cease your noisy talking, O ye sons of men, and hear what God will say to you! Cease your work, that you may be wrought upon by Him who alone is able to work in you to will and to do the right!

Indeed, a refusal to rest and be still on the sabbath is an indication of the most arrogant self-conceit. It is saying virtually to God, "I must talk seven days in a week, but I have no need even for one day to be talked to. I must work seven days in the week; but I have no need even for one day to be wrought upon." The fool is one who not only "says in his heart, There is no God," but who is forever chattering with his tongue of his own importance. The wise man is he who knows enough to shut his mouth, and open his ears, when God says, "Be still, and know that I am God. I will be exalted among the heathen, I will be exalted in the earth."

Having said that rest is an essential condition of worship, I wish to notice the kind of rest that is essential. For there are two kinds of rest, — the rest of sleep and the rest of recreation. When we lie down at night to slumber, the whole man, the mind and the body alike, passes into repose. That is the rest of sleep.

When the student becomes wearied with his intellectual efforts, he leaves his books and his thinking, and gives
himself to some vigorous bodily exercise. Or, when the
laborer is tired of his manual toil, he sits down, and regales
himself by reading some pleasant story. This in either
case is the rest of recreation. The rest of sleep is the
cessation of all activity; the rest of recreation is an
exchange of activities, relieving one by exclusive use of
the other.

Now, such in kind is the rest to which God invites us
on the sabbath. Man is a threefold being, with spirit,
soul, and body. During the week the body is taxed with
labor, or the mind with severe study or thought, according to our occupation. On the sabbath God says, "Come,
O children of men, relax the muscles of the body from
their burdens; release the intellect from its heavy strain
of thinking; and let both find rest in the exercise of the
soul." Bend the affections to praise and adoration; bring
the spirit's powers into the exalted work of contemplating God and studying his attributes and acts. Rouse the
soul's faculties to the most intense and strenuous worship
of which they are capable, and so find rest for body and
mind in the holy toil of a worshipping heart. That is
the rest to which God calls us on his day. Not the rest
of sabbath idleness or sleep, not the yawning *ennui* of
sacred sluggishness: nay, just the contrary is the scripture exhortation. "Therefore let us not sleep as do others,
but let us watch and be sober. For they that sleep, sleep
in the night; and they that are drunken, are drunken in
the night. But let us who are of the day be sober, putting on the breastplate of faith and love, and for an hel-
met the hope of salvation." So binding is this, that I
believe that a man violates the sabbath just as effectually
by sleeping away his Sunday hours as by employing them
in work. In the one case he disturbs God's rest by his

snoring, and in the other by his pounding; and the first is more odious, if any thing, than the second. Away with the sacrilege of slumbering out the Lord's Day hours, and calling it rest! The rest to which he invites us is found in the alert and tireless use of the spiritual powers. The worship that is in spirit and in truth is infinitely restful. As "David took a harp, and played with his hand, and Saul was refreshed and made well, and the evil spirit departed from him," so the high praises of God's sanctuary, its songs and psalms and hallelujahs, refresh the weary body, and heal the tired and thought-sick mind.

Having considered the character and uses of the sabbath as related to the glory of God, let us consider it, secondly, as related to the happiness and well-being of man. For this is the evident thought in the words, "the sabbath was made for man," that God ordained and adapted the day for the comfort and blessing of his children in all time. Instead of being a day for the binding of burdens, it is a day of release from burdens; instead of being a ceremonial yoke upon the neck of man for tying him up to hard and exacting service, it is an ordinance of emancipation from earthly toil and hardship. And in this fact we find, I think, one of the highest religious uses of the sabbath. It is a commendation of God's love and compassion towards us his burdened and toiling sons. For whatever is humane in God's religion commends that religion as divine. "I know that this Bible is God's book," said Arthur Hallam, "because it is man's book; because it fits into every turn and fold of the human heart." And so we may say in regard to God's day. The highest proof of its divinity is its humanity. It is not an institution set up by God's arbitrary will, and to which man must bend at whatever cost. It is an institution, rather, which is cast in the mould of man's necessities, and fashioned to the end of his blessing and comfort. Its requirements fit the human heart, as the casting fits the matrix in which it was shaped. So that one of the most evident proofs that the sabbath was made by God is that it was made *for* man.

This line of argument was a favorite one with Vinet as applied to the whole system of Christian evidences. He contended that the highest indication of the supernatural character of the gospel is its marvellously natural character; so that the "Christian religion and humanity, when rightly apprehended, each leads back to the other; faith towards nature, and nature towards faith." But the institution of the sabbath is to my mind the most conspicuous illustration of this idea. It is God's answer to humanity's "universal instinct of repose." It comes to vindicate man from the oppressor's exactions, and to defend his cause against the taskmaster's tyranny.

Thus the sabbath becomes one of the most powerful of the Christian evidences. It is an argument from the heart of God, to the heart of man. "Come unto me, all ye that labor and are heavy laden, and I will give you rest," is Christ's message to a weary and sin-burdened world. "Who art thou, Lord, that we should come?"—"I am he that giveth thee one day for rest when thy masters would give thee none: I am he that removeth thy shoulder from the burden, and delivereth thy hands from the pots, when they who rule thee would make thee grind in perpetual servitude. I am he that saith upon the sabbath, 'Break every yoke, and let the oppressed go free,' when men have bound heavy burdens upon thee, and refused to lift them with one of their fingers. Return unto thy rest, O tired soul! For this is a statute for Israel, and a law of the God of Jacob."

Just here is where the Christian has an immense advantage over the infidel in the discussion of the sabbath question; for the plea which he makes for Christianity is at the same time a plea for humanity.

In a recent anti-sabbath convention held in this city, I heard several well-known free-thinkers appealing vehemently to the people to rise up against the tyranny of Sunday laws and restrictions. "Let the day be as free as any other," they demanded. "Let the cars and steamboats run *ad libitum*, for conveying the tired people on excursions into the fields and upon the waters. Let the reading-rooms and theatres be open for the entertainment of the weary working-people. Let the shop-keeper be free to take down his shutters, and sell his fruit and refreshments to the hungry and thirsty crowds that shall pass by." This was the plea of the liberals, for emancipation from the Sunday yoke.

But let us analyze it for a moment. If the cars and steamboats run on the sabbath, the engineers and stokers and brakemen and conductors and drivers must work to keep them running. If the reading-rooms and theatres are open, the librarians and door-keepers and waiters and performers must be at their posts. If the stores are open, the clerks and porters and book-keepers must be on hand to carry on the business. In the encroachments upon the sabbath which have already taken place, all this has been proved true. There are hundreds of men in our cities, as I know from investigation, who are compelled to work every Sunday against their will, or lose their situations. And the number has increased just in proportion as the sabbath restrictions have relaxed. Is not it strange, that men who assume the name of "advanced thinkers" should put forth a plea for liberty, which is so utterly and thoughtlessly self-contradictory as this? They assume to be friends of the working-man, and then clamor for a freedom that shall compel him to work seven days in the week. They call themselves the defenders of the laboring classes, and then demand that all laws shall be expunged from the Bible and from the statute-book, which may prevent the taskmaster from exacting the entire time of the servant in toil, and giving him none for recreation. Surely *"the tender mercies of the wicked are cruel."* The merciful Framer of the world devised a system for giving rest to his creatures when they should need it. Men have tried to improve upon it, and to supersede it in the name of liberty; but every such attempt has proved in the end a concession to tyranny. "The sabbath," it has been beautifully said, is "the smile of creation." That smile can be truly found only upon the upturned, restful face of the obedient worshipper of God. The smile which the infidel is trying to bring upon the countenance of society will prove only the counterfeited smirk of men and women who are trying to look happy, while they are tiring themselves out in the effort to find rest, and wearying both themselves and their Creator with their sinful dissipations, and calling it recreation. There is, there can be, no rest for man but in obedience to the laws of Him who made him. "Oh that thou hadst hearkened unto my commandments! then had thy peace been as a river, and thy righteousness as the waves of the sea." "But the wicked are like the troubled sea when it cannot rest, whose waters cast up mire and dirt. There is no peace, saith my God, to the wicked."

I have said that in the controversy concerning the sabbath, the Christian has an immense advantage on the humane and philanthropic side over the infidel. The advantage is this: The Christian, in asserting the sanctity of the sabbath, and urging its maintenance, is simply retracing the lines of a law which, however dimmed and faded, is deeply written on the human heart. The infidel, in assailing the sabbath, is contending both against revelation and against nature. He must not only desupernaturalize the Bible, but he must denaturalize nature. I think it must be clear to any one now, that the sabbath has a most powerful religious use in mediating between God and man.

If *religion*, according to the common opinion, means to *bind back*, the sabbath constitutes a double bond between the Creator and man. It binds and braids together natural and revealed religion into a single twofold cord. With its claim for man's homage, it unites a proffer of divine good-will. With the command, "Thou shalt worship the Lord thy God," it joins the invitation, "Come unto me, and rest." With the requirement that man shall look to God in worship and adoration, it unites the assurance that God is looking down from heaven upon man, to give the hireling respite from his toils, and to give the maiden release from the service of her mistress. Thus, whatever conflicts and disagreements the soul may have with God, the sabbath constitutes a perpetual meeting-place of reconciliation. It is the one point and the one place where the word of God and the heart of man find nearest agreement.

Thus the Sabbath is of the highest use as an evidence of the truth of revealed religion. Two witnesses establish a fact. When your watch as you take it from your pocket is found to agree to a second with the town-clock, you are strongly assured that you have the true time of day. So, when the dial of nature is found to agree with the dial of revelation, what conviction it awakens of the truth of the Bible! If the pulse-beats of the heart tick with the seconds of God's sabbatic time, so that when God's clock strikes seven, the heart says seven also, how the conviction is strengthened and deepened that God must be the author and regulator of both! One of the most interesting narratives of conversion which I have ever read was effected by just this line of reasoning: a man who had defied and trampled upon the sabbath, arrested at last by a law in his own nature, and compelled to take rest on the Lord's Day, and, from the relief and blessing which he experienced, convinced of the beneficence of God, and

the truth of the Bible which has enjoined such a rest-day.
And I presume the annals of the Church are full of such
instances.

God's seventh-day law is thus seen to be written on the
heart of man. It may be written, in the case of many,
only as with invisible ink. But when by the light of
some powerful revelation, or by the fire of some great
affliction, the letters are clearly brought out, what conviction they bring as they are found to be the exact
transcript of God's holy law! and as God calls the weary
world to rest, how does man's deepest heart respond,
"Return unto thy rest, O my soul! *for the Lord hath
dealt bountifully with me.*"

THE SABBATH IN THE WORD OF GOD.

THE SABBATH OF THE OLD TESTAMENT: ITS GROUNDS AND METHOD OF INFLUENCE.

BY REV. THOMAS ARMITAGE, D.D., OF NEW YORK.

MOSES attributes the crowning act of God in the making of man, to the sixth day, in the order of creation, thus making the seventh the first full day of his existence; and as the seventh was chosen for the sabbath, it is coeval with man.   Whatever period of time may be covered by the word "day" in the Mosaic account of the creation, is immaterial to this discussion, since it is clear that the sacred writer uses the period represented by a "day," having a definite beginning and end, "an evening and a morning," as a symbolism to represent the periods of the divine labor and rest; and so it is immaterial to this discussion, whether the symbol were clothed in the costume of the literal or not.   In any case, the word "day" is a human term under which the sublime mystery of divine work, and cessation therefrom, is couched.   "And God blessed the seventh day, and sanctified it; because that in it he had rested from all his work which God created." [1]   Then the first sabbath dawned upon our earth before it was blighted by the curse; and on its peaceful

[1] Gen. ii. 3.

morning, Adam awoke from his first night's repose to celebrate the wisdom and power of God, as they burst upon
his soul from this wonderful universe, with his first sunrise. Phidias, the renowned sculptor, so intertwined his
own name with the curious work on the shield of Minerva,
over the portico of the Acropolis of Athens, that it could
not be cut away without destroying his whole work. In
like manner the eye of man read the signature of the
great Architect everywhere, when the sun flooded the new
creation with glory, and before a muscle of his body was
toilworn, or a faculty of his soul clouded by sin. The
whole creation was to him Jehovah's infinite argument,
that he was man's Maker. Thus the Adamic sabbath
was generic, was made for man in his individuality as
man; for no social or national relations then existed. It
was to work out for him both conviction and joy, even in
his innocency. The first purpose of the primeval sabbath, then, was the commemoration of Jehovah's creative
attributes, a standing monument of that great monotheism
which underlies both human responsibility and divine
revelation. This purpose of the sabbath was infinitely
worthy of its Founder; for, when "the heavens and the
earth were finished, and all the host of them," it stood an
eternal protest against every possible form of materialism,
pantheism, and atheism. The first sabbath commanded
man to stand still, while the "heavens" declared to him
"the glory of God, and the firmament" showed "forth his
handiwork." It challenged, "Why lookest thou so earnestly on us, as though by our own power we had made
ourselves? Jehovah is the maker of us all." The first
sabbath attested to man that the world was not its own
creator, that an unbridgeable gulf stretches between unconscious things and the living God, — between divine
volitions and the eternity of matter. Its mute eloquence
witnessed for God, then as now, and barred out all idea of

pagan adoration to strange gods and all worship of nature, by claiming man's first homage for the Creator of heaven and earth.

Again, the law of the original sabbath is written on the framework and constitution of man for the most benevolent ends in his whole nature. The foundations of the sabbath rest are laid deeply and permanently upon the needs of humanity, and exert an elementary hygienic power over the physical, mental, and moral man, without which his highest well-being cannot be promoted; proving that it is not an arbitrary human expedient, but a vital necessity for the government of his life. He was not made to stagnate in idleness, but to be energetic; and one day's rest in seven was granted, to refresh, enlarge, and enrich all his faculties. Physical exhaustion is insured to him by the very delicacy of his bodily tissues. All the channels by which the mind performs its functions must clog under its exactions on the brain and its gossamer congregation of nerves. These, with the perturbed fever of the moral nature, all prove the truth of Aristotle's philosophical statement, "that the end of labor is to gain leisure;" and the sabbath commands that leisure after each week's labor. It follows as a consequence, that the natural liberty of man is outraged whenever a materialistic plutocracy attempts to disturb this balance of natural forces; for by robbing him of his weekly rest he is reduced to a socialistic machine, and left without his chief defence against avarice, overwork, and heartless oppression. From the beginning of man's existence to this day, no human legislator has submitted a law of property, whereby a slave, or a free laborer, or even the beast of burden, should surrender a seventh part of their toil as a voluntary concession to their inherent rights: human greed and heartlessness have never made this possible. No: the sabbath springs from the nature of things, as they are expressed in the human constitution, and the benevolent considerations which govern man's creaturely relations to God. This preconformation between man and his rightful sabbath is as unique and benevolent as that between his eye and the light, his lungs and the air. It links up a sense of creaturely frailty with the omnipotence of the Creator, which, when once removed, leaves man to work seven days in and seven days out, until for sheer want of repose his whole nature sinks.

An ingenious attempt has been made to show that the Mosaic record of the Adamic sabbath is not historical, but anticipatory of what actually took place on Sinai, in the giving of the Fourth Commandment, twenty-five hundred years afterwards. But the honest simplicity of the record itself makes this a part of the history of the creation, quite as much as the other parts, and sets aside the supposition that the sabbath was an after-thought. As becomes a faithful historian of facts, Moses throws no guard around his statement to warn us against the supposition that the sabbath was a pre-existent institution, but leaves the impression that, as established facts, the sabbaths of Eden and Sinai are identical. His consecutive arrangement of facts, in the history of creation, properly cuts off all speculation here, and shows that the antiquity of the sabbath is parallel with the antiquity of the man for whom it was made; so that it both antedates and outlives the Jewish system. Many passages in Genesis not only indicate that the patriarchs kept the sabbath, — such, for example, as those which speak of time as divided into "weeks," — but this position draws support from the fact that the substance and spirit of the other nine words of the Decalogue were obeyed from the beginning, without the exact formulation of the Sinaitic tables. God said to Abraham, "I am the Almighty God: walk before me, and be thou perfect." What is this but that he should have

no other God but him, according to the First Commandment? When Jacob insisted upon the removal of idol
images which Rachel his wife had stolen from Laban, had
he not in view that jealousy of Jehovah against idolatry,
which the Second Commandment sets forth? The patri-
arch took the solemn legal oath in the name of the Lord,
an act which implies that reverence for the divine name,
which the Third Commandment enforces. In what spirit
did the children of Noah and Abraham "honor their
father," but that of the Fifth Commandment? The full
animus of the Sixth Commandment is amply seen in the
treatment of Cain for the murder of his brother. Were
the requisitions of the Seventh Commandment ever more
devoutly obeyed than by Joseph, in rejecting the blandish-
ments of his master's wife under the protest of "great
wickedness and sin against God"? When the same Joseph charged theft upon his brethren, their denial contains
the substance of the Eighth Commandment, "Thou shalt
not steal." Pharaoh's reproof to Abraham, for deceiving
him in saying that Sarah his wife was his sister, forbids
"false witness," in the spirit of the Ninth Commandment;
and the discovery that she was his "neighbor's wife"
appears to have ended his covetous desire for her, in
keeping with the demands of the Tenth. But if the very
essence of these nine enactments of Sinai was in action,
and the Fourth Commandment, found in the very heart of
this legislation, was non-existent, from Adam to Moses,
the exception is most unaccountable in every way. The
fact is, that a new world without a sabbath for five and
twenty centuries, would have made the home of man as
imperfect as to have left it without a law forbidding theft,
adultery and murder; as imperfect as he himself would
have been without its ever-recurring septenary rest and
health and strength. But whether these sins were forbidden in so many words, or not, we find that, by the very

first sabbath institute, man rendered to God the natural act of moral submission, and came to the royal enjoyment of sabbatic holiness. Besides, whatever may be the genesis of a ceremonial ordinance, or its fluctuations, the prime attributes of moral law are its eternity and immutability. But, if the right of God to one-seventh part of man's time was not known through the long stretch of the patriarchal ages, on what moral ground does he require a sabbath now that was not operative then? We must reach the conclusion that a patriarchal sabbath enforced his right then, and that, to men in that age as well as afterwards, he vouchsafed sabbatic rest for his worship, his honor and blessing.

The fact that the sabbath is not specifically mentioned in the Old Testament, between the account of the creation and the exodus from Egypt, no more shows it to have been unknown then than it was during the silence of the six hundred years which ran through the time of the Judges, and the administrations of Samuel and Saul. During those six centuries, kings, priests, prophets, and the Jewish nation itself were sacredly observing the day, and yet it is not mentioned once. It is not at all likely that the Egyptian taskmasters allowed the Israelites a sabbath rest in their bondage. But the law of the sabbath seems to have been fully known to them before the giving of the Decalogue. Two months before the Israelites reached Sinai, we find them distinguishing the sixth from the seventh day, and gathering twice as much manna on the sixth as on other days. And when the elders inquired of Moses whether they had done rightly in this forecast, he said, "To-morrow is the rest of the holy sabbath. Six days ye shall gather it, but on the seventh day, which is the sabbath, in it shall be none;" and so on the sixth day they gathered enough for two days. But some of the people went out on the sabbath to gather manna notwithstanding; and the Lord remonstrated against their wilful disobedience, saying, "How long refuse ye to keep my commandments and my laws?" a form of remonstrance which showed them to be acquainted with his sabbath law, and also their deliberate refusal to keep it. The whole air of familiarity thrown around the narrative, proves their acquaintance with the sabbath as an established fact, and that it was not a new revelation. Then, they ask no questions as to what its meaning was, why it existed, how to keep it, or what its benefits were ; all of which questions must have attended a new institution. The simple fact is stated, that the seventh day is the sabbath ; and they show themselves to be sufficiently familiar with all its claims, to honor its observance.

We now come to look at the grounds and methods of the Old-Testament sabbath as we find it in what is called the Jewish, or Mosaic form, under the theocracy. When the Jewish provisions of the sabbath law were promulgated, the Hebrews were not only a religious people, but also a civil nation, and lived under the direct municipal, religious, and regal government of Jehovah himself. The Mosaic form of the sabbath law is found in Exod. xx. 8-11 : "Remember the sabbath day, to keep it holy. Six days shalt thou labor, and do all thy work: but the seventh day is the sabbath of the Lord thy God: in it thou shalt not do any work, thou, nor thy son, nor thy daughter, thy man-servant, nor thy maid-servant, nor thy cattle, nor thy stranger that is within thy gates : for in six days the Lord made heaven and earth, the sea, and all that in them is, and rested the seventh day : wherefore the Lord blessed the sabbath day, and hallowed it."

These words were written on stone by the finger of God himself, and laid up in the ark, in token of their solemn grandeur, as the perfect and imperishable law of Jehovah on this subject. They hold a middle place in the ten great words, between the things of God and man, and are a link of love which joins the two tables, in securing glory to God and blessings to humanity. The word "remember," as used here, implies, to keep in mind the day specified, as one with which they were familiar. Although the article is omitted in the Hebrew syntax, the specifying word which follows carries with it the face of the article, conveying the same meaning to the Jewish ear, that the words, "remember sabbath day," would convey to the English. When we take the Fourth Commandment into association with various other Old-Testament passages, we are safe in saying of the Mosaic sabbath, that, —

1. *It covered an entire day.* The element on which God is legislating here is time, which he divides into seven parts ; and the same number of hours which constitute a whole day in any of the six parts form also the seventh. That day was to be just as long as any other day ; no more, no less. Lev. xxiii. 32, says, "From even unto even shall ye celebrate your sabbath," an entire day of twenty-four hours.

2. *Its negative character carries with the words, "In it thou shalt not do any work," the suspension of all secular toil and business.* (1) The Jews were not allowed to travel on the sabbath, excepting to the house of God. "Let no man go out of his place on the sabbath day." [1] (2) They were not allowed to go to market, or to buy and sell goods on that day, or to expose them for sale. Some avaricious Israelites were impatient for the day to pass, and said, "When will the new moon be gone, that we may sell corn ; and the sabbath, that we may set forth wheat ?" [2] But the law was inexorable. Nehemiah says that he testified against the traders of Jerusalem when he saw some "treading wine-presses on the sabbath, and bringing in sheaves, and lading asses ; as also wine, grapes

---

[1] Exod. xvi. 29.   [2] Neh. viii. 5.

and figs, and all manner of burdens, which they brought into Jerusalem on the sabbath day."[1] Others brought "fish and all manner of ware, and sold on the sabbath." "Then I contended with the nobles of Judah, and said unto them, What evil thing is this that ye do, and profane the sabbath day?" "When the gates of Jerusalem began to be dark before the sabbath, I commanded that the gates should be shut, and charged that they should not be opened till after the sabbath; and set some of my servants at the gates, that no burdens should be brought in on the sabbath." He says that "the merchants and sellers of all kinds of ware" lodged outside of the gates "once or twice;" but he threatened them that if they did so again he would "lay hands" on them as a magistrate; and, with the jail in view, he says that "from that time forth came they no more on the sabbath." (3) They might not kindle a fire on the sabbath. "Ye shall kindle no fire throughout your habitations upon the sabbath day."[2] (4) They were not to embalm or bury their dead on that day. The women at the burial of Jesus returned from his tomb, "and prepared spices and ointments, and rested on the sabbath day, according to the commandment."[3] (5) They were not allowed to plough their land or gather their harvest on the sabbath, however plausible the necessity might appear. "On the seventh day thou shalt rest; in earing time (the time of ploughing) and harvest thou shalt rest."[4]

3. *The positive side of the Fourth Commandment devotes the day to absolute rest and religious uses.* All pleasure-seeking, diversion, and idleness were to be cast aside, to make it a day of pre-eminent sanctity. The law "hallowed" it, that is, made it God's own day; for the leading thought in hallowing is, to separate, to consecrate. It was time "blessed" and "sanctified," made sacred to sacred

---

[1] Neh. xiii. 15–21.   [2] Exod. xxxv. 3.

[3] Luke xxiii. 54–56.   [4] Exod. xxxiv. 21.

purposes. The solar, or sun-dividing mark, was not a radical and broad enough line of demarkation to characterize it from its fellows. It must stand alone, be "kept holy." "Ye shall reverence my sabbaths." "Not doing thine own ways, nor finding thine own pleasure, nor speaking thine own words." [1]

4. *This sanctity was to evince itself in acts of public worship.* "The seventh day is a holy convocation." [2] This phrase, "holy convocation," is always used to designate the religious gatherings of Israel, in distinction from their political and other gatherings. Then, special sacrifices were to be offered in the sanctuary on the sabbath. "On the sabbath day two lambs of the first year, without spot, and two tenth deals of flour, for a burnt offering, mingled with oil, and the drink offering thereof. This is the burnt offering of every sabbath, besides the continual burnt offering." [3] Particular force is given to the injunction, "Ye shall reverence my sanctuary," by specifying the particular gate of the sanctuary which should be used for these double sacrifices on the sabbath. "Thus saith the Lord God; The gate of the inner court that looketh towards the east shall be shut the six working days; but on the seventh it shall be opened. . . . And the prince shall enter by the way of the porch of that gate without, and shall stand by the post of the gate, and the priests shall prepare his burnt offering and his peace offerings, and he shall worship at the threshold of the gate: then he shall go forth, but the gate shall not be shut until the evening. Likewise the people of the land shall worship at the door of this gate in the sabbaths." [4] The New Testament throws light upon the Jewish sabbath worship in the synagogue, after the captivity. Jesus, "as his custom was, went into the synagogue on the sabbath day, and stood up to read." [5] And

---

[1] Isa. lviii. 13.   [2] Lev. xxiii. 3.   [3] Num. xxxiii. 9, 10.
[4] Ezek. xlvi. 1–13.   [5] Luke iv. 16.

the Apostle Paul says, "Moses of old time hath in every city them that preach him, being read in the synagogues every sabbath day."[1]   Reading the Scriptures was a part of this worship.

5. *There are intimations that the family engaged in social as well as public worship on the sabbath.* The home is put in conjunction with the "holy convocation," in the words,[2] "It is the sabbath of the Lord in all your dwellings." The family tie, which is mentioned so carefully in the Fourth Commandment, seems also to indicate this household privilege, as belonging to the whole family, — an inheritance of rest, comfort, instruction, and worship. This right is secured to labor as well as relationship ; the "man-servant," the "maid-servant," the "stranger," as well as "thou," "and thy son and thy daughter."

6. *Sabbath observance was enforced by an appeal to Hebrew gratitude.* When the commandment said that the Lord "rested on the seventh day," it did not carry the gross idea to the Israelite that he was weary, and needed repose after the work of creation, but, that he had brought his work to a definite end, and had ceased to work.   And in the same sense he summoned their better nature to the observance of the sabbath, by the additional consideration, that, when they left Egypt, their toils of bondage were consummated, and they rested from bondage.   They were to commemorate that completed work in the sabbath.[3] "Thou wast a servant in the land of Egypt, and the Lord thy God brought thee hence, through a mighty hand and by a stretched-out arm: therefore the Lord thy God commanded thee to keep the sabbath day." This makes their sabbath not only a commemoration of creation, but also a national monument to their personal and national liberties.   This beneficent humanity made Jehovah not only the Lord of the sabbath by creation, but

---

[1] Acts xv. 21.   [2] Lev. xxiii. 3.   [3] Deut. v. 15.

by the endowment of a great nation with all its distinguishing privileges and rights. Eminent writers have
claimed that their slavery ended in Egypt on the sabbath
day, and that therefore they were to celebrate it as the
time of a new national creation, with an animated and elevated gratitude. Their new-found liberties made it jubi-
lant with honors, humanities, and enjoyments. It was to
remove their commonwealth as far as possible from the
grinding toils of a sabbath-less Egypt.[1] "See that ye
keep my sabbath, because it is a sign between me and
you in all your generations." The doctrine that the sabbath was a "sign" to the Jews, taught that their exodus
from slavery was followed by the restful sabbath, just as
God himself ceased from the work of creation on the sabbath. With this grateful and cheering view, the weekly
returning "sign" must have thrilled every household, for
the sabbath was made one of the great social influences
which kept the national sentiment of freedom alive and
fresh, removing from the home all that was gloomy and
austere. The "sign" of the sabbath filled every family
with a free, breathing patriotism; for its sanctity chas-
tened every feeling, filled every house with the cheerful
song of deliverance, and knit the circle into friendship and
the serenity of love. And this happiness was to be abiding; for the Lord said to them,[2] "From one new moon to
another, and from one sabbath to another, shall all flesh
come to worship before me, saith the Lord." Creation
and liberty were the joint note of their sabbath.

7. *Jehovah deprecated sabbath-breaking as a grievous sin,
and severely punished the offender.*[3] "Ye shall keep the
sabbath holy. Every one that defileth it shall surely be
put to death. . . . Six days may work be done, but in the
seventh is the sabbath of rest, holy to the Lord: whoever
doeth any work in the sabbath day, he shall surely be put

---

[1] Exod. xxxi. 13.   [2] Isa. lxvi. 23.   [3] Exod. xxxi. 14, 15.

to death." The death-penalty was inflicted on one man who desecrated the day:[1] "All the congregation brought him without the camp, and stoned him with stones, and he died; as the Lord commanded Moses." Nay, the Lord threatened the very existence of the Hebrew state, if the nation profaned the sabbath:[2] "If ye will not hearken unto me to hallow the sabbath day, and not to bear the burden even entering in at the gates of Jerusalem on the sabbath day, then will I kindle a fire in the gates thereof, and it shall devour the palaces of Jerusalem, and it shall not be quenched." This particular sin is one of the counts in the indictment on which his ancient people were sent into captivity, as numerous passages from the prophets show, both before and after that calamity. When the sabbath was honored, kept "holy," and held as the "delight" of the people, the nation prospered politically; but, when it was prostituted, stern retribution followed. Nehemiah says that after the return from captivity he[3] "contended with the nobles of Judah, and said unto them, What evil thing is this that ye do, and profane the sabbath day? Did not our fathers thus, and did not our God bring all this evil upon us, and upon this city? Yet ye bring more wrath upon Israel by profaning the sabbath." Much has been said against the moral obligation to perpetuate the sabbath under the provisions of the Fourth Commandment, on the ground that these terrible adjuncts imposed under the Mosaic law, must have made the institution temporary and local. But the abolition of these civil penalties can in no way have set aside the moral principle which conserves the fitness of the sabbath for all its humane and religious designs. And therefore it becomes an important question: Why Jehovah looked upon all sabbath desecration as so great a wickedness? Let us examine this point for a moment.

---

[1] Num. xv. 36.   [2] Jer. xvii. 27.   [3] Neh. xiii. 17.

To begin with, sabbath-breaking was not the only crime for which death was inflicted under the Jewish theocracy. Adultery, murder, and disobedience to parents, were all capital crimes under that order of jurisprudence : because each of these undermined the honor and safety of society, while the Hebrews continued to be a nation and a theocracy. But when their nationality came to an end, temporal death was no longer judicially inflicted for sabbath-breaking, because legislation on the *civil* sabbath dropped, with the other rights to inflict the death-penalty, into the hands of the state ; while the religious sabbath fell back upon the eternal principles of morality, which had governed the sabbath in pre-Mosaic times. The death-penalty for the violation of the sabbath was a part and parcel of the political and local regulations of the theocracy. While Jehovah was the only Lawgiver of the Jews, he constituted the sabbath a civil institution as well as a religious obligation ; and hence, its desecration was an act of downright treason against their only King. He had but recently brought them out of the slavery of centuries. He had given them the lands of those who practised polytheism, and worshipped false gods ; he had made their law the depository of a pure theism and worship, and he had based all their national politics upon moral law. Their sabbath was both a sign and a test of his kingship : therefore he determined that if his own people, for whom he had done so much, should publicly insult him, by setting that covenant sign at defiance before the mocking heathen, their bold presumption should be punished with the utmost rigor. Such conduct flaunted defiance in the face of Jehovah : it was an act of Deicide, and treasonable in the highest degree. For this reason, offenders endured these heavy penalties when they worshipped idols, blasphemed his name, disregarded the obligations to parents, and violated the sabbath, as well as when they took human life.

Now, take the case of the man who was stoned to death for gathering sticks on the sabbath. It evidently came under this daring character, and his punishment was a judicial sentence. This man sinned neither through ignorance nor infirmity, mistake nor impulse: if he had, some of the sacrifices ordained in such cases would have atoned for him. John Selden takes the ground that he was cutting up the roots of trees, rather than "gathering sticks;" and the Hebrew word מקשש may mean "chipping," or "splitting wood," as Arnheim suggests. In that case, his act defined a direct and positive labor on the sabbath. God had put him to this test of allegiance, and, having deliberately chosen to commit high treason, he was given over to the nation to be dealt with in this summary manner; and the whole congregation, for the welfare of the commonwealth, executed the sentence of death to expiate his political crime against their King. The relation of God to the Jews was not general and spiritual only, but temporal and national also: it was such a relation as he has never assumed towards any other nation. He was their legal and political King, as well as their chosen divinity: therefore his right to his own sacred day, as their monarch, was inviolable. Where, as slaves, they had no day to call their own, he had given them six in each week, only reserving one for himself; and the sabbath-breaker would deliberately rob him of that. He blessed them and protected them, and guarded all their sacred liberties, after he had become the acknowledged Founder of their nation; and he beneficently intertwined the sabbath with all their temporal, political, and religious institutions; and so most justly made it the channel for the public recognition of his magisterial authority as their only Lord and Lawgiver.

8. *Jehovah enforced the sanctity of the sabbath by rewarding those who kept it holy.* For this purpose he

renewed the original benediction which he pronounced
upon the sabbath again and again. " Blessed is the man
that doeth this, and the son of man that layeth hold on
it ; that keepeth the sabbath from polluting it. For thus
saith the Lord unto the eunuchs that keep my sabbaths,
and choose the things that please me, and take hold of
my covenant, even unto them will I give in mine house
and within my walls a place and a name better than of
sons and of daughters."[1] "If thou turn away thy foot
from the sabbath, and from doing thy pleasure on my holy
day, and call the sabbath a delight, the holy of the Lord,
honorable, and shalt honor him, . . . I will cause thee to
ride upon the high places of the earth, and feed thee with
the heritage of Jacob thy father."[2]

9. *Sometimes there was a perfect rebound from the wilful non-observance of the sabbath, amongst the Jews, to
the most superstitious and fanatical observance of the day.*
But this did not occur until the spirit of the institution
had been entirely lost in its letter. By tradition and the
teachings of the Talmud, they added all sorts of fantastical
provisions to the commands of God concerning the external observance of the day. They would not even defend
themselves against an invading army on the sabbath,[3] nor
countenance the use of the healing art for the restoration
of the sick.[4] If an egg was laid on the sabbath, it might
not be eaten, because it was "prepared" by the hen in
sacred time.[5] There were many similar extravagances.
To some extent this over-scrupulous abuse of plain ordinances had been foreseen and provided for ; as, for example, in the case of sabbath military guards. "A third
part of you that enter in on the sabbath, even they shall
keep watch of the king's house. And two parts of all
that go forth on the sabbath, even they shall keep the

---

[1] Isa. lvi. 1-7.   [2] Isa. lviii. 13.   [3] 1 Macc. i. 11-15, 39-45.
[4] John v. 18.   [5] Smith's Bib. Dic., art. " Pharisees."

watch of the house of the Lord about the king. And the captains over the hundreds did according to all things that Jehoiada the priest commanded ; and they took every man his men that were to come in on the sabbath with them that should go out on the sabbath." [1]

There can be no doubt from the teachings of the New Testament, that the Old-Testament sabbath was a type of better things to come ; but the Jews did not so understand it at the time, and did not observe it for that reason, or in that spirit. This great application of the sabbath is a New-Testament revelation. But the sabbath of the Old Testament appears to have laid its grounds and methods of influence chiefly, if not entirely, in the principles and modes of operation indicated in the above observations.

[1] 2 Kings xi. 5, 7, 9.

CHRIST'S CONNECTION WITH THE SABBATH.

BY REV. HENRY W. WARREN, D.D., OF PHILADELPHIA.

THE theme naturally divides itself into four parts : viz., I., the ideal sabbath as enjoyed by God, and communicated to men; II., the perverted Pharisaic institution afterwards called sabbath ; III., Christ's connection with that then existent institution ; and, IV., his relation to the sabbath subsequent to his life on earth.

The initial idea of the sabbath, as of all things else, is derived from God (Gen. ii. 2). That text takes pains to repeat that God rested from the work that he *had* made, not from all work. The word *shabath* means resting from the work immediately preceding, because now complete. There had been struggle with chaos, formlessness, and darkness. The result of divine power was order, beauty, light ; and the divine judgment said, "It is very good." God saw all things conformed to his idea, ready for finer developments, and ceased from the work he had done. For six days he had ploughed with earthquakes, terraced with mountain-ranges, put oceans for reservoirs, appointed winds and clouds to water continents, had seeded the earth for flowers and fruit, and had created millions of sentient creatures to enjoy them. That cycle was complete. Now he needed only to preserve and enjoy. That is the first part of his sabbath, a blissful contemplation and preservation of a material universe. Well do we sing of God amid the grand march of shining stars.

> "Thy temple is the arch
> Of yon unmeasured sky;
> Thy sabbath, the stupendous march
> Of vast eternity."

But we have a very incomplete idea of God's sabbath, unless we realize that he therein entered upon a new and higher kind of work; a work moral and spiritual, impressing his nature on souls, as he had impressed his power on matter; a work distinct from all previous work, and but for which no previous work would have been undertaken. This communication of personal holiness and power to spiritual children is God's rest-day work, going on through thousands of years as one day; and it was of this especially that the Saviour said, "My Father worketh hitherto," or up to now. And this constitutes the clearest and sublimest illustration of what the true sabbath is, and for what it is appropriately used.

After the exodus the term "sabbath" came to be applied mainly, if not altogether, to a certain definite keeping of the seventh day of the week. *What was that sabbath?*

In order that there might be a cessation from work, it was first enjoined, "Six days shalt thou labor," an injunction too apt to be forgotten. It was then ordered, negatively, that the people should not light a fire in their dwellings, nor go out of the camp to gather manna nor to do any work. Infraction of this law was punished, in one instance at least, with death.

The sabbath was an enjoined rest, provided by God's authority, not only for the Israelites, but also for servants and even for beasts. It was designed to prevent the emancipated Israelites from practising the hard and bitter lessons they had learned as slaves, on those who should afterwards serve them. It was an assertion that servants and slaves had rights, as well as masters, and that God designed to vindicate them in those rights. It was an attempt on God's part to recuperate the vigor of a part of the race that sin had so frightfully damaged, and restore it to something of its pristine vigor.

Besides these negative regulations for the people, it was

positively enjoined that the priests should double the laborious and difficult sacrifices of the tabernacle on this day, and that they should bake new show-bread, and place it on the table for the week to come. It is easy to see that the restrictive rules about labor and lighting fires did not apply to religious service. Instead of saying as the Jews did, that there was no sabbath in holy things, we would say that in holy things it was a perpetual sabbath, and that for the worship of God and the sanctification of men all possible labor was devout sabbath-keeping.

When we come to the great religious revival under Nehemiah, after the Babylonish captivity, we find the people gathered on a holy day, to hear preaching, or expositions of scriptures, by Ezra. They were told not to mourn and weep, but go their way, eat the fat, drink the sweet, and send portions to those for whom nothing was prepared; "for this day is holy unto the Lord : neither be ye sorry, for the joy of the Lord is your strength." Hence rose the custom of giving feasts on the sabbath. To these the rich and poor were invited, or were free to come. Altogether it was a day of social joy, religious worship, and the best attainable rest, that is, a perfect rest from secular toil for gain, and a refreshing labor, inspired by the spirit of love, for the religious profit of others.

But in the course of time this ideal sabbath formed upon the model of God's rest-day was changed. The Pharisaic spirit, which becomes intensely religious in some points as it becomes intensely wicked in others, that offers to God anise and cummin, and to its own avarice the widows' houses it devours, set about making the rest-day one of torture. They had read in Jeremiah, "Take heed to yourselves, that ye bear no burden on the sabbath day," referring to traffic through the gates of Jerusalem. So they decided that men might wear shoes not nailed, as a protection for their feet, but that nailed shoes were a burden, and he who had only such must go barefoot. They might not carry a fan to drive away flies, for that would be a burden. A handkerchief might be worn as a girdle, or pinned to any part of one's apparel, and so be a garment; but, if loose in the pocket, it was a forbidden burden. They read that Moses enjoined every man to abide in his place on that day, and not go out of his place. So they set about enlarging his place, so that he could go, and not disobey. They said a man's place extended two thousand paces in every direction, and that far he might journey on the sabbath day. But, if a man found himself more than two thousand paces from his home on Friday night when the sun went down, there must he abide over the seventh day, whether he had food and shelter, or not. Nevertheless, if a man had carried food two thousand paces from home on the sixth day, he might on the sabbath make that a new point of departure for another sabbath-day's journey. They read in the commandment, "In it thou shalt not do any work." So they enacted that men must not walk the permitted journey on the grass, lest they do threshing; and must not catch troublesome fleas, lest they do hunting. Thus they laid burdens on men's shoulders grievous to be borne, but, by applying the same farcical reasoning, managed to exempt themselves from touching these burdens with one of their fingers. It was an attempt to please God by splitting the hairs of one's head, instead of serving him with the heart. Judaism was fast lapsing into the Pagan idea that God was to be pleased by bodily discomfort and torture, and was teaching men that he was vindictively exact about straining out gnats, and utterly unmindful of swallowed camels; that he was painfully precise about insignificant details, but regardless of men's passing by justice, righteousness, and the weightier matters of the law.

To such a farce of sabbath-keeping, both ludicrous and

wicked, came the Lord of the sabbath. We shall find in his words and deeds the true ideal of the proper keeping of the day.

We notice first of all that even in his preparatory ministry it was his custom to go into the synagogues, and expound the word of God. He would have made the day memorable above all the concentrated Fourths of July of all nations, if he had done nothing else than to announce at Nazareth that epitome of the objects of his coming: "The Spirit of the Lord is upon me, because he hath anointed me to preach the gospel to the poor; he hath sent me to heal the broken-hearted, to preach deliverance to the captives, and recovering of sight to the blind, to set at liberty them that are bruised, to preach the acceptable year of the Lord." All the ages do well to keep holy the day that brings such blessed declarations to a groaning creation.

We observe secondly that Christ attended at least one of the feasts men were wont to give on that day. Probably the meat was that of a slain sacrifice. Jesus did not rebuke the custom, and he made it an occasion of healing the sick, teaching good manners and the true humility.

We find thirdly that Christ was accustomed to walk about the city and fields on this day. We find him with a multitude near the pool of Bethesda. It was no place of religious gathering, except what he made it by his holy presence. But into that idle crowd he brought the power of holy words and deeds. He said to one who had been an invalid thirty-eight years, "Willest thou to be made whole? Rise, take up thy bed, and walk." He settled the whole question of forbidden work just as Nehemiah did nearly five hundred years before. He forbade treading wine-presses, bringing in sheaves, lading asses, i.e., ordinary work from the ordinary motive, hire or gain. The Pharisees were alert; but in the frenzy of their sabbatarianism they let the offending burden-bearer go, that they might wreak their hate by putting to death the one giving the command. Christ's defence at once vaults to the highest authority, "My Father worketh up to now, and I work." The Father constantly fills all spheres of being with himself. And the Son by the word of his power continually upholds all things, and by him all things stand together: all the planets fly, vegetative processes go forward, life sings and leaps its happy round of existence. And from both proceeds the Holy Spirit, flooding all spiritual beings with a perpetual sabbath influence.

Indeed, Christ did work on the sabbath. He did no less than seven or eight of his great miracles on that day. He did them on the sabbath defiantly, ostentatiously, when there was no special reason for haste. The Jews said, "Come on one of the six days, and be healed, and not on the sabbath day;" but, just to pour his contempt on their style of sabbath-keeping, Christ wrought these cures on the sabbath. He healed the demoniac in the synagogue at Capernaum, rebuked the fever of Peter's wife's mother, he made whole the man's withered hand, loosed the daughter of Abraham whom Satan had bound for eighteen years, and cured the man of dropsy in the home of one of the chief Pharisees. And it was the light of the blessed sabbath day that first reached the darkened soul of the man who was born blind. I greatly fear that Christ's followers, in their Jewish ideas of no work on the sabbath, forget the sublimity of Christ's work for the good of the souls and bodies of men. Christ cites the case of the priests who labor on the sabbath and are blameless, goes over a masterly argument, and reaches the sublime conclusion, "Wherefore it is lawful to do well on the sabbath day."

It is not to be thought for a moment, that Christ said aught against the day as a divine institution; but his hot-

test anger burned against the men who perverted mercy
to cruelty, and exalted an institution above the man.
Hence he thunders at them, "The sabbath was made for
man, not man for the sabbath." Institutions are given to
be kept, modified, or abolished if need be, for man's good;
and not man to be stretched or mutilated on the Procrus-
tean bed of an institution. The Son of man is lord of the
sabbath, and in that high capacity he illustrates its proper
observance as has been detailed. He saved all the Mosaic
rest-day, but tore off the grave-clothes with which they had
bound it. When the Christian Church shall have truly
copied the sabbath-keeping of its Lord, no lonely patient
in the hospital shall lack the visit of a friend, no worthy
poor for whom no portion is prepared shall lack his food,
and probably no crowd of idlers in the city park will lack
its faithful Christian missionaries. And unless we use the
day more for missionary work, and less for ecstasy and
mental titillation, there is great occasion to fear it will be
taken away from us.

Christ also showed his lordship over the sabbath by
changing the day of its observance. As the Creator hallowed the day on which he, having finished creative, commenced spiritual work, so Christ hallowed the day on
which he, having finished re-creative work, commenced
the eternal sabbath of spiritual development.

We find ourselves keeping another day for a rest-day.
Has it any divine authority, or is it a matter of individual
choice? The only authority that concerns us to-day is
whether Christ gave this new day for man's keeping. I
confess there is no definite command of his on record to
change the day. But we do find custom which seems
based on sufficient authority. It is clear that the apostles
immediately commenced to keep the first day of the week
in that manner in which they had previously observed the
seventh. Seven texts, or instances, can be adduced in

proof of this. Neither the apostles nor the early fathers assert that Christ changed the sabbath from the seventh to the first day, but circumstances all point that way. On the first day of the week Christ rose from the dead : his work, greater than speaking a world from nought, was finished. He appeared five times that day to his followers. On the following first day he appeared again ; and there is no record that he appeared to them in the intervening six days. Then on the day of Pentecost, that day of spiritual power worthy of perpetual celebration, Christ once more distinguished the first day of the week.

At Troas, years after, Paul abode seven days ; and upon the first day of the week, when the disciples came together, Paul preached unto them. That it was the custom of the early Church to gather on the first day of the week, is still further illustrated by Paul's exhortation to the Corinthians, to make their collection for the poor on that day. St. John said of himself, that he was in the Spirit on the Lord's Day. This was the first day of the week. Thus it was the practice of the disciples of the Lord to keep holy the day of his sabbath rest, the day of his resurrection from the dead. They not only did this, but Paul wrote to the Colossians not to allow any man to judge them — the early Christians — in regard to keeping the former sabbath or the seventh day. He says the Jewish sabbath was a shadow of which the body is Christ.

We find also the early fathers for two centuries accepting without dispute or question the Lord's Day, and doing therein their holy duties, while the seventh day gradually fell into the same estimation in which other days were held. It is a fair inference, that, while the whole Church obeyed the divine commandment to remember the rest-day and keep it holy, they followed the indication of Christ himself in regard to what particular day should be so observed.

The main point to be noticed in Christ's connection with the sabbath is the fact that he recognized its authority, and raised it to a higher range of honor and use. He stood over its grave, and authoritatively bid it come forth. He stripped it of the mummy-cloths in which the Jews had fettered it for a thousand years. He then restored its true idea as being hallowed of God. Thus the day allied the child to its Father; the work of the day put him in sympathy with God's spiritual work, and the work of the other six days associated him with his Father in material work. Oh, happy man who feels that his six-days' toil is not only God's appointment, but analogous to God's brooding over darkness and chaos, to call out order and light! Then the creation of roses from soil, houses from clay, and temples from the quarry, is really Godlike. Oh, thrice happy man who can feel that his seventh day keeps pace with God's higher work for spiritual and immortal ends!

We shall naturally expect, as we go forward from Jewish to Christian dispensations, that there will be a marked advance; there will be an enlarged liberty of manhood to those whose childhood has been well taught by the Mosaic schoolmaster. Those who learned law under Moses will find more amplitude under the greater grace and truth of Christ. As the passover flowered into the Lord's Supper, so will the significance of the sabbath, and its mode of keeping, bourgeon into greater beauty and worth.

Christ takes some of the commandments of the older dispensation, and tells their wider meaning and richer spiritual significance in the new kingdom. "Ye have heard that it was said to the men of old, Ye shall not kill; but I say unto you, that whosoever is angry with his brother without a cause, is in danger of the judgment; and, if angry enough to say, Thou fool, he is in danger of hell-fire." So he takes the laws against adultery and perjury, and makes them cover the thoughts and intents of the heart; takes the law of loving friends, and stretches it till it covers enemies and persecutors; takes the universal law of human nature to trust in gathered treasure, and raises it to a perfect trust for food and raiment in the source of all treasure, even God. He exalted the law written in stone, transgressions of which were atoned by the blood of slain victims, till now no man feels that he can bring his heart clean to God till it has been washed in the atoning blood of Christ.

Did he so amazingly exalt the sabbath? Yes, indeed, he did it by his whole life and by the inspirations of his disciples. What sublime sabbath-work he did before his death! Human language has not words to convey the sweet messages of rest that he brought to toiling men. The weary and heavy-laden have ever since heard him saying, "Come unto me, and I will rest you." They find indeed that it means more than our version says, " give you rest." Christ taught that in him should men find a perpetual sabbath for the soul. He inspired his apostle to declare that there is a sabbath-keeping for the people of God; not in the future world, but in the present, for we who have believed do enter into rest. And Paul in writing unto the Romans ventures to commend equally him who esteemeth one day as a sabbath, and him whose sublime likeness to Christ esteemeth every day as raised to a sabbatic rank. The dim hints which are scattered through the whole volume of sacred writ, of a coming sabbatic condition for all the holy, grow so clear and possibly real in Christ's personal teaching and that of his disciples, that some think it may be realized on this earth. Some believe in a long sabbath of a thousand years, when swords shall be beat into ploughshares, and spears into pruning-hooks, and nations learn war no more. Whatever may be true in that respect, it is certain that all that is essential in the

figure shall be realized here or hereafter. Already Job's
far-off, uncertain place where the wicked cease from trou-
bling, and the weary keep a sabbath, grows clearer under
Christ's promise, till it becomes a Father's house with man-
sions prepared for individual men. There by the river of
life shall all the wounds of earth's wars and labors be
healed, and one blessed sabbath, such as God enjoys, be
man's forever.

For this grand consummation the earthly sabbath is a
preparation. How shall man use it so that it shall minister to the designed end? It is obvious that Christ did not
commit the Pharisaic error of specifying a mode of keeping the day holy. He left it as a divine institution, and
permanent in human history. But its mode of observance
may be varied to suit man's individual development, or the
form of civilization. He knew that any true keeping of
the sabbath must come from the state of one's heart, and
not the condition of body. Indeed, no one can truly keep
a sabbath, who is not, like John, in the Spirit on the
Lord's Day. Men may enact laws for the cessation of
labor, for the stoppage of traffic and every pursuit of
gain, and it is all very well. But how far short of God's
idea is this! Had this been all, Christ might have said
the sabbath was made for *bodies.* But, in saying it is for
man, he presented an ideal as much above this as souls
are above bodies. No man has a right merely to rest his
body, or merely to refine his taste, or merely to enlarge
his intellect. He is to grow in the whole of his being,
especially in the highest part thereof. How is the soul
to grow?

What a blessed proof of our tireless immortality, that
the rest of the spirit is exercise! When man's body no
longer aches with toil, when all the powers of the mind
are sweetly calmed to rest, then the tireless spirit comes
out to its restful activity. Love brings no weariness.

Sacred awe never tires. Blessed adoration knows no fatigue. Purified spirits above *continually* do cry, "Holy, holy, holy!" They cease not day nor night, for they need no rest in such blissful growth. Here, then, is the sabbath of the Lord, — opportunity for the exercise of our noblest faculties, and for the development of our spiritual being. Let, then, the labor for gain stop, and the labor for God go on ; and, superinduced upon mere quiet for refreshment, let the joy of the Lord be your strength. Thus shall we share the invigoration that makes the ceaseless praises of heaven possible, the tireless rapture and growth of the immortal spirit a realized hope.

Christ would say to his followers I am sure, Rest your body, strengthen it with the rapture of the joy of the Lord ; labor God's sabbath works, that is, any labor that is proper on other days, — with this difference only, that they shall be a direct means of spiritual growth to self, or work of mercy to others. "Call the sabbath a delight, the holy of the Lord, honorable, not doing thine own ways, nor finding thine own pleasure therein, nor speaking thine own words. Then thou shalt delight thyself in the Lord, and I will cause thee to ride on the high places of the earth, and feed thee with the heritage of Jacob thy father ; for the mouth of the Lord hath spoken it."

ST. PAUL AND THE SABBATH.

BY REV. WILLIAM DE LOSS LOVE, D.D., OF SOUTH HADLEY.

ALTHOUGH this seems to be, and is, a large subject, it is singular that we have only three scattered verses of Scripture that give us much light upon it, and in each of those three there is only an incidental allusion to it. We have to work our way out to large conclusions from small premises in the outset. Many statements now to be made must be a mere abstract. Lack of time compels the omission of many proofs; and the statements must in general be in the most brief and positive language. I could desire more time for the circumlocutions of modesty and rhetoric.

The Apostle Paul, after his embrace of Christianity, continued regularly to attend religious services with the Jews on the seventh-day sabbath, and on such occasions to preach the gospel at every opportunity; but in no instance do we find him, or any of the apostles, holding a meeting with the disciples by themselves on that day. There is no evidence that the seventh-day sabbath after Christ's resurrection was ever regarded or treated as a specifically *Christian* day, although it was some time before its services were omitted even by any Christians. But we *do* find the Apostle Paul holding a meeting with Christians on the *first* day, and in circumstances indicating that they customarily held meetings each week on its recurrence.

The first record we have of Paul's connection with the first day is in Acts xx. 7: "And upon the first day of the week, when the disciples came together to break bread,

Paul preached unto them, ready to depart on the morrow;
and continued his speech until midnight." The term "first
day" here is significant. How came the phrase into use?
Christ prophesied that he would rise on the "third day"
(Matt. xx. 19), and he reminded his apostles of his prophecy when he first met them after his resurrection (Luke
xxiv. 46). Angels spoke of it at the tomb (Luke xxiv.
7); the two disciples going to Emmaus told the Saviour
of it (Luke xxiv. 21); Jews heard of it, and observed it
in setting their guard at the sepulchre (Matt. xxvii. 63).
The Evangelists make record of that "third day" eight
times. It was the common expression at the period of
the resurrection, and nothing is heard of "first day"
then. The Evangelists wrote their Gospels from twenty
to forty years after; and then the expression everywhere
is, that Christ rose on the "first day of the week." Each
of the Evangelists thus speaks of it, and Mark twice.
Luke in his Gospel four times speaks of the prophecy that
Christ would rise the "third day:" yet some thirty years
after he speaks in the Acts incidentally of the "first day"
as though that were a term then in common use (Acts xx.
7). And about that same time Paul in First Corinthians
also speaks of the "first day" (xvi. 2). This marked
change from "third" to "first" day suggests a contrast
already begun between the seventh and the first day.
That contrast suggests the early Christian keeping of the
first day, and the religious character of it, as somewhat
like that of the seventh day.

Many have claimed from this passage in Acts xx. 7,
that Paul and his companions travelled from Troas to
Assos on Sunday, thus showing they did not regard it as
sacred. "Ready to depart on the morrow." Was that
morrow Sunday, or Monday? The answer depends upon
whether Luke reckoned by Jewish or Roman time. The
claim that it was of course Jewish is mere assumption.

The best of authorities, as Horne some time ago, and Smith's dictionary now, say that the Jewish chronology at this period was modified by the Roman, which dated the day at midnight as we do, and not at sunset as the Jews did. An example of change is this : Old Testament passages show that by the Jewish reckoning there were only *three* watches in the night (Lam. ii. 19; Judg. vii. 19; Exod. xiv. 24; 1 Sam. xi. 11). In Christ's time, by *his* language in one case (Mark xiii. 35), and Matthew's in another (Matt. xiv. 25), there were *four* night watches. Hegewisch [1] and others say that Jewish chronology was also modified by the Babylonian, and the Babylonians and Persians commenced the day with sunrise instead of sunset. Reasons for believing that Luke in this passage used Roman or Babylonian, and not Jewish computation, are : —

1. He wrote the book of Acts chiefly of Gentile churches, and mainly for them, and was likely to use the same chronology that they did, which was Roman.

2. The *morning* of the day was made conspicuous by Christ's resurrection, and his disciples would not be likely to begin the celebration of it the night previous ; certainly not out of special regard to Judaism just then. If there were any choice in chronologies, as there was, Luke would be likely to employ that which was *not* Jewish.

3. The Evangelists did in a similar instance use Roman or Babylonian chronology, and not Jewish ; and therefore Luke probably did in this. The instance is as follows : The Apostle John, having recorded Christ's resurrection, says that he suddenly appeared in the company of the disciples, "the same day at evening, being the first day of the week" (John xx. 19). Was this the evening of the first day by Jewish reckoning, or Roman ? It was probably after sunset ; for the doors were shut "for fear of the

---

[1] Introduction to Chronology, pp. 17, 71.

Jews," and they probably had sought cover of the shades of evening. The two disciples who went to Emmaus that day had there "sat at meat" with Jesus "towards evening" (Luke xxiv. 29, 30); then had gone to Jerusalem several miles distant, and there had found the disciples before Jesus appeared among them. It cannot reasonably be supposed that all this was done previous to sunset. Further, the Jews did not usually take their evening meal until their day's work was done, which was at sunset; and when Jesus appeared in the midst of his disciples they were sitting at meat, and on such a day, full of strange events, they would be likely to eat after, rather than before, their usual time. Therefore, again, it was doubtless after sunset. Yet more, John expressly says it was ὀψίας (xx. 19), late, the later evening, when Christ appeared among his disciples. The Jews had *two* evenings, — one between three P.M. and sunset, and one after sunset, immediately following the former. Christ's appearance being in the later evening, it is *certain* that it was after sunset. I have named four reasons for believing it was after sunset, and they culminate in *certainty*. But John says, it was "the same day at evening, being the first day of the week." He reckons the later evening, the one after sunset, as part of the day preceding it, and *not* as the beginning of another day. A fifth reason settles the question absolutely. Christ rose the first day. The evening of the "same day" on which he rose would have been, by Jewish reckoning, the night before he rose; since with the Jews the evening was the first part of the day. Therefore the Apostle John in this instance wrote by Roman or Babylonian chronology, and not the Jewish. But Luke, in the Acts, would be *more* likely than John to use Roman reckoning, because he wrote more of and for Gentile or Roman churches. Paul held the meeting, now in question, at Troas on an evening, and certainly continued it after sunset ; for he did not close it till after midnight. They celebrated the Lord's Supper on that occasion, and seem to have waited "seven days" for the usual time. It was an occasion very similar to that when Jesus met his disciples on the first evening after his resurrection. In the latter instance the apostle John puts the evening with the day preceding ; and, in the case of Paul at Troas, Luke would be still *more* likely to reckon the evening with the day preceding. If he' did so reckon, then Paul and his companions did not travel to Assos on Sunday, but on Monday. This passage rightly interpreted, then, brings weighty evidence against both the seventh-day sabbatarians, and those who have used it to show that the early Christians did not keep the first day sacred.

In 1 Cor. xvi. 2, we read : "Upon the first day of the week let every one of you lay by him in store, as God hath prospered him, that there be no gatherings when I come." Though each one was to decide upon the amount of his gift at home on the "first day," there were to be "gatherings" of the contributions, and these were most naturally on the first day also. This is made nearly or quite certain by the fact, that about three-fourths of a century after, according to the definite testimony of Justin Martyr, one part of the regular services of Christians on each first day, in connection with the Lord's Supper, was this : "They who are well to do, and willing, give what each thinks fit ; and what is *collected* is deposited with the president, who succors the orphans and widows, and those who through sickness or any other cause are in want, and those who are in bonds, and the strangers sojourning among us, and, in a word, takes care of all who are in want." [1] This custom no doubt originated with the apostles, and perhaps at Pentecost. In Justin Martyr's time

[1] Ant.-Nic. Lib., vol. ii., pp. 65, 66.

the collection was made on the *first* day of the week. The entire probability is, that it was made by the Corinthians through Paul's direction on the first day. The passage at least shows a marked distinction given to the first day in the apostle Paul's time. The collection, being taken in connection with lengthy religious services in Justin Martyr's day, was probably similarly taken in Paul's day. But the apostle gave the same "order to the churches of Galatia" (1 Cor. xvi. 1), — to more than one church, — and no doubt the "first day" part of it was included. And he commended the example of the Corinthians in their contributions, to the believers of Macedonia (2 Cor. ix. 2); and probably the "first day" was not there omitted. And the Macedonians seem to have followed the example of the Corinthians; for Paul commended the example of both Corinthians and Macedonians to the disciples at Rome (Rom. xv. 26). Paul commenced his original direction thus: "Upon the first day of the week." The *day* comes first and foremost. Was he likely to omit that part in his directions and commendation to the churches of Galatia, and the believers in Macedonia and at Rome? Not at all. Then the first day of the week was a very noted time in all those Gentile churches, and doubtless among all Christians. The Gentile Christians in all these churches, previous to conversion, had been unaccustomed to any marked *septenary* division of time. The meeting at Troas, and the laying by in store at home, and the collections of contributions in so many churches on the first day of the week, render it certain that that day was in some sense sacred and religious among the early Christians. If, now, it were germane to add concerning the apostle John's utterance respecting the "Lord's Day," we should much increase the accumulating evidence. But, keeping to the Pauline limitations, we find *much* proof of distinctively Christian meetings very frequently held. Glancing at a few chapters in First Corinthians alone, we can easily number a dozen instances where religious assemblies are spoken of. They were meetings of Christians, and not ordinarily, if at all, held on the Jewish sabbath; for Christians continued more or less to attend Jewish services. When were these many Christian meetings held, except on the Lord's Day? And, if thus held, that day of necessity became religious to the believers. This Pauline *example* of holding services on the first day, and treating it as a noted and a sacred day, was by inspiration, and is *precept* for us, *binding wherever the gospel goes.*

Turn to the third and last passage from Paul, concerning this subject, found in Col. ii. 16: "Let no man therefore judge you in meat, or in drink, or in respect of a holy day, or of the new moon, or of the sabbath days." All agree that the phrase, "Let no man therefore judge you," makes it *optional* for Christians to observe, or not, those several customs and feasts and days; optional to observe the "sabbath days," or not, whatever they were.

Two classes say that "sabbath days" mean Jewish feast-days, not seventh-day sabbaths. They are seventh-day sabbatarians, and first-day sabbatarians who fear the first day will suffer if the sabbath in any respect is meant in this passage.

That the word "sabbath days" does *not* refer to Jewish festivals, appears from the following: 1. The word "holy day" refers to such festivals, and another word for the same is not probable in the same phrase. 2. The word "sabbath days," in English or Greek, does not elsewhere mean such festivals in the whole New Testament. This all must admit. 3. It elsewhere, in the nearly fifty instances, means seventh-day sabbaths. 4. Jewish feasts are often spoken of in the New Testament, but not one of them anywhere is called a sabbath, or credited with the

nature of the sabbath.   5. In the Old-Testament Hebrew
none of those feast-days are ever termed a sabbath, save
the day of atonement twice.   That was indeed a full sabbath in its manner of being kept.   6. There is a mistrans-
lation in the English in the case of the feasts of trumpets and tabernacles, where they are called sabbaths
(Lev. xxiii. 24, 39).   The Hebrew for sabbath is *shabbath,*
or, *shabbath shabbathon.*   The feasts of trumpets and
tabernacles are termed merely *shabbathon,* — a sabbatism,
or partial sabbath, or rest only.   7. The Septuagint notes
this distinction, not translating these feasts by the Greek
σαββάτων, but by ἀνάπαυσις, rest.   8. A member of the Old-
Testament Bible-revision committee has recently said,
"The distinction between שַׁבָּת and שַׁבָּתוֹן, in Lev. xxiii.,
will be marked in the new revision by a difference of
expression.   What it will be, I am not at liberty to say."
9. The Targums on the Pentateuch, that is, the transla-
tions of it by ancient Jews into the Chaldee language,
make like distinctions with the Septuagint.   10. The
phraseology in Col. ii. 16, "Of a holy day, or of the new
moon, or of the sabbath days," is in substance a *copy* of
language in Ezekiel (xlv. 17), and there the word for "sabbaths" in the Hebrew is *not* for feast-days, but for *full*
sabbaths; and a rational inference is, that real seventh-
day sabbaths are meant in Colossians.   "Holy day" in
Colossians should be "feast-day," as, in the other twenty-
six instances in the New Testament, the original is rendered "feast."   In six other places in the Old Testament
the word for sabbaths is joined to those for "feast" and
"new moon," and in each case the original means "sabbaths," and not "sabbatisms."   11. In the nearly one
hundred and fifty texts in the Bible where the word "sabbath" or "sabbath day," singular or plural, is used, there
are only *two* where it is properly applied to any day except
the sabbath, and, in those, to the day of atonement, and

in the single book of Leviticus.   One hundred and fifty against two!   The day of atonement occurred *once*, while the sabbath occurred fifty-two times.   Was it that isolated day of atonement that the apostle meant?   What violent hands they are, though not so designed, that take that one text, and affirm it means Jewish feast-days, and then build a doctrine on it, and a new observance on it!   Some seventh-day sabbatarians admit that if this word in Colossians does not mean feast-days, their theory cannot stand. It is the one brick in the row, that, tipped over against them, knocks down all their other proofs.

But the non-sabbath Lord's-Day men here meet us. They say the word does mean seventh-day sabbaths, and that Paul set them aside; and from that they take the tremendously illogical leap to the conclusion that he set aside the Fourth Commandment.   What! was that sabbath, kept by the Jews after Christians were keeping the first day; that sabbath which the Talmudist doctors of the law buried with excrescences and perversions; that sabbath which Christ disowned as Pharisaism held it, — was that sabbath the one given by the Lord on Sinai? Much depends on the meaning of this word "sabbath days."   We may well call this passage the Rosetta stone of interpretation on this subject.

We need to get into the very notion of the sabbath as it was in Christ's and the apostles' time.   The Lord of heaven might not heal the sick, nor loose a poor crippled woman from her bonds, upon that day, without suffering the charge of sabbath-breaking.   A healed man, when mercy came to him away from home, might not carry his bundle of a bed with him as he went to tell the news to his family.   Hungry men might not pick and shell in their hands a few heads of grain, and eat the kernels, as they passed by the field in going from one meeting to another.   One might not wear sandals on the sabbath over those flinty Palestine paths if they had nails in the sole, for that would be breaking the law by bearing a burden. One might not carry a pail of water to his thirsty animal, for that would be bearing a burden; but he might *lead* the animal to the water, for then *it* would bear the burden, and there was no law against horses or camels carrying water after they drank it. One might not walk on the grass, for the bruising of it would be a kind of threshing, as was the shelling of wheat in the apostles' hands. The Essenes would not remove a dish or vessel on the sabbath, for that would be bearing a burden; and some of them would not move themselves if caught away from home Saturday night, but stay there in the street or anywhere else the full twenty-four hours. Oil might not be taken internally as a medicine on the sabbath, though it might be used externally for perfuming the person. One might not catch a biting flea, for that would be hunting. Thirty-nine rules — and these are some of the minutiæ under them — those doctors of the law had against labor on the sabbath.

Now, when the apostle said, "Judge for yourselves about keeping the sabbath," it was *such* a sabbath, the one right there, known to him and the people. And is it right to say, that, when he made that sabbath optional, he swept away the whole Fourth Commandment? Nay? When God said to the apostate Jews, "The new moons and sabbaths, the calling of assemblies, I cannot away with," did he mean the sabbath of the Fourth Commandment, and did he revoke it?

Again, at the time Paul wrote, the new dispensation had come in; a new day had appeared, better, dearer by far than the old. It told of the glorious resurrection of the Son of God; it assured of like resurrection of his saints, or of their quick change and transition to glory. That noted day, full of the memory of wonders, the Christians deemed the light of heaven, and in some sense were keeping it sacred, as by divine authority. Was omitting the seventh-day observance *then* all the same as omitting it before Christ came? Was making the mere *seventh day* optional then all the same as pronouncing the Fourth Commandment abolished? Was it the same that it would have been under the old dispensation? No! Circumstances alter cases. Observe that neither Paul nor any of the apostles say that the Fourth Commandment is abolished; and the question is, whether *men* now can be justified in saying so, on the ground that Paul releases from obligation to keep the seventh when the new and clean first day is given.

But some go further, and tell us the whole Decalogue is abolished. They prove it, they say, from Paul, where he says, "Ye are not under the law, but under grace;" "We are delivered from the law;" "If ye be led of the Spirit, ye are not under the law." On the basis of such texts they say the law is abrogated. Does a comprehensive view of the Scriptures justify their conclusion? Is not rather this the meaning? "We are not under the ceremonial law, to obtain salvation through its ceremonies and sacrifices; nor under the moral law, to be justified and saved by our good deeds, or be lost; nor under it as unwilling subjects to be driven by its penalties, — because love is the fulfilling of the law, and the love of Christ constraineth us." To say we are not under the law, in being obligated by its principles of right and righteousness, that it is abolished so as not to be to us an ever-living testimony of God's will, that the Ten Commandments are no more to us a guidance to the divine pleasure, — is it not theoretical antinomianism? But Archbishop Whately says the law of the Decalogue was intended for the Israelites exclusively;[1] and Dr. R. W. Dale says the

[1] Difficulties, St. Paul, p. 147.

Fourth Commandment was given to the Jews only.[1] The inference is made, that, the Jewish economy having passed away, the Decalogue is abrogated. The Jewish ceremonial and civil laws have passed away; but *moral* laws stand on a different basis. "Moral *duties*," says Bishop Butler, "arise out of the nature of the case itself, prior to external command." Then, moral duties engrossed in the Decalogue existed *before* their engrossment, and exist after it forever, because the case of man's moral obligations is not changed. Whately says the moral law written in our hearts is unabolished, and that moral precepts are binding on all in all ages.[2] Dr. Bushnell says, "Plainly enough the law of God never can be taken away from any world or creature; for with it, in close company, goes abroad all the conserving principle, moral and physical, in which God's kingdom stands."[3] Then God's moral law in the Decalogue cannot be taken away. No matter though engrossed specially for the Israelites, as it was, it was engrossed for *man*. No matter when or where God's *moral* law breaks forth: it is for mankind. Tertullian well exclaims, "Why should God . . . be believed to have given a law through Moses to one people, and not be said to have assigned it to all nations?" He speaks of the moral law, and declares, "He gave to all nations the self-same law."[4] But is the Fourth Commandment a *moral* law? Two classes of errorists are here: one class call it wholly moral; the other, wholly positive. It is in part *both*. But can both kinds of elements be united in the same law? Yes. See an example in the next neighbor to the Fourth: "Honor thy father and thy mother" (moral and perpetual), "that thy days may be long upon the land which the Lord thy God giveth thee" (positive and temporary). Paul changed it from Canaan to "earth."

[1] Ten Commandments, p. 93. [2] Difficulties, St. Paul, pp. 150, 159.
[3] Forgiveness and Law, p. 119. [4] Ant.-Nic. Lib., vol. xviii., p. 200.

In the Fourth are rest, physical and spiritual, worship, holiness. But the *septenary* element is not moral, it is positive. God can take it, and put the first day in place of the seventh, and still be immutable. Yet those moral elements that live in all ages, that cannot be taken away, where are they now? Not in the seventh day, for inspired Paul tells us the seventh-day sabbath is now only optional. Paul makes sacred the first day, John calls it the "Lord's Day," primitive saints observed it: are not the sabbatical elements in it? Those moral elements exist without being re-appointed. The apostles never did so foolish a thing as to re-enact them.

But admit for a little that the Fourth and *all* the Commandments are abrogated, as some assure us. When circumcision passed away, Paul did not appeal to it as in force any more. When laws become dead on our statute-books, abrogated by our law-makers, our magistrates do not undertake to enforce them, do not appeal to them as authority. Surely the apostle will not appeal to the abrogated Decalogue! He will let it slumber with the dead past. Look, now, over the pages of his Epistles to the churches. See them swept clean of all the Commandments! But what! has Paul gone back to legalism? Has his inspiration failed him? Fallen from grace is he, or fallen from doctrine? Some years after telling us that we are not under the law, he actually appeals to the law for authority and for the rule of righteousness: "Honor thy father and thy mother; *which is the first commandment with promise.*" And in the same *book* where he tells us, "We are delivered from the law," he afterwards appeals to that law again: "Thou shalt not commit adultery, thou shalt not kill, thou shalt not steal," and on to the end. And this *Pauline* summons of Sinai is equalled by the Apostle James's like appeal (ii. 8–11). And, in the very Epistle where some claim that the law is abolished, Paul himself refutes them by affirming, "The law is holy, just, and good." "Do we, then, make void the law through faith? God forbid; yea, we establish the law." Profess- or G. P. Fisher says, and others say, the change from seventh to first day was by no explicit ordinance.[1] Truth; but it requires *more* truth. The *change* from passover to supper, from animal sacrifice to the one sacrifice of Christ, was by no explicit ordinance. The new was com- menced, the old gradually passed away. But there were certain moral truths underlying the old in each case, which are embraced in the new. So the moral elements in the seventh-day sabbath are contained in the Lord's Day. Some positive elements in all the old are changed to other positive in the new.

Is the interpretation of the Pauline Scriptures now given, consonant with the testimony of the early Chris- tian fathers, and is it the *only* interpretation that is agree- able thereto? Beginning with the death of the apostle John, within one century eleven of the fathers testify to the keeping of the Lord's Day by the Christians; and within about three and a half centuries nearly fifty tes- tify to it. The first of them was contemporary with the apostle John. Some of them testify that Sunday observ- ance *began* with the *apostles*. Within about three centu- ries after the apostolic age, some twenty of the fathers testify that the Christians generally did not consider the observance of the seventh day obligatory. These facts are utterly inconsistent with seventh-day sabbatarianism. A portion of them overthrow the modern theory of some, that the early Christians did not specifically keep *any* day sacred. They also condemn the view that the early Christians were at variance among themselves, whether to keep the first day or not. The testimony of the early fathers is absolutely inconsistent with modern declara-

[1] Beginnings of Christianity, p. 562.

tions that the early Christians prosecuted their secular business on Sunday. They spoke of the first day as holy, and sacred, and chief. It was their great delight. Tertullian specifically says in substance that secularities should be refrained from on the first day. On this point the statement of Theodore Parker should have weight. Treating of the keeping of Sunday by the early Christians, he said, what can be corroborated, "The Romans, like all other nations, had certain festal days in which it was not thought proper to labor unless work was pressing. It was disreputable to continue common labor on such days without an urgent reason."[1] Did the primitive Christians care less about their chief of days than idolatrous worshippers did about theirs?

But did the fathers teach that the Fourth Commandment was abolished? Some say they did. I do not believe *one* sentence can be produced sustaining that position. Their writings are misinterpreted. They argue that the Fourth Commandment in respect to keeping the *seventh* day is no longer binding. And that is just what we now hold, whether or not maintaining that that command is still obligatory in other respects. The *point* of their argument has by many been missed. They were in controversy with those who said, "You must keep the seventh day, generally then called sabbath." Yet Tertullian, on this very question, after naming "sabbath" explains himself by saying "seventh day."[2] It shows what he was about, trying to refute those who troubled many Christians by saying they ought still to keep the seventh day. He and other fathers labor to show in substance that there was nothing sinful *per se* in not keeping the seventh day, and that they were now released from it. He cites the case of the Israelitish army marching around Jericho seven

---

[1] Sermon on Christian Use of the Sunday, p. 22.

[2] Ant.-Nic. Lib., vol. xviii., p. 211.

days in succession, of course one day being the sabbath ; and thence infers that it does not break up the foundations of all things not to keep the seventh day. But he does not say that the Fourth Commandment is gone.

The question is not whether the sacred day of the new dispensation is the Jewish sabbath of the old, nor whether apostles gave the Judaistic day to the Christian Church. No one claims that they did. To debate it were missing the point. But it is, whether certain moral sabbatic elements of the Decalogue — which is *not* the whole of the Jewish sabbath — are not divinely given in the Lord's Day. The Fathers plainly indicate that sacred time, rest, spirituality, holy convocations, religious services, and the Lord's Supper, especially belonged to the Lord's Day, which makes that day, in their conception, at least akin to the Decalogue sabbath. The discussions of their time necessarily put the seventh and the Lord's Day in some contrast with each other ; and in that connection the Fathers indicate that the Lord's Day was religious, as much or more so than the seventh day. For example, Ignatius speaks of the Christian "observance of the Lord's Day ;"[1] and Tertullian, of the sacred rites of the Lord's Day.[2] The Fathers also *compared* the two days, giving the religious superiority to the Lord's Day. (See Irenæus,[3] Clement,[4] Origen.[5]) The Fathers, in describing the Lord's Day, used ideas and phraseology formerly employed to describe the sabbath of the Decalogue. Dionysius speaks of the "Lord's *holy* day."[6] His word for "holy" has the same root that the Septuagint — both being Greek — employs for "holy" in the Fourth Commandment. Athanasius speaks of the command to keep the sabbath, and then says, "So we *honor* the Lord's

---

[1] Ant.-Nic. Lib., vol. i., p. 180.   [4] Ibid., vol. xii., p. 284.

[2] Ibid., vol. xv., p. 428.   [5] Comm. Ex. Patrologiæ, tom. xii., p. 385.

[3] Ibid , vol. ix., pp. 162, 163.   [6] Patrologiæ, Euseb. Eccl. Hist., b. iv., c. 23.

Day." [1] The council of Laodicea, deprecating Judaizing
on the then Jews' sabbath, says Christians ought to give
the "chief honor to the Lord's Day." [2] But carefully
observe, that, in all cases, the Fathers speak of the Jewish
seventh day in their time, and do not affirm or assume
that their view annuls the totality of the Fourth Commandment. They may not have had full conceptions of the
true philosophy of the case ; but they seem to have been
kept by a gracious divine Providence from affirming false-
hood on this subject. Scrutinize the matter, and you will
see that the Fathers in fact retained in the Lord's Day
all the *moral* elements of the sabbath of the Decalogue,
though not retaining the seventh-day *number*. The Fathers recognized the distinction between the moral and
ceremonial law. The evidence is too much for present
space. But Irenæus says, "The Lord did not abrogate
the natural precepts of the law ;" "Preparing man for this
life, the Lord himself did speak in his own person to all
alike the words of the Decalogue ; and therefore, in like
manner, do they remain permanently with us, receiving, by
means of his advent in the flesh, extension and increase,
but not abrogation." [3] If Irenæus and other Fathers, in
speaking of the Jewish seventh day, or sabbath of their
time, had meant by it the equivalent in all respects of the
sabbath of the Decalogue, and had intended to say that
it was abrogated, would Irenæus have stultified himself
by affirming that even Christ in his advent did nothing to
abrogate the words of the Decalogue ? Utterly impossible ! He would have made exception of the Fourth Commandment if he held that that *was* abrogated, either by
Christ himself or his apostles. But Dr. Hessey, very
learned in Patristical lore, tells us that, after Paul's

---

[1] Patrologiæ, Ath., tom. iv., p. 138; De Sab. et Cir., 4.
[2] Conc. Laod. Can., 29; Morris's Lib. Faths. St. Ephræm, p. 391, note.
[3] Ant.-Nic. Lib., vol. v., pp. 412, 424, 425.

teaching on the subject, the "sabbath was of obligation
no longer."[1] He interprets the Fathers as substantiating
that view. Both he and Professor Hopkins seem to have
overlooked most important evidence on this point. Bishop
Archelaus, A.D. 277, replying to an errorist named Manes,
describes his error as an "effort directed to prove that
the law of Moses is not consistent with the law of Christ,"
and says, "As to the assertion that the sabbath has
been abolished, we deny that he has abolished it plainly,
(*plane*), for he was himself also Lord of the sabbath. And
this (the law's relation to the sabbath) was like the servant who has charge of the bridegroom's couch, and who
prepares the same with all carefulness, and does not suffer
it to be disturbed or touched by any stranger, but keeps
it intact against the time of the bridegroom's arrival ; so
that when he is come the bed may be used as it pleases
himself, or as it is granted to those to use it whom he
has bidden enter along with him."[2] Deducible from this
passage is the following : 1. Christ could abolish or change
the Decalogue sabbath. 2. The law kept it for him till
he came. 3. One thing he did *not* do : he did not abolish it. 4. The true sabbath, therefore, in some sense
remains, though the followers of Christ do not keep the
seventh, but the first, day. Archelaus had the question
whether the *law* of Moses, in respect to the sabbath,
was abolished. Other Fathers had the different question,
whether the Fourth Commandment now required the keeping of the seventh day. I cannot find that Drs. Hessey
or Hopkins, or others, who hold, that, according to the
Fathers, the Fourth Commandment is abolished, have ever
seen this language of Archelaus. It is not beneath their
notice. It is utterly inconsistent with their theory. Dr.
Hessey says in substance that the Lord's Day was not
regarded as a sabbath until at least after the fifth cen-

---

[1] Sunday, p. 37.　　　　[2] Ant.-Nic. Lib., vol. xx., p. 373.

tury. Not *generally;* but he should have noticed that
Clement of Alexandria, not a century after the last of
the apostles, recognized the first day as substantially a
sabbath, and indicated his anticipation that it would yet
be called such.[1] We do not find his thought questioned
by those around him. It must have been shared by
others.

This line of interpretation now presented runs harmoniously through, I think, the whole Scriptures, and as
well through the literature of early Christianity. And
I am confident that no other theory, substantially different from this, can ever be made to do it. Moreover, the
non-sabbath Lord's-Day men seem in substance to confess judgment against themselves, or to yield the point
in debate, when they are not content without falling back
to the law of holy rest that they admit underlies both the
original sabbath and the Lord's Day ; or to those *principles* which they acknowledge were in the Fourth Commandment, and may still be appealed to in support of the
first day. That "law," those "principles," we maintain,
are the *moral elements* of the original and the Sinaitic
sabbath, existing still, and ever to remain.

NOTE. — This subject, and others concerning the sabbath, are to
be more fully discussed in a series of articles in "The Bibliotheca
Sacra," of the present year, published by W. F. Draper, Andover,
Mass.

[1] Ant.-Nic. Lib., vol. xii., p. 386.

OBLIGATION OF ONE REST-DAY IN SEVEN : SO THAT
THE SEVENTH-DAY REST IS OBLIGATORY, IF THE
FIRST IS NOT.

BY REV. PROF. HENRY LUMMIS, OF WATERTOWN.

MORAL law is binding, not because it is found written in
a code, but because of its place in the nature of things, as
the order of God. There are sources of the Mississippi
more original than Itasca Lake, or than the brooks by
which the lake is fed. The springs which from depths
in the earth bubble up, and form the primitive streams, are
the true sources of the great river.

So there are principles of law more fundamental than
any code. The code, in regard to many of its enactments,
may be binding simply because of the authority of the
lawgiver ; the principles, if they belong to moral law, are
authoritative without enactment or promulgation. Moses,
Lycurgus, Solon, were eminent lawgivers. Once their
legislation had supreme authority. To-day it is null.
But the principles embodied in their statutes, so far as
they were moral, are as binding now as they were twenty-
four hundred or three thousand years ago. So it must be.
Statutory laws will be continually changing, with changing
times : the underlying principles, if sound, are permanent
because they belong to the immutable and eternal nature
of things.

The obligation of one day's rest in seven does not grow
out of legislation: it lies deeper ; it is found in man's
nature. Long before, " Honor thy father and thy mother,"
had been formulated, reverence was due to parents. The
obligation grew out of the relationship, and was as incum-

bent before, as after, the words had been written in stone by the finger of God.

Ere the law of Moses contained, "Thou shalt love the Lord thy God with all thy heart, and with all thy soul, and with all thy might," it was man's duty to render supreme love to his Creator.

In the primitive book of God's *work*, older, obscurer, it may be, than that supplemental volume, God's *word*, is the unwritten law wherein must be found the primary ground of obligation for a rest-day for man, if it is to be found. We need not seek it in Genesis, nor in Exodus, in the Gospels, nor in the Epistles. It antedates human documents, and is earlier than a knowledge of letters.

The Mosaic legislation presupposes it, though it may not have been clearly apprehended by man prior to the giving of the law.

There were great principles evidently not yet understood when Moses promulgated his wonderful system. The principle of prohibition of vinous liquors needed clearer light to find a place in Jewish statutes. Up to the time of David no severe word had been recorded against the use of wine. Even the principle of monogamy, now so clearly understood, was in the shadow, and polygamy found toleration under the legislation of Sinai. Still monogamy was the righteous principle *then*, as really as *now*. If man's well-being requires one day's rest in seven, that rest was the fitting and so far the obligatory thing, for man, prior to the code of the Hebrew lawgiver. The lapse of forty-three hundred years, however much it has added to human knowledge, has originated no principles.

It may be asked, "What is the evidence of the need of one rest-day in seven?" The reply is: Such need has become so evident, that eminent statesmen, successful merchants, and enterprising manufacturers have long since conceded the fact, simply on the ground of political economy. It is shown by the joint admission of employers and employees, that in the long-run the wages of a week of seven days is only equal to the wages of a week of six, and that the work is no more in the longer week than in the shorter.

Lord Macaulay in his speech on the Ten-Hour Bill, delivered in the House of Commons in 1846, declares that when a Puritan Government in England had swept away Easter, Whitsuntide, and Christmas, it felt obliged to institute new holidays; and that when the French Jacobins decreed that Sunday should no longer be a day of respite from toil, they substituted every tenth day for every seventh. Though they annulled the saints' days, they put in their place days sacred to Genius, to Opinion, and to Industry. These men did not fear God, but they did recognize the necessity of days of rest. After mentioning the fact that the Sundays of three hundred years would give fifty years of labor, if devoted to labor, Macaulay says, " For my own part, I have not the smallest doubt that if we and our ancestors had during the last three centuries worked just as hard on the Sundays as on the week-days, we should have been at this moment a poorer people, and a less civilized people, than we are; that there would have been less production than there has been, that the wages of the laborer would have been lower than they are, and that some other nation would have been now making cotton stuffs and woollen stuffs and cutlery for the whole world." " Of course," he adds, " I do not mean to say that a man will not produce more in a week by working seven days than by working six days; but I very much doubt whether at the end of a year he will generally have produced more by working seven days a week than by working six days a week. . . . We are not poorer, but richer, because we have through many ages rested from our labor one day in seven. That day is not lost. While

industry is suspended, while the plough lies in the furrow,
while the exchange is silent, while no smoke ascends from
the factory, a process is going on, quite as important to
the wealth of nations as any process which is performed
on more busy days.   Man, the machine of machines, the
machine compared with which all the contrivances of the
Watts and the Arkwrights are worthless, is repairing and
winding up, so that he returns to his labors on Monday
with clearer intellect, with livelier spirits, with renewed
corporal vigor.   Never will I believe that what makes a
population stronger, and healthier, and wiser, and better,
can ultimately make it poorer."   Note that Lord Macaulay
spoke not as a clergyman, but as a political economist, presenting the question not from the religious but from the
financial view.

William Wilberforce, in a letter bearing date Oct. 8,
1818, addressed to Christophe, King of Hayti, writes : "I
well remember that during the war, when it was proposed
to work all Sunday in one of the royal manufactories, for
a continuance, not for an occasional service, it was found
that the workmen who obtained government consent to
abstain from working on Sundays executed in a few
months even more work than the others."   This testimony to a matter of fact, from an eminent civilian, has
great weight.   It finds confirmation from documents, both
in our own country and in France.   It has been conclusively shown that the public work of these nations continued through seven days of the week was a losing enterprise.

Further testimony freely given by men of large business
experience, and showing clearly the economy of a rest-day
during the week, might be given, did the assigned limits
allow.

Eminent men of this convention, to whom special assignment has been made in regard to the law and advantages

of periodic rest, render it less important that this point be elaborated here.

It scarcely needs to be said, that if just as much worldly gain can be secured by six days work per week, as by seven, it is better to have a rest of one day in seven. No sensible man can be anxious to work seven days, if he earn just as much by the work of six. Will it be said, "While it is evident that one day's rest in seven is better than *no* rest, it does not follow that one day in seven is better than one day in ten or one day in six"? True, it does not follow. But France tried the experiment of one rest-day in ten, and found the amount of productive labor diminished by the change.

Attention is called, in Smith's Bible Dictionary, to a remarkable pamphlet by Pierre Joseph Proudhon, a noted French socialist, who maintains with singular ability the advantage of one rest-day to six work-days, and the inconvenience of any other proportion that could be arranged. This monograph is of special value, and, coming as it does from an extra-ecclesiastical source, must be deemed altogether disinterested testimony. It meets the demand properly made for the reason of one rest-day in seven, rather than in some greater or less number.

It may also be asked, naturally enough, "Why the first or seventh day, rather than the third or fifth?" Saturday has, almost from time immemorial, been the school recreation day; but Wellesley College, without censure, adopts Monday as its day of recreation. May the demand for one rest-day in seven be met with entire fitness by taking Wednesday or Thursday as that day of rest? So far as unwritten law answers, it seems to give an affirmative. Any one day of the seven, properly observed, is all that is called for by that law founded in the constitution of man. The special *day* must be determined by some circumstance of fitness, or by positive enactment.

The usage of different nations recognizes the principle of one rest-day in seven. But the great diversity in regard to *the day* shows that no specific day is naturally indicated.

Every day in the week, somewhere or other, seems to have been separated from the rest as a sacred day. The great body of Christians observe the first day of the week, the people about Ormaz and Goa solemnize the second, the tribes of Goa observe the third. Certain Christians of the early Church kept the fourth with fasting and with public assemblies for prayer. The tribes in the territories of the Mogul kept the fifth. The Mohammedan festival is on the sixth, and Friday in the Catholic branch of the Christian Church at least appears to have had special honor since the days of Constantine. The sacred day of the Jews is the seventh, and several respectable bodies of Protestant Christians are at one with them in regarding that day as the sabbath. In the valley of the Nile to-day, both Saturday and Sunday are kept sacred by the Abyssinians.

Have we well-established grounds for making one day rather than another the day of rest? Christians certainly find in the first day of the week a fitness for the day of rest. Eminent among the grounds of that fitness is the fact that thereon Christ rose from the dead. Bishop Wordsworth thus enumerates the reasons for regarding the Lord's Day as the *consecrated* day of the week : —

1. Christ rose from the dead on this day.

2. He appeared twice in succession on this day.

3. He gave special evidence of his resurrection on this day.

4. He gave earnest of the Spirit on this day.

5. He sent the full effusion of the Holy Ghost to his Church.

He subjoins : "Our Lord does not seem to have shown

himself to his disciples in the intervening six days. Thus he distinguished the first day from all other days of the week as his own day. And the Holy Spirit in recording those appearances in holy Scripture, and by calling it the Lord's Day, has consecrated that day to him."

These reasons are not without weight. Unless greater or at least equal reasons exist in regard to some other day, this first day of the week is entitled to precedence, as a matter of fitness.

There are, it must be admitted, some difficulties in regard to the reasons assigned above; not for preferring this first day of the week as a memorial day of the Lord's resurrection, but for its preference over the seventh as a rest-day. The asserted authoritative change is a difficult point to establish, as is felt throughout Protestantism.

Men cherish days on which great benefactors were born. The people of this country reverence the 22d of February. Men regard the days on which good sovereigns had a birth. England shows special respect to the 24th of May. There is surely reason why we should reverence the day on which Jesus Christ became the first-born of the dead. Herein men can agree. But, in the absence of any definite word in respect to the change, can we be quite *sure* that he meant that the first day of the week should take the place of the day signalized as the rest-day for at least fifteen hundred years, possibly for four thousand or even five thousand or more? With all respect for those who may deem the problem simple of solution, I confess to a consciousness of obscurity here. And it grows, the more I study the history of the seventh and of the first day. Is it evident that Christ, without mention of the fact, should have desired and ordained that this first day of the week should become the most honored and sacred of all days? Nazareth was under odium all his lifetime, yet he never uttered a word to free his own and his mother's home from its reproach.

Bethlehem, the place of his nativity, honored as the home of his great ancestor David, he never seemed to give especial honor to, himself, nor to solicit honor for from others. The day on which he was born he has suffered to remain in such obscurity, that, though the Christian Church has agreed for centuries to honor Christmas, no one among all the hundreds of millions of Christendom *knows* the day of the week, nor of the month, and no one knows either the month or the year, in which the Redeemer had his birth. I believe that the apostles would naturally regard the *day* as well as the *fact* of their Lord's resurrection with profound interest : I think I can see reasons why John at Patmos might first among the disciples call the first day of the week the Lord's Day ; and I find no occasion for doubting that there were religious services connected therewith, and that this Lord's Day gradually took precedence of all the days of the week; but that in the absence of specific command the first day of the week took forthwith the place of the ancient rest-day, and that without controversy between the adherents of the old and the maintainers of the new, is so out of the ordinary course of human proceeding, that if not inexplicable, it must be admitted to be very strange.

The *clear*, definite, unmistakable divine assignment of the seventh day of the week as the rest-day is in striking contrast with a want of assignment in the case of the substitution of the first for the seventh, if it has been really made. No man who believes the sacred record has ever doubted that the Israelites were commanded to keep the seventh day sacred as the weekly rest. But many good, many learned men, gravely question whether an authoritative voice has ever enjoined such keeping of the first day. "Remember *the sabbath* day to keep it holy," was written on tables of stone. If that divine command be still binding, can it be fairly read, "Remember *a* sabbath day to keep it holy"? If one jot or tittle has passed from the law, has it not thereby become defective? if it has been fulfilled, is it longer binding? If "The sabbath was made for man," be the enunciation of the universal and everlasting obligation of the sabbath law, can it be other than the original law given to Moses in the midst of the smoke and the fire and the thunderings of Mount Sinai? And, if that original law is still in force, is it legitimate to construe it, "*A* sabbath was made for man"? If the Saviour's conclusion, "Therefore the Son of man is Lord even of the sabbath day," be deduced from a premise affirming the universal obligation of the sabbath, he evidently disregarded the canons of Aristotle.

Again and again the duty of observing the seventh-day rest was urged and enforced upon the people of Israel. Its neglect was censured and threatened; the benefits of its observance are proclaimed; and the sin and the folly of its desecration are declared. Hear the prophet speak for Jehovah: "If thou turn away thy foot from the sabbath, from doing thy pleasure on my holy day, and call the sabbath a delight, the holy of the Lord, honorable; and shalt honor him, not doing thine own ways, nor finding thine own pleasure, nor speaking thine own words: then shalt thou delight thyself in the Lord; and I will cause thee to ride upon the high places of the earth, and feed thee with the heritage of Jacob thy father; for the mouth of the Lord hath spoken it" (Isa. lviii. 13, 14).

"The sons of the stranger that join themselves to the Lord to serve him, and to love the name of the Lord, to be his servants, every one that keepeth the sabbath from polluting it, and taketh hold of my covenant: even them will I bring to my holy mountain, and make them joyful in my house of prayer; their burnt offerings and their sacrifices shall be accepted upon mine altar; for mine house shall be called a house of prayer for all people" (Isa. lvi. 6, 7).

"If ye diligently hearken unto me, saith the Lord, to bring in no burden through the gates of this city on the sabbath day, but hallow the sabbath day, to do no work therein; then shall there enter into the gates of this city kings and princes sitting upon the throne of David, riding in chariots and on horses, they and their princes, the men of Judah, and the inhabitants of Jerusalem; and this city shall be inhabited forever" (Jer. xvii. 24, 25).

In these specific mentions of the rest-day it was *the* sabbath, — the day indicated in the Decalogue. Would it not seem that a change, if made, would have been as specific as was the original designation of time in the law? Do not the expedients resorted to, to adjust the problem, indicate the uncertainty of the thing attempted to be explained? Would a Jew be at any loss to point out his ground for observing *his rest-day?*

It is certainly questionable whether the use of the expression "*the sabbath*" for the first day of the week does not imply a conclusion not warranted by the premises in the case.

Perhaps it will be asked, "Does not the essayist observe the Lord's Day as a day of rest?" If he answer, "Yes," how can he consistently keep the first day, and yet hold the seventh to be more evidently binding?

Men are not always consistent. Embarrassments may be found on both sides of a question. The following escape from the dilemma is suggested: —

The legislation of Moses was not in reference to one day in seven: it named a specific day, the day which God originally hallowed, because on it he had rested from his work. This was to be to the Hebrews a memorial of their escape from the bondage of Egypt, a land where they had enjoyed no rest-day. If God dealt with them as one deals with children that need specific direction, rather than as with enlightened men able to comprehend

principles, this clear statement of written law in the code
of Moses was just what might be expected to be given
to this comparatively undeveloped people. Take an illustration : I say to my boy of eleven, "I wish you to practise your music from ten to eleven o'clock in the morning ;"
to my adult daughter I say, "Arrange the time for your
study and practice for yourself." Both are bound by a
principle, — the one under the specific detail of a definite
time indicated by a specific command, when he will be
fresher and better fitted to do his work than if a later hour
in the day were assigned, after long play had brought weariness if not exhaustion : the other is free to choose her time,
whether morning or evening ; her developed intelligence,
and clear apprehension of the importance of progress,
keep her at work as fully as would the specific command.

The principles of the law were as obligatory in the
days of Paul as they were in the days of David ; but circumcision, which under the law was enjoined with severe
penalties in case of its omission, had become a matter
of so little moment in the days of the apostle, that he
dared to assert the nothingness of circumcision. If the
Decalogue unchanged still binds, I see no escape from
breaking the divine law except by a prompt return to the
observance of the seventh day. It may be asked, "Does
the Decalogue, then, cease to be binding ?" May we not
answer, "Yes, as specific legislation, not in the underlying principles"? Is it not conceded that the law, outside
of the Decalogue, is abrogated ? But the principles contained in that law outside of the Decalogue, prohibiting
the intermarriage of near blood, bind to-day as really as
if they were found in the Decalogue itself. And are not
the principles therein requiring tenderness to animals
authoritative to-day? Those enactments are not law in
this land ; but the principles may wisely be embodied,
by such benefactors to the dumb animals as Mr. Bergh,

in the legislation of Pennsylvania and of New York and of Massachusetts. So, throughout the entire Mosaic law, its fundamental moral principles will bear re-formulating for the statutory laws of this nineteenth century.

Without doubt the constitution of man requires a day of rest. It did so originally. If the specific law given to the Israelites is binding now as really as it was then, must we not all plead guilty to the habit of disregarding that law so far as *the* sabbath is concerned? If, under the principle of the need of one day's rest in seven, we have liberty to take the day on which Christ arose from the dead, a day hallowed by the early Christian Church, and regarded with reverence almost universally for eighteen centuries, consecrated by the associations and memories and usages of the saintly and the wise for fifty generations, and honored by God's providence as really as was the day of rest under the Mosaic legislation, we meet the natural want as truly as if we were observing in the most rigid conformity to the command of the Decalogue the very day anciently sanctified.

If, as is conceded by the best intelligence of the nations, man's well-being requires a seventh-day rest, the duty of observing such a rest is imperative even in the absence of formal statutes. If the days of the Jewish dispensation have passed away along with their code, and if, under the bond of natural obligation and evident fitness, we choose the Lord's Day as our weekly rest, are we losers? Are we not rather great gainers? Fostering in our hearts grateful love and glad remembrance of our Redeemer, we elect to honor his resurrection-day. We even name the day, as is done in Russia, "the resurrection." We hold fast to the day and its observance, not under a statute enforced by the death-penalty, but as a weekly Easter in which we chant our joyful anthem, —

"The Lord is risen indeed!　Hallelujah!"

No other rest-day, it must be conceded, has the recorded divine authority which belongs to the seventh day. Here it stands supreme. On the other hand, no other day of worship has the *consensus* of so large a part of the human family, no other day is in such harmony with the customs of the nations through many centuries, as the first day. Even the Mohammedans, with a host of one hundred and eighty millions, have no such showing for their sacred weekly festival. The first day may claim on various grounds the foremost place of the days of the week among hundreds of millions of Christians. And no other day than the seventh or the first has claims that can pretend to transcend or even to equal those of either of these.

If the highest intelligence of the highest civilization, and if the uniform laws of the highest civilization, in this nineteenth century, grant the need of a rest-day in every week, and if this law be written in our bodies and minds as well as recognized in our statutes, we have sufficient evidence of the obligation to observe one day in seven ; if no days but the first and seventh present so high claims as do these, if none have any claim if these do not, then it must be granted, that, if the first day of the week is not *the* day for a day of rest, the seventh is ; if the seventh is not, then the first is.

THE SABBATH AND THE LORD'S DAY: THEIR PERMANENT ELEMENTS AND LEGITIMATE UNION.

BY REV. EDMUND K. ALDEN, D.D., OF BOSTON, HOME SECRETARY A.B.C.F.M.

THE sabbath question of the times fundamentally is this: Has God appointed one day in seven as a sacred day set apart in a special sense for divine worship? or is the distinction put upon one day in seven, setting it apart from the other six, a human ordinance, having its important uses, but not of divine authority?

We readily see that all subordinate inquiries as to the appropriate methods of observing the day must come back to this fundamental question.

In order to settle the main question we need, *first*, to discern clearly the divine appointment and design of the Old-Testament sabbath; *second*, the divine appointment and design of the New-Testament Lord's Day; and, *third*, the divine appointment and design of what has descended from both of these, — the permanent Christian Lord's-Day sabbath.

We shall then be prepared to consider the appropriate mode of observing the day, that it may occupy the fundamental position which belongs to it as related to the individual, the family, the church, and the state.

I. THE DIVINE INSTITUTION AND DESIGN OF THE OLD-TESTAMENT SABBATH.

1. *The Old-Testament sabbath was a sacred day.* This is indicated in the record of the original institution of the sabbath (Gen. ii. 2, 3), also in the official proclamation in the wilderness (Exod. xvi. 23, xx. 8).

The fellowship with God in worship is part of this "hallowing." Upon the sabbath the morning and evening sacrifices, by command, were doubled, and the show-bread kept upon the table in the sanctuary, indicating fellowship with God, was renewed. It is also specially enjoined (Lev. xxiii. 3), that the people come together for worship, "a holy convocation, a sabbath of the Lord in all your dwellings : " i.e., not merely in your own domestic habitations, but wherever your residence may be, the sabbath is to be a day of holy convocation ; you are to assemble for divine worship. Note also the significant juxta-position of the repeated precepts (Lev. xix. 30, xxvi. 2), "Ye shall keep my sabbaths, and reverence my sanctuary." This association of the holy day with the holy place indicates a day sacred to worship. Consider also the significance of the fact that the observance of the sabbath is spoken of as "a sign" between God and his people (Exod. xxxi. 16, 17). The recognition of such a covenant, a sign between the soul and God, is an act of worship (Ezek. xx. 12, 20; Isa. lviii. 13). And.yet it has been maintained, by some flippantly, by others seriously, that the Jewish sabbath was not a day specially appointed for religious worship.

In the history of Elisha we find an interesting inci-dental allusion which suggests the manner in which in his day the sabbath was observed by the devout Israelites (2 Kings iv. 23). The afflicted Shunammite woman is about to hasten to the prophet; and her husband, not knowing of the affliction, inquires, "Wherefore wilt thou go to-day, seeing it is not the sabbath ?" implying that on the sab-bath day the praying people gathered about the prophet for instruction and worship.

The ninety-second Psalm, entitled, "A Psalm or Song for the Sabbath Day," commences, "It is a good thing to give thanks unto the Lord, and to sing praises unto thy

name, O Most High ;" and moves on to the declaration,
"Those that be planted in the house of the Lord shall
flourish in the courts of our God," as though worship constituted an important part of sabbath-day observance.

After the establishment of synagogues, during the
period of Jewish history subsequent to the captivity, coming down to the days of Christ and his apostles, it is a
well-known fact of history that it was the custom to
gather in those synagogues regularly upon the sabbath
day, the Hebrew scriptures being there read and expounded. To this custom our Lord himself conformed,
thus honoring the sabbath day as a day specially for religious worship (Luke iv. 16, vi. 6, xiii. 10; see also Acts
xvii. 1, 2).

We reach an important conclusion in relation to the
whole sabbath question, when we see clearly that the original Old-Testament sabbath was appointed by God primarily as a sacred rest-day, — a method by which individuals,
families, and communities were to be lifted up into abiding fellowship with the holy God. Whether or not the
institution is perpetuated in the modern history of the
world, this sabbath of the old covenant was certainly a
remarkable provision by which God indicated his will that
men should find their true rest in communion with himself.

2. *The Old-Testament sabbath was not only a sacred, it
was a beneficent day.* Emphasis is put upon release from
work one day in seven. Those who might be overlooked,
servants, strangers, brute beasts, are particularly mentioned, so that all may be included in the merciful arrangement (Deut. v. 14, 15 ; Exod. xxiii. 12).

Whether or not this divine provision for man is perpetuated, there was a period in the history of the world
when God tenderly lifted from men the burden of continuous toil.

3. *Being a sacred and beneficent day, it was appointed
also to be a joyous day,* — the joy not worldly, but joy in
God ; "a festival of holy rest," the divine repose breathed
into human hearts and homes, thanksgiving and praise
ascending from these hearts and homes in delightful worship ;

"Heaven once a week."

Whether or not the Old-Testament sabbath has been
substantially preserved in the history of the Church, let us
be grateful for the rich provision once bestowed.   It was
a marvellous gift of God's grace to man.

Has God in righteous judgment taken it away from
man ?   Can it be that Christianity has lost this blessed
institution ?   Does it not look as though God intended it
for the whole human race, during all ages, since he instituted it at the close of creation ; since he honored it by
giving it a place in the proclamation of the great Ten
Words from Sinai ; since the reasons why it was good for
man in one period of the world abide the same at all
periods ; and since our blessed Lord himself, who honored
it throughout his earthly ministry, and released it from the
appended burdens which man, not God, had put upon it,
declared emphatically that "the sabbath was made" not
for one clan, or one generation, or one nation, but "for
man"?

Are there not indications also in the glowing prophecy
of Isaiah, looking on to the days of gospel triumph, that
in something which corresponds to the glad sabbaths,
God's gracious gift to ancient Israel, the Gentiles too
shall share, when he writes, "From one sabbath to another shall all flesh worship before me, saith the Lord"?
(Isa. lxvi. 22.)

It certainly does seem as though the good Lord would
not take away from the children of men, unless he has

given them over to a curse, so wonderfully gracious a provision as that of the holy sabbath. It certainly does seem as though Christianity, which is the heir of all the rich heritage of former days, must have also inherited in some form this especially munificent gift of God to man.

Leaving the Old-Testament sabbath for a time to stand forth by itself in its own radiant beauty, let us look at another object of equally radiant beauty, one which rises gradually before us along the history of the Christian Church, —

II. THE NEW-TESTAMENT LORD'S DAY.

On the first day of the week the glad proclamation went forth for all the coming ages, "He is not here: he is risen." This was the day, when, according to Levitical law, a sheaf of the first-fruits of the harvest was brought to the priest, and he waved the sheaf before the Lord, that the Lord might accept it in their behalf (Lev. xxiii. 11). By special appointment of God it is pre-arranged from the foundation of the world, that the Lord Jesus Christ shall rise from the dead, not on the sacred seventh day, but on the succeeding morning, the eighth day, when the first-fruits of the harvest are waved before the Lord.

Another illustrious honor is in reserve for this day. It was Levitical law, that, from the morrow after the pass-over-sabbath, the day of the wave-offering of the first-fruits, seven sabbaths should be counted complete, and upon the morrow after the seventh sabbath, — the fiftieth day, Pentecost, — there should be another wave-offering, "two wave-loaves" before the Lord (Lev. xxiii. 17–20). Then God came down in the inauguration of his third sublime manifestation of himself, the great outpouring of the Holy Spirit.

Consider now the startling significance of the fact, that for these two remarkable events, fundamentally connected with the institution of the Christian Church, the resurrection of the Lord Jesus Christ, and — what was the divine attestation that the risen Saviour was exalted to dominion at the right hand of God — the advent on earth of the Holy Comforter, henceforth to abide as the guiding, presiding Presence and Power over the Lord's people, — that, by special divine appointment for both these momentous events, the sacred seventh day is passed by, and the first day is thus doubly crowned.

We cannot be at all surprised at what follows. For some reason the first day of the week becomes, among believers in Christ everywhere, the stated day for Christian worship. No statute is enacted appointing it; no proclamation is made announcing it: it needed neither statute nor proclamation. It followed the resurrection of Christ and the descent of the Holy Spirit just as regular Christian worship itself followed, — the spontaneous blossoming-forth of the joyous Christian heart delighting in the risen glorified Redeemer, unfolding in peculiar beauty upon the first day of the week (Acts xx. 7; 1 Cor. v. 4, xi. 17–34). The most significant and beautiful allusion of all is given incidentally, and therefore more impressively, by the Apostle John in the introduction to his Revelation: "I was in the Spirit on the Lord's Day." Just as the sacramental feast, commemorative of the crucified Christ, had begun to receive the expressive name, "the Lord's Supper" (1 Cor. xi. 20), so the day when Christians were accustomed to assemble in worship to commemorate their risen Redeemer received the equally appropriate name, "the Lord's Day."

All this is confirmed by the well-attested history of the primitive Church. No fact is more indisputable than that the early Christians did observe the first day of the week as their particular day for stated weekly worship, and that this day, rising to pre-eminence as a joyous day of devout thanksgiving in honor of their risen Redeemer, was called "the Lord's Day."

The testimonies are as interesting as they are instructive.

Pliny, writing to the Roman emperor, A. D. 109, mentions the fact that the Christians met on a stated day, " *stato die,*" for the worship of Christ as God.

Justin Martyn, about fifty years later, says, "Those who live in the city and those who live in the country are all accustomed to meet on the day which is denominated Sunday, for the reading of the Scriptures, prayer, exhortation, and communion. They meet on Sunday, because this is the first day, on which God, having changed the darkness and the elements, created the world ; and because Jesus our Lord on this day arose from the dead."

Tertullian at the close of the second century attests, "We celebrate Sunday as a joyful day. On the Lord's Day, we think it wrong to fast or to kneel in prayer."[1]

Clement of Alexandria writes : "A true Christian, according to the commands of the gospel, observes the Lord's Day by casting out all bad thoughts, and cherishing all goodness, honoring the resurrection of the Lord which took place on that day."

Dionysius of Corinth, A. D. 170, mentions the "faithful observance of the Lord's Day, and reading of the Scriptures " in the assemblies then gathering.

Reasons for observing this day are more fully presented by Leo the Great (fifth century) : "On this day the world had its origin. On the same day, through the resurrection

---

[1] " Nos vero, sicut accepimus, solo die dominico resurrectionis non ab isto tantum [geniculis adorare] sed omni anxietatis habitu et officio cavere debemus, differentes etiam negotia, ne quem diabolo locum demus." Neander finds in the passage indications of a transfer of the Jewish law of the sabbath to the Lord's Day.

of Christ, death came to an end, and life began. It was upon this day also that the apostles were commissioned by the Lord to preach the gospel to every creature, and to offer to all the world the blessings of salvation. On the same day came Christ into the midst of his disciples, and breathed upon them, saying, 'Receive the Holy Ghost.' And finally on this day the Holy Ghost was shed forth upon the apostles. So that we see, as it were, an ordinance from heaven evidently set before us, showing that on this day, on which all the gifts of God's grace have been vouchsafed, we ought to celebrate the solemnities of Christian worship."

It will be noticed that the early Christians were not accustomed to call their stated day of worship the sabbath, but gave it a new name, — "the Lord's Day." This was intentional on their part, for obvious and important reasons. The seventh-day sabbath was still an existing institution in the world, and was still observed ; and the early Christians carefully distinguished the two. As to the observance of the first day of the week, the Lord's Day as the stated day for Christian worship, there was no discussion. The whole Christian Church sprang up in acclamation to welcome this day, and so it continued. But as to the observance also of the seventh day, the Jewish sabbath, there was difference both of opinion and of practice, not only in the apostolic age, but for several subsequent centuries.

The rites of the Jewish Church did not suddenly come to an end, and the observances of the Christian Church suddenly take their place ; but the change was gradual. The two for a time went on together. All believers heartily entered into the Christian observance ; some retained for a time also the Jewish. We find the apostles, after the day of Pentecost, going up to the temple at the regular hours of morning and evening prayer. We find them also frequenting the synagogues for worship upon the seventh-day sabbath. Some of the early Christians continued to observe the passover and other Jewish feasts. Some continued the practice of circumcision and various rites of purification (comp. Acts xxi. 20, xxiii. 5, xxiv. 12, xxv. 8, xxviii. 17). Moreover, some began to insist on these observances as essential, and to impose them as a yoke upon Gentile believers.

This explains the language of Paul in the fourteenth chapter of Romans, the fourth of Galatians, and the second of Colossians. The discussion as to the observance of days refers to the matter in hand, the compulsory observance of Jewish days, having reference to its several feast-days, including the seventh-day sabbath.

These injunctions guard against adding to Christian institutions compulsory Jewish appendages binding the Christian conscience; e.g., against adding to the Lord's Supper the Jewish passover, and adding to the Lord's Day the Jewish sabbath, — a most important principle; but no question is raised as to the observance of the Lord's Supper or the Lord's Day.

As an actual fact in the history of the Church, the observance of the seventh-day sabbath in addition to that of the first Lord's Day continued down to the fifth century, with this difference, — that in the Eastern Church both days were regarded as joyous, but in the Western Church the Jewish sabbath was kept as a fast.

Theodoret (fifth century, first part), writing of the Ebionites, says, "They keep the sabbath according to Jewish law, and sanctify the Lord's Day in like manner as do we." Both days were solemnized by public religious assemblies for instruction and spiritual edification, and the observance of the Lord's Supper; the Jewish sabbath chiefly by Jewish converts adhering to the custom of their fathers, — a custom gradually discontinued and at length denounced as heretical. The Council of Laodicea, A. D. 350, uses these words : " Christians ought not to act as Jews, and rest from labor on the sabbath " (i.e., Saturday), " but should work on that day, and, giving pre-eminent honor to the Lord's Day, they ought then, if they can, to rest from labor." The Abyssinian Church still observes both the Jewish sabbath and the Christian Sunday. (*V.* Stanley's Eastern Church, p. 97.)

The best historical summing-up of Christian usage is given by Eusebius, early in the fourth century, commenting upon the ninety-second Psalm. "The Word [Christ] by the new covenant translated and transferred the feast of the sabbath to the morning light, and gave us the symbol of the true rest, the saving Lord's Day. . . . On this day, which is the first of the Light and of the true Sun, we assemble after an interval of six days, and celebrate holy and spiritual sabbath ; even all nations redeemed by him throughout the world assemble, and do those things according to spiritual law which were decreed for the priests to do on the sabbath. All things which it was duty to do on the sabbath there we have transferred to the Lord's Day as more appropriately belonging to it, because it has the precedence, and is first in rank, and more honorable than the Jewish sabbath. It is delivered to us, handed down by tradition, that we should meet together on this day ; and it is evidence that we should do these things announced in the ninety-second Psalm."

The main point pertaining to this part of our discussion seems to be established beyond question, — that in the Christian Church one day in seven, the first day of the week, was set apart as a day for stated Christian worship ; that it specially commemorated the resurrection of the Lord Jesus Christ from the dead, and received the appropriate name "the Lord's Day." Without express statute it came forth in the gladness of Christian believers beholding their risen Redeemer, and in the reception of the great out-pouring of the Holy Spirit, as the spontaneous expression of the Lord's people pouring out hearts full of adoring praise to Him who had bought them with his precious blood, and who was worshipped as the exalted Prince and Saviour, — a day for the exuberance of Christian joy in the Lord Jesus Christ.

May we not reasonably infer a divine intention in the method of this appointment of the Lord's Day in the Christian Church as a sacred day? And may not one part of that intention be that the beauty and glory of the Old-Testament sabbath might be preserved and made permanent in the superior beauty and glory of the New-Testament Lord's Day? This would be in harmony with every thing else pertaining to the gradual passing-over of the Old-Testament dispensation into the New.

The manner in which the Christian Church was founded, and Christian institutions were established among men, suggests that the method of divine revelation was intended both to test and to train those to whom it was communicated. It tests their docility; it trains them to a delicate, thoughtful appreciation of evidence. No loud proclamation was heard from heaven, saying, "Here endeth the Old-Testament dispensation; here beginneth the New." The one ripened and perfected in the other, the same divine life being in both. The roots of the new go back to the beginning of the old; the blossoming and fruitage of the old go forward to the final glory of the new.

He, therefore, who looks for something sharp and abrupt in the termination of the Jewish Church, and the planting of the Christian at the same point of time, so that just then and there all that was Jewish ceased, and all that was Christian sprang into instant life, will look in vain. For the wisest reasons, some of which it is not difficult to discern, this was not God's method. A unity pervades the whole divine plan, reaching back through all the centuries since the foundations of the earth were laid, looking forward through all the centuries unto the period of the new heavens and the new earth. There are no antagonisms between any of its parts : each contributes to the whole. Like the growth of a tree, certain parts, having finished their work, drop off and decay ; but what in their hour gave them their life is in the tree, and abides permanent, their very decay contributing new life to the root and so passing again into the life of the ever-growing tree. Thus the life of the New Testament springs out of the life of the Old ; and we are not to look for a set of authoritative statutes, saying, "Here Jewish institutions end, and Christian institutions begin ; henceforth no more law, all is gospel ;" but we are rather to look for such an intermingling of the two, that somehow, we can hardly tell how, the beauty and glory of the old abide in the superior beauty and glory of the new.

Now, it is in accordance with this interesting divine method of revelation, that, as we have already seen, the first day of the week, called "the Lord's Day," rose into prominence in the history of the Christian Church, and at length practically took the place of the Old-Testament sabbath. There is no command in the New Testament to observe the first day of the week as a day of Christian worship. There is no direct re-quotation of the Old-Testament command, "Remember the sabbath day to keep it holy." There is no positive declaration saying that the seventh day has ceased to be binding, and that the first day henceforth is obligatory. It would be contrary to the whole method of divine revelation in the institution of the Christian Church if there were. He who declares that he will not be convinced that there is any divinely-authoritative sacred day under the Christian system unless you can show him the express command in chapter and verse saying, "Remember the first day of the week to keep it holy," will remain unconvinced. That is not the style of evidence which God has given ; and it is as foolish as it is impious to try to force it into the Scripture contrary to what is the far better and, to the docile inquirer, far more conclusive evidence, which God has given.

It is worthy of special consideration, that precisely the same reasons which lead us to desire the permanence of the Old-Testament sabbath as something so precious for man, lead us to desire the permanence of the New-Testament Lord's Day as something equally precious, and lead us also to desire that these two may be one. We want the emphasis put by the Old-Testament sabbath upon the beneficent provision of rest from labor, commemorating the sublime repose of God after the creation of the world : we want, also, the emphasis which is put by the New-Testament Lord's Day upon the exultant worship of the Lord Jesus Christ, the risen Redeemer.

Let us elevate our expectations. May we not reasonably hope that somehow these twain are one in substantial principle and in divine intention, and that we can retain them both in delightful harmony as the Christian Lord's-Day sabbath ? We love the dear name "sabbath," the rest of God, suggesting our rest in God. We love the dear name "Lord's Day," honoring our risen Redeemer, suggesting our own resurrection in Christ. What if that God, who not only "commanded the light to shine out of darkness," but who hath also "shined in our hearts to give the light of the knowledge of the glory of God in the face of Jesus Christ," mindful of his people's necessities, should have given us both in a glorious conjunction !

May it not be true that God has not only blessed the Old-Testament sabbath, and hallowed it, has not only blessed the New-Testament Lord's Day, and hallowed it, but that he has also "blessed the banns" by which these twain are one?

III. Having thus far considered the distinctive beauty of two institutions, the Old-Testament sabbath and the New-Testament Lord's Day, and having observed how in the providence of God they have historically come together, let us now behold the surpassing beauty of the two united, —

THE PERMANENT LORD'S-DAY SABBATH.

1. *There remains to us the observance of one day in seven as a day of glad worship.*

Methods of divine worship have in some respects changed as God has revealed himself more fully to men; but the substantial worship remains, rising in significance, and increasing in spirituality, as the divine character and will are more clearly manifested. Christian worship is a higher style of worship than the antediluvian, the patriarchial, or the Mosaic; for what was only foreshadowed in the ancient sacrificial system is fulfilled in the one sacrifice offered upon Calvary. "God, who in sundry times and in divers manners spake in time past unto the fathers by the prophets, hath in these last days spoken unto us by his Son:" the Son has breathed upon his believing people, saying, "Receive ye the Holy Ghost." Christian worship is the Old-Testament worship sublimely elevated through the delightful revelation of God as Father, Son, and Holy Spirit. It is a worship which pre-eminently magnifies Christ, through whom alone we approach the Father.

Now, as worship permanently remains in the history of the Lord's people on earth by being elevated into Christian worship, it seems appropriate that the one sacred day in seven should remain by being also elevated so as to put peculiar honor upon what is distinctively Christian worship. Since to the record of the first verse of Genesis, "In the beginning God created the heaven and the earth," Christianity adds the first verses of the Gospel according to John, "In the beginning was the Word, and the Word was with God, and the Word was God. The same was in the beginning with God. All things were made by him ; and without him was not any thing made that was made," — it seems appropriate that the one day in seven which commemorates the divine Creator, participating in the elevation given to worship through the additional revelation of Christianity that "by Christ were all things created," should somehow specially honor God in Christ. This in a most interesting manner is effected by the observance of the first day of the week as the Christian's sacred day, extolling the risen Redeemer. Recognizing also the advent of the Comforter upon the same day, remembering that in the creation of the world "the Spirit of God moved upon the face of the waters," we gratefully discern the peculiar fitness of the Lord's Day to the worship of a God who has been pleased in these latter times to manifest himself in his triune glory as "Father, Son, and Holy Ghost." All this is ours in the observance of the first day of the week as the Christian's sacred day, while the original appointment of one sacred day in seven commemorating the finished creation remains.

If any importance be attached to the divine appointment at the close of the six-days' creation, re-affirmed in the proclamation of the moral law cut into the tables of stone, of one day in seven set apart as a day of sacred rest for the divine worship, this remains permanent and fundamental for the glory of God and the good of man in the Christian Lord's-Day sabbath.

2. *There remains to us a sacred seventh day, which requires for its appropriate observance rest from the secular labors of the six-days' work.*

It contemplates the gathering together of people for associated worship, "a holy convocation." It contemplates a special sustained outpouring of Christian hearts in praise to the Lord who hath bought them. It contemplates the proclamation and hearing of the divine word, continuous periods of reverent communion with God, and happy Christian fellowship with his people.

Whatever constitute the best methods for the appropriate observance of a day specially set apart by God for restful worship, they necessarily imply cessation from the secular labors of the week. For there can be no general gathering of all the people for divine worship one day in seven, unless there accompany it a general laying-aside of the six-days' labor. It is not only true that man, physically and mentally, needs the rest, but he cannot perform the duties and enter heartily into the privileges of the sacred day without the rest. That pre-eminent joy in the Lord which is appropriate to the day can be known only by the surrender of the entire being, free from ordinary secular obligations, to delightful spiritual worship.

This emphatic provision in the ordinance of the Old-Testament sabbath, cessation from servile work, to which no allusion is made in the New-Testament mention of the Lord's Day, is thus permanently secured as an absolute necessity for the appropriate observance of a day whose distinguishing feature is that all the people shall assemble for associated Christian worship. This, therefore, abides as one of the essential features of the Christian Lord's-Day sabbath.

3. *There remains to us a sacred seventh day, which not only permits, but requires, the performance of whatever labors may most efficiently promote its most appropriate observance.*

This was the principle emphasized by Christ in interpreting the spirit of the Old-Testament sabbath. It is the principle frequently reiterated in the administration of the divine government, both Old Testament and New. What Christ said of the sabbath is true of every divine ordinance : the ordinance was "made for man, not man for the ordinance." "I will have mercy, and not sacrifice," is a universal principle in the divine government, the illustrations of which are various. Christ reminded those arrogant teachers of the Jewish law, who, that they might lord it over God's heritage, had taken pains to forget this principle, that it had always been true, as related to the law of the Old-Testament sabbath. It was no new thought he was uttering, but something which belonged essentially to the institution, both in the past and the future : viz., that the law forbidding work, and enjoining rest in God upon the sabbath day, not only did not exclude, but required, acts of mercy, e. g., relieving pain and satisfying hunger ; and also that it not only did not exclude, but required, the labors necessary for the best religious observance of the day, — it being, as they all knew, in certain respects, an unusually hard-working day for the priests, and for the servants of the tabernacle. No fire was to be kindled in their habitations for the performance of mere secular work ; but the show-bread was to be baked, and presented anew, every sabbath morning. No secular work was to be done ; but the extra-religious work — offering the sacrifices, attending the altar, and caring for the worship of the assembled convocations — was to be done with special diligence and fidelity.

Since Christian believers are all priests of the Lord, are all the appointed servants of the tabernacle, whatever is necessary to make the one day in seven the most efficient and useful day for Christian worship is not only a permission, but a duty ; and from some of the Lord's servants it calls for no inconsiderable amount of hard work. What was true under the Old-Testament dispensation being more emphatically true under the New, this principle abides in the Christian Lord's-Day sabbath.

4. *There remains to us a sacred seventh day, whose appropriate observance is essential to the permanent establishment among men of the kingdom of Christ.*

It is vitally connected with all Christian institutions, particularly with the growth, the spirituality, and efficiency of the Christian Church, and with the successful proclamation of the gospel throughout the world. No statement can be more clearly established than that the Lord's-Day sabbath is central and fundamental, as related to the highest welfare of the individual, the family, the church, and the commonwealth; and as such it abides permanently a divinely-appointed institution among men, one of God's most precious gifts.

No generation of men has yet appreciated this gift as it ought to be appreciated. Some have grossly abused it. We all need to re-invigorate our faith as to what this one day in seven is, contemplating its beauty as it comes forth from its two divine sources, — the Old-Testament sabbath and the New-Testament Lord's Day harmoniously united, a permanent divine benediction among men. Whatever else it may be, or may not be, these principles abide: (1) It is a sacred day, set apart by God, in a special sense, for elevated Christian worship. (2) In the accomplishment of this design, it necessarily requires cessation from the secular labors of the six-days' work. (3) It both permits and demands the performance of all labor necessary for the best appropriate observance of the day. (4) Its appropriate observance, according to its beneficent design, is essential to the permanent establishment among men of the kingdom of Christ.

INFERENCES.

I. *The theory which would make the Lord's Day a day for amusement, for recreation, for an agreeable change of worldly pursuits, or for idleness, has no foundation at all upon which to rest.*

It is a sacred day set apart for divine worship, or there is no such day at all. Men may pervert it into a holiday, they may abuse it as a day in which sin shall not only not be restrained, but shall run riot; or they may be grateful for it as a day of leisure, each man to use it according to his own taste, — some in reviewing the business of the week, finishing up their accounts and planning for the week to come, some in mere rest of body and of mind, some in reading up the news or in literary pursuits, some in social entertainments, and so on. These things may be appropriate for the observance of a holiday, or a day of leisure; but they do not constitute the observance of the Lord's Day; they do not constitute holy repose of the soul in God, nor the joyous worship of the risen Redeemer.

Whatever be the theory of the origin of a special seventh day, whether it come from the Old-Testament sabbath, the New-Testament Lord's Day, or the spirit of the two united, it makes no provision for a day of worldly recreation and amusement. If that is needed, we must provide for it in some other way. This provides that one day in seven shall be a sacred day set apart for special worship, the hearts of men gladly engaging in the continuous praise of God, and for this purpose uniting in Christian assemblies.

This, then, becomes the simple, practical sabbath-question: How shall Christian communities so observe the one day in seven as to make it most efficient for Christian worship? How, as individuals, as families, as congregations, shall we best praise the glorious Redeemer? How shall we lead others to do the same?

To this test bring your practical inquiries as to methods of sabbath observance, and most of them are easily answered. Are they expressions of Christian worship, and do they contribute to make the day a day set apart for Christian worship, so distinguishing it from the other days of the week? If so, they are not only permitted, they are required. Sabbath observance is not negative. Sabbath observance is positive; the special outpouring of grateful hearts in praise of the Lord of the sabbath. The test-question, then, as to sabbath-day excursions for pleasure, riding, walking, visiting, opening and frequenting places of amusement, opening and frequenting public libraries or galleries of art, and all similar inquiries, is the same simple question in every case: Are these the expressions of Christian worship, and are they, in a social community, helpful to Christian worship? If so, they are not only permitted, they are required, just as some walking, some riding, and some preparation for religious worship, are required. If not, then these cannot constitute the appropriate observance of the Lord's Day. Whatever else may be said of the application of this principle, it certainly excludes the theory that the one day in seven is to be regarded as a day of worldly amusement, recreation, mere idleness, or change of pursuit. If there be any such day at all as the Lord's-Day sabbath, it is a sacred day set apart for Christian worship.

II. *It is equally plain that such a day as this, a day set apart for worship, to Christian hearts is not a servile, burdensome day, but an exceeding great joy.*

It was so under the Old-Testament dispensation; it is so still more emphatically under the New.

Men talk about the severity of the ancient Jewish sabbath. Where did we get the eighty-fourth Psalm, the ninety-second Psalm, the one hundred and nineteenth Psalm, the one hundred and twenty-second Psalm?

One of the distinguishing characteristics of the Christian heart is joy in the Lord : to have the privilege of expressing this in worship, is the sweetest delight. It continually breaks forth through all the necessary labors of the six days ; and, when the opportunity of one whole day in seven comes, it runs to the Lord like a released child, so glad to be at home in the abiding fellowship of Christ and his people, finding here a foretaste of the anticipated blessedness of an everlasting heaven. If the spirit of joyous worship in the Lord is not in the heart, then, indeed, a day set apart for the expression of that worship may be burdensome and servile ; and this may tell the story as to the heart that finds it so.

Much has been said, repeated, and continued to be repeated, in certain quarters, as to the severity and servility of the New-England Pilgrim and Puritan sabbath, the revered Lord's Day set apart for worship. With some, this is a favorite theme for pert or sarcastic remark. I venture to call in question the competence of these self-appointed critics. Why not take the testimony of the Pilgrim and Puritan himself?

When our fathers drew toward Plymouth Harbor in the cold and storm, beating their way up from Cape Cod coast in the shallop, landed on Clark's Island early Saturday afternoon, so as to make preparation for the coming rest-day, and then spent that day in devout worship, who imagines that this was to them a severe and servile day? Their hearts poured themselves out in prayer and praise to that God whose Fourth Commandment they so delighted in, that they left Holland, and came to this unknown land, for the avowed purpose of keeping sacred the holy sabbath day. This is the first of the five reasons which induced them to emigrate, as given by Secretary Morton : "Inasmuch, that, in ten years' time, whilst their church sojourned amongst them, they could not bring them to

reform the neglect of the observance of the Lord's Day
as a sabbath, nor keep their own families from the sur-
rounding infection." Read the testimony of Gov. Brad-
ford, himself one of the eighteen explorers, who, after their
perilous escape, kept that grateful sabbath. " But though
this had been a day and night of much trouble and danger
unto them, yet God gave them a morning of comfort and
refreshing (as usually he doth to his children); for the
next day was a fair, sun-shining day, and they found themselves to be on an island, secure from the Indians, where
they might dry their stuff, fix their pieces, and rest themselves, and give God thanks for his mercies in their manifold deliverances. And, this being the last day of the
week, they prepared to keep the sabbath." Picture them
adding a new music to that of the waves and the winds,
the high-sounding praises of God, as Deacon John Carver
"lines a psalm," which all sing with uplifted heart and
voice, accompanied with prayer and elevated discourse
upon the great themes of God and godliness.

Take the testimony of one of the descendants of that
mate of "The Mayflower," for whom Clark's Island is
named.

"We do the Puritans great injustice to suppose that in their
strict, punctilious life on the Lord's Day, they were acting under any
other restraint than that of the love they bore to the Lord of the sabbath; which did, indeed, constrain them to keep their hearts and
hands disencumbered, as far as possible, from the world, that they
might the more readily 'be filled with all the fulness of God,' and
which, by imposing a truce on their social intercourse, left them more
free to commune with Christ. When, in accordance with prevailing
usage in New England, they suspended all secular toil at the going-
down of the sun on Saturday, and began their sabbath service with
an evening prayer, a psalm, and a season of solitary self-examination,
it was with more gladness of heart than that which Burns ascribes to
the 'Cotter's' children on coming home, after the week's drudgery is
over, to exchange salutations around the old hearthstone, and receive
anew the paternal benediction. . . . In like manner, with a keen

spiritual relish for holy time, holy acts, holy pleasures, they arose the next morning earlier than on other days, revolving in their hearts the words of David: 'Awake up, my glory: awake, psaltery and harp: I myself will awake early.' And so through the day, 'private meditation, family devotion, and public worship engaged their delighted and unflagging souls till the sun went down.' "—Dr. Joseph S. Clark, *Congregational Quarterly*, 1859.

Add the testimony of a representative of Puritanism, on the other side of the water, John Owen: —

"For my part, I must not only say, but plead, while I live in this world, and leave this testimony to the present and future ages, that if ever I have seen any thing of the ways and worship of God, wherein the power of religion or godliness hath been expressed; any thing that hath represented the holiness of the gospel, and the author of it; any thing that looked like a prelude to the everlasting sabbath, and rest with God, which we aim, through grace, to come unto,—it hath been there, and with them, where and among whom the Lord's Day hath been held in highest esteem, and a strict observation of it attended unto as an ordinance of our Lord Jesus Christ."

Bring in the testimony of our beautiful sabbath-hymns. What kind of hearts wrote them? What kind of hearts have sung them with most exultant joy?

"One day amid the place
  Where my dear Lord hath been
Is sweeter than ten thousand days
  Of pleasurable sin."

When I hear a man speaking depreciatingly of what he calls "the hard, stern, strict sabbath" of the pious Jew, the godly Puritan, or the devout Scotch, I feel like saying to him, "Sir, speak for yourself; but do not undertake to speak for the holy men and women whose whole souls went out in praise to God, hailing the day you call 'hard and strict,' as a type of the heaven of whose blessedness they are now participants." Hard, servile, and strict, to worship God one day in seven? Speak for yourself, O

wise man of the nineteenth century, but not for your
godly sires. When you know as they knew — God grant
you may! — what the worship of God is, what the exultant
joy of a soul resting in the risen Redeemer is, you may
speak for them who know the same ; and, when you do,
you will testify that there is no day so joyous to the
Christian heart as the sacred day of the Lord.

III. *We see the cause of the main practical difficulty
as to the sabbath-question.*

It arises from the endeavor to adapt God's sabbath to
the unrenewed human heart, to make a day specially set
apart for the joyous worship of God agreeable to those
who have no joy in the worship of God. It is a tough
problem to solve.

Suppose we try the same experiment with the Lord's
Supper. " The Lord's Supper, as now observed, is a dry,
uninteresting service, — exceeding servile to sit still, take
a bit of bread, taste of a little wine, and have long prayers
over it." So some would say. Now what? " The Lord's
Supper is a Christian ordinance, and we ought to observe
it. It should be made interesting to everybody. Therefore change it to a social festive entertainment, which will
be universally popular;" i. e., degrade and desecrate the
sacredness of the service, to make it pleasing to sinful
hearts. This you pronounce sacrilege.

Apply the same reasoning to the sacred Lord's Day, a
holy day, set apart for divine worship. Are people to be
elevated and trained to its joyous appropriate observance,
or is the day to be desecrated, to be made agreeable to
sinful hearts? This is the sabbath-question of our times.
Shall we have a sacred day, honored by God as a day for
glad Christian worship, and shall we seek to be in the
appropriate spirit for such a day, so that we shall delight
in such a day, and so shall we be lifted up by this blessed
provision of divine grace for needy man? or will we pull

down God's day to our own pleasure? It is a momentous
question as related to all dear to Christian hearts, Christian homes, and a Christian commonwealth. It touches,
as has been appropriately said, "the spinal column of the
body politic."

IV. *We see the need of recognizing divine authority,
giving divine sanction to the sacred observance of the
permanent one day in seven as the Christian Lord's-Day
sabbath.* Man needs not only the invitation and the privilege, but the command, just as he needs other commands.
Sinful man is wilful and wayward, and requires restraint
as well as guidance. He requires admonition as well as
invitation. Christian believers need the command as well
as the invitation; for some of us have but little grace as
yet, and the best of us are exceedingly imperfect.

No man, however holy, has yet observed God's sabbath
as he ought to have observed it. No community has yet
observed it as it ought to be observed. We are far from
having learned how much of the riches of divine grace for
man is wrapped up in this one day in seven, thrice blessed
as the sabbath, as the Lord's Day, and as the twain made
one. We need reverently and heartily to accept this
munificent divine gift, both as an authoritative command
and as a precious trust; to prepare for it by making the
six-days' work contribute to its growing spiritual life; to
make the most of it in all its possible efficiency as a day
of Christian power in worship, and in the proclamation of
the divine word; and then sacredly to guard it as something fundamental, vitally related to the home, to society,
to the permanence of all Christian institutions, and to the
extension of Christ's kingdom on earth.

God hasten the promised time when the blessed one day
in seven shall not only be permanently secure to those
who love it, but when all men shall love it; when, as the
morning of each Lord's Day dawns, with its serene divine

benediction, upon every nation and kingdom and people and tongue, the fulfilment of the glowing prophecy of Isaiah shall illumine the whole world with a belt of light! "FROM ONE SABBATH TO ANOTHER SHALL ALL FLESH COME TO WORSHIP BEFORE ME, SAITH THE LORD."

> "Oh! let me take thee at the bound,
>   Leaping with thee from seven to seven,
> Till that we both, being tossed from earth,
>   Fly hand in hand to heaven."

II.

HISTORICAL.

THE SABBATH IN HISTORY.

THE PRE–MOSAIC SABBATH.

BY REV. JOSHUA T. TUCKER, D.D., OF BOSTON.

IT is immaterial to the purpose of this essay, how long the appearance of man on this planet, as a reasonable and responsible being, may have antedated the Hebrew exodus. Nor does it now matter what may have been the method of that appearance; whether as an instantaneous creation of man in physical and spiritual completeness, or the in-breathing from God of a rational and moral nature into a previously existing and properly developed anthropoid. It is enough for this discussion to fix this starting-point, that, by the will of God, a date was reached in time when this earth became the abode of a man who was "a living soul," capable of mental growth, susceptible of moral impressions, endowed with an accountable will, and, so far forth as is possible to the finite, standing in the image of his Maker.

The next event in the record, after the advent of man, is the formal declaration of the resting of God from his creative work (Gen. ii. 1–3). It does not matter to the force of this fact upon our present inquiry, what may have been the length of the periods called days in this earliest narrative. Be they longer or shorter, they severally mark some limit in duration, — a beginning and an ending.

And, when the sixth had completed itself, then to the seventh and last period God gave the distinctive character which separated it from the others as a day made holy, by his example and implied precept, for other uses than the former. If this rest-day of the Lord far exceeded in duration any thing known to us as a day, it would not follow that this was not intended as an institutional act, set up at the very commencement of human life, by which to model a regularly recurring interval of sacred repose and worship during all succeeding generations of humanity. For the question of the sabbath stands quite clear from cosmogonic theories. Its essential element is not a time-element, but a spiritual idea and obligation. Hardly any one now will dispute the scientific conclusion that those primeval evenings and mornings were age-long successions, rather than a modern calendar week. Hence it is inferréd by some, that, as. our sabbath cannot have any such prolonging as that divine sabbath, no reasoning is admissible from it to ours, as holding us to this observance. This is putting the matter on a very mechanical basis. A better view of it is this, that a comparison is here obvious between God's time and works, which are projected on a divine scale, and man's time and works, which are finite and of earthly limitations. God made the universe in six of his mysteriously measured days, and rested on the seventh. The working and the resting were each on the scale of his own infinitude. Man works out his six short days on the small circle of a human and mortal life, and keeps his sabbath at their end. God, out of his own immeasurable life, gives us a pattern to follow in our narrow term of being. Whether the story as we have it in Genesis be history or allegory, it carries this moral instruction, that He who made all things by regular stages of progress, through what we may call his creative week, ceased from his accomplished labor at its close, and kept a sabbath commensurate with that labor and with his own uncreated being. Therefore man, his child, made in his likeness and for the same spiritual ends, should regulate his activities on the same plan of working and resting, conforming thus to the example of the highest wisdom, both in the sphere of a natural and a spiritual existence. In this we are entitled to see not an arbitrary arrangement, but the revelation of an absolutely essential law of rational life in its dependent forms.

The argument so far is rather from analogy than from express commandment. The line of thought is legitimate, for it is formally brought forward as an argument in the Decalogue. Whether the Old-Testament sabbath forms any obligatory ground for the Christian Lord's Day or not, the connection between the creation-sabbath and the Mosaic is unquestionable, as is also the reason for that connection. When Jehovah, through Moses on Sinai, had enjoined upon Israel the keeping of a specified day of holy time, he added this enforcement of the precept: "For in six days the Lord made heaven and earth, the sea, and all that in them is, and rested the seventh day; wherefore the Lord blessed the sabbath day, and hallowed it." This positive enactment, uttered some twenty-five hundred years, according to the popular chronology, after the ending of creation, is linked by a firm bond with the day which God then blessed and sanctified. The sabbath of Moses is a clear outcome of the earlier institution. The great World-Builder, who needed no rest, because he neither faints nor is weary, puts himself, in this statute, as if on a level with his working and wearied offspring, and condescends to a repose from his long days of unfatiguing toil, that he may give the force of a divine sympathy as well as the authority of a divine mandate, to his chosen people, to conclude every sixth of their brief week-days with a blessed and hallowed seventh like his own. "Like his own," that is, so far as the two cases can be brought into parallelism. For it is captious, and not critical, to demand an exact correspondence between these lines of comparison. As there was a most natural, if not necessary, diverseness between the periods of the divine week in Genesis, and the subsequent sun-divided days of man's appointed week, which nevertheless did not break the analogy between them ; so there is an absolutely necessary difference between God's sabbatic rest and ours, while the resemblance is strongly marked, and the innermost meaning of both is identical.

This is the interpretation put upon the pre-Mosaic sabbath by the Fourth Commandment : God rested on the seventh day ; so should the Hebrew. God made that day a separated, a sacred day ; so should the Hebrew. We go back, then, to the beginning, and ask for the significance of this divine blessing and hallowing of the creation-sabbath. Did the Lord make that day holy for himself, or for men ? " The sabbath was made for man," said Jesus ; the rest-day of divine ordaining and re-ordaining. To confine this sanctifying of the primeval, the Edenic rest-day, to its divine Institutor (as some attempt), thus cutting it off from subsequent human relations at least until the Mosaic epoch, is to make it meaningless. We can attach no idea to a God-sabbath, whether of holy rest or devotion, except as related to the human offspring of God. He blessed and hallowed his own sabbatic day as something which should project itself into the days to come, for the use and enjoyment of others. "Blessing the day means blessing it for some purpose : it is the expression of God the Creator's love to it as a holy and beneficent thing among the things of time, as carrying ever with it something of God, some idea of the Blesser, and of the love and reverence due to him as the fountain of all blessedness and of all blessed things. So the blessing upon man (in

the day of his creation, male and female, in the divine likeness, Gen. i. 26, 27) looks down through all the generations of man." [1] God made the seventh part of time holy,
by reserving it for his own peculiar worship and service :
not for self worship and service, but for these as a homage
from his children and subjects. The whole arrangement
has a paternal and filial aspect, — the benediction of the
Eternal Father upon mankind through this ever-returning
memorial of his creating and sustaining care. " It is elevating a portion of the human time to the standard, or in
the direction at least, of God's own eternal sabbath ; " [1]
so to bring up humanity to the plane from which it is far
enough removed at present, when all its days shall be
thoroughly hallowed by the spirit and works of righteousness, as are the ages of the ever holy and blessed Lord.
That were a consummation devoutly to be wished ; but the
way to make every day a true sabbath is not by abolishing
what remnant of Sunday we still have.

It seems to be a morally unavoidable conclusion, for
which we now are ready, that the sabbath announced in
Eden was intended to be of perpetual obligation ; that,
whether or not the Sinaitic sabbath was ordained for Gentile as well as Jew, the original rest-day was made universally for the human race. This, however, is not my special
line of inquiry. Having found a sabbath at each terminus
of the pre-Mosaic period, it is now in order to ask how
this benign institution fared in the interval thus bounded ?
The line of travel through this piece of history is not very
open and easy ; but something may be done in the way of
its satisfactory exploration.

Two facts pertinent to the subject stand out clearly on
that early record. The first is *a sevenfold division of time.*
This was not confined to the Hebrew race, though of common mention in its remotest annals. The same thing

[1] Tayler Lewis.

belonged to all the Shemitic peoples, to the Egyptians, and even to some of the South-American tribes. What was the origin of this septenary time-table? In some of the later registers and other documents of those ancient nations, this arrangement of time is referred to astronomical phenomena, to the movements of the moon and other celestial bodies; but this appears rather to have been a subsequent conventional explanation of a long-recognized fact, than a true accounting for that fact. To get at the root of the mystic pre-eminence of the number seven requires a deeper search than to say that seven was the number of the primary planets, or that the eight tones of the musical scale are divided by seven intervals. A week of seven days, from the very dawn of time, is not adequately explained as the division of a lunar month into four parts. For the twenty-nine and a half days of a regular lunation, divided by four, does not give an even quotient, but leaves a continual balance of troublesome fractions to disturb the reckoning; while the successive quarterings of the moon are not sharply enough cut to serve for an accurate weekly measurement. Back of all these "afterthoughts," as they have been aptly called, a much more elementary cause is required. The Hebrews had it, and recognized it, in the creation-week of seven evenings and mornings constituting the cosmogonal days. There is no question that the Jewish week was counted from the sabbath, from the beginning. It is reasonably supposable that this primitive division of time into seven days went over by tradition, after the deluge, into the recollection of the nations which were organized subsequently to the dispersion at Babel, just as the fact of the deluge itself was perpetuated through nearly the whole earth in this way, even into its most barbarian corners. And this meets the objection that the earlier Hebrews could not have gotten their seven-day week from the genesis, because the biblical Genesis was not written until the Mosaic age. It was written in the living thought and speech of the race as incrasably as was the Flood, or the migration of Abraham. From the same source, also, came the septenary adjustments of religious and national festivals in Palestine; and the well-known mystical completeness ascribed to the number seven among this people. How did seven thus come to be a sacred or perfect number? There is nothing in itself to give it this distinction or value. It has no arithmetical claim to such importance. Running back from it the scale of numeration, some reason may be discovered why one of the previous numbers might have been so dignified. Thus, six is the double triplet or triad; five told off the digits, whence sprung the decimal notation; four marked the square; three the triangle; two terminated the line; one is the initial point, the all-combining unit. Each of these has more apparent title to the place assigned to seven than it can show; yet seven was the Hebrew "perfect number," without any inherent justifying quality, as far back as history reaches.[1] It seems too obvious to need more than a statement, that this was a consequence of the same seven-fold creative work which gave the sons of Adam their week of seven days, the earth over; the last of which days, and the date of all succeeding reckonings, was the sabbath.[2]

The second fact is the equally constant reference to *formal acts of religious worship* during the pre-Mosaic age. It will hardly do to infer (as some have done) a weekly service of public devotion from the words in Gen. iv., "Then began men to call on the name of the Lord," even if this were the right rendering of the text; much less when it should be read, "Then began men to call out, to proclaim, the name Jehovah," as the divine name for

---

[1] The following are some of these early references: Gen. iv. 15, vii. 3, 4, viii. 10, 12, xxi. 30, xxix. 18, 20, 27, 30, l. 10; Job ii. 13, xlii. 8; Exod. vii. 25.

[2] Comp. Lange on Genesis.

the future, instead of Elohim, the creating God. (See Lange's "Genesis.") But even earlier than that we have a sabbatic hint in the offerings which Cain and Abel brought to the Lord "at the end of days,"—a weekly custom already, one might think, without any severe straining of the record. Compare with this ending of days the not unlike intimation in the Book of Job: "There was a day when the sons of God came to present themselves before the Lord." This was for sacrificial worship, as was the other; and it is every way probable that these solemn appearances "before the Lord" were on fixed days, without which such observances have never been permanent. Three times, "at the end of seven days," Noah sent forth the dove from the opened window of the ark. This proved that the old voyager kept up his weekly reckoning; and it is not presumable that so long and faithful "a preacher of righteousness" would have forgotten when the sabbath came around. The patriarchal history is full of the building of altars unto the Lord, wherever Abraham and his children travelled or abode. It is hardly conceivable that their Bethels should have had no sabbaths.

But against this view the objection of Paley and others, who wish to make the sabbath an exclusively Jewish affair, is still urged,—that no express mention of this seventh-day rest is found from Adam to the exodus. If this be literally true, it does not shut out an inferential recognition of the day, as we have seen. Strange as this silence seems at first glance, it is to be considered that the entire record of at least twenty-five centuries is compressed into what would make a thin pamphlet of some sixty or seventy pages, where only the bare skeleton of what took place during that long period could have mention. Professor Phelps has reckoned that the sabbath is mentioned only five times in the Hebrew scriptures from Moses to the return from the Babylonian captivity, some one thousand years of much more stirring interest. From Joshua to David, five hundred years, the day is not once referred to,[1] yet certainly it was then a regular institution. Some things have to be taken for granted in writing out such memorials ; and the things apt to be omitted are those which, by common consent, are looked upon as matter-of-course occurrences. It is very probable that sabbath-keeping habits fell off into much neglect during the bad times of antediluvian violence and of the Egyptian bondage. But the silence of Scripture, whether in enjoining this observance, or in reproving its cessation, does not prove that there was no sabbath then. On the contrary, there is good proof that the sabbath survived the irreligious influences of those many centuries. It is found in the significant word with which the fourth command of the Decalogue begins : "Remember the sabbath day to keep it holy." This is not the phrasing of a new injunction. No statute *de novo* of Church or State commences so. Nobody can remember what never happened. It was not a caution for the future, but a precept for the then present. It did not say, "By and by, when you shall be in danger of forgetting this commandment, don't do it." It bade them primarily and at that hour to *remember* the sabbath rest and worship which had been the precious heirloom of their race since God blessed and hallowed the seventh day in Eden ; which was now to be re-enacted under more impressive sanctions in connection with those other nine everlasting words of Jehovah. Turn back now from the twentieth chapter of Exodus, where these commandments are recorded, to the sixteenth, which narrates an event that occurred some weeks before. It was the supplying of Israel with the daily manna. Notice the following language when it was reported to Moses that, on the sixth day, the people had gathered a double

---

[1] Phelps on the Sabbath, p. 31.

measure, contrary to general orders. "And he said unto
them, This is that which the Lord hath said : To-morrow
is the rest of the holy sabbath unto the Lord : bake that
which ye will bake to-day, and seethe that ye will seethe ;
and that which remaineth over, lay up for you to be kept
until the morning. . . . And Moses said, Eat that to-day ;
for to-day is a sabbath unto the Lord. . . . Six days shall
ye gather it ; but on the seventh day, the sabbath, in it
there shall be none." This is the language of recognition,
not of institution ; and it is in entire keeping with the
command to "remember" the day of rest. In the light of
these plain recognitions, it is not a forced exegesis which
holds that the attempt of Moses in Egypt was to lighten
the oppressive burdens of Israel by securing for them the
seventh-day rest. That was Pharaoh's charge against the
Hebrew chiefs : "Behold, the people are many, yet ye
make them sabbatize (rest) from their burdens." So,
when the petition was pressed at the court of Pharaoh,
that the people should be let go to hold a feast of sacrificial worship in the wilderness, it seems to have been
mainly this, — that they might keep unmolested the hallowed day to which their awakening religious feelings were
urging them ; which they could not do in presence of
their pagan enemies who held as deities the very animals
which the Jews slew upon their altars.

According to the view thus presented, the separating
of a seventh part of time to God, in cessation from needless labor, and in the services of religious worship and
well-doing, did not begin with the apostles, nor at Sinai
under Moses, but had its origin and authenticating seal at
the end of creation, as necessary then for man's right
physical and spiritual growth ; therefore presumably necessary ever since. Even Dr. Hessey, while strenuously
denying any formal connection between the Lord's Day
and the Jewish sabbath, concedes that there is a moral

element in the Fourth Commandment, and hence some moral obligation to observe it religiously; and, further, "that the creation labor and rest were exemplary, typical, and consolatory, and were so understood by the writers of Holy Scripture, and by the Fathers."[1] It may be added, that, so far as we can understand its spirit and method, the pre-Mosaic sabbath was, at many points, in closer harmony with the Christian Lord's Day than was the Levitical sabbath. The latter was the sabbath, specifically, of a national-political dispensation, carrying forward into this theocratic *régime* the religious purpose of its predecessor, and much more besides. The sabbath of the patriarchs, and of yet earlier saints, was of a simpler spirituality, a freer, more elastic devotion; less bound by formal restrictions; more in tone, as should be ours, with the worship, the rest, the service, of the second and perpetual Paradise.

[1] Bampton Lectures, pp. 23, 24.

THE SABBATH IN JEWISH HISTORY.

BY REV. ALVAH HOVEY, D.D. LL.D., PRESIDENT OF NEWTON THEO-
LOGICAL INSTITUTION, NEWTON CENTRE, MASS.

WE may begin our sketch of the sabbath in Jewish history with recognition of the fact that there is evidence
of an ante-Mosaic and primeval sabbath, intended for all
mankind. This evidence is comprised in a remarkable
passage of Genesis (ii. 2, 3), which declares that God rested
from the work of creation on the seventh day, and hallowed that day; in traces of a weekly division of time,
especially among the descendants of Shem, but also in
Babylon before the era of Moses; and in traditions of
reverence for the number seven, as pre-eminently sacred.

But while the passage in Genesis, and the traces of a
primeval sabbath just named, are sufficient to warrant a
belief that a weekly day of rest was instituted by Jehovah
in Eden, there is evidence, on the other hand, that in the
time of Moses this day was no longer remembered and
kept as holy by any large part of mankind. It is even
probable that the children of Israel had gradually ceased
to observe it during the later years of their sojourn in
Egypt. A long period of prosperity in a land where idol-
worship and self-indulgence prevailed must have tended
to darken their minds and corrupt their manners; while
the subsequent period of dreadful suffering, under a jeal-
ous monarch and heartless taskmasters, must have rendered any outward observance of the sabbath impossible.
It cannot therefore be surprising if, as we suppose, a
sort of Egyptian darkness settled down upon the religious life of the Israelites, and if, in consequence of this,

there was little, if any, worship at set times during the later years of their residence in Goshen.

Accordingly, when the sabbath was re-instituted at Sinai, it must have seemed to the people who were truly devout a fresh gift from God, and, to the undevout, a new check upon their worldliness. Naturally enough, though the command to "remember the sabbath day, and keep it holy," was assigned a place on the tablets of stone, there were some who disregarded it in the wilderness, and brought upon themselves the just judgment of God. But we walk in twilight, even though we have the Pentateuch in our hands, if we seek to discover many traces of the holy day in the life of Israel under Moses. Yet there is good reason to believe that it was generally observed, at least by resting from secular employments, during the period of wandering in the desert, and from the entrance into Canaan until the death of Joshua and his contemporaries. But the same cannot be said of it in the stormy and unsettled times that succeeded the death of this great captain and of the elders that outlived him. For, when the people "did evil in the sight of the Lord," and "followed the gods of the nations round about them" (Judg. ii. 11), as they did at intervals until the days of Samuel, it is to be presumed that they desecrated the sabbath by doing forbidden work and by offering sacrifice to idols. Yet the twilight of history continues; for there is no reference to the sabbath in the books of Joshua, Judges, and Ruth ; and all we can do is to infer a disregard of the sabbath from the general disorder of the times and from the asserted idolatry of the people. It would, however, be unreasonable to suppose that there were none who remembered the former days, and worshipped the God of their fathers.

From the time of Samuel until the nation was rent in twain, the weekly day of rest must have been generally

observed. Though nothing is said of it in the books of
Samuel, or in the first book of Kings, there is sufficient
evidence in the character of the prophet-judge, and in the
devout spirit of David, as well as in the organized temple-
worship under Solomon, to justify a very confident belief
that the sabbath was remembered by the nation, and hallowed by those whose hearts were true to Jehovah. This
period of nearly two hundred years was the golden age of
Israel; and throughout these generations of increasing
strength and fame the seventh day of the week, as all
reverent and impartial scholars must admit, was honored
as a day of rest and worship. And it was this observance
of the sabbath, together with their religious life in other
respects, which made the nation prosperous.

But the wisdom of Solomon, and his royal provision for
worship in the house of the Lord, did not prevent his
tolerance of idolatry from corrupting the morals of the
people, and weakening their reverence for the law of
Moses. The heavens began to be dark in the latter part
of his reign, and predictions of evil were uttered by one
at least of the prophets of Jehovah. Yet the holy day
was doubtless kept by most of the nation till the death
of this sagacious but splendor-loving and degenerate monarch.

From the division of the nation until the Jews were
carried away captive into Babylon, we find here and there
indications that the sabbath was known to the people,
and kept when the other statutes of the Mosaic law were
kept. But the language of Isaiah, Jeremiah, and Ezekiel,
if carefully examined, will prove that the holy day was
profaned much of the time by many of the people. Under
irreligious kings true worship was neglected, and multitudes treated the seventh day of the week like any other
day.

Thus it is said of Ahaz, who reigned sixteen years in

Jerusalem, that he walked in the way of the kings of Israel, that he sacrificed and burnt incense in high places, that he made his son to pass through the fire, that he cut in pieces the vessels of the house of God, that he shut up the doors of the temple, and that he made himself altars in every corner of Jerusalem (2 Kings xvi. 2–4; 2 Chron. xxviii. 1–4). Under such a king the sabbath was certain to be desecrated. He was followed on the throne by the good King Hezekiah; but, when Hezekiah died, Manasseh took the kingdom, and reigned fifty-five years in Jerusalem, doing what was evil in the sight of the Lord. For he rebuilt the high places which his father had destroyed, together with altars to Baal and all the host of heaven, placing the latter in the two courts of the temple. He also worshipped all the host of heaven, made his son pass through the fire to Moloch, used magic and divination, and dealt with necromancers and wizards (2 Kings xxi. 2–6). He was succeeded by Amon, a son after his likeness, who reigned but two years; and then by Josiah, his pious grandson, who came to the throne at eight, and reigned till he was twenty-six before the book of the law was discovered in the house of the Lord. So universal and complete had been the apostacy of Judah, during the years of Manasseh's reign, that Josiah had never seen a copy of the book of the law, or heard that such a book was in existence. We may therefore, making all due allowance for the special wickedness of the royal family at that time, be certain that for half a century the sabbath was either deliberately profaned, or quietly ignored, by a majority of the Jews. That other times were similar to this, can scarcely be doubted. Yet the impression which the sacred literature concerning the southern kingdom makes on a reader's mind justifies us in believing that the people of almost every generation had some knowledge of the law, and that there were always a few devout souls that sought to obey it.

But in the northern kingdom idolatry prevailed from first to last; and so great was its influence under the worst kings, that the worshippers of Jehovah were obliged to live in concealment. Yet, in the darkest hour, when Jezebel was supreme, there were "seven thousand" in Israel who had not bowed the knee to Baal. But as they were known to God, and not to Elijah, we must conclude that they served the Lord in secret, without attempting to let their light shine abroad, and perhaps without resting from their customary labors on the sabbath.

Whether the sabbath was honored by any considerable part of the Jews during their captivity in Babylon, we have been unable to ascertain. A cloud rests upon their history in this respect, and we do not learn that a single ray of light from modern discoveries has pierced that cloud. How eagerly would any of us welcome satisfactory evidence on this point! And it is possible that such evidence may yet be discovered in the wonderful ruins of the East.

The Jews who returned from Babylon to the holy city, by permission of Cyrus, were doubtless, for the most part, men who cherished a very high regard for their religion, as well as for their fatherland. Their leaders were men zealous for the law, and ready to encourage a strict obedience to its requisitions. On their arrival at Jerusalem an altar for burnt-offerings was set up at once, and the building of the second temple was presently undertaken. Religion was treated as a chief concern of the people. They were instructed as to the law of their fathers, and the sabbath was strictly observed by many.

Yet they were not all faithful. Accustomed to intercourse with the heathen in Babylon, and encompassed in their recovered city by idolaters, they found it no easy task to walk according to all the ordinances of the law, blameless. Some of them had taken heathen wives, and had yielded in many things to their seductive influence. It is not therefore surprising that we read these words in Nehemiah, referring to the state of religion about one hundred years after the first company returned from Babylon : " In those days I saw in Judah men treading wine-presses on the sabbath, and bringing in sheaves and lading on the asses, even both wine, grapes, and figs, and all burdens, which they brought into Jerusalem on the sabbath day. And men of Tyre dwelt therein, bringing fish and all kinds of wares, and selling on the sabbath to the sons of Judah. And I contended with the nobles of Judah, and said unto them, What is this evil thing that ye do, even profaning the sabbath day?" To put an end to such traffic, Nehemiah ordered the gates of Jerusalem to be shut before the sabbath began, and to be opened only after it was past. At this the merchants and sellers of all kinds of wares lodged without Jerusalem once or twice ; but, when Nehemiah threatened to lay hands on them if they should do this again, they gave up the contest, and from that time forth came no more on the sabbath (Neh. xiii. 15 *sq.*). From this narrative we do not infer that all the Jews were ready to engage in labor or traffic on the sabbath, but rather that a minority, composed of irreligious men, would do this ; and, though it is certain that such a minority was always present among the people from the days of Ezra to the time of Christ, — a period of five hundred years, — the few references to the sabbath in the Apocrypha, in Josephus, and in Philo, warrant the conclusion that the weekly day of rest was strictly observed by devout Jews through this half-millennium of their history.

In support of this statement, we appeal to their conduct in time of war, to the Rabbinic interpretation of their sabbath-rest, and to the mystical reasons for rest on the seventh day presented by Philo.

1. Their conduct in time of war. According to Jose-

phus, Ptolemy, the son of Lagus, who was one of the five
that divided between themselves the empire of Alexander
the Great, entered Jerusalem without resistance, partly
because the Jews were unwilling to take up arms on the
sabbath, and partly because they were not sure that he
was an enemy to them ("Antiq." xii. 1, 1). Again, when
Antiochus had polluted the temple, and had undertaken to
compel all the Jews to worship false gods, the Asmonean
heroes — Mattathias and his sons — refused to forsake
the law of Moses, and repaired to mountain fastnesses for
safety. Others of kindred spirit followed their example,
and took refuge in caves of the wilderness. These were
surrounded and attacked upon the sabbath ; and as they
would not even stop up the entrance to their caves, or
hurl a stone at their assailants, they were ruthlessly slain
to the number of a thousand people, with their wives, their
children, and their cattle. Hearing the particulars of this
slaughter, Mattathias and his friends took the matter into
consideration, and decreed that, "Whoever shall come to
make battle with us on the sabbath day, we will fight
against him, neither will we all die as our brethren that
were murdered in secret places" (1 Macc. ii. 19–41 ; Josephus, "Antiq." xii. 6, 1). But this decree, which was thence-
forth accepted as compatible with the law by most of the
Jews, did not authorize them to repair or strengthen their
own defences on the sabbath, nor even to assail an enemy
who was pushing forward his works on that day. Hence
Josephus testifies that the Romans under Pompey, when
besieging the temple, would not have been able to fill the
chasm north of it, had not Pompey observed that the Jews
abstained from all sorts of work (save that of repelling an
assault) on the seventh days ; and, restraining his soldiers
from fighting on those days, employed them in filling up
the chasm and raising the necessary embankment (Josephus, "Wars of the Jews," i. 7, 3 ; ii. 16, 4). Thus the

right of self-defence against an actual attack was made of little service by a denial of the right to oppose preparations for attack. Moreover, a passage in the Life of Josephus shows that some of the Jews believed it unlawful to repulse an assaulting foe on the sabbath (Life, § 32).

2. The Rabbinical interpretation of the Fourth Commandment. This appears to date from the period of the second temple. It was current and respected in the time of Christ, though some part of it is more modern. The Mishna, which gives the substance of this interpretation, divides the work which must be avoided on the sabbath into thirty-nine heads, such as "ploughing, sowing, reaping, binding sheaves, threshing, winnowing, sifting, grinding, kneading, baking," and so on through all the principal departments of useful labor. It also pronounces every kind of work that can be classed under any of these thirty-nine heads unlawful. Thus, under the head of "ploughing" is put every similar work, as digging, delving, planting, watering, weeding, pruning, and the like. The ramifications of prohibition are thus almost endless; and a great number of particulars are specified, some of which seem to us trivial, if not absurd. For instance, no person is allowed to carry or convey any thing on the sabbath from a private place, say an ordinary dwelling-house, to a public place, like the highway, — or the reverse. But this carrying or conveying is not a complete or perfect action for which one is guilty, unless the *same person* who takes an object from the one place deposits it in the other. Suppose, then, that a beggar stands in a highway just outside a private house, and the owner stands within. If the beggar should put his hand through a door or window into the house, and put something into the owner's hand, or take something out of his hand into the street, the beggar would be guilty, but the owner of the house free from guilt. On the other hand, should the owner of the

house reach his hand out of the same, and put something
into the beggar's hand, or take something from it, and
draw his hand back, the owner would be guilty, and the
mendicant free from guilt. But, should the beggar put
his hand in, and the owner take something from it, or
put something into it, and the beggar then withdraw it,
both are free. Or, should the owner reach out his hand,
and the mendicant take the gift from it, both would be
free from guilt. For, in neither of these instances does
the owner of the house, or the beggar, perform the complete act of conveying any thing from one kind of place
to another. ("Eighteen Treatises of the Mishna," translated by the Rev. D. A. De Sola and the Rev. M. J. Raph-
all, xii. ch. 1.) Thus, for doing half a piece of work one
is innocent; for doing the whole of it, guilty; or, in
other words, divide the sin, and you annihilate it, — a
new illustration of the motto, "Divide and conquer." But
the fact that these details were patiently considered and
determined by some of the most eminent sages is satisfactory evidence of two things: viz., *first*, of the profound
respect which was felt for the law of Moses concerning
the sabbath; and, *second*, of the extreme difficulty which
there is in laying down special rules as to what may or
may not be done on a day of holy rest. Certain it is that
Jesus Christ refused to comply with some of the regulations which had already been prescribed by Jewish teachers, though many more regulations were subsequently
added. For instance, it was lawful, in the time of Christ,
for the owner of an ox that had fallen into a pit to lift him
out of the same on the sabbath; but, according to the orthodox Judaism of later times, the animal cannot be taken
out unless it is likely to perish by remaining where it is
until the morrow.

3. The writings of Philo afford proof of the high esteem
in which the sabbath was held by Jews out of Palestine in

the first century of our era. In his treatise " On the Crea·
tion of the World " (ch. 30), he says, " After the whole
world had been completed according to the perfect nature
of the number six, the Father hallowed the day following,
the seventh, praising it, and calling it holy. For that day
is the festival, not of one city or of one country, but of all
the earth ; a day which alone it is right to call the day
of festival for all people, and the birthday of the world." ·
In his treatise " On the Life of Moses " (ch. xxvii.) he
remarks that " in accordance with the honor due to the
Creator of the universe, the prophet hallowed the sacred
seventh day, beholding, with eyes of more acute sight than
those of mortals, its pre-eminent beauty. For this reason
the all-great Moses thought fit that all who were enrolled
in his sacred polity should follow the laws of nature, and
meet in a solemn assembly, passing the time in joy and
cheerful relaxation, abstaining from all works and from
all acts that tend to produce any thing, and from all business connected with securing the means of living, that
they should keep a complete truce, avoiding all laborious
thought and care, and devoting their leisure to . . . the
study of philosophy." Again, " On the Ten Commandments " (ch. xx.), he says, " The Fourth Command refers to
the sacred seventh day, that it may be passed in a sacred
and holy manner. Now some states keep the holy festival
only once in the month, counting from the new moon, as
a day sacred to God ; but the Jews keep every seventh
day regularly after each interval of six days. . . . For the
sacred historian says that the world was created in six
days, and that on the seventh day God desisted from his
works, and began to contemplate what he had so beautifully created ; therefore he also commanded the beings
who were destined to live in this state to imitate God in
this particular, . . . applying themselves to their works
for six days, but desisting from them, and philosophizing,

on the seventh day." Philo now proceeds to explain what he means by philosophizing, thus: "They devote their leisure to contemplating the things of nature, and to considering whether in the preceding six days they have done any thing which has not been holy, bringing their conduct *before the judgment-seat of the soul*, subjecting it to a scrutiny, and making themselves give an account of all the things which they have said or done, — *the laws sitting by as assessors and joint inquirers*, in order to the correcting of such errors as have been committed through carelessness, and to the guarding against any similar offences being hereafter repeated." It would detain you too long if I should read all the words of Philo touching the sacred and mystical qualities of the number seven, which seem to be in his view the great reason why God hallowed the seventh day by resting from all his work. A single paragraph must suffice: "The number seven consists of one and two and four, numbers which have two most harmonious ratios, the twofold and the fourfold ratio; the former of which effects the diapason of harmony, while the fourfold ratio causes that of the double diapason. It also comprehends other divisions, existing in some yoke-like combination. For it is divided first of all into the numbers one and six; then into the two and five; and last of all into the three and four. And the proportion of these numbers is a most musical one; for the number six bears to the number one a sixfold ratio, and the sixfold ratio causes the greatest possible difference between existing tones, the distance by which the sharpest tone is separated from the flattest. . . . Again, the ratio of four to two displays the greatest power in harmony, almost equal to that of the diapason. . . . And the ratio of four to three effects the first harmony, that in the thirds, which is the diatessaron." By such and still more mysterious properties in the number seven, does Philo undertake to account for the rest of the Creator on the seventh day. How puny and childish they appear beside the majestic simplicity of historical truth in the Book of Genesis!

From the strict and almost fanatical regard which the Jews paid to the sabbath in time of war, as we learn it from the Apocrypha and Josephus; from the minute and complicated rules which were laid down by the Rabbis to guide the people in their sabbath rest, as we learn them from the Mishna and New Testament; and from the philosophical rhapsodies of Philo on the sacred number seven, on the rest of God after creation in the seventh day, and on the Fourth Commandment, requiring the Jews to hallow that day by abstaining from all productive or fatiguing labor, — it must be evident, to an impartial student of history, that the sabbath was scrupulously observed by pious Israelites in the time of Christ. It must likewise be evident that the Saviour did not condemn sabbath-keeping in itself, but only the Rabbinic regulations by which it was made unnatural and sometimes cruel; regulations which were at least trivial, and the observance of which may be fitly compared with their tithing of mint, anise, and cummin, while neglecting the weightier matters of the law, — judgment, mercy, and truth.

Since the time of Christ the Jews have kept the sabbath in about the same spirit and manner, speaking generally, with which it was kept by their ancestors who rejected our Lord. A large majority of the race have honored the instruction of the Rabbis, and have observed, with singular faithfulness, the specific rules prescribed by Rabbinic wisdom. Through evil report and good report, in times of persecution and in times of peace, they have clung to the traditions of their fathers, and have bowed to the authority of their teachers. "Circumcision" and "sabbatizing" distinguished them from Christians in the time of Justin Martyr, and have continued to do the same from that day to this.

Yet there have been some Jews in almost every age who have hesitated about receiving the Mishna and Talmud as of no less practical authority than the law of Moses. By such the words which Longfellow puts into the mouth of Gamaliel would not be accepted as true :—

> " Great is the Written Law; but greater still
> The Unwritten, the Traditions of the Elders,
> The lovely words of Levites, spoken first
> To Moses on the mount, and handed down
> From mouth to mouth, in one unbroken sound
> And sequence of divine authority,
> The voice of God resounding through the ages.
>   The Written Law is water; the Unwritten
> Is precious wine; the Written Law is salt,
> The Unwritten costly spice; the Written Law
> Is but the body; the Unwritten, the soul
> That quickens it, and makes it breathe and live."

This language, which represents, not unfairly, the spirit of extreme Rabbinic orthodoxy, would have been rejected by a considerable fraction of the Jews in almost every century since the advent of Christ. Yet the sabbath has been held in honor by this fraction of the people, as well as by the far greater numbers that have received the Mishna and Gemara. With remarkable unanimity have the many sects of this remarkable race persevered in calling the sabbath a delight; and, in circumstances fitted to shake the constancy of any but the firmest, have they recognized their obligation to abstain from labor during the seventh day of the week. In face of odds the most hopeless, and of hatred the most relentless, and of persecution the most cruel, they have testified their reverence for the day of rest. Even when they have purchased a continuance of life by submitting to baptism, and professing to be Christians, they have, in many instances, retained their regard for the seventh day.

Of such Jews, in the time of Ferdinand and Isabella,
Milman thus speaks : " They attended the services, they
followed the processions, they listened to the teaching of
the Church ; but it was too evident that their hearts were
far away, joining in the simpler services of the synagogue
of their fathers ; and, in their secret chambers, the usages
of the law were observed with the fond stealth of old
attachment. To discover how widely Jewish practices still
prevailed, nothing was necessary but to ascend a hill on
their sabbath, and look down on the town or village below.
Scarce half the chimneys would be seen to smoke: all that
did not were evidently those of the people who still feared
to profane the holy day by lighting a fire " (iii., 308).

We may perhaps be aided in our attempt to appreciate
the steadfastness of the Jews in keeping their holy day,
by looking at a few particulars. They have always been
a thrifty people, eager to buy and sell and get gain. It
was therefore an act of no little self-denial when they
rested on the sabbath in countries where markets were
held on that day. Yet they did this in France, previous
to the reign of Louis the Fair, and probably in many other
parts of Europe (Milman, iii., 146). In estimating the
significance of their conduct in this respect, we must bear
in mind three facts : *first*, that trade was their business,
their livelihood, their passion ; *second*, that the people then
did most of their trading on market-days, coming into the
towns and cities from the country round about, for the purpose of disposing of their produce, and purchasing what
they needed ; and, *third*, that Christians would not engage
in traffic on the first day of the week, and that Jews were
rarely permitted to do so. It will be seen, therefore, that
reverence for the sabbath led this people, during long centuries of oppression, to conquer the strongest impulse of
selfishness. In many instances, however, this was not
their severest trial. Thus, according to Grætz' History

of the Jews (iv., p. 392), they were sometimes required by generals to provide fresh bread for the hungry legions every sabbath day; and this could not be done by them without breaking their holy rest by the kindling of fires and much other labor. Yet the requisition must be met, or pillage and death would ensue. We are therefore glad to learn from the Jewish historian that the anxious Rabbis found means to relax the strictness of their interpretation of the law, instead of demanding punctual obedience in the face of certain ruin.

It would require more time than is allotted to this address, to describe the various methods which have been employed by the foes of Judaism to render the worship of the synagogue on Saturday a source of peril and of loss; but it may properly be remarked that the bitterness of Christians towards Israelites has not been chiefly due to the fact that the latter have kept their ancient sabbath, but rather to such facts as these: that they have crucified and blasphemed the Christ of God; have treated the day of his resurrection and glory with contempt; have separated themselves in domestic life and sympathy from all men of alien faith; have been usurers, greedy of gain, in every nation and age; and have been suspected at times, though without sufficient reason, of being "haters of mankind," and guilty of horrible crimes. Hence they have often been assailed *by means* of their sabbath-keeping, though not *on account* of it. Yet it would, no doubt, be going too far, if we should say that their observance of the seventh day of the week instead of the first has not been a serious annoyance to the Christian world, and that it has not led, with other things, in rougher times than ours, to unjust treatment of them. Nay, we are constrained to admit, that, in some parts of our own land to-day, the statutes forbidding labor and trade on the Lord's Day are scarcely just to Israelites and others who believe themselves under religious obligation to make the sabbath a day of rest.

Having spoken of the sabbath in Jewish history, as if it had been carefully observed by all the Israelites, it is perhaps necessary for me to state that there have always been exceptions to this general fidelity. Not all the Jews have been religious according to their own standard of religion. Thus we are informed, that, in the fourth century, Saturday was the day for theatrical entertainments in Alexandria, and that Jews flocked to these entertainments which were also frequented by Gentiles; and this, I am confident, was incompatible with a strict observance of the sabbath. In modern times, if we are not misinformed, Jews have often been associated in business with Christians, so that, while they rested themselves on their sabbath, the work of the firm went on, and the profits of trade came into their possession. If, then, they were able to contribute something to the firm by their toil on the Lord's Day, and perhaps by traffic in a quiet way with their brethren, and with others who had no religious convictions — why, so much the better for the firm! But it may be questioned whether Jews or Christians who are in earnest about their religion would be wholly satisfied with such an arrangement. Furthermore, it is said that many "reformed Jews" of our own day do not hesitate to continue their business on Saturday, especially since that is the best day in the week for trade.

Yet, after making all necessary qualifications, it remains a fact that the Israelites have exhibited through eighteen centuries a most remarkable and praiseworthy regard for the sabbath of their fathers. We can only commend them for doing this as long as they remain Jews in religion, believing in Moses but not in Christ. But we must deeply regret that Jesus of Nazareth is still to them a root out of dry ground, without form or comeliness.

Our sketch of the sabbath in Jewish history leads us to the following reflections: *First*, that rest from secular work during one day in seven is conducive to health and thrift. For nothing in the history of the Jews is more noteworthy than their mental and bodily vigor, and their success in acquiring wealth. And, though the former as well as the latter may have been due in part to the vital force of the original stock, we must ascribe them in a still larger measure to the blessed influence of their weekly rest. The opportunities of gain which they have missed by keeping the sabbath have been more than balanced by the health and endurance which it has given them for the other days of the week. And so their history, apart from the question of religious duty, is a strong argument for making one day in seven a period of rest from ordinary work. But, whether the full benefit of such a weekly rest can ever be secured without religion, is another question. Certainly we have no satisfactory evidence that a weekly holiday for idleness and dissipation would bring the repose and blessing of the sabbath. We remark, *secondly*, that the conscience of Jews in keeping their sabbath ought to be regarded by the State as no less sacred than the conscience of Christians in keeping the Lord's Day. If Christians are more numerous than Jews in any nation, it is manifestly proper for "the powers that be" to make the first day of the week the legal day of rest, for the physical, the mental, and the moral good of the people; but the Jews should be suffered to engage on that day in any kind of lawful work which does not disturb the worship of Christians. For the State should treat all peaceable citizens as nearly alike as is practicable; and therefore it should not compel those who think themselves under religious obligation to keep the seventh day of the week, to keep the first also. History proves that no degree of legal restraint will prevent persons who are Jews in faith from keeping their sabbath, and that no decree of civil constraint will force them to keep the Lord's Day while they disbelieve in Christ Jesus, who on that day entered Jerusalem in triumph, and on that day rose from the dead.

THE CHANGE OF THE SABBATH TO THE LORD'S DAY.

BY REV. PROFESSOR EGBERT C. SMYTH, D.D., OF ANDOVER.

EVERYWHERE in Christendom the first day of the week is recognized as a day of special religious observance. Various opinions exist respecting the grounds and the extent of the obligation thus to set it apart from the other days of the week. But its recognition is practically universal. And wherever it is observed, the obligation to keep the seventh day as a Sabbath of the Lord is regarded as terminated.

The question upon which I have been requested to speak, viz. : " The Change of the Sabbath to the Lord's Day," is best approached, I think, by noticing this broad and patent fact, that Christianity has, in some way, brought about such a substitution of days, and by inquiring, first of all : How has this change been accomplished ? As the change is itself a fact of history, and also is not, like other facts which lie at the foundation of the Christian religion, announced and explained directly and authoritatively by the writers of the New Testament, it is specially incumbent that our investigation should be, in the first instance at least, rigidly and impartially *historical*, rather than *dogmatic*.

Our Lord, during the period of His earthly ministry, carefully conformed to the requirements of the Mosaic institute. No fault could be found with Him in any of His relations to the Jewish law. He fulfilled all righteousness. He led His disciples in the same path. His teaching, indeed, spiritualized the commandments of the law.

He claimed to be the Lord of the Sabbath. He plainly pointed to vast religious changes which were to come. He finally commissioned His disciples to proclaim a universal religion. Yet, *salvation is of the Jews*. The Apostles were to tarry in Jerusalem until endued with power from on high. Not during Jesus' lifetime on earth, — not even in the interval between His resurrection and ascension, — did He ever, so far as appears, formally release His disciples from their special obligations as Jews.

It need not surprise us, therefore, that the Apostles themselves were somewhat slow in discovering the change which in principle and potency had been fully brought about by the crucifixion, resurrection, and ascension of their Lord. They were Jews. They followed their great Teacher's example in frequenting the temple, in observing its ritual, in keeping the national feasts, in hallowing the Sabbath. Soon, we may believe, — just how soon we cannot tell, — the Apostles, at least, were made aware that their special mission to their own countrymen was ended. There is a tradition which possibly may have some foundation in truth, that after twelve years they went forth into the world.[1] Yet it seems reasonable to believe that the Church of Jerusalem, down to the destruction of the Temple, and perhaps even later, continued to observe the Jewish law, including the hallowing of the Jewish Sabbath. With the leaders of the Church, at least, — probably with the majority of its members, — this observance was increasingly a matter of expediency. It rested on the principle which Paul declared: "To the Jews I became as a Jew, that I might gain the Jews."[2] The hope was entertained of a collective conversion of their countrymen, and perhaps of a retention by the Jewish nation of its place of privilege and honor in God's covenant. So long as this result seemed possible, it was desirable to avoid every thing which would

---

[1] Clem. Alex., *Stromata*, vi. 5.   [2] 1 Cor. ix. 20.

excite prejudice and needless hostility. There was of course danger in such a line of conduct, — the exposure to an identification of Christianity with Judaism, and even to apostacy from Christ. But it was not in principle and motive such an identification. For again and again the Church of Jerusalem recognized the liberty of the Gospel, and the Christian standing of Gentile converts who observed none of the ceremonies required in the law. The course pursued, therefore, was, as I have said, a natural and expedient one until, in the Providence of God, the success or non-success of the mission to the Jews should be decisively settled.

While this state of things continued, it is reasonable to suppose that the Sabbath — the hallowed rest of the seventh day — was scrupulously observed at Jerusalem, and by all the Jewish Christian churches. That there was also some commemoration of the day on which Jesus rose from the dead, seems not improbable. But there is no *evidence* of the fact, and, whatever may have been the custom, it can scarcely have assumed either such significance or proportion as belongs to the observance of a Sabbath.

It is one of the many signs of the genuineness and thorough trustworthiness of the Acts of the Apostles, that the first indication, with a single exception, of a special remembrance of the first day of the week appears incidentally, in connection with a distant Pauline church in Asia Minor, and about the year 57 of our era. Paul was returning for the last time to Jerusalem. Sailing from Philippi to Troas he had an unexpectedly long passage, and arrived after the first day of the week was past. He tarried seven days, — apparently, in part at least, that he might be with the church on "the first day of the week, when the disciples came together to break bread," the bread of holy communion. The natural implication is, that the first day of the week was, in Troas, a season set apart for the celebration of the Lord's Supper, the most distinctive rite of Christianity. Such a day would inevitably, for this reason, if for no other, receive the appellation of the Lord's Day. Yet, in the narrative, this term does not occur. The day is simply called : *the first day of the week.*

A little earlier — perhaps a year before — Paul writes to another of the churches under his care, the Corinthian, and directs that on the first day of the week every one should set aside a contribution to be ready upon the Apostles' arrival.[1] Similar instructions, it is also stated, had been given to the churches of Galatia. It is thus evident that already the first day of the week was of wide-spread distinction as a day of special religious service.[2]

Less than a decade after this direction was given, the writer of the Epistle to the Hebrews exhorts a community of Jewish Christians to attendance on distinctively Christian gatherings.[3] It is natural to suppose that such Christian assemblies were held on a distinctive day.

If, as many scholars now suppose, the Apocalypse of John was written about the same time with this exhortation (A. D. 68 or 69), it is all the more noticeable that, in a book so conformed in diction and symbol to *Jewish* conceptions,[4] occurs the phrase, *the Lord's day.* Its appearance in such a relation intimates that one of the apostles, who had been a pillar in the Jewish branch of the Christian Church, recognized the first day of the week

---

[1] 1 Cor. xvi. 2.

[2] If we interpret the command to mean that the offerings were to be set apart by each one in his own home, and so the whole sum of his gifts be available for the Apostle on his coming, the first day of the week must have been of some peculiar significance to these Christians to be thus designated. If — as seems most congruous with the Apostle's design in giving the direction — we suppose that the gifts were put into a common fund each first day of the week, we have an additional trace of Christian assemblies for worship on such a day. Cf. Bishop Ellicott's *N. T. Com. for English Readers,* vol. ii., p. 353.

[3] Heb. x. 25.

[4] Cf. Bishop Lightfoot's Com. on Galatians, p. 343.

as belonging peculiarly to the Lord, and that he was familiar with a Christian custom of thus observing it. For a name could not thus incidentally, and without explanation, be used of one day in the seven unless the habits of Christians at the time — Jewish as well as Gentile — interpreted the name ; unless, in a word, the special religious observance of the day was already an established fact.

And in this connection it is worthy of notice with what particularity the Apostle John, in his Gospel (which, however, was not written until toward the close of the century), marks the appearance of Jesus to His disciples not only on the day of His Resurrection, but also "after eight days," [1] — that is, on the first day of the week ; and how carefully the Apostle also records that "on the same day," or "that day," — i.e., the day when He rose, — "being the first of the week," [2] Jesus breathed on His disciples, and said to them : *Receive ye the Holy Ghost. Whose soever sins ye remit, they are remitted unto them, and whose soever sins ye retain, they are retained.*

It is thus evident from the facts which have been adduced : —

First. That in Christian Churches superintended by the Apostles of our Lord — particularly the Apostles Paul and John — the custom sprang up, with their approval, of setting apart the first day of the week for special religious observances.

Second. That this day received a specific name, characterizing it as peculiarly connected with the remembrance of Christ, the Lord.

Third. That it commemorated the event by which was attested the Redeemer's victory for mankind over sin and death, His resurrection from the tomb ; and that it was also associated with the Gift of the Holy Spirit, the Inspi-

---

[1] xxi. 26.   [2] xx. 19.

ration and Commission of the Apostles, and thus with the Founding of the Christian Church.[1]

These results are amply confirmed by testimonies which exhibit the practice of the Church in the period immediately subsequent to the Apostolic Age. I will not cite them, for they have been often adduced, and are easily accessible. They show the continued existence of the Lord's Day as a day commemorative of the Resurrection, and also that it was used for special religious services.[2] An acceptance of the day so universal, uninterrupted and undisputed, implies, it may be fairly argued, that it was received as a part of Apostolic Christianity.

On this basis the day had, for a time, a natural and legitimate development. It grew into the proportions of a Christian Sabbath, a Sabbath fulfilling the spiritual intent of the ancient day of rest as interpreted by the prophets, and by our Lord. This quiet growth of the day in its extension with the Christian Church, and in its appropriation of time from secular pursuits and cares, is a striking feature of the history. It is more noticeable, because, as we shall see, the Early Church sharply and decisively discriminated the Lord's Day from the Jewish Sabbath. The assimilation of the two days was through an inward spiritual law, and in view of religious necessities which demanded satisfaction.[3] When, at a later stage of

---

[1] The question whether the Pentecost of Acts ii. 1 fell on Saturday or Sunday, is still an open one, though the probability is in favor of the former. Some recent writers (Drs. William Smith, Lechler, Plumptre) recognize the 15th of Nisan as the date of the Crucifixion, yet, with Mr. Lewin (*Fasti Sacri*, p. xli.), claim that the following Pentecost occurred on the first day of the week. But the fifty days are better reckoned from, and inclusive of, the 16th of Nisan, so that Pentecost falls on the same day of the week with it. This, according to Oehler (*Theol. d. Alt. Test.*, p. 552), is the Jewish practice. In any event, however, the Early Church made no mistake in closely connecting the festival of Pentecost (Whitsuntide) with that of the Resurrection. Cf. Neander, *History of the Christian Religion and Church*, i., p. 300, *sq.*

[2] I do not recall in the earliest writers any allusion to its connection with the Descent of the Spirit.

[3] See Origen, *Cont. Cels.*, viii., 23.

the history, there began to be an outward conformity, maintained by an appeal to ancient commandments, as though these were still in force, the Church itself was far on the road to the legalism of the Mediæval era. But the first process to which I have referred, though not wholly pure, was in the main a spiritual one, and the fact of such a development has not, perhaps, received the attention it merits.

The first observance of the Day is associated with the celebration of the Lord's Supper and of the Agape. The time of holding these services appears to have been the evening.[1] From Pliny's letter to Trajan (c. A. D. 111, possibly a little earlier), we learn that services were then held "on a stated day before light," and that after separating it was the custom to re-assemble for a common and harmless meal. The indications are that the Lord's Supper was now observed in the early morning, and the Agape afterwards, probably still in the evening.[2] A generation later Justin Martyr gives us a somewhat detailed account of the weekly worship of the Christians.[3] The hour is not specified, but it is most natural to assume some time in the course of the day. The service was a protracted one. And though there was probably then no uniformity in this matter, and all arrangements were increasingly liable to disturbance from the growing hostility of the Empire, it is involved in the general progress of Christianity that the common worship would become more and more a matter of formal arrangement. Passing on to the next century, we find the services yet more elaborate and sufficiently protracted to occupy a considerable portion of the early morning hours.[4] And just upon the

---

[1] 1 Cor. xi. 20; Acts xx. 7. Cf. the Alexandrian custom noticed in *Dict. of Christian Antiq.*, i., p. 41.

[2] Cf. Dr. Plumptre's comment on Acts xx. 7, in Bishop Ellicott's Com.

[3] *Apol.* i. 67 (Ante-Nicene Christian Library, ii. 65).

[4] See for details the very graphic and full description given by Dr. Pressensé: *Chr. Life and Practice in the Early Church*, p. 324, *sq.*

threshold of the century we hear Tertullian's exhortation : "But we, as we have received, ought, on the day of the Lord's Resurrection alone, to beware not only of that,[1] but also of every habit and office of anxiety, postponing even our business lest we give any place to the Devil." [2] The religious commemoration of the day of the Resurrection was thus drawing in its train, as a necessary consequence, abstinence from all that would interfere with such observance. A century later, and Eusebius, in an Exposition of the Ninety-first Psalm,[3] uses language which might seem at first to imply his belief in a complete transference, by Divine authority, of the observance of the ancient Sabbath to the Lord's Day, but which, upon closer examination, shows only how naturally and readily a Christian use of the latter takes on a Sabbatic form. In this same century, also, the first ardor and purity of Christian love having subsided, and the "Peace of the Church" through Constantine and his successors having brought a great mass of formal worshippers into its membership, ecclesiastical councils found it necessary to prescribe disciplinary rules for absentees from Christian worship and from the Lord's table, and finally this canon appears : "Christians should not Judaize, and rest on the Sabbath, but should labor on that day. But, preferring in honor the Lord's Day, they should rest as Christians, if, indeed, they are able (so to do). But if they should be found to be Judaists, let them be anathema from Christ." [4] So near to the ancient Sabbath even in outward form did the desire to secure a religious remembrance of a risen Redeemer and of His passion, bring the observance of the Lord's Day, at a time when it was still necessary to guard against a confusion of Christianity and Judaism. And Hilary but expresses the

---

[1] i.e., praying kneeling instead of standing.
[2] *De Orat.*, xxiii. (A.-N. Lib., xi., p. 199).
[3] xcii. of our version.   [4] c. 29.

natural result of a process not yet robbed of its inward
spiritual motive, when he says — speaking of keeping the
Lord's Day — that on it Christians " enjoy the felicity of
a perfect Sabbath." [1]

We are now prepared to deal more directly with the
question I have proposed, viz. : How was the change from
the ancient Sabbath to the new brought about ?

It is the opinion of some persons that the change presupposes a sense perpetuated in the Church of a continued obligation of the Fourth Commandment.   Some have
maintained that the literal interpretation of this command
requires simply a hallowing of one day in seven, leaving
the particular day to be otherwise determined.   Others
have admitted that the specific requirement of the seventh
day contained in the law was authoritatively repealed, but
claim that the observance of one day in seven was still
prescribed.   In addition, it is supposed that the specific
day which fulfils this obligation was for this purpose authoritatively appointed by our Lord through His Apostles.

Such an interpretation of the change I deem untenable
in view of the facts of the history.   And since an erroneous theory of the change is prejudicial to the cause we
are assembled to promote, I may be pardoned for stating
somewhat fully the reasons for believing that the Lord's
Day began its history and became established in the Christian Church with less dependence upon the ancient Sabbath than is sometimes supposed.

(I.) A *legal* transfer of the requirements of the Fourth
Commandment from the seventh day of the week to the
first could only have taken place by divine enactment,
duly communicated by competent authority.   There is no
evidence that such an enactment was made and promulgated.

The will of God can be made known in other ways than

[1] *Prol. in Psal.*

by statutes and ordinances; but we cannot claim that it is revealed in the form of a command, or as a formal part of a commandment, without a divine authorization to this precise effect.

The Fourth Commandment requires the consecration of one particular and specified day to religious uses. It defines this day to be the seventh. It prohibits on this special day the work of life which is appointed for the other days of the week. If another day was substituted for the seventh, and made binding on the conscience as the requirement of this commandment, in the same way that previously the seventh day had been on the conscience of the Jew, the change could only have been effected by the same authority which enacted the original law. And, if made, it must have been duly authenticated to all whom it bound. But in respect to such a transfer and publication the New Testament is utterly silent. The Apostles give directions as to Baptism and the Lord's Supper, as to the duties of parents, and children, and masters, and servants, and slaves. They re-affirm, at least in principle, all of the other commandments of the Decalogue. But there is no injunction to keep the first day of the week *as a Sabbath.* The fact, when rightly understood, is perfectly consistent, as I hope to indicate, with the continued religious observance of one day in seven, and with its maintenance as of Christian obligation, but we cannot claim for the first day of the week any positive prescription to this effect, nor directly appropriate to it the law given on Mount Sinai. For that law does not require the observance of the first day of the week, but that of the seventh. Nor is this a mere accident of the command, but a part of its substance, and is founded in the reason which is given in the book of Exodus for its institution. Nor has any one but the Giver of the law any right to alter it. Nor can any modification of it become legally binding, —

that is, obligatory as an explicit ordinance, and as a part of this command, — which has not been enjoined as such by Him.

A recent writer [1] has recalled a mediæval legend which discloses men's consciousness of the need of such a sanction, if the law of the Christian Sabbath is to be literally the Fourth Commandment, with merely a change of day. Somewhere about the eighth century, probably, a letter appeared which purported to have been written by Christ in Heaven, and dropped so that it fell, according to one version of the story, in Jerusalem, according to another, in Rome. In this letter the Lord commanded His people on earth, under the severest penalties, for time and eternity, to keep Sunday by abstinence from all labor, by diligent attendance upon public worship, and in general by an increased punctiliousness in the performance of all duties prescribed by the Fourth Commandment. The legend is only an expression of what, in some form, must have taken place, if the Christian Sabbath was to rest on the same legal basis as the Jewish.

(II.) The early Jewish-Christian observance of the seventh-day Sabbath is inconsistent with the opinion that the Apostles prescribed the first day as a change of Sabbaths.

As I have already intimated, among the Jewish-Christian churches the Sabbath of the old dispensation was probably kept until either their amalgamation with Gentile Christianity, or their withdrawal as isolated and to some extent heretical fragments.[2]

Whatever commemoration of the day of the Resurrection became established, — and the allusion in the Epistle to the Hebrews to assemblies for Christian purposes, as

---

[1] Zahn: *Gesch. des Sonntags*, p. 8.

[2] Cf. the Appendix to Richard Baxter's treatise, *The Divine Appointment of the Lord's Day proved:* Works, vol. xiii., p. 495. The whole treatise deserves to be kept in remembrance.

already noticed, affords a presumption that there was a
stated time for such meetings, — it is not probable that
the Lord's Day, in this portion of the early Church,
could have been regarded as the Sabbath of the Fourth
Commandment transferred to the first day of the week.
The Jewish Sabbath, though kept from motives of expediency, was nevertheless observed as a Jewish institution,
as the Sabbath of the Decalogue. While thus hallowed,
another day could not have been celebrated as itself equally and alike the Sabbath of the Commandments. Whatever interpretation may be given to the Fourth Word
spoken in the Mount, no Christian Jew could have supposed that it commanded the keeping of two days of the
week, — the seventh and the first. Nor while he was
hallowing the seventh day as the requirement of Jewish
law, could he have supposed himself to be fulfilling the
same law in the observance of the first day. Nor is there
the slightest trace anywhere to be found that he regarded
the latter as a successor to the former, and its keeping as
a compliance with the legal requisitions of the other.[1]

The only way, if I do not misjudge, by which this position can be questioned, is by disputing the alleged conformity of Jewish Christians to the Mosaic ordinances.
But this is not a matter of uncertainty. It is clearly
evinced in the inspired record given us in the Book of
Acts, and is reflected in the early traditions of the Church.
Not to review the evidence, it will suffice for my purpose
to refer to the narrative of the last visit of Paul to Jerusalem, recorded in the twenty-first chapter of Acts. Paul,
we are told, met James and the elders of the Church, and
declared *what things God had wrought among the Gentiles
by his ministry. And when they heard it, they glorified
the Lord, and said unto him, Thou seest, brother, how*

---

[1] Cf. Zahn, op. cit., p. 33; also Professor Fisher's statements in *The Beginnings
of Christianity*, pp. 561, 562.

many thousands of Jews there are which believe; and they are all zealous of the law. And out of deference to this zeal, extending to the national "customs," as the narrative states, Paul went so far as to participate in the temple sacrifices. Though the Sabbath is not specified, it is unquestionably included.

(III.) If we turn now to those churches where the observance of the Lord's Day first distinctly appears, and assume that the custom noticed at Corinth and at Troas represents a usage prevalent in the Gentile churches, we are impressed by the fact that nowhere in the Pauline Epistles is there any association of this usage with the Jewish custom respecting the seventh day. And more than this. The Apostle repeatedly asserts, against influences coming into the churches directly or indirectly from Judaism, the non-obligation of the Jewish Sabbath. And I think he goes farther. To understand his language, we need to recall the nature of his mission. He was the Apostle of the Gentiles. He had to deal with men whose whole religious training had been in the bondage of ceremonialism. Heathenism was in its essence, as Paul met it, a servitude to forms, a matter of rites, and days, and prescribed usages. The great Apostle's energies were strenuously devoted to the gigantic effort of extricating these men from their life-long bondage. He strove to break fetters which had been forging for generations, to reverse and purify and elevate *habits* of thought and feeling and life which had the fixedness given by centuries of induration. He proclaimed the Gospel as above all times and seasons, all forms and ceremonies, all questions of days, and meats, and drinks. For him to have made the observance of a particular religious day a continuation of the Jewish Sabbath; for him to have repeated, as though it had been proclaimed from a Christian Sinai: "Remember the Sabbath day to keep it holy. Six days shalt thou labor, and do all thy work; but the first day (the day after the Jewish Sabbath) is the Sabbath of the Lord thy God; in it thou shalt not do any work, thou, nor thy son, nor thy daughter, thy manservant, nor thy maidservant, nor thy cattle, nor thy stranger that is within thy gates," — for him, I say, to have thus legislated, would not only have made it necessary that, like Moses and Joshua, he should first have led his followers into some land made open, not without miracle, to their possession, where they could set up the new economy unconstrained by the laws of the Roman Empire, it would also have required that the Apostle should himself have embarrassed his own great endeavor to raise men by the inward spiritual power of Christianity from the bondage of ceremonialism to the glorious liberty of the children of God.

Paul, I think we must believe, gave his pagan converts no command to keep the first day of the week as a Sabbath of the Law.

(IV.) Nor is it put in any such relation, so far as I am aware, by any teacher of the Christian Church in the early centuries.

What the primitive conception was, may be definitely learned from authentic testimony.

Ignatius, who presided over the Church of Antioch at a time when it was not inferior in importance to any church, writes as follows to the Magnesians:[1] "Be not deceived with strange doctrines, nor with old fables which are unprofitable. For if we still live according to Jewish law, we acknowledge that we have not received grace; for the divinest prophets lived according to Jesus Christ. . . . If then they who were conversant with ancient things came to newness of hope, no longer sabbatizing, but living according to the Lord's [Day],[2] on which also our life sprang up by Him and His death, . . . how can we live without

---

[1] c. viii. (A.-N. Lib., i., p. 179.)   [2] *Al.*, life.

Him? . . . Therefore, having become His disciples, let us learn to live according to Christianity. . . . For Christianity did not believe into Judaism, but Judaism into Christianity. . . ."

Not more than a generation later, Justin Martyr — who has left us the well-known description of the. primitive worship on Sunday — engages in discussion with a Jew. The latter expresses surprise that the Christians, professing to be pious, do not keep the festivals, and the Sabbath, nor practise circumcision. Justin, in his elaborate reply, nowhere alludes to the Lord's Day as a fulfilment of the Sabbath. He argues that the ancient covenant is abrogated; that the law of Moses was not essential to piety, for it was unknown to Abraham ; that it was given on account of transgression, and hardness of heart; that Sabbaths were instituted as a sign ; that their spiritual meaning is realized in a life of constant piety ; and in the spirit of Paul, and in a way illustrative of the whole position at that time of the question of ceremonial requirements, of sacred rites and holy-days, he says : "The Lawgiver is present, and you do not see : the poor are evangelized, the blind see, and you do not understand. You need a second circumcision. . . . The new law requires you to sabbatize every day, and you, because you are idle for one day, think that you are pious. . . . The Lord our God does not take pleasure in such things. If there is any perjured person or a thief among you, let him cease ; if any adulterer, let him repent : then he has kept the sweet and true Sabbaths of God." [1]

And so, even when pressed by his opponent with Isaiah's declaration of the divine approval of those who keep the Sabbath spiritually,[2] Justin simply reiterates his opinion that such observance was enjoined upon the Jews

---

[1] *Dial. c. Tryph.*, xii. (A.-N. Lib., ii., p. 101).
[2] Isa. lviii. 13, 14; *Dial.* xxvii.

on account of their hardness of heart. Whatever we may think of his interpretation of the prophetic utterances, it is clear that he had no idea that the Sabbath was hallowed in the worship offered by Christians on the Lord's Day.

And to precisely the same effect is the testimony of Tertullian, in a treatise which has been inadvertently cited to establish a different opinion. Referring to the saying of the Jews that God sanctified the Sabbath from the beginning, and that this fact explains the word "Remember" in the Fourth Commandment, Tertullian comments : "Whence we" — i.e., Christians — "understand that we are under special obligation to observe a Sabbath from all servile work *always*, and not only every seventh day, but through all time,"[1] and so, he continues to explain, the question arises what Sabbath God would have us keep. For the Scriptures designate a Sabbath eternal and a Sabbath temporal. The temporal, or temporary, Sabbath is the one prescribed in the Decalogue.[2] The eternal Sabbath, foreshadowed and foretold from the beginning, is fulfilled in the times of Christ, — not, evidently, in the hallowing of the Lord's Day as another weekly Sabbath, but, as he has just intimated, in the *entire* consecration of the believer through all time to the love and service of God.

And precisely this is the teaching of that ancient Father — the disciple of Polycarp, the disciple of John — the saintly Irenæus, a man whose testimony is of more value than almost any other because of his reverence for apostolic tradition, and his freedom from any spirit of ambitious leadership or partisanship, or speculative interpretation of inspired teaching. The Decalogue, he main-

---

[1] *Adv. Judæos*, iv. (A.-N. Lib., xviii., p. 211).

[2] Manifestum est . . . non æternum . . . sed temporale fuisse præceptum, quod quandoque cessaret.

tains, is of perpetual obligation. He distinguishes it from "the laws of bondage," and from ceremonies which were a sign to the Jews. Yet it remains — not in its literal form and special provisions — but so far as it is an embodiment of laws which are "natural, and noble, and common to all," and as expanded and increased by the teachings of Christianity. Sabbaths were given for a sign. But this sign is not unmeaning nor without purpose to the Christian. It was given, he says, by a wise Artist. The Sabbaths of the Law teach the Christian that he should continue, or persevere, *day by day* in the service of God.[1] The solemn setting apart of one day of the seven is a symbol that all our days belong to Him.[2]

It is not necessary to my purpose that I should defend the Patristic view of the ancient Sabbath. The Fathers, I am ready at once to concede, in their antagonism to a Judaism which was hostile to Christ may not have fully appreciated a Judaism which was preparatory to His coming. We are in a better position than were they to see the true relations of the new economy to the old. And, to say the least, their interpretation of the relation of the Lord's Day to the teaching of the Old Testament is no final authority for us. I have not adduced their testimonies for any such exegetical purpose, nor in any such relation of authority. I appeal to them simply as witnesses that the early Church betrays no consciousness of a legal institution of the Lord's Day by the Apostles. And I cannot but think it impossible that they should have appointed the Lord's Day as a continuation of, or literal substitute for, the Sabbath of the Commandment, and the early churches have remained in ignorance of the fact, and the early Fathers have written as they did.

---

[1] *Adv. Haer.*, iv. 16.

[2] The opinions of the Fathers are exhibited with candor and sound learning by Dr. Hessey, "Sunday, Its Origin, History, and Present Obligation."

(V.) And once more — if we consider the circumstances in which the Gospel won its first converts, and made progress, we shall see that it is improbable that such a commandment as the Fourth could have been regarded as of legal obligation.

The first triumphs of Christianity were largely achieved among the poor and degraded. Celsus, in the second century, mocks at the new religion, because it was recruited from the ranks of the ignorant and low, and from slaves. There is an unbroken line of slaves, it has been said, among the Christian martyrs. Christianity, moreover, was proclaimed as a *universal* religion. The Church was conscious of a mission to evangelize all nations. The enforcement of a positive commandment like the Fourth would have been an impossibility in the early propagation of such a religion. It would have been necessary to interpret the statute in such subordination to the higher law of mercy as practically to have suspended its operation. Those who needed an express command to quicken their consciences would have readily made the exception the rule, and with the excuse that the exception would practically have become the rule ; while the conscientious would have been constantly exposed to the snare of legalism, or burdened with questions of casuistry.

Moreover — and the fact I am about to state is very significant — the Apostolic Epistles and the early Christian literature bring to light many a question of practical duty about which the Christian mind of those days was more or less perplexed, but there is no trace of such discussions as must inevitably have arisen had the law of abstinence from labor on the Lord's Day for master and slave, and ox and ass, been regarded as obligatory upon Christians in the same way that it had been upon Jews.

The view, therefore, which I am constrained to take of the change of the Sabbath to the Lord's Day is, that the

Apostles approved of and perhaps instituted the latter as a day of special religious observance, but left its development into usages and needful auxiliary regulations, its establishment as a *Christian* Sabbath in social, political, national, and religious life, to the free development of Christianity itself as a world-subduing power. Christianity, they seem to have believed, would care for its own day.

They did not legislate concerning it, but they did something far wiser and better. They implanted *principles* in men's minds, so that the Lord's Day has become everywhere recognized as a Christian Institution. Men may neglect it, as they do all the other blessings of the Gospel. They may misinterpret it, now in this direction, now in that. Yet it stands secure, for its roots are in the Christian's love for his Redeemer, its branches are sheltering, and its fruits healing.

When we think that the Apostolic method carried the observance of the Lord's Day victoriously into every city and town and village and hamlet which had been ruled by Greek and Roman Paganism, that it changed the calendars of the nations, that it controlled legislation, that it has secured for the slave, the down-trodden, the ignorant, the prisoner, the despised and outcast, the immunities and the privileges of a weekly day of rest from toil and of opportunity for spiritual instruction and worship, — we need not fear that an adherence to their wisdom will jeopard the day.

The revelations of God's will in act and history are no less authoritative than specific commands. A principle which commands our reason is no less sacred and imperative than a statute. The Resurrection of Jesus was a divine act, of commanding significance to the ancient Church, and it should be so to us. It may well be the foundation of a commemorative observance no less obligatory than that required in the Decalogue. The *Logos* of

the new creation is the *Logos* of the old. Redemption is
a higher revelation of God than Nature. This august
counsel and purpose of Divine Love is celebrated by the
Church on the Lord's Day. The intrinsic reasonableness
of such a celebration is a divine authorization of it. Its
CHRISTIANITY is reason enough for him who is willing —
to use Ignatius's most expressive words, — to "*live according to Christianity.*"

Yet this is not all. The observance of the day of the
Resurrection goes back to the time when Apostles guided
by their personal direction the forming customs of the
churches. It has, at the lowest, their approval. When
we recall the early universal acceptance of the day, it is
fair to presume that — indirectly at least — it was of their
institution. When we add the recognition it has had
from Christian hearts, the Christian's love for it, — how
it enters into prayers and hymns as well as creeds and
confessions, — we find, if we have any right and reverent sense of God's authority in the evolution of the
history of His Church, a sanction which is a seal of His
Spirit. I can see how a specific commandment might
convey to a thoughtless mind a quicker sense of authority. I can imagine that to some the darkness and tem-
pest and thunder of Sinai, the sound of a trumpet and
the voice of words, might be more instantaneously impressive than the calm, resistless rising of Jesus from
the unopened tomb, *declared to be the Son of God with
power;* more impressive even than the mighty attractions
of His Person, lifting, for all believers, all the days of all
the centuries into the light of His hallowing Presence;
or than the descent, noiseless as the wings of light, of
His creative and inspiring Spirit, calling into being, on
the very day which is supposed to have commemorated
the giving of the law, the *Christian* CHURCH, with its
tongues of flame, and its law of the Spirit of life, and its

fellowship in truth and love, with its holy sacraments and hymns and prayers, and its universal mission, and its risen Lord of the Sabbath, the Rest of all that labor and are heavy-laden, and its weekly commemoration of His Resurrection, the rhythmic modulation of its unceasing song of gratitude and praise, and its vision of the Jerusalem which is above, and free, and the mother of us all. I can imagine, I repeat, how men can still mistake the synagogue for the church, and be more restrained for a time by a prohibition than by a principle. But I cannot understand how the Mosaic and Sinaitic mode of revelation and institution can be deemed more authoritative than the Apostolic and the Christian, or more effective than that by which the Church of Christ has actually been led to commemorate His Resurrection, and, that it may do this more perfectly and fruitfully, has also been led to make the day of this remembrance a period of rest from distracting care and toil. Nor can I esteem the former method to be as distinctively Christian, or as congruous with Christianity, as the latter. Indeed, I suspect that if any thing of the former sort were discovered in some alleged ancient manuscript claiming to be the record of such Apostolic legislation, this character of the document would at once stamp it as a forgery.

Let me add, — though it may carry me for a moment upon ground assigned to other essays, and simply to guard against misapprehension, — that I do not conceive that the argument for the observance of the Lord's Day should be wholly sundered from the teachings of the Old Testament respecting the Sabbath.

There is a historical connection between the new and Christian day and the older Jewish Sabbath. The Apostles and early Christians found a religious cycle established for their use. The idea of the week as a season of alternate labor and rest, and the adjustment of the due pro-

portion of time to be allotted to each, were conceptions
and regulations too beneficent to be lost in the current of
human history. The Apostles left this religious cycle to
make its way by the force of its past history, and of its
intrinsic reasonableness and usefulness. And to-day socialists are defending it on grounds of humanitarianism.
It is a fine saying, which has been quoted from "some of
the wisest Jewish teachers:" "*He who breaks the Sabbath
denies the Creation.*" [1]

The Apostles also, as did our Lord, gave to the Christian Church the Old Testament as a divine Revelation.
In that Revelation is the Decalogue, — a disclosure of
universal and permanent principles of religion and morality. Irenæus, as we have seen, distinguished these commandments from the rest of the Jewish law in so far as
they are a summary of natural precepts from the beginning implanted in mankind, and of unceasing obligation.
The Apostle Paul interprets the Fifth Commandment as
containing a promise to all obedient children, and changes
its specific reward to one of universal application. "Children, obey your parents in the Lord: for this is right.
Honor thy father and mother (which is the first commandment with promise), that it may be well with thee,
and thou mayest live long *on the earth.*" [2]

Though the Apostle has not interpreted authoritatively
for us the Fourth Commandment in the same way, and
we may not make our reasoning upon it identical with a
divine ordinance, we may nevertheless find in it instruction of permanent importance. Though no longer literally binding, it is a revelation to us of a creative counsel
and purpose of God in which we have a part as well as the
chosen people. Though limited as a statute, it suggests
universal maxims. Though no longer formally prescrip-
tive, it is still directory. Though not for us an outward

---

[1] Speaker's Commentary, i. 341. [2] Eph. vi. 1, 2.

ordinance, it discloses permanent and authoritative principles, to be conscientiously applied, *as principles*, to the
regulation of individual, social, ecclesiastical, national life.

The Fathers, as we have seen, interpreted it as institut-
ing a type of the Christian's constant obedience, and of
the heavenly rest. But it has other meanings and relations. It bids us remember that man, in his present sub-
jection to the law of labor, needs a regularly recurring
season of rest ; that in his present necessity of solicitude
and toil respecting earthly things, he requires a weekly
day of repose for the special contemplation of things
heavenly and divine ; that in a sphere of existence where
the relations of parent and child, of employer and employed, of the strong and the weak, are in danger of being
ruled by worldliness and selfishness, it is the duty of every
parent, and every employer, to see that those dependent
on him have opportunity for the cultivation of that life in
which there is neither bond nor free, but Christ is all and
in all.

And then, as thus interpreted in the light of the Christian Dispensation, the Sabbath links the primal Creation
with the new, redemption from the bondage of Egypt with
redemption from sin, the rest of God with the peace of
the believer in Christ. And so, by all that was promised
in Eden, by all that was typified and signalized in the
Divine resting on the seventh day, by all that was commanded in the Decalogue, by all that was fulfilled in the
Resurrection of our Lord from the dead on the first day
of the week, and in the inspiration of Apostles, and the
gift of the Spirit, and by all that the Christian Church has
won of beneficent power through its commemoration of
this day through the centuries, and by all that the Christian Sabbath now is to human welfare, the Lord's Day is
commended to the reason, and the conscience, and the
love of mankind.

Let us not mistake its obligation, because God now deals with us on principles of liberty.[1] Let us not forget that Christianity is not without its sanctions of terrific force. Ever, for all abusers of its sacred freedom ; ever, for all violators of its holy covenant of spiritual obedience and unselfish devotion to the highest welfare of our brother man, sounds forth the inspired word : *He that despised Moses' law died without mercy under two or three witnesses : Of how much sorer punishment . . . shall he be thought worthy who hath trodden under foot the Son of God ?* In whatsoever respect or regard the keeping of the Lord's Day is of vital importance to mankind, it is of permanent obligation ; in whatsoever it blesses man, it is a duty to Christ. And the perfect law of liberty, which is the law of Christian love, is of all laws the most severe in its sanctions, as it is of all laws the highest in its authority.

[1] Irenæus, after developing the spiritual and noble interpretation of the Decalogue in its relation to Christian righteousness, which is found in the Fourth Book of his work *Against Heresies*, closes by reminding his readers that those who have received in Christ "the power of liberty" are thereby more severely tested than were men under the ancient law, — *magis probatur homo, si revereatur et timeat et diligat Dominum.*

CONSTANTINE AND THE SABBATH.

BY REV. FRANKLIN JOHNSON, D.D., OF CAMBRIDGE.

THE influence of Constantine on the religious thought of the world, though not now so great as it was during the latter part of his reign, is remarkable. His victories and his civil policy no longer affect us deeply; "but a considerable portion of the globe," to use the words of Gibbon, "still retains the impression which it received from the conversion of that monarch; and the ecclesiastical institutions of his reign are still connected, by an indissoluble chain, with the opinions, the passions, and the interests of the present generation." To the great body of his subjects he was known as a man of perfect physical proportions; as the possessor of health which no exposure could impair, and which he preserved from infancy to age; as a monarch whose majestic form, whose affability combined with dignity, and whose fondness for splendor, became the purple; as a soldier unsurpassed in military genius, in courage, and in celerity; as the ablest politician of his age; as a diplomatist who read the secrets of other courts at a glance; and as a ruler who could be cunning, stern, vindictive, and even cruel, but whose virtues, when contrasted with the hideous vices of his immediate predecessors, seemed angelic. To the few who were admitted to a more intimate acquaintance he appeared also as a lover of learning, though his early education had been neglected. Even in the camp he spent his evenings in study, and the Christian writings secured his diligent attention. In process of time he became an ardent defender of our faith. The lustre of his position, the extent of his authority, his habit of imperious command, his aptitude in religious controversy, and his determination to protect the churches from their persecutors and to establish them on firm foundations, combined to make him, towards the close of his life, prevalent in their counsels.

Yet, great as was his influence on ecclesiastical affairs, and great as it continues to be, it is sometimes overrated and misjudged. By many he is called the author of things which existed before his birth, and which he did but sanction. By many, in such hatred do they hold his memory, any opinion or any measure with which his name is connected is at once condemned; and with these persons it is a sufficient refutation of a view to refer its origin, whether with strict truth or not, to one for whom they cherish a boundless antipathy. His attitude towards the Christian sabbath is specially worthy our consideration, since it is not always understood, and since it may afford us lessons of importance. Let us consider, first, his legislation concerning the holy day; second, his motives in its enactment; and, third, the light it should shed on the theme of this convention.

His first and principal edict in reference to the day of rest was published in March, A. D. 321, in the eleventh year of his reign. Whether this was before or after his adhesion to Christianity, it is impossible to decide, since the date of his conversion is unknown, if, indeed, he may be said ever to have become a disciple in the evangelical sense. For ten years, at least, of his career as Emperor, while he was an admirer of the Christians, and an appreciative observer of their growing political power, he was a regular worshipper in the heathen temples.[1] His vision of the cross, and his adoption of it as his banner, did not mark his desertion of idolatry, in whose practice he continued long, like those Samaritans that "feared

[1] Gibbon, ii. 250.

the Lord, and served their own gods." The law is as follows :

"Let all judges, inhabitants of the cities, and artificers, rest on the venerable day of the sun. But husbandmen may freely and at their pleasure apply to the business of agriculture, since it often happens that the sowing of grain and the planting of vines cannot be so advantageously performed on any other day ; lest, by neglecting the opportunity, they should lose the benefits which the divine bounty bestows upon us."

The decree is extremely moderate, affecting only the business of justices, of artificers, and of large towns, but leaving the greater part of the people at liberty to prosecute their affairs on all days alike. Three or four months later it was modified in the interests of mercy. The courts being closed, no slave could be freed until Monday, for the legal forms necessary to the change were quite elaborate. The emperor therefore published another edict which must have rendered the Christian sabbath the jubilee of the oppressed :

"As we conceived it most unfitting that the day of the sun, which is venerable and famous, should be taken up in wrangling suits and hurtful altercations, so it is most grateful and pleasing that those things should be done on it that are most desirable. Therefore it is our pleasure that all our ministers have leave to emancipate and manumit on that holy day, and enter all such acts as concern the same."

It is probable that another modification was made. On the fragments of a bath rebuilt by Constantine, and now a second time ruined, has been found an inscription in which it is said that "by a pious provision he appointed markets to be held on the day of the sun throughout the year." "Thus," writes Charles Julius Hare, "Constantine was the author of the practice of holding markets on

Sunday, which, in many parts of Europe, prevailed above a thousand years after, though Charlemagne issued a special law against it." The decree establishing markets on Sunday seems to have been later than those I have considered already; for, had it been followed by the decree forbidding business in the larger towns, the markets would have been closed at once, and would not have been found in the subsequent centuries.

In our received text of Sozomon it is stated that Constantine commanded his people to honor Friday, as the day of Christ's death, equally with Sunday as the day of His resurrection. In our received text of Eusebius it is stated that he enjoined for Saturday the same cessation of business. But the statements of both Sozomon and Eusebius are viewed with doubt by the more careful critics, not only because the text of both is corrupt, but also because no such law concerning Friday or Saturday is found either in the Justinian or the Theodosian code. In short, we know of nothing more in his public life even indirectly relating to our subject, unless, perhaps, we should mention, in a word, his requirement that his armies offer prayer on Sunday, without naming any particular deity as its object,[1] and his care for the observance of days in memory of apostles and martyrs. exhibited chiefly in his later years, when his repeated crimes made him eager to find in external rites some solace for a troubled conscience.

The legislation of Constantine, when viewed as a whole, is seen to have been extremely mild. The courts were left open on Sunday for the manumission of slaves. All persons outside the large towns were permitted to pursue their ordinary vocations. And even the cities transacted so much business as was deemed necessary to supply the table with fresh provisions, and to secure the pecuniary

---

[1] The form of the prayer is given by Eusebius, Life of Constantine, iv., 20.

interests of the agricultural population, for whose prosperity the Emperor was ever solicitous.

The motive of Constantine in the legislation I have
reviewed could have been nothing else than the desire to
satisfy his Christian subjects, without arousing the opposition of the heathen. This is evident on the very face
of the principal decree. He applied it to the cities; he
exempted from its operation the country-people. Christianity was known almost exclusively in the cities: it was
assumed that a countryman was an idolater; and hence the
word "pagan" meant originally a dweller in a village, a
countryman; for the country-people lived then, as throughout Europe they do now, in hamlets and villages. Neither
party would be displeased with a law which expressed, at
least in some degree, the convictions of the Christian,
without violating the convictions of the heathen. The
Christian rested in order to celebrate the resurrection of
his Lord: the heathen had been accustomed to a festival
on the same day, and counted it no hardship to rest in
honor of his god, when the fields and vineyards did not
require his toil. The language of the edict is chosen
with the nicest skill: the Emperor refrains from any expression that might seem to indicate a Christian regard for
the day; he uses no word peculiar to the Christian; he
says, "the day of the sun," employing a phrase quite
familiar to both Christian and heathen, and obnoxious to
neither. He had been known as a zealous worshipper of
the sun; he had filled the temples of Apollo with his
offerings; [1] and, while the Christian would interpret the
law as an expression of favor to his faith, the heathen
would interpret it as an evidence of devotion to the deity
the Emperor had always regarded with profound venera-
tion. The subsequent decree, permitting the manumission
of slaves on Sunday, would meet the hearty approval of

[1] Gibbon, ii., 251.

the Christian; and the establishment of markets would satisfy the demands of the heathen. As if to guard, with almost timorous care, against the suspicions of the priest-hood which represented the old mythology, in the very year that he pleased the Christians by commanding the observance of Sunday, he pleased the heathen by com-manding the regular consultation of the aruspices. The whole transaction exhibits the hand of a politician who had two parties to govern; the Christian, as yet in the minority, but compact, vigorous, enthusiastic, aggressive, growing; and the heathen, corrupt, savage, eager to per-secute, and, though not well organized or well led, con-scious of being in the majority. He did not legislate as a Christian: there is no evidence that at this early date he had adopted our religion, and it is certain that but one year before he was bowing down to stocks and stones. His attitude is simply that of a shrewd ruler seeking the harmony of his people.

We are prepared now to ask what light our discussion casts on the questions this Convention has met to con-sider. What errors should it enable us to correct? What truth should it enable us to enforce?

Many writers, hostile to the Christian sabbath, refer its origin to the first edict of Constantine. They maintain that the disciples of our Lord, while they assembled on Sunday for worship, did not rest on any day of the week until commanded by the Roman Emperor.[1] I will not pause to cite the Fathers in answer to this assumption: it is only necessary to consider the decree itself, the charac-ter of the monarch who made it, and the disposition of those who are said to have received it in such a docile

[1] See, for instance, Cox's Literature of the Sabbath Question, i., 257, notes; also The Sabbath Question considered by a Layman, p. 37. Other writers seek to create the same impression by words less direct: see, for example, The Sabbath, by Sir William Domville, i., 277.

spirit, and to have adopted it at once, without a word of dissent, of discussion, or even of inquiry, as a part of their creed, and as their rule of conduct. The decree, by its terms, was operative only in cities and large towns; and it was in these that our religion had become predominant. Its author was the shrewdest statesman of his age. The churches had been purified but a little while before by the fires of persecution, and were composed of persons ready to die rather than suffer the least infringement of that which they held to be the true faith; for, though often in error as to what the Gospel teaches, they were ever ready to defend with life itself what they supposed to be its doctrines. Now, we are asked to believe that the most astute ruler in the world undertook, with no conceivable motive, to deprive the Christians of a right they had derived from the Apostles; to force on them, by a useless law, a rest to which they had been utterly unaccustomed. We are asked to believe that he directed his legislation specially against the Christians, while he favored the pagans by exempting the larger part of them from its operation. We are asked to believe that the Christians bowed meekly to the mandate, partial as it was, unjust as it was, subversive of their rights as it was. This is to read history backward. We know that Constantine, even while yet an idolater, favored the Christians so far as he could consistently with his views of wise policy. We know that, as they had withstood his predecessors to the death, so they were ready to withstand him, should he impose on them practices contrary to their convictions. Every thing leads to the conclusion that his decree was a concession to their views, rather than a violation of them. They would rather perish than enter the courts for ordinary business on Sunday, and hence the courts were closed. They observed the day as one of rest, and hence he enforced rest in those places where they were most numerous.

Christianity does not owe its sabbath to Constantine; Constantine borrowed the sabbath from Christianity.

Some opponents of the Christian sabbath go to the opposite extreme in their hostile statements, and represent the decree of Constantine as the "result of the corrupt union of Church and State." [1] That is, instead of imposing the day of rest upon the Christians, the Emperor suffered them to impose it upon him, as a condition of the bargain by which the ecclesiastical and the civil organizations became one. We need only look at the date of the edict in order to discover the error of such statements. It was published long before the union of Church and State; and, in fact, within a year of the time when the Emperor is known to have been an idolater. Here, again, we are driven to the conclusion that he acted in this affair simply as a statesman, anxious to preserve the harmony of his subjects.

Equally erroneous is the view of those Seventh-Day Baptists who maintain that the early Christians observed the Jewish sabbath until the reign of Constantine, and were induced to transfer their rest to the first day of the week by his mingled persuasion and authority. He had no motive whatever for seeking to effect such a translation; and, in fact, no reason intelligible to us has ever been adduced by those who find his hand, rather than that of God, in the change. His character and his policy alike forbid us to suppose that he undertook the Herculean task. At the time his edict was published, he was so little identified with the Christians, that his influence upon their doctrines and practices, however great it became afterwards, was insignificant. We know the fierce tenacity with which they held fast their views even in the presence of fire and sword; and we infer that his prospect of suc-

[1] The History of the Institution of the Sabbath Day, by William Logan Fisher; p. 54.

cess would have been slight, had he made the effort attrib-
uted to him. It is of all things the most idle to say, as we
must if we adopt the view now under discussion, that the
whole Christian world, compacted by persecution, ready
for the crown of martyrdom, punctilious to a fault, bowed
meekly to the edict of an Emperor to whose garments
still cleaved the stains of idolatry, disobeyed a plain command of Scripture, and broke away from their immemorial
traditions, without a whisper of debate or dissent.

And, lastly, our reverence for antiquity might lead us to
regard the legislation of Constantine as a model. But, on
sober reflection, we shall dismiss it as inadequate to our
wants. We must have far more than it provides. It was
a step in the right direction; and, at a time when Christian and pagan were pitted against each other in fierce
opposition, it was perhaps the best that could be done. It
was adapted, however, to be but a temporary expedient,
and the progress of events has rendered it no longer useful. We demand a civil sabbath which shall abolish the
concert-room, the rum-shop, and the gambling-hell, which
shall protect from every disturbance the quiet necessary to
repose and to worship, and which shall bring to all the
sons of toil, whether in city or country, God's boon of
rest.

THE EUROPEAN SABBATH BEFORE AND SINCE THE REFORMATION.

BY REV. WILLIAM RICE, D.D.

THE close connection between the religious condition of a people and the character of their Lord's-Day observance is very generally recognized, and has often been made the subject of comment. It certainly cannot be questioned, that the moral and religious welfare, alike of individuals and nations, is greatly affected by the improvement or neglect of this sacred day. It is none the less true, though less often remarked, that the character of Sunday observance, both in the case of nations and individuals, will depend upon the speculative theories which they adopt with reference to the day, and the degree of spirituality which they possess. A right observance of the Lord's Day can but be beneficial to life and character; but such observance can only come from one who is "in the Spirit on the Lord's Day," and errors in theory have ever led to mistakes in practice. This principle finds its illustration in the varying and checkered history of Lord's-Day observance in Europe; and to understand aright the spectacle presented at the Reformation, and the later history of the day in Europe, a brief sketch of its earlier history is requisite. The contrast between ancient and modern practice will thus be seen, and the causes revealed which have gradually yet surely wrought the change.

In the first few centuries of the Christian era, both the seventh and the first days of the week were quite generally observed, especially by the converts from Judaism, though the observance of the latter was never more than permissive.

In the Western Church, and among the European nations especially, the Jewish Sabbath ever occupied a very subordinate position, and its strict observance was early and emphatically condemned. Shorn of its real authority and significance, it prolonged for a time a lingering existence, a life in death. The first day of the week, on the contrary, was held in the highest esteem, and universally observed. In the language of the Fathers, it was the "regal day," the "queen of days," the day of public assembly, and of joyful religious worship. Unlike the Jewish Sabbath, especially in its Pharisaic type, it was a day of liberty, not of bondage. With little of prescription or prohibition, by what seems to have been a voluntary and spontaneous movement, the day had been made a joyous festival, commemorative of the resurrection of the Lord, and of his finished work of redemption; and its observance formed an essential part of the religious life of those who embraced the Christian faith. All the Fathers whose writings have come down to us from the time of the Apostles are in harmony in their testimony on this point. Ignatius, and Justin Martyr, and Dionysius, Irenæus, Clement, Tertullian, Origen, and Cyprian, all declare that the Lord's Day was observed as a sacred day, and that upon this day special religious rites were practised by Christians of every sect and name. Whatever their circumstances or surroundings, however great the obstacles to be encountered, however limited their control over their own time, — for many of those early Christians were employed as soldiers, or held as slaves, — they nevertheless "remembered the day which the Lord had made, to rejoice and be glad in it," and "forsook not the assembling of themselves together," though ofttimes compelled to find in darkness and concealment the only opportunity for their united worship. Thus, while pre-eminently a religious day, it was felt to be rather a day of privilege than of obligation. During the first three centuries, there is no question in respect to this fact. While the Lord's Day was never called the Sabbath, or confounded with the Jewish Sabbath, while it was distinguished from it as an institution of the new dispensation, to be observed with different rites, and in a different spirit, all Christian authorities speak of it, as of other things received from Christ and the Apostles, with simplicity, and yet with assurance. They celebrated the Lord's Supper on that day ; and he who absented himself from the Lord's Supper virtually severed himself from the "body of Christ." Indeed, ecclesiastical history records this fact, that one of the test-questions put by the Roman persecutors to those suspected of being adherents of the new religion was, "Dominicum servasti?" ("Hast thou kept the Lord's Day?") And the expected answer, that sealed the death-warrant of so many martyrs, was in these simple and yet sublime words, "Christianus sum, intermittere non possum" ("I am a Christian, I cannot omit it"). We do not find, during this period, exhortations or appeals for the observance of this day. It is assumed that the Christian will observe it ; and no man would have been recognized as a Christian who failed to "remember the Lord's Day."

The edict of Constantine, A. D. 321, marks the beginning of a new era in the history of the Lord's Day.

The day which has heretofore found its sanction in apostolical authority and example, and made its appeal to the individual conscience of the believer, is now protected and enforced by civil enactments. The Church is growing more powerful, but less spiritual. It can now claim the right of self-protection, and demand the removal of all hinderances to its peculiar services and worship ; but it begins also to manifest a disposition to impose unwarrantable restrictions upon those who are unwilling to embrace its teachings. That the members of its own communion

are losing something of their former spirit of devotion is
also painfully apparent from the civil and ecclesiastical
enactments which now follow each other in close succession, imposing restraints and regulations relative to the
observance of the Lord's Day upon those who but now
were "a law unto themselves." With the growth of ecclesiastical power, there begins to be also a demand for more
of pomp and circumstance in the religious ceremonials of
the Church. This demand becomes more imperative as
the attempt is made to dazzle the eyes, and gain a moral
conquest over the minds, of the barbarous tribes by whom
the Roman Empire is being rapidly overthrown. Sacred
festivals and holy-days are multiplied, and some of them
begin to exceed in apparent importance the day of the
Lord's resurrection.

Meanwhile the Church is growing in arrogance and
pride, as well as power, and begins to assume an independent authority, alike over the belief and the life of its
members. The holy-days of its own appointment being
assumed to be of equal sanction with the primitive Lord's
Day, it follows naturally that all obligation for the observance of the latter, save that which emanates from the
authority of the Church, is soon denied, or, at best, ignored.

A worse than Jewish formalism begins to pervade the
ceremonies of the Church; and the Lord's Day is no
longer welcomed with the joyful enthusiasm, and observed
with the heartfelt devotion, which marked its earlier history. Like the Galatian formalists in the days of Paul, the
Church is turning again to the "weak and beggarly elements whereunto it desires again to be in bondage," and
"observes days, and months, and times, and years." The
result that followed was inevitable. It would scarcely
have been possible for a people as devoted as were the
early Christians to keep reverently the multitude of holy-
days which the Roman Church established. In the low

state of spirituality into which the Church had fallen, such an observance was manifestly out of the question. As all could not be regarded, all were alike neglected, or only observed in outward form and hollow ceremony. The words of Christ to the Pharisees might with truth have been again repeated: "This people honoreth me with their lips, but their heart is far from me." In defence of the festivals inaugurated by ecclesiastical authority, Jewish analogies in Old-Testament history were first pleaded, and at length attempted identification took the place of analogical reasoning.

Thus, in theory, the Jewish Sabbath was grafted upon the Lord's Day ; but the only practical effect of the unnatural and unauthorized alliance was to "lade men with burdens too grievous to be borne " by adding to the meaningless restrictions with which the day was burdened, and in which its sanctity was made largely to consist. Again, as in the days of the Pharisees, in the "tithing of mint, anise, and cummin," "the weightier matters of the law " were omitted.

The re-action against this ecclesiastical Sabbatarianism, which strove by church authority to substitute the letter of the Jewish Sabbath law for the spirit of the Lord's-Day observance, led to the unbridled license which has continued up to the present time to disgrace the history of Papal countries, and, by exerting an undue influence upon the minds of the reformers, produced in Protestant Europe the evils which will a little later engage our attention.

The change in theory and practice which we have thus briefly sketched was a gradual change, effected only after the lapse of centuries, and meeting, at every stage of its progress, the most decided opposition from those who still clung to the simplicity and spirituality of the primitive Lord's Day. At the time when the Reformation began, it was complete and well-nigh universal. The Lord's Day was nothing but a festival of the Church, with no higher sanction than that claimed for the innumerable other days created by its authority, and even sharing with other festivals its identification with the legal days of the Jews, as their legitimate successors. As I write, a catechism lies before me, containing the question, "What are the days which the Church commands to keep holy?" and the answer, beginning with "Sunday, or the Lord's Day," enumerates a long list of feast-days, and fast-days, and saints' days. The Fourth Commandment itself, though called into requisition, was so travestied as to read, "Remember the festivals." It is not to be wondered at, therefore, that the Lord's Day had lost its hold upon the affections and reverence of the people, and was either openly desecrated, becoming, in the worst sense, a holiday instead of a holy-day, or, at best, was but formally and slavishly observed.

With the Reformation, a new era opens. Luther, Calvin, and the other reformers strove to emancipate the minds and souls of men from ecclesiastical bondage. They protested against the assumed authority of the Church, by which the superstitions of men had been in great measure substituted for the oracles of God, and led their followers back to the word of God as the fountain-head of wisdom, and the only infallible guide, alike in doctrine and in life. They therefore rejected the vast array of holy-days which the Church had called into being, regarding them as of no obligation, and little, if any, value. Their very resemblance to the Old-Testament festivals, and the attempted identification of the one with the other, were rightly regarded as reasons for their abrogation rather than continuance, since the legalism thus countenanced was in complete opposition to the true spirit of Christian liberty. The mistake of the reformers lay in their failure clearly to distinguish the Lord's Day from the Church festivals of merely human origin. The Church, by its own authority, demanded observance for all alike; and, in refusing obedience to what they regarded as an unjust usurpation of power, they failed to recognize the pre-existent sanction of the Lord's-Day observance, which had been obscured by the false claims of the Romish hierarchy. Conceiving the day to be of purely ecclesiastical origin, they denied that it was of divine appointment, or indispensably necessary. They saw too clearly its moral and religious value, to favor its abolition; and yet defended its continuance on low grounds, basing their arguments largely on considerations of expediency. While, on the whole, they deemed it best that the day already selected by the Church for rest and worship should not be changed, they yet considered the particular day to be a matter of indifference, since, as they claimed, one day is no more sacred than another. The grand facts intended to be commemorated by the Lord's Day, namely, the resurrection of the Saviour, and his finished redemption, were thus to a great extent forgotten or ignored. The sanctions of the Lord's Day which appeal most powerfully alike to the intellect and the conscience were denied.

Luther says: "No day is better or more excellent than another. Some one day, at least, must be selected in each week for attention to *these* matters (viz., worship and instruction); and, seeing that those who preceded us chose the Lord's Day for them, this harmless and admitted custom must not be readily changed: our objects in retaining it are, the securing of unanimity and consent of arrangement, and the avoidance of the general confusion which would result from individual and unnecessary innovation."

Again he says: "The gospel regardeth neither Sabbaths nor holy-days, because they endured but for a time, and were ordained for the sake of preaching, to the end God's word might be tended and taught."

Still more strongly the same principles are affirmed by Luther in a passage often quoted : —

"Keep the Sabbath holy for its use both to body and soul ; but if anywhere the day is made holy for the mere day's sake, if anywhere any one sets up its observance upon a Jewish foundation, then I order you to work on it, to ride on it, to dance on it, to feast on it, to do any thing that shall remove this encroachment on the Christian spirit and liberty."

How well these principles have been reduced to practice by the countrymen of Luther, we shall soon see.

The Augsburg Confession, prepared by Melanchthon, and adopted in 1531 by the whole body of German Protestants, declares : "Those who judge that in the place of the Sabbath the Lord's Day was instituted as a day to be necessarily observed, are greatly mistaken. Scripture abrogated the Sabbath, and teaches that all the Mosaic ceremonies may be omitted, now that the gospel is revealed. And yet, forasmuch as it was needful to appoint a certain day, that the people might know when they ought to assemble together, it appears that the Church destined the Lord's Day for this purpose."

The Helvetic Confession, drawn up in 1566, declares substantially the same doctrine : —

"In the churches of old, from the very time of the Apostles, not merely were certain days in each week appointed for religious assemblies, but the Lord's Day itself was consecrated to that purpose, and to holy rest. This practice our churches retain for worship's sake, and for charity's sake. But we do not thereby give countenance to Judaic observance, or to superstition. We do not believe, either that one day is more sacred than another, or that mere rest is in itself pleasing to God. We keep a Lord's Day, not a Sabbath day, by an unconstrained observance."

Calvin himself claims that "Christians should have nothing to do with a superstitious observance of days," and that, after the introduction of Christianity, "it being expedient to overthrow superstition, the Jewish holy-day was abolished." Of those who claim that "nothing was abrogated but what was ceremonial in the commandment, while the moral part remains, viz., the observation of one day in seven," he says, "But this is nothing else than to insult the Jews by changing the day, and yet mentally attributing to it the same sanctity, thus retaining the same typical distinction of days as had place among the Jews."

"These," he declares, "go thrice as far as the Jews, in the gross and carnal superstition of Sabbatism; so that the rebukes which we read in Isa. i. 13 apply as much to those of the present day as to those to whom the prophet addressed them."

I might multiply authorities on this point, but time forbids. This whole matter is quaintly and yet forcibly put by old Richard Baxter : —

"The Devil," he says, "hath been a great undoer by overdoing. When he knew not how else to cast out the holy observation of the Lord's Day with zealous people, he found out the trick of devising so many days, called holy-days, to set up by it, that the people might perceive that the observation of them all as holy was never to be expected. And so the Lord's Day was jumbled in the heap of holy-days, and all turned into ceremony by the Papists, and too many other churches in the world, which," he adds, "became Calvin's temptation (as his own words make plain), to think too meanly of the Lord's Day with the rest."

In the case of the reformers themselves, and their immediate followers, it is true that errors of theory were to a great extent counteracted by high-toned spirituality and fervent piety; and, despite their doubts as to the

sacredness and necessity of the day, they made a good
use of the privileges and opportunities for spiritual growth
and religious culture which it afforded. When, however,
the religious fervor of the Reformation began to subside,
those who had accepted their doctrines without imbibing
their deep religious and devotional spirit were hardly
likely, from mere considerations of expediency or utility,
to observe in a fitting and Christian manner a day regarded by their Fathers as so unessential to the system
of Christianity, and so devoid of divine sanction. We find,
therefore, that, wherever in Protestant Europe the influence of these principles has been predominant, looseness
in Sabbath observance has prevailed.

Many have been the attempts to correct the existing
state of things, on the part of those who have been led to
adopt higher ground with reference to the Lord's Day;
but their efforts have met with but indifferent success.
In Holland, indeed, the "orders for the observation of the
Lord's Day," adopted by the Synod of Dort in 1618, did
much to elevate both theory and practice upon the subject,
though they led to a long and acrimonious discussion,
and never received more than a very partial acceptance
from the theologians of the country. In Germany, the
re-action in favor of a more truly Christian Sabbath was
more than counteracted by the steady growth of rationalism, which has carried to the farthest extreme the lati-
tudinarian views of the reformers.

In Great Britain alone have the divine sanction of the
Lord's Day, and the religious character of its observance,
been fully recognized. Here the influence of Luther and
Calvin was less felt than elsewhere in Europe, and the
Reformation, though more slowly effected, was more complete. The Puritans, it is true, adopted extreme Sabbatarian views, which have given to the Lord's Day —
especially in Scotland, where those views were quite gen-

erally adopted — altogether too much the character of
the Sabbath of the Pharisees. In England, however, the
violent conflict which for many years raged between the
Puritans and the Established Church issued at length in
the very general acceptance of the theory that the Lord's
Day is of divine appointment through the authority and
example of the Apostles, and in the recognition of its
religious observance as obligatory upon all.

Having thus briefly sketched the history of the Lord's
Day in Europe throughout the nineteen centuries of its
existence, and traced the varying influences which have
left upon it their impress, and given character to its
observance, it only remains for us to take a rapid review
of the actual state of Sabbath observance in Europe at the
present time.

The condition of things, it must be confessed, is most
deplorable. " As for the Continental Sabbath," remarks a
recent traveller, "I do not think there is much of any.
Railroads run generally on the same time-tables as on
week-days, save that extra excursion-trains are put on for
pleasure-seekers. Those who can afford it take a holiday
on Sunday : those who cannot afford to take a holiday keep
at work."

Bad as is the state of things throughout Continental
Europe, there are yet degrees of badness, and the Papal
countries stand much lower in the scale than the Protestant. This is doubtless attributable in great measure
to the fact that in Protestant countries the Sunday is not
buried under a mass of other church festivals, as it is in
Papal countries. It should also be remembered, that, in
the Protestant countries, while there is far too much of
dead formalism and materialistic infidelity, there is yet
more of real spiritual life than can be found in nations
which have never thrown off the blighting and deadening
influence of Catholicism. Since the churches are open

every day in Catholic countries, and more largely attended on some of the feast-days than on Sundays, the traveller sees little on Sunday to remind him what day it is. "One Sunday evening in Venice" (says the writer I have already quoted), "we met a young Congregational clergyman who had lost his reckoning, and had been sight-seeing all day. He had observed no unusual phenomena of any kind, and was only made aware of his sabbath desecration by being reminded of the day by his American friends in the evening."

Says Professor Prentice, speaking of Germany: "In the country, Sunday seemed to me better observed than in the towns, because the Church finds fewer rivals for the attention and interest of the people. Still, Sunday is everywhere a holiday of the most open character. In some cities, it is true, business-places are closed during the morning, especially during the church service; but the rest of the day is given to labor, hunting, fishing, theatre-going, haunting beer-gardens and public-houses. On this account, many a poor German woman dreads to have Sunday come. Her husband, who has worked hard and kept sober through the week, finds it a much more perilous affair on his weekly respite, and returns home from his Sunday recreation and dissipation in no favorable mood for domestic peace." [1]

"Pleasure," says Newman Hall, "is the authorized Sabbath-keeping of the Continent, and is the special worship of the French. Shops of all kinds are open till noon, when the entire population turn out for amusement."

"Sunday in Paris," says Dr. Durbin, "is the great day for fêtes of all kinds, horse-racing, theatres, balls, parties,

---

[1] A writer in the Bibliotheca Sacra, in a review of Müller's sermons, asks: "Can the sermon ever produce its legitimate effect in Germany, where the Sabbath is desecrated as it is; or, rather, where the Sabbath is both theoretically and practically regarded as scarcely more holy than the other days of the week?"

concerts, and excursions; nor is business generally suspended, although in the after-part of the day you will find but few shops open. All this we cannot but regard as both the index and the cause of immorality."

The distinguished Proudhon thus speaks of France: "Sunday in the towns is a day of rest without motive or end, an occasion of display for the women and children, of consumption in the restaurants and wine-shops, of degrading idleness, of surfeit and debauchery. The workmen make merry, the grisettes dance, the soldier tipples: the tradesman alone is busy."

The Abbé Gaumé, a Catholic authority, speaking of the Sabbath in France, asks: "Where now do these men, women, and children, free now as to their time, resort?" He answers: "Ask the barriers, the theatres, the taverns, the places of debauchery. The tables of surfeit and excess have with them displaced the holy table; licentious songs are their sacred hymns; the theatre is their church; dances and shows engage them, instead of instruction and prayer. Thus, by a disorder which cries for vengeance to Heaven, the holy day is the day of the week most profaned."

What is true of France is largely true also of Spain, Portugal, Austria, Italy, and the other Papal portions of Europe.

In Russia, Poland, and Greece, where the Greek Church is dominant, the condition of Sabbath observance is no better. It is no unusual thing in these countries to see gross drunkenness and debauchery following the church service, and participated in by the clergy.

Indeed, everywhere in Continental Europe, there is great lack of a real appreciation of the religious significance of the day. If kept at all, it is but as a day for rest and recreation. Where work is suspended, amusements and dissipation take its place. Even attendance at the church services, which seems to constitute about the only religious feature of the day anywhere, is in many places sadly neglected, and the entire day is spent in idleness and pleasure-hunting.

Professor Von Schulte, in a recent article in " The Contemporary Review " on the religious condition of Germany, declares that " the Protestant churches are often deplorably empty, and are never crowded, except when some celebrated preacher is expected." He states, also, that, while it is true, as a rule, that " the Catholic worship throughout Germany is better attended than the Protestant," it is also true that " there are many thousands in the towns who never enter a church, except now and then at weddings, funerals," &c., and that " this is true alike of Catholics and Protestants." He adds, further, what will be found to be the fact wherever the Lord's Day is disregarded, — that there is in Germany an " entire lack of religious home-culture."

In portions of Switzerland, in Holland, and also, though in a less degree, in Denmark, Norway, and Sweden, the Sabbath is more carefully observed than in most of the European countries. The church services are more generally attended, and less time is devoted to business and amusement. Yet even in Protestant Switzerland, the popular elections are held on the Lord's Day.

In Great Britain, however, alone of European countries, can any thing like a satisfactory observance of the Lord's Day be found. Until within a few years, it might have been said that the English Lord's Day was the counterpart of the American; but to-day, I fear, the comparison would hardly be in our favor. The Continental Sabbath has never, since the days of the Puritans, gained so firm a hold in England as it has already obtained in our great American cities. England clings firmly to the religious idea of the Christian Sabbath, and, though compelled con-

stantly to meet the attacks of latitudinarianism and the
fierce assaults of infidelity, has thus far maintained this
principle in its integrity.

The European sabbath of to-day is thus the exponent
of the religious condition of the nations of Europe, and
of the Sabbath theories which they have respectively
adopted. Papal countries, bound fast in a dead formalism,
and making of the Lord's Day but one among many church
festivals, have lost the substance, while they still grasp the
shadow, of the apostolical institution. The Protestant
countries that share in great measure the spiritual dead-
ness and blindness of their sister states of the Papal faith,
share likewise with them the loss of the Christian Sabbath.
Those nations only which unite with religious zeal a deep
appreciation of the divine sanction and spiritual significance of the Lord's Day, and are able to say with the
Psalmist, "This is the day which the Lord hath made ; we
will rejoice and be glad in it," — those only find this day
to be a power and a blessing, and reap the rich benefits
which it was intended to confer.

When the nations of Europe shall recognize in the
Lord's Day not only a day of convenient rest from toil,
but also a day of joyous religious worship, divinely sanctioned, coming down from the Apostles, and intended to be
to the Christian more than was ever Sabbath to the Jew,
and when they shall celebrate the day which commemorates the grandest event in human history as those only
can who "know the power of Christ's resurrection," —
then, and not till then, will a true Christian Sabbath be
enjoyed.

THE AMERICAN SABBATH.

BY REV. EDWARD S. ATWOOD OF SALEM, MASS.

IT needs only slight alteration of accent to change holy-day into holiday; and yet what practical shift of emphasis of that sort has been effected in regard to the American sabbath has been wrought by a multitude of factors working through more than a century of national life. That the general estimate of the Lord's Day has undergone serious modification, is beyond question; that the present trend of popular thought is towards a more exhaustive denial of its special sanctity, is equally evident. There is reason for sorrow and alarm in the fact that the nation has been swept so far from its original status; there is ground for comfort and hope in the fact that the drift has been so slow in spite of the push of almost irresistible winds and tides.

The actual decline in sabbath reverence is best measured by contrasting initial and terminal facts. In 1620 a company of Pilgrims, after a wearisome voyage, making an exploration for a place to land, are driven by stress of weather to an unknown island, and, finding themselves unable to regain the ship before the sabbath, spend the Lord's Day unsheltered in the bleak, wintry air, rather than seem to trespass on holy time. In this year of grace, great excursion-steamers plough through the same waters on the sabbath, loaded with pleasure-seekers, and the shores of Clark's Island echo back the sound of careless laughter and the crash of bands. In 1621, when the very existence of the colony seems to depend upon friendly relations with the Indians, chief Samoset and a company of his braves make their appearance on sabbath morning, and commence overtures of peace by a proffer of traffic ; but, in spite of the imminence of the crisis, the sturdy Pilgrim refuses to desecrate the Lord's Day by business, and the embassy retire in ill-humor, leaving the aspect of affairs more threatening than ever. In this year of grace, on each sabbath day, railway-trains are thundering north, south, east, and west ; metropolitan post-offices are alive with a corps of busy workers ; manufactories are taking advantage of the time to make repairs in the machinery ; steam-presses are clattering with preparation for the issue of the morning journals ; the cry of the newsboys with their Sunday papers dins the ears of the worshippers on their way to church ; public pleasure-resorts find it their most profitable day for business ; restaurants and saloons have a thriving trade ; and sacred (?) concerts and a variety of entertainments fill out the last of the holy hours. I am aware that this is a partial showing of American sabbath observance : there is another side to the matter ; but these things *are,* and must be set in contrast with the things that *were.* An almost equal difference is noticeable in the legislation of the two periods. The first codification of the laws of the Massachusetts Bay Colony was made in 1648, in the framing of which Bellingham and Cotton had a large share. In the first draught of those laws by Mr. Cotton, among the crimes punishable with death was "Prophaning the Lord's Day in a careless or scornful neglect or contempt thereof." This penalty was erased by Winthrop, and it was "left to the discretion of the court to inflict other punishment short of death." In Connecticut it was enacted in 1643, that "Profanation of the Lord's Day shall be punished by fine, imprisonment, or corporal punishment ; and, if proudly and with a high hand against the authority of God, with death." The earlier legislation of New York, as represented by the

"Decrees and Ordinances of Peter Stuyvesant," 1647–48, makes special provision for securing the sanctity of the sabbath. All of the original States of the Union had sabbath-laws on their statute-books, and the same thing has been true in the growth of the Republic. Every commonwealth in the land makes formal recognition of the Lord's Day in its laws ; and the general government adds the weight of its sanction, in its provision for a rest-day for its employees. But in this year of grace stormy mass-meetings demand the abrogation of these laws, and widely circulated journals and pamphlets declaim against this infringement of the rights of man. The provisions still stand on the statute-book, but, as "inter arma silent leges ;" so in this war of opposition they are not executed, and to a great extent, all over the land, the sabbath-law is a dead letter so far as its restraint upon individual conduct is concerned.

During the first century and a quarter of American history, the shift in popular sentiment in the direction of looseness in the matter of sabbath observance was exceedingly slow and comparatively insignificant. No small stress has been laid on the demoralizing influence of the war of the Revolution, and by many it is thought that the 'first damaging blow was then struck at the Puritan idea. It is questionable, however, whether far more mischief was not wrought by the epidemic of French infidelity which set in immediately after the recognition of the Republic, — a sneering, mocking unfaith in every thing sacred, which became the vogue in high circles, and numbered among its adherents men of brilliant talents and foremost station, like Aaron Burr and Thomas Jefferson. The religious criticism and disbelief of the times were hardly likely to leave undisturbed in the popular reverence the institution of the sabbath, which was one of the mightiest pillars of the temple they were endeavoring to overthrow. Through the open door of American gratitude, French infidelity found an easy entrance, not to say a courteous welcome. The absence of any reference to God in the National Constitution ceases to be such a wonder when we take into account the atmosphere of religious distrust with which its framers were encompassed. It *was* an atmosphere, and not an assault, and all the more deadly for that reason. It was the breath of that malaria, more than the smoke of the battle-field, which weakened the popular estimate of the Lord's Day, and which, if it had been suffered to spread over the land without arrest, might have made America what France has since been, the arena for the most extravagant excesses of theory and the wildest outbreaks of lawlessness and violence. Fortunately there were "giants in the land," in the pulpits of that day ; and Samuel Hopkins of Newport, and Nathan Strong of Hartford, and Timothy Dwight of New Haven, in the latter part of the last and the early years of the present century, made a masterful stand against the drift of the times, and were in no small degree successful in arresting it.

The second period in the history of the American sabbath may be loosely said to cover a period of some forty years, commencing with the revival and wonderful stimulation of the material prosperity of the country after the close of the war of 1812. There had been a previous development of industrial enterprise, but it seems trivial in the light of to-day. The hum of the spindles had not yet been heard in Lowell and Lawrence, and Manchester and Fall River, and the great manufacturing centres of New England. Buffalo and Chicago, and the teeming cities of the West, had not yet entered even into the dreams of the most enterprising capitalists. Commerce crept slowly in diminutive vessels from port to port. A ship of five hundred tons was considered a wonder. Railways and steamboats and telegraphs and labor-saving machinery were yet to

come. But they came; and between 1820 and 1860 there
was in America the most amazing development, the most
magnificent flowering-out of industrial enterprise, which
the world has ever seen. The financial depression of 1837
arrested the progress for a moment, and then the push
onwards was more impetuous than before. In the hurry
and fever of that hot race, sacred things lost their sanctity.
The spiritual was subordinated to the material. It is true
that within this period religion caught something of the
same spirit of enterprise, and concreted and crystallized
its enthusiasms in great benevolent organizations, like the
American Board and similar corporations. At the same
time, it is undeniably true that a process of disintegration
was going on in the religious sentiment of the people.
Spirituality was losing its hold, and business was tighten-
ing its grip. The money-making day was getting to be
more highly esteemed than the Lord's Day. But along
with this, and more than this, immigration was introducing
a vast alien element into the population of the country.
The ocean was turned into a vast highway, over which
day and night tramped the unending procession of those
who were seeking these shores. They came from lands
where the sabbath is a holiday, and they brought their
sabbath with them. The elasticity of American laws
regulating religious liberty allowed them large license in
this matter of sabbath observance. The coercion of the
civil statute went no farther than the restraint put upon
open business, and the requirement of non-disturbance of
worshippers. It was nearly equivalent to no restriction.
Between those two poles there was room for a whole globe
of laxity. Sabbath pleasure-resorts began to multiply;
sabbath entertainments were inaugurated in the great
cities. The roads grew thick with the dust, and the
harbors were white with the sails, of the holiday seekers.
The desecration of the day was bad enough in itself, but

it was worse in its influence. It continually stood out as
a protest, and flaunted its defiance at the American idea
of the sabbath. More than that, by contrast, it had its
fascination. It was attractive to the young and thoughtless. Its freedom and sparkle were tempting to the man
whose confining labor had indisposed him to serious
thought. And so, gradually, the European theory began
to color and modify the American theory, encroaching
more and more, and striking its stain deeper and deeper,
until the panic of 1857 broke upon the country, and over
the *débris* of ruined fortunes and shattered business the
Spirit of God marched through the land, and, through the
new-born religious enthusiasm of thousands, the day recovered something of the old reverence of the popular
heart.

The third period in the history of the American sabbath — the period in which we are now living — commenced with the war of the Rebellion. In a paper read
before the National Sabbath Convention at Saratoga, in
1863, Dr. Philip Schaff said, "The severest trial through
which the American sabbath ever had to pass, or is likely
to pass in the future, is the civil war which has now been
raging with increasing fury for more than two years. The
desecration of the sabbath soon after the outbreak of the
war increased at a most alarming rate, and threatened the
people with greater danger than the Rebellion itself."
The accuracy of the prophecy has been abundantly proved.
Probably no great war was ever carried on in which such
strenuous endeavor was made to secure the *morality* as
well as the morale of the army. The "orders" of some
of the commanders, conspicuous among which are "general orders" of the President himself, read like sermons
eliminated of their dulness. A corps of the Christian
Commission marched with every brigade and division of
the grand army, and pitched their tents or built their

chapels for sabbath worship. Religious books and news-papers were widely circulated. In field and hospital alike, devoted chaplains labored to keep alive reverence for God and his laws. The postal service transmitted thousands of letters filled with religious counsel. The whole atmosphere was tremulous with prayer. And yet, in a little more than a decade after all this, the outlook is so threatening, that a convention is in session in the metropolis of New England, to devise measures to re-establish and perpetuate the sanctity of the Lord's Day.

History repeats itself. Just as after the war of the Revolution French infidelity saw and was quick to embrace its opportunity to infatuate men with its frivolous criticisms upon Christianity, so in the last decade English materialism and German mysticism have taken advantage of the relaxed condition of the popular thought to push themselves into prominence, and secure acceptance. Next to the Word of God, the SABBATH is the Gibraltar of the Christian system, the imperial fortress that secures the whole Mediterranean of revealed religion. It is therefore nothing surprising, that the assaults upon it should be so sharp and so persistent. Materialism and mysticism both see that it is easier to induce men to loosen their grip upon an institution than it is to persuade them to renounce a system, especially where their hold upon that institution has been relaxed by some great strain of national history ; but materialism and mysticism see with equal clearness that with the sabbath swept away, or essentially modified in its observance, complete victory is only a question of time. Happily, but none too soon, the Church of God sees it also, and is beginning to prepare itself for the coming Armageddon of American Christianity.

There are three things that at the present time specially stand in the way of the perpetuity of the American sabbath : —

(I.) *The impotence of the civil law.* To what extent it is wise and well to push the endeavor to secure the observance of the Lord's Day by legislation, it is not the province of this paper to discuss ; but so long as restrictive regulations stand upon the statute-books, and are not adjudged illegal or unjust, *they should be enforced*, and their annexed penalties inflicted, whether the violator be an individual or a great corporation. That they are operative, except in a trivial and farcical way, no man pretends. Now and then some poor beggar is under arrest for card-playing on the sabbath ; but the managers of great Sunday excursions, that turn out to be perfect pandemoniums, coolly pocket their profits, and defy the authorities to touch them. The inaction of the law breeds contempt of the law and of that which the law is set to guard. The paralysis of the civil arm encourages outrage. The danger in this quarter is incalculable. Few men have even *read* the sabbath-laws of this Commonwealth, and fewer still have urged their enforcement. It is well judged by interested parties, that the inefficiency of the statutes is due to the fact that there is no solid public sentiment that supports them ; and, where this is lacking, the technic of the code is as powerless as the Pope's bull against the comet.

(II.) A second danger lies in *the false notions of personal liberty*, that are obtaining with great masses of the population, and which are humored, if not fostered, by political leaders, for party ends. The clamor in New York and Cincinnati and Chicago, against sabbath-laws as an infringement upon the rights of the individual, is not sporadic, but symptomatic. Communism is half-sister of republicanism ; and those subtle and perilous theories of freedom, that privilege every man to do as he pleases under a representative government, have made surprising headway. Restraint on what seems to be the *religious*

side is peculiarly obnoxious. Political fallacies re-enforce
personal preferences in the attempt to secularize the sabbath ; and in a country like ours that constitutes a for-
midable alliance. That central truth of state-craft, liberty
under authority, imperatively calls for re-affirmation. The
subordination of individual right to the general good, the
limitation of personal privilege by the common need, are
integral elements in a stable national life : but in some
directions there is strenuous endeavor made to remand
them to obscurity ; and especially in the matter of abro-
gating or neutralizing sabbath-law, in the name of liberty,
there is surprising persistence and enthusiasm.

(III.) The third and perhaps greatest peril is the *apathy
of the Christian Church.* The assembling of this convention might seem to refute that statement, but at most it is
only a late confession of sin. From time to time some of
the pulpits of the land have been outspoken on the subject,
and ecclesiastical bodies have formulated their faith, and
then buried it in the sepulchre of a series of resolutions ;
but the work has too often been merely perfunctory, and
seldom if ever has been followed by the edge and flame of
enthusiastic effort. Our dearly-bought rights in this matter, inherited from the fathers, have many of them been
wrested from our hands ; and the Church has made its
little moan over the theft, but has uttered no strong protest,
and put forth no mighty endeavor to recover its lost jewels.
As we contemplate the future of the American sabbath,
the darkest cloud that looms above the horizon is the indifference of the nominal Christianity of the land. The
Church of God is the one sovereign human instrumentality
by whose efficiency or inefficiency the position of the
Lord's Day, in the estimate of the coming generations,
is to be settled ; and, since the beginnings of Christianity,
no graver responsibility has been laid upon the disciple-
ship than rests upon it at this hour and in this particular.

It has been the peculiar boast of the Christianity of the land, that in no country was the actual so nearly the ideal sabbath as in America. There have been times when that was true. The shrewd French observer Duponceau once said, that, "of all we claimed as characteristic, our observance of the sabbath is the only one truly national and American." That boast is not wholly without warrant still. The closed doors of the Centennial Exhibition at Philadelphia preached a manly and eloquent sermon. The sabbath stillness in the halls of magistracy, in banks and custom-houses, in great manufactories whose din and smoke fill the air the other six days, the church-bells that ring out in city and village, and the thousands that gather for worship, — these things must not be forgotten or undervalued. And yet undeniably there is a vast drift of popular sentiment the other way, — a drift that is steadily growing in volume and momentum, which has already gone too far, which must be arrested soon, or it will become irresistible.

If the imminence of the danger be not sufficient stimulus, there is enough in what has been wrought out by the American sabbath in the past, to inspire unstinted effort to realize its possibilities in the future. There is a myth concerning an old painter, that by happy chance he compounded one day a certain mordant, which, colorless itself, possessed the power of heightening every color with which it was mixed. By the help of his discovery, from being a commonplace artist he became a master. His works were renowned for the marvellous brilliancy of their tints. On his canvas was reproduced in exactest hue the waving emerald of the forest, the silver gleam of the river, the swimming light of the sunset, the infinite azure of the sky ; and everywhere and always the charm of the picture was due to that colorless nurse of color, that, by its strange alchemy, transfigured the crudeness and coarseness of the common tint. It is not mere ecclesiastical prejudice which asserts that the American sabbath has similarly wrought in American life. The student of our legislation, the observer of our domestic and social prosperity, the inquirer into the excellence of our educational systems, finds everywhere the influence of reverence for the Lord's Day. Often unrecognized in its workings, the sabbath is the element that has wrought out the choice beauty of the best things of which we boast. To it, and largely, we are indebted for juster laws, better schools, happier homes, greater security of social order, than can be found in other lands; and therefore let it be perpetuated. Therefore let good citizens organize for its defence against any and all comers. Therefore let the Church of God recognize the critical hour, and prove equal to the emergency.

III.

CIVIL AND SOCIAL.

THE SABBATH IN THE STATE AND IN SOCIETY.

CIVIL LAW AND THE SABBATH.

BY REV. PRESIDENT THEO. D. WOOLSEY, D.D., LL.D., OF NEW HAVEN, CONN.

SINCE the time when the English colonies were first planted in America, there has been a great change of opinion in respect to the relations between Church and State. The colonists, whether in New England, New York, Virginia, or South Carolina, agreed in the duty of the state to protect religious establishments, religious institutions, and days of public worship; to provide for, or to require that the people in their parishes should provide for, the support of ministers; and even to regulate the conduct of individuals, by requiring attendance on worship, and by punishing neglect of it. And, besides these outward acts, opinions came within the sphere of legislation; errorists of different kinds were fined, or driven beyond the borders of the colonies.

As for the laws touching the observance of the Lord's Day, the colonies did not essentially differ from the mother country. In England, laws passed in the reigns of Elizabeth and James I. imposed a penalty of a shilling for absence on any one Lord's Day, and twenty pounds for such absence through a month. And so in Virginia, absence from church on Sunday rendered a person liable to pay fifty pounds of tobacco as a fine ; but Quakers and other recusants, who totally absented themselves, were liable to the penalty of twenty pounds sterling above spoken of, which was imposed by a statute of 23 Elizabeth. These laws seem to have been passed in order to keep dissenters, by means of penalties, out of the colony. The Sunday laws of the Puritan colonies had a higher motive, — that of bringing all classes of men within the reach of religious truth. The almost universal belief in these northern colonies seems to have been that the Lord's Day rested on the same divine command with the Jewish seventh day ; and they held that the state ought to see that it was kept holy according to the law given to the Jews, although they by no means claimed that every religious or moral obligation, even of an outward nature, ought to be enforced by civil law and penalty.

These ancient statutes have gone out of use, or have been repealed in great measure. There still remain, however, on the statute-books, laws forbidding certain actions on the Lord's Day, or the Christian day of rest. Let us see by the statutes of Connecticut, as revised in 1875, and by those of New York and Massachusetts, what these laws actually are.

1. First, we notice, as it respects Connecticut, a provision which is to be found, probably, in all the laws of English-speaking states, that "all civil processes issued or served between sunrise and sunset on Sunday shall be void." Not only the laws of the several States, but those of the United States, secure this immunity from civil processes on the first day of the week. And it is to be defended, apart from any desire to sustain the institutions of Christianity, by the importance, both to civil officers and to private persons, of a day of rest, and, in the case of the latter, by the necessity, on the day devoted to reli-

gion, of being free from harassing cares, as well as by the difficulty of making such arrangements as a civil process might require, if served on a day when men in general are away from their places of business. In other words, the law must, in a practical way, consider the business-habits of society, whatever they may be, and accommodate itself to them as far as is consistent with general justice.

The other statutes in the present code I will give *verbatim* (General Statutes of Connecticut, revision of 1875, title 20, chap. ix., sects. 57–63, pp. 521, 522) : —

" SECT. 57. Every person who shall travel, or do any secular business or labor, except works of necessity or mercy, or keep open any shop, warehouse, or manufacturing or mechanical establishment, or expose any property for sale, or engage in any sport or recreation on Sunday, between sunrise and sunset, shall be fined not more than four dollars, nor less than one dollar ; but haywards may perform all their official duties on said day.

" SECT. 58. Every person who shall be present at any concert of music, dancing, or other public diversion on Sunday, or on the evening thereof, shall be fined four dollars.

" SECT. 59. Prosecutions for violations of the two preceding sections shall be exhibited within one month after the commission of the offence.

" SECT. 60. Every person who, within the hours of twelve o'clock Saturday night and twelve o'clock Sunday night next following, shall keep open any room, place, or enclosure, or any building, or any structure of any kind or description, in which it is reputed that intoxicating liquors are exposed for sale, or that any sports or games of chance are carried on or allowed, shall be fined forty dollars, to be paid to the town where the offence is committed, or imprisoned thirty days or both.

" SECT. 61. All prosecutions for a violation of the preceding section shall be determined by a justice of the peace, or police or city court.

" SECT. 62. Every proprietor or driver of any vehicle not employed in carrying the United-States mail, who shall allow any person to travel thereon on Sunday between sunrise and sunset, except from necessity or mercy, shall be fined twenty dollars, to be paid to the town in which the offence is committed.

"SECT. 63. No person who conscientiously believes that the seventh day of the week ought to be observed as the sabbath, and actually refrains from secular business and labor on that day, shall be liable to prosecution for performing secular business and labor on such day (i.e., on Sunday), provided he disturbs no other person while attending public worship."

By decisions of the courts, it is settled that notes given or contracts made on Sunday are void; any money loaned cannot be recovered; that an apprentice compelled to violate Sunday is not bound to remain with his master; but that the value of a horse hired on Sunday, and killed by the hirer, may be recovered.

The first of these provisions belongs to the year 1702; the second and third, to 1784; the rest, to this century. And especially the law against drinking-places, &c., open on Sunday, is quite recent, having been enacted in 1872. This recent date of the law shows not that law was loose before, but that such things have crept into the State in the more modern times.

The Sunday laws of Massachusetts and New York, in their principal provisions, are as follows : —

First, The Sunday laws of Massachusetts, in the digest of 1860, were in substance as follows : —

"SECTION 1. Any one who keeps open a ware or work-house, or engages in any labor, business, or work, except works of necessity or mercy, or is present at any dancing, or public diversion, show or entertainment, or takes part in any sport, game, or play on the Lord's Day, shall be punished by a fine not exceeding ten dollars.

"SECT. 2. Whoever travels on the Lord's Day, except for necessity or mercy, shall be punished, not exceeding ten dollars for each offence."

Sect. 3 has been superseded.

"SECT. 4. Persons present at games, &c., except concerts of sacred music, on the evening of the Lord's Day or the evening next preceding, unless such sport or game, &c., is licensed by persons authorized to grant licenses, shall be punished, not exceeding five dollars for each offence.

"SECT. 5. No person licensed to keep a house of public entertainment shall entertain, in his house or any place appurtenant thereto, any strangers not being travellers, drinking and spending time there on the Lord's Day or the evening preceding. The penalty to the innholder for so entertaining is not to exceed five dollars for each offence.

"SECT. 6. Civil processes are not to be executed on the Lord's Day; the person executing to be liable to the party aggrieved in the same damages as if he showed no process.

"SECT. 7. Rude or indecent behavior within a house of public worship on the Lord's Day may be punished by fine not exceeding ten dollars."

Sect. 8 makes it the duty of sheriffs, grand-jurors, and constables, to inquire into, and inform of, offences against this act.

Sect. 9 exempts those who observe the seventh day of the week from penalties, provided they refrain from business on that day, &c., and disturb no other persons on the Lord's Day.

"SECT. 10. Prosecutions for violations of those laws relating to the Lord's Day must be commenced within six months after the offence.

"SECT. 11. Innholders or victuallers keeping or allowing on their premises gaming-implements, who on the Lord's Day use or allow said implements to be used, shall for the first offence forfeit not exceeding one hundred dollars, or be imprisoned in the common prison; and for every successive offence be imprisoned in a house of correction for a time not exceeding a year; and shall give securities for good behavior, and especially not to repeat this offence.

"SECT. 12. The Lord's Day is defined as continuing from midnight succeeding Saturday until the next midnight."

The Sunday laws of New York are in substance as follows (Fay's Digest, 1874) : —

No process or warrant, &c., shall be served or executed on Sunday, except in cases of breach of the peace or apprehended breach; or for apprehension of persons charged with crimes and misdemeanors, except when specially authorized by law.

There shall be no sporting, hunting, fishing, playing,

horse-racing, frequenting tippling-houses, or unlawful exercises or pastimes, on the first day of the week, called Sunday; nor shall any person travel on that day, unless in cases of charity or necessity, or in going to or from some church or place of public worship within the distance of twenty miles, or in going for medical aid or medicines, or in visiting the sick and returning; or in carrying the mail of the United States, or in going express by order of some public officer, or in removing his family or household furniture when such removal was commenced on some other day. Nor shall there be any servile labor or recreation or working on that day, except works of necessity and mercy, unless done by some person who uniformly keeps the last day of the week, called Saturday, as holy time, &c.

The penalty for each offence is one dollar in the case of persons over fourteen years of age.

The selling of goods, fruits, herbs, &c., on Sunday, except meats, milk, and fish, before nine o'clock, is forbidden. Articles exposed for sale on that day are forfeited for the use of the poor, &c.

No keeper of any inn or tavern, or of any ale or porter house, or grocery, or any person authorized to retail strong or spirituous drinks, shall on Sunday sell or dispose of any ale, porter, strong or spirituous drinks, except to lodgers or persons legally travelling on that day by law, under penalty of two dollars and a half for each offence.

A law of special application to the city of New York, passed in 1860, forbids various kinds of exhibitions on Sunday, under heavy penalties.

A law passed in 1872 forbids processions on Sunday, except funeral processions and such as go from churches in connection with religious services there, on penalty of twenty dollars.

These laws, which seek to secure the quiet and rest of the Lord's Day, do not aim at regulating the conduct of individuals within their own premises, or at enforcing in any direct way the observance of the day for the purposes of worship. The inquiry, however, naturally arises, whether even this is not inconsistent with the liberty of individuals ; and this inquiry runs back to a more general one, — whether any restraint whatever on the outward action of the individual, on the Lord's Day, can be compatible with the true idea of the limits of public power.

1. We must answer, first, by saying that legislation is not confined within the sphere of outward and material good. The ideal good is as much to be protected by the laws of society as the good of the body and the temporal possessions. Otherwise all that department of law which relates to education, to the prevention of certain immoral habits, such as obscene exposure of the person, to cruelty towards animals, to blasphemy, could not be defended. The conception of man as a moral, intellectual, æsthetical, and religious being, has something to do with the conduct of his fellows towards him or his towards them, and may call for the protection of this part of his nature, just as the sensual and outward part of his nature calls for his protection in other respects.

2. In the second place, we remark that the state's function in its laws and penalties has three sides to it : it may require something to be done by the individual ; or prevent him by penalty from doing — that is, prohibit him from doing — certain things ; or, again, it may, without directly coming into contact with the individual, perform certain actions of its own.

In regard to moral and religious actions, the state's province of requiring individuals to perform certain actions is exceedingly small. No positive action is required of a person as to the observance of the Lord's Day by the laws of the States which have been read. And such commands as that of attending church, or not walking abroad, or abstaining from certain employments, provided they do not affect or involve the conduct of other individuals, do not now appear on the statute-books.

3. Prohibitory legislation, or that which forbids certain acts, is a restraint on personal freedom; and there is no use in restraint *per se.* Hence the inquiry always is, whether there is sufficient good to be gained to justify the prohibition. Laws concerning conduct on the sabbath are not peculiar in this respect. If a man is forbidden to walk on the green turf of a public park, or to walk across a bed in a public garden, the reason is that the state or municipality has a right to maintain such park or garden, and the conduct of the man tends to injure causelessly what the public authority has a right to preserve from injury. If an obscene exposure of the person in a public place is prohibited, the reason is that the act is at once causeless and wrong. Some might state the reason of the prohibition to be, that it is revolting to the taste and moral sense of men. I would not quarrel in this case about the exact reason for the prohibition, and will only say here that an action so entirely revolting to the moral sense is a wrong action, and would not be revolting unless it were wrong. Again, cruelty to animals is prohibited because it is inhumane, not because it makes a man feel badly who sees it. He feels badly because it is inhumane, and therefore wrong.

These examples, which might be multiplied, show that prohibitory laws do not all rest on just the same grounds; and the actions forbidden are not all of the same kind. There may be in some cases several reasons for the same prohibition. Thus laws relating to dram-shops are justified by the harm done to individuals, by the evils, such as poverty and crime, entailed on society, and, it may be, by the injury inflicted on families by such resorts.

4. There may be, then, and there are, various reasons

for laws touching the observance of the Lord's Day, or the day of rest. But is there any need of such laws in the statute-book? Christ says the sabbath was made for man. And, in consistency with this declaration of our Lord, it would seem that the benefits of the day for man are the comprehensive reason why the day should be protected by legislation. This reason implies, that if a considerable part of the people of a state acknowledge the truth of the Christian religion, and actually observe the Lord's Day, it ought so far to be protected by law that its benefits should not be lost.

And here I observe, in the first place, that the habits, or rather the fixed habits, of a people, as long as they are not deleterious to social order, have a right to demand protection for themselves from the state by appropriate laws. If Chinamen have a right — as they have by treaty — to come into this country, they have a right to come and stay with their cues on, just as our fathers had a right to their cues and wigs. So, if a man or his wife give a party, there is no right of assemblage and noisy disturbance before his door. The office of preserving public order extends to every thing in the nature of an institution, whether set up by the state or voluntary, unless it is hurtful to public interests or injures some private rights. This principle is more wide-sweeping than that similar political one, that the people or portions of it have a right to assemble to discuss their grievances, and present petitions to the government. The right of peaceable gatherings for religious worship is a most important right, because it is essential to such worship. Whether a man believes in any thing but cellular development, or not, let him be an Agnostic in regard to all invisible things, he must still admit that the mass of men do believe that public worship is of immense importance; and that they must be protected in this right, if any one is to be pro-

tected in any rights.   But the limit here, — for there must
be limits to all rights, — implying that men gather together, cannot be found in the truth which is taught ; for
the nation or its officers cannot teach mere opinion, but
only in the orderly and moral conduct of the persons
assembled, and in the fact that the object of the meeting
is not to do, or incite others to do, direct injury to individuals or to the Commonwealth.

Second, If persons ought to be protected in their religious gatherings on the Lord's Day, it is necessary that
they should have buildings for the purposes of worship,
which they may own, or at least control, for the time
being.   This is a power, or right, which every corporation for every legitimate purpose, every club and association, may exercise ; and the only question is, whether
the privilege, now conceded to a great extent, of exemp-
tion from taxes on houses of religious worship, should
be granted ; or, at least, whether church-buildings, put up
at a certain moderate cost, should be so exempted.   If
this is granted, the grant must rest on the conviction of
the importance of public worship, upon a day of rest from
labor, to all the highest earthly interests of the community.
The interests, in fact, of all the members of society depend
on stated outward days of worship, more, even, than on
schools and places of refuge for the poor ; and, until a
large portion of society becomes hostile to Christianity,
this will be generally admitted.

Third, A more difficult question arises touching public
sports, travelling for unnecessary purposes, opening shops
and exposing articles for sale ; in fact, touching all laws
by which a distinction is made, in regard to outward acts,
in any way, between the Lord's Day and the other six
days of the week.   Here several considerations present
themselves, to which we devote a few very brief remarks.

A day of rest from labor is invaluable for all who are

occupied in bodily labor through the week. In a farming community, perhaps, the mere rest from toil on one day is not so important as it is for operatives ; and, again, those who carry on their own business of producing that which they sell by their own bargains, can, to some extent, command their time, and rest when they are weary. But all operatives, clerks, domestic servants, persons engaged by others in transportation, and, we may add, children in schools, older students, and professional men, need such rest as the Lord's Day affords. It is admitted to be eminently a humane institution.[1] To a humane person, it is a joy that beasts of burden and transport share in man's weekly rest. If there is a public habit of rest, the business of the world is not affected ; nay, it is probable that as much work is done in six days as would be done in seven. It is for the health of man. A day of religious rest is again eminently a social institution. By bringing men together in worship, it unites society, opening the hearts of the community to the noblest truths, and helping them to resist the influences of mere earthly occupation. A day of common rest may thus be a blessing to man and beast, to all whose vocation calls to bodily or mental labor, to the bodily and to the spiritual natures. But a day of common rest cannot well arise, except for religious pur-

---

[1] Bismarck, who is not at all strict in his views on the observance of Sunday, expresses himself thus in Dr. Busch's book (1,222 American ed. of transl.) : —

"I, too, am not at all against observances of the Sunday : on the contrary, I do all I can, as a landed proprietor, to promote it ; only I will not at all have people constrained. On Sunday, no work should be done, not so much because it is against the commandment of God, as on man's account, who needs repose. This, of course, does not apply to the service of the state, especially not to the diplomatic service ; for despatches and telegrams arrive on Sunday, which must be attended to. Nor is any thing to be said against our peasants bringing in their hay or corn on a Sunday, in the harvest, after long rain, when fine weather begins on a Saturday. I could not find it in my heart to forbid this to tenants in the contract ; although I should not do it myself, being able to bear the possible damage of a rainy Monday. It is thought by our proprietors rather improper to let their people work on Sunday, even in case of necessity."

poses. Man may have occasional and irregular festivals, or holidays, in a land of atheists; but religion gave us and keeps up for us the Lord's Day. It thus, in all Christian lands, forms the habits of the community.

Now, a habit so important and universal cannot exist without having some relations to law; and the legislator who deserves the name, one who feels the necessity of supporting all civil interests on a basis of morality and religion, and who discerns the intense morality of the Christian religion, will be most ready to protect the Lord's Day on account of its use, because "it was made for man."

Let us now look at some of the ways in which the Lord's Day is protected by law. One is the protection of the laborer against his employer. Men are now agreed that the state may be required to regulate the daily number of hours' work in a factory, especially for women and children; and the law, in Connecticut, provides not only against overworking young children, but against using up all their school-time in manual employments. The necessity of law in such cases arises from the fact that in contracts for labor one party, the employer, has an advantage over the other. If the laborers wear out through excess of toil, and are incapacitated for work, the employer has had so much the more profit from them, provided he pays them by day's work; and then society, acting on humane principles which are above the doctrine of rights and obligations, must help them to live. For two reasons, then, such cases may be noticed by law, — for the sake of the laborer and for the sake of the community.

And again, within certain limits, all those demands on men's time, which require particular persons to use up the day of rest in serving the mere pleasure or the pecuniary interests of others, may come under the regulation of law. Such cases would be free travelling on rail or other roads; free use of hired carriages, requiring hostlers to do more than supply food to horses (which is an act of humanity); the employment of men in pleasure-excursions on the Lord's Day; every kind of work which without necessity takes away from men the possibility of rest or of worship. For the protection of such persons, as well as for the general good derived from worship and the inculcation of Christian truth, laws like those in the statute-books, which have been read, are entirely justifiable; nay, they are needed, because without such props the character of society would become worse. Such laws are, in fact, a protection of outward religious and moral habits, and society is paid for them by the defence of all civil order and civil institutions which religion and morality afford. In fact, an unbeliever in revelation, who felt the importance of cherishing the moral and religious convictions for the maintenance of public order and safety, might be rationally in favor of protecting the Lord's Day by institutions and laws, although he drew no benefits from it himself.

Another description of laws which will meet with general commendation are those which forbid, under penalties, the opening of gambling and drinking houses on the Lord's Day. A day even of religious rest may have its temptations for those who will not spend it for the purposes contained in its original institution. The tired laborer may welcome the suspension of work, but may use the day in criminal self-indulgence, ruinous to him and his family. Thus for the workingmen, especially in large towns, severer laws are needed on Sunday, in regard to gambling and drinking, than in the rest of the week.

Suppose, now, such a general spirit of unbelief to prevail as would render all Sunday-laws obsolete, if not repeal them altogether: Christianity would by no means lose its day of rest, but a state of things would ensue, much worse for society than the severest sabbath code that ever was enacted. In such a state of things Christians would be forced into closer unions than now exist. They would form societies within society. As they would have no laws to support their institutions, they would combine the more easily to protect themselves. If, for instance, the unbelieving part of society bought and sold, drank and gambled, on Sunday, they would undoubtedly deal with no such traders, but would draw all their supplies from men within their own communities. That this would promote hypocrisy and hatred, is very likely; but it would be the inevitable result of the new state of things, unless the Christians should dwindle into an insignificant sect, or by the putting of their life and character to the test it would enable them to recover their old place in society.

We will recapitulate what we have to say on Sunday-laws in a few formal statements : —

First, Religion being the highest interest of man, and the Christian religion bringing with it social institutions, it is impossible for civil law to ignore them and pass them by on the other side.

Second, A weekly day of rest and worship is essentially connected with social gatherings of Christians, with an intelligent and efficient ministry, and with the maintenance of religion in the world. So far as the rights of social public worship are concerned, the gatherings, the house, the day necessary for this purpose, must be respected and protected by law. This must and will be done, until society shall come to believe that religion rests on no real truth concerning God and man, and that it is hurtful to society.

Third, For its own sake as well as because it is a guardian of habits and institutions in which a large part of the community share, the state may make laws such that worship be not disturbed ; and, if a day of rest be one of those habits, the State must see to it that rest itself be not made a curse instead of a blessing by the opening on that day of sources of dissipation.

Fourth, The compulsory closing of shops, and forbidding of travel and transport for business purposes on the Lord's Day, goes still further. Such prohibitions are defensible on the ground that a day of rest is an institution full of benevolence, of moral and religious good for clerks, servants, and all persons employed in labor, sale, or transportation. A day of rest, on which the spiritual interests of man can be attended to, is necessary, as we believe, for the morals and uprightness of character of all persons who labor through the week, as well as for their health and social respectability. Society, dreading the evil to its own best interests, and especially to the classes that are burdened by the week's manual labor, gives them an opportunity to recruit themselves on Sunday, both by rest and by change of thoughts and interests.

Fifth, It is not true that Sunday-laws, as we have defended them, contain any residuum of a connection between Church and State. They provide only for the rest from labor of manual workers on one and the same day; but demand nothing in the shape of worship, nor even of rest, so far as it is not public or preventive of the rest of others. If a state where the mass of men believe in the importance of religion, and of a day of rest for religious and other purposes, cannot do as much as has been laid down, its sphere of action must be limited indeed. We should have to go much farther than the abandonment of all Sunday-laws, in a backward legislation founded on such an idea as this.

Sixth, Individuals must be left aside from Sunday legislation, so far as they do not prevent others from receiving the advantages of a day of rest. The old English fines for non-attendance at the parish church, and every thing like them, have disappeared from the world. But history shows that the nations which have been strict without narrowness in the observance of Sunday have had the purest morals, and have clung to their faith in times of religious decay ; so that, if they had faults and follies in their severe codes which tended to bring back a Jewish sabbath, they were yet, on the whole, right in protecting the Lord's Day by legislation.

THE SABBATH AND FREE INSTITUTIONS.

BY REV. PRESIDENT E. G. ROBINSON, D.D.

THE word "sabbath" will be used in this paper in the sense of the Christian Sunday, and without any reference whatever to the question of the relation of the day to the Jewish sabbath.

By free institutions will be meant a free government and all the institutions, civil and religious, which a free government either directly establishes, or simply fosters and protects. And by a free government will be meant a government which is not only dependent on the will of the governed for its existence, but which secures to every one who is subject to it his personal liberty and all his personal rights. Governments are not necessarily free because democratic in their origin, nor because republican in form. Democracies can trample on individual rights: they have often proved most arbitrary and tyrannical. A government, in order to be free, must not only derive its authority from the will of the governed, but that will must be so enlightened, and so controlled by its enlightenment, as to insure the enactment and enforcement of equal and just laws for all. A government of the people, for the people, by the people, will be a free government only and always in exact proportion to the intellectual and moral enlightenment of the people.

Now, in respect to the relation of the Christian sabbath to free institutions as we have defined them, it is first of all to be remembered, that the institutions of our own country clearly had their origin in the Christian Sunday, and the uses that were made of it. There had been

democracies and republics before our own, which had
known no sabbath. But they were republics in which the
sacredness of the rights of the individual was not recognized and protected by fundamental law. It is the glory
of our land and its institutions, that before the law every
man is the equal of every other. And for this we are indebted to the Christian sabbath, — not as a day of mere
rest, but as a day devoted to worship and to religious
instruction. Before the Reformation in England, it was
little that Englishmen knew of personal rights and personal freedom, and still less of a sabbath in which Christian truth was unfolded to them in its fulness. To establish the sabbath as a day of public religious teaching, was
one of the first steps of the first reformers in England.
To accomplish this end, they wrote catechisms; they
preached; they procured Acts of Parliament; they left
no legitimate means untried. With Luther and Calvin,
in their ideas of Sunday, the first English and Scotch
reformers were utterly at variance. They held it to be a
day in which the people should be publicly taught as well
as prompted to worship. Out of the sabbath-teaching
begun by the first English reformers sprung the commonwealth of England; and out of the sabbath which
gave the commonwealth to England sprung the free institutions of America.

What the Christian use of Sunday has originated, it can
help to conserve. Let us glance briefly at two or three
of the ways in which this conservative. influence may be
exerted.

First, As a day of mere bodily rest it is useful. To
observe it even as a day of compulsory cessation from
labor, and from whatever disturbs the public quiet, is both
politically and morally wholesome. To observe it even in
obedience to the State, as a day of public worship, pro-
motes the public tranquillity, and so contributes to the

stability of the government and of all that government protects. The Christian Sunday with any kind of religious observance of it, and even with an observance of only a few of its hours, cannot fail to help in conserving all that is politically and socially dear to us. A worship that should be only ritual, that should address simply·the æsthetic taste, and never a word to the intellect or the heart, would be infinitely better than no worship, and would contribute its proportion to the preservation of all that is sacred and good. To recognize God at all, and especially to reverence him in some kind of worship under the authority and protection of the State, teaches reverence for law, and fosters a love for the order and security and peace which obedience to law alone can secure.

Second, Again, a right and Christian use of Sunday will conserve free institutions by giving to men right ideas of freedom. The most perfectly free institutions, including free governments, which can exist among men, are those in which every individual citizen fulfils all his obligations to every other citizen, and each respects the rights of all. The most perfect freedom that any nation can know is that in which all the laws, formulating the eternal principles of right and wrong, are spontaneously and punctiliously obeyed by all. The highest conceivable freedom will always be coincident with the strictest obedience to law. The freest people will always be the most law-abiding. And where among all the sources of knowledge open to man will you find so simple, so lucid, and so complete a statement of the immutable principles of right and wrong for the individual, and of justice and equity for the state, as in our sacred Scriptures? And where among men have these principles been enunciated with more distinctness, or urged on the attention of men with more cogent reasoning or with more impressive and persuasive eloquence, than in the Protestant pulpits and on the Chris-

tian sabbaths of the past three centuries? And where
among all the nations of the earth have free institutions
been so firmly established, or so beneficent in their influence, as among the peoples where Protestant pulpits on
Christian Sundays have proclaimed and enforced the
duties and the rights of men?

Third, Again, thirdly, the Christian sabbath, rightly
used, conserves free institutions by giving to men a just
appreciation of their rights; and it does this by constantly reminding them of their duties. The rights of man,
in defence of which, real or imaginary, life has been so
freely sacrificed, kingdoms convulsed, and governments
overthrown, can be rationally explained and intelligently
maintained only as the duties of man are clearly understood and accepted. Man has rights only as he has duties.
Every right grounds itself in an inexorable duty. The
theory which grounds rights in personality mistakes by
regarding personality as its own end. The truth is, that
to be a man is to exist after a given type. Personality
exists only as the embodiment of an ideal being; and to
realize that ideal in accordance with the will of God, is the
highest end of man. To realize the typical ideal of manhood, just so far as may lie within his power, is the one
all-inclusive and inexorable duty of every human existence.
To whatever is necessary to the realization of that ideal,
every man has a God-given and inalienable right. The
clearest perception of rights, therefore, and the most in-
domitable will in maintaining them, will ever be his who
perceives most clearly and feels most keenly the duties
from which he cannot escape.

He, accordingly, who points out to men most plainly
their duties, not only gives them the most just appreciation of their own rights, but also a regard for the rights
of others. To listen to the unappeasable demands of duty,
and to perceive clearly our right to whatever we may need

in doing our duty, is to take the first step towards appreciation of the sacredness of the rights of the race. But
to remind man of his duties alike to God, to himself, and
to his fellow-men, and to give him time to reflect on them,
were the chief ends for which the sabbath was instituted,
and for which its observance should be perpetuated. And
to explain and to urge on the consciences of men their
duties, is unquestionably one of the highest uses to which
the day can be devoted.

Fourth, Again, our Christian Sunday helps to keep man
in mind of the complication of his rights with the rights
of other people. The rights of man are manifold and
complex, but the just rights of no one will conflict with
the just rights of another. The supposed rights of one
may conflict with the supposed rights of another. It is
the business of government to decide between them, and
to decide what is just. This prerogative every government entitled to be called a government, whether tyrannical or free, assumes and exercises. And any assumed
right of one, which invades the recognized right of another, is dealt with as a crime. Even personal vices which
are clearly seen to be the results of crimes are treated as
punishable offences against the common rights of all.

Of this complication of the rights of the individual with
the rights of society, it is one of the chief functions of the
Christian sabbath to keep men constantly in mind. It
does this by giving them opportunity to reflect on questions of duty which, without a day of rest and reflection,
might be left unsettled and in confusion ; and, more than
all, it enables them to hear the great principles of religion
and morality so stated and discussed, and so yoked together in harmony, that what seemed obscure and contra-
dictory is made plain and accordant. " The speediest
courser on the road to despotism is a principle ridden
without reins," says a philosophical German in a recent

work on the constitutional and political history of the United States. To save from this abuse of single and isolated principles, is one of the great offices which our Christian sabbath is capable of doing for our American population, and so for the perpetuation of all that is dear to us in our political and religious institutions.

Now, in what we have thus said, it is of course taken for granted that the sabbath shall be properly used. The day will be serviceable in conserving free institutions in proportion as it is intelligently used. An intelligent use will also accord with scriptural example. Whatever our theory of the origin of the Jewish sabbath, or of the relation of the Christian to the Jewish, both Testaments of our Scriptures may justly teach us as to a rational use of the day.

Just how the earliest Jews observed their day, beyond mere cessation from labor, is not altogether apparent. During the times of the prophets, especially the earliest of them, there are reasons for believing that the people resorted to them on that day for instruction. After the Babylonian captivity, and the institution of synagogues, the people, we know, were accustomed to resort to these on the sabbath, to hear their sacred Scriptures read and expounded. At the beginning of the Christian era, the Jews, we know, were accustomed to resort to their synagogues on the sabbath, not only for worship, and to hear the Scriptures read, but to hear the teachings of the Scriptures enforced by any competent expounders who might chance to be present. Out of this Jewish use of the day, sprung undoubtedly the earliest and true Christian use of the Christian's Sunday.

An intelligent and rational use of the day in our time is, we think, just this primitive Christian use, so far modified as the growth in religious knowledge, and the natural development of Christianity and of the Christian life, have clearly made necessary. But the day is not intelligently used when merely devoted to the observances of a ritual which appeals to the æsthetic and emotional parts of our nature, but enforces neither duty nor doctrine. This is to restore the temple, and abolish the synagogue; to dismiss the apostles, and call back the priests. Nor yet is that an intelligent or a scriptural use of the day, which would devote it exclusively to worship, though a worship in which all the people should join; or which should make worship so to preponderate over all other uses, as to limit religious instructions to mere homilies on the commonplaces of religion. If we be told that the worship of God is the one use to which all others should be subordinated, our reply is, that, granting this to be true, the questions arise: Which is the more acceptable to God, the worship offered in blindness and without reflection, or the worship born of discernment and conviction? Who are the people who will worship with most reverence and devotion, if not they whose hearts have been moved through enlightenment of their intellects? Who will feel their obligations, if not they who under intelligent guidance have sought to understand them? And when, if ever, will they seek or be able to understand them, if not on stated days set apart for the study of them, and the study of them under the tuition of men who are able to teach?

Nor does that use of the day seem any more rational which aims only at the production of fervid emotions; which supposes that the highest use of the day is to be reached in the delivery of an emotional sermon; which supposes that the great end of Sunday, of all preaching, and of Christianity itself, is attained when men are converted. Vital as is the doctrine of the new birth, it is not the only great doctrine of Christianity; nor is any man the more likely to be made sensible of his need of a new heart by perpetually harping upon the necessity of it. The symmetry of character into which it is the aim of Christianity to chisel the soul of man is wrought by use of no single truth, nor of any single group of truths, but of every truth that has come to us from above.

But there is a use of the Christian sabbath supported alike by reason and by Scripture. It is that use which not only devotes the day to cessation from toil, to prayer and praise, to the study of the word of God, and to the moral and religious instruction of the young, but also to a public proclamation and enforcement, by competent and well-trained teachers, of all those great truths which constitute at once the foundation and the structure of the Christian religion, and on a sure recognition of which the destiny of nations as well as of individuals must always depend.

The function of the Christian pastor of to-day, though essentially one with that of the early heralds of the gospel, yet differs from it in many a broad particular. At the beginning, Jews and Gentiles alike needed minute and repeated explanations of the very elements of Christian truth. Now Christianity forms a part of the very civilization into which we are born. Its elementary principles are embodied in the first lessons of our childhood. To-day the evangelist, the lay preacher, and the Sunday-school teacher relieve the pulpit of no small amount of its work of elementary teaching; and by so doing they lay upon it the severer task of dealing with subjects more difficult and more complicated, but none the less necessary, than any which the early heralds of the gospel were called on to discuss. The thousand agencies now at work among us for the diffusion of religious knowledge have lifted up the average intelligence of the people to a level where the pulpit, if it is to command attention and to control the public heart and will, must deal in something else than commonplaces. There are higher regions of thought, and higher levels of Christian activity and character, than the Church has yet reached; and up to these levels the pulpit is summoned of God to raise the people.

And so again, in a government like ours, the very foundations of which rest on the assumed sacredness of the rights of the individual, and the stability of which is dependent on an abiding consciousness among the people of individual responsibilities,—a government which, though totally separate from the Church, was yet the direct and natural product of Christian ideas,—it is evident that the pulpit sustains a relation to the national life such as was never sustained in any other nation. The great ethical and theological ideas of which the nation was born, which this generation is so disposed to forget, by recurrence to which the national conscience alone can be quickened and public morals be purified and conserved, need to be enunciated and enforced as never before. And where and by whom can they be so enunciated and enforced as to reach the public conscience, if not in Christian pulpits and on Christian sabbaths by the ministers of our holy religion? And in doing this there need be no preaching of politics, nor of any thing else than the teachings of Christ and his apostles. Nor need there be any departure from the models of apostolic preaching farther than this: that whereas the apostles preached truths which vanquished heathenism, and overthrew arbitrary and despotic governments, we would so preach the same truths as not only to save the souls of men, but to purify and perpetuate all that the good God has intrusted to us of civil and religious liberty.

To accomplish all this, it will not be denied that the pulpit will need to be relieved of some of the labor which long-established custom has imposed on it. It is idle to expect from it two sermons a Sunday such as the men of this generation will listen to. No man of average intellect and attainments, in this age of universal religious knowledge among church-goers, can preach for a long series of years two sermons a Sunday which are worth listening to. Nor is it the function of the pulpit alone to press home on men the need of personal regeneration as a condition to personal salvation. This is one of the first truths of Christianity, and is proclaimed in the family, in the Sunday school, by lay teaching and preaching everywhere. The higher function of the pulpit now is, to train up a sacramental host who shall everywhere, by the fireside and by the wayside, in the schoolroom, in the counting-house, and the market-place, reiterate the elementary truths of the gospel to all who will hear. Let the pulpit teach and build up all Christian people in Christian knowledge and enduring character, and they will daily and hourly, both by example and word, press home as the pulpit never can, on the unthinking world, its need of a practical acquaintance with the gospel of Christ. Let the pulpit be so used on the sabbath, and all lay teaching and preaching now employed be continued, and there will go forth from the sabbath a train of influences which, reaching the heart and conscience of the nation, will conserve to us and transmit to posterity of our free institutions all that is sacred and worth preserving.

The Christian Church to-day provides for the education of her clergy as never before. Whether their ministrations are correspondingly superior to those of all their predecessors, it is not the province of this paper to inquire. But the opportunities of the clergy at this day and in this country have been exceeded by those of no century in our era. That they are summoned to works of patience and faith by voices from the past, the present, and the future, such as no clergy ever before heard, no one who has diligently considered the past, the present, and the future, can fail to perceive.

Passing now from the service which the sabbath is capable of rendering to the State, let us ask : What is the relation of the State to the sabbath? What should be its attitude towards it? What does the state owe it, and what can a free government render it, in the way of legislative protection and authorization? Let us see what the state can and ought to do for the Christian sabbath.

It is self-evident that the only permanent foundation of a republic like ours is to be found in the intelligence and virtue of its citizens. So universally is this recognized, that the right of a republican government to tax its citizens for the support of free schools, and thus to protect itself against the dangers arising from ignorance, is accepted by all, except a few political fanatics, as an unquestioned principle. Self-defence is a first law of life, whether of the individual or of the nation. A true republic, which is only the national life embodied, has a right to protect itself by compelling its citizens to educate their children, by whose want of intelligence the life of the republic would be imperilled.

But mere intelligence insures permanence to no form of government, free or despotic. No republic has yet perished, in which intelligence was not more general and higher at its overthrow than at its founding. The truth is, that knowledge without virtue, intelligence without conscience, warrants neither appreciation nor respect for the useful, the just, or the sacred. To discipline the intellects of men as a protection to the state, while we neglect their hearts, is like building dams upon quicksands.

If free governments can be justified in protecting themselves against the contingent dangers of ignorance, still more in protecting themselves against the undeveloped force of passion and vice, — a danger against which the free school has presented as yet no sufficient barrier, and against which neither our state governments nor our national government have made any direct provision. It is idle to say that the free school *should* train the heart as well as the intellect, that it *ought* to forestall vice as well as supplant ignorance. The truth is, the great body of teachers in the common school suppose, and will continue to suppose, their tasks completed when they have seen to it that their scholars know their lessons. If they venture on the *rôle* of teachers of morals, it is to perform a task which the letter of their contracts does not exact, or which, if exacted, would probably be irksome and so be only perfunctorily performed. The State can never provide itself with moral defences against revolution and anarchy by any amount of provisions for free schools. Perhaps it never can provide them directly by any kind of statutory provision. Forbidden by organic law to establish any form of religion, or to enjoin any species of religious instruction, the only morality the State with us can foster will be the morality of prudence and of calculated chances. But a morality without God, without a supremely perfect Being who is at once its source and its standard, is a morality that will change with the changing opinions of men.

But the State can indirectly protect itself morally by statute, and by statute which its fundamental laws will sustain. It can enact that one day in seven shall be devoted to moral and religious uses, and shall not be secularized. And, by so enacting, it does not trench on the personal liberty of the citizen any more than when it enacts (as it is conceded to have the right to do) that every citizen shall give to his child some degree and kind of education, and that he shall give it on certain days and hours of the week. It simply enacts that one day in seven shall be reserved for moral and religious instruction, but leaves every citizen to determine for himself with absolute freedom in what manner and by whom that instruction shall be given. And whoever may scrupulously object to the day which the State, in compliance with the wishes of an overwhelming majority, may appoint, shall be protected in his observance of any other day which he may select. But the State cannot, consistently with its educational laws, tolerate any man, or any body of men, in refusing to provide moral and religious instruction for themselves and their children, or in contumaciously abusing a day which the State may set apart for such instruction.[1] No reason can be alleged against the right of the State to set apart such a day, and to shield it by statute from abuse, which cannot be pressed with greater force against the right of the State to demand that some years of every childhood shall be given to mental training, and that all real estate by whomsoever owned, citizen or foreigner, shall be taxed for the cost of it. If the State may justly protect itself against the danger of ignorance, still more may it, and ought it, to protect itself against the incomparably greater dangers of irreligion and immorality.

The truth is, this is a Christian nation, whether the Constitution may in so many words avow it or not. The very corner-stone of the national fabric rests on faith in

[1] John Stuart Mill in his volume "On Liberty," chap. iv., characterizes "sabbatarian legislation" as "an example of illegitimate interference with the rightful liberty of the individual;" and with strange intellectual perversity affirms that "the only ground on which restrictions on Sunday amusements can be defended must be that they are religiously wrong." And yet, in chap. v. of the same treatise, where he deals with "applications" of his principles, we have a vigorous defence of "compulsory education." He regards it as "almost a self-evident axiom, that the state should require and compel the education, up to a certain standard, of every human being who is born its citizen." He declares that "the objections which are urged with reason against state education do not apply to the enforcement of education by the state, but to the state's taking upon itself to direct that education; which is a totally different thing." Precisely so is it in respect to what Mill stigmatizes as "sabbatarian legislation." The state ought not to give, in this country the state is prohibited from giving and from requiring to be given, any distinctive form or species of religious instruction; but, if it can and ought to enforce education of the intellect, it certainly can and ought at least by legislation to recognize and protect by law from abuse a day which may be set apart for the education of the moral affections.

the Christian's God. All our indigenous institutions, civil and religious, more or less distinctly recognize this faith. The Christian sabbath has been from the beginning an integral part of all that has been distinctively national in our history. To that sabbath let us cling both by statute and by reverent observance of it as one of the sure safeguards of all our liberties. If foreigners come to us without a sabbath, and with unwillingness to observe ours, let us say to them, "If you like our national life well enough to desire to become a part of it, we insist that you must accept all the institutions embodying that life, our sabbath included."

In conclusion, let history and observation teach us. Historically we know that by no people on the globe, and at no period, was the sabbath ever more strictly, or, on the whole, criticise as we may, more rationally, kept than by the people of New England a half-century ago. And among no people were the blessings of a free government, and of all the institutions which free governments insure, ever so conspicuous. Nowhere were crimes ever less common; nowhere were property and life ever safer. The culture of the people was by no means high; their tastes were not refined; their manners were rude: but they were honest; they were lovers of justice, and always law-abiding. Their government was not perfect; themselves were not faultless: and yet we are justified in affirming that nowhere else on this earth was there ever presented a nearer approach to ideal free government,—a government free in the origin of its powers and administration, and securing personal freedom and equal rights to all the governed,—than in the New-England township as it existed before the influx of foreigners and of foreign ideas and practices. But for all this New England was indebted, more than to all else, to her unyielding regard for the sabbath, and to the sound teaching which her respect for the sabbath led her to listen to from her pulpits. To her sabbath and her use of it, above all else, has New England been indebted for all that has justly distinguished her in the annals of our common country.

What history thus teaches positively, observation teaches negatively. Where there is no sabbath, and no sabbath ministrations from the pulpit, free institutions are either impossible, or can maintain at best but a feeble and precarious existence. To a perception of this truth the living statesmen of France are awaking as their predecessors never awoke. In our own land, wherever the sabbath is misused, our institutions are recognized as in peril. That there is in all parts of our country an increasing decay in the popular regard for the sabbath, and a growing indifference to the sabbath instructions of the pulpit, will not be denied. Neither will it be denied that there is a corresponding decay, even here in New England, of that old jealousy for the honor and dignity and purity and stability of our distinctive institutions, which was once characteristic of its humblest citizens. There was a time here in Massachusetts when political knaves, whatever their ability, would not have had the audacity to attempt what they now venture on boldly and without a blush.

THE LAW OF REST FOR ALL NECESSARY TO THE LIBERTY OF REST FOR EACH.

BY LEONARD WOOLSEY BACON, D.D., OF NORWICH, CONN.

MR. CHAIRMAN AND FELLOW-CITIZENS, — I purpose scrupulously to refrain from overstepping the narrow limits of the thesis on which I have been asked to speak, in any such way as to encroach on ground occupied by others. But there is one point essential to a right understanding of this and of many other parts of the subject before us, which, through the regretted absence of Judge Strong, has failed to be formally set before the Convention,[1] and which, therefore, I may be permitted to illustrate by an incident that occurred in the first International Sabbath Congress, held three years ago at Geneva.

After many hours of conference and discussion, the Congress had been brought to the point of adopting the platform of a permanent international sabbath league ; and of this platform a conspicuous article was the one embodying a " scriptural basis " (as it was called) consisting of the Fourth Commandment and the declaration of our Saviour, " The sabbath was made for man." The question being on the adoption of this article, a fair-haired, near-sighted, and broad-shouldered gentleman, who had been thus far an earnest and useful member of the convention, arose, and very modestly and courteously asked (in the German language) that no basis of organization should be insisted on which would exclude him and those whom he represented from co-operation in a work so beneficent as

---

[1] Judge Strong of the Supreme Court of the United States had been expected to read a paper on " The Civil and the Religious Sabbath."

the maintenance of a weekly day of rest. He himself was a rationalist pastor from Bremen : he was the representative of an "Arbeiterverein," or some sort of working-men's organization of a socialist complexion ; and neither he nor the Bremen working-men had any kind of faith in the "scriptural basis," in Old Testament or New, which was proposed as a condition of co-operation. Only they felt that a weekly day of rest, guarded and guarantied by law, would be an immense blessing to the working-man and to the whole public ; and they asked the privilege of doing what they could, in their own way, and acting from their own point of view, in co-operation with those who differed from them in opinion, to promote the end which they all sought in common.

With many expressions of personal respect, the Congress nevertheless voted by an overwhelming majority to allow their unorthodox brother no part nor lot with them in their efforts to promote a social and legislative reform. But I have the satisfaction of assuring you that this action was not taken without an energetic remonstrance from the representative of the United States, who objected to hearing America cited as an example of enforcing religious duties by secular laws, and declared that our American Sunday legislation, which they so admired, was founded, not on the principle of enforcing a religious duty by civil law, but on the democratic principles of liberty, equality, and fraternity, — principles which we believe that we understand quite as well in America as they do in Geneva or Paris. A religious basis, he declared, was considered in America to be essential to co-operation in religious movements ; but that we did not always find it necessary to quote Scripture in a political manifesto, though this was sometimes done. It was important, he said, that those who undertook to deal with the sabbath-question should remember that the sabbath-question is not one question,

but two questions; that the religious sabbath, consecrated
to worship and to divine commemoration, and the civil
holiday, maintained by force of law, have this in common,
that, in many countries, they coincide upon the same day,
but they are not the same : the former cannot be enforced
by secular legislation, and the last cannot, in this age, be
sustained merely by Bible-texts.

It was not much of a speech, but it made something of
an impression ; and the speaker was entirely contented
with the result of it when, in the great closing assembly,
the most eloquent *conférencier* in the French language,
Ernest Naville, took this distinction for his text, and in a
discourse of more than an hour's duration commended the
religious sabbath to the observance of every good Christian, and the civil sabbath to the support of every right-
minded citizen, Christian or not. I wish this exquisitely
lucid address might be added, in English, to our scanty
stock of good popular literature relating to the subject.
It might help to supersede some of the superstitious and
fanatical literature now or lately current, from the effects
of which the sabbath cause is suffering.

Let me ask you, in order to avoid the misunderstanding
which will otherwise be inevitable, to keep this distinction
in mind, and remember, that, throughout this paper, I am
speaking primarily not of the religious, but of the civil,
institution.

I shall presume, then, on your good sense and clear
apprehension in this matter, taking for granted that you
are wiser than the narrowness of the International Congress, and that on the enforcement of the external quiet
and repose of the civil Sunday (which I understand to be
the aspect of the question on which I am invited to speak)
you are willing to entertain a line of argument broad and
liberal enough to demand the adhesion and support of
every reasonable man, whatever his views concerning the
religious sanctions of the day.

The question is one of — what shall I say? work-ing-men's rights, I was about to say, except that this expression has become so smutted in the dirty hands of demagogues, that one loathes to take it up after them, — the question is one of personal liberty ; how to secure for every citizen the liberty to rest one day in seven.

There is a very free and easy answer to this question on the tongue's end of some wise people, who deliver it as an axiom that the short and ready way to universal liberty of resting is simply to keep hands off, not to meddle with the matter by legislation, and let everybody do as he pleases about it. What can be simpler?

The temptation is irresistible, to answer these people according to their folly, and condemn them out of their own mouths. For it happens, curiously enough, that many of the very people who are clamoring against our *six-day law*, as an unwarrantable interference with indi-vidual liberty, are just as clamorous in favor of an *eight-hour law* of their own invention. "What do you want," let me ask, "of an eight-hour law? Why not leave the matter to every man to decide for himself, whether he shall work eight hours, or ten, or fifteen? Don't let us have any meddlesome legislation. 'The best government is that which governs least.' Surely, if your reasoning is good concerning days in the week, it is equally good con-cerning hours in the day!"

This argument has been curiously and admirably antici-pated in the speech of Macaulay in defence of the princi-ple of a ten-hour law, in the House of Commons, in 1846. The right and expediency of guarding the liberty to rest, by legally limiting the time of labor, was vindicated against this very objection by the analogy of the Sunday-laws. Objectors said, "If this ten-hour limitation be good for the working-people, rely on it that they will themselves estab-lish it without any law." — "Why not reason," answered

Macaulay, — "why not reason in the same way about the Sunday ? Why not say, 'If it be a good thing for the people of London to shut their shops one day in seven, they will find it out, and will shut their shops without a law'? Sir, the answer is obvious. I have no doubt, that, if you were to poll the shopkeepers of London, you would find an immense majority, probably a hundred to one, in favor of closing shops on the Sunday ; and yet it is absolutely necessary to give to the wish of the majority the sanction of a law; for, if there were no such law, the minority, by opening their shops, would soon force the majority to do the same."[1]

How curiously the wheel of this discussion has come around, so that now there is a party of people soberly alleging what that famous orator enunciated as an absurdity, and claiming as an axiom what he proved from the premises which they are trying to knock away !

This whole subject gets its liveliest illustration when, from time to time, some one of those vocations which the general convenience allows to be excepted from the general law of Sunday rest seeks to be included within the law. Repeatedly, for instance, there have been memorials from all the barbers of a town, asking to have their own shops shut by law. Very absurd, isn't it ? If they want their shops shut, why don't they shut them ? This was the view taken by one enterprising young colored man in a Connecticut town, not long ago. There was a movement, among his competitors in the profession, to have all the barbers' shops shut on Sunday. "All right !" he said, "you go right on, and shut your shops. Never mind me." And so all the shops had to be kept open.

Another illustration of a like character comes to me from a similar quarter. A coal-dealer, near a certain

---

[1] Speeches of Macaulay, ed. Tauchnitz, ii., 208, 209. The whole speech is worth reading for its close relation to our subject.

steamboat-landing, finds that in the competitions of business his Sunday rest has been completely taken away from him. All the little tugs and propellers find that they can get their coal put in on Sunday, and so they come Sunday in preference to any other day. Says he, "I don't so much as get time to go to early mass, and I am compelled to keep busy from morning till night. I can't refuse them; for if I do they will quit me altogether, and I shall lose my business. *I wish to heaven that some one would prosecute me!*" A clearer illustration of the value of the law of rest for all, in securing the liberty of rest for each one, can hardly be asked for, than this case of a man who wants to be prosecuted himself in order to protect him from the necessity of doing what he does not want to do, but has to do because he is at liberty to do it.

I put it to the whole trade of labor-reformers, who want to begin their reforms by breaking down the best existing safeguard of the working-man's liberty of rest and leisure. I put the question to them, and beg for an answer if there is one to be given. After you have succeeded — I do not say in amending or repealing, but in defying and nullifying, our *six-day law*, how much good is your eight-hour law likely to do you, supposing that you get it passed? You succeed, by mere defiant law-breaking, in trampling down a statute venerable with use, anchored deep in the traditions of the people, and consecrated by many a solemn religious sanction. And you propose to set up in place of it a novel invention of your own called an " eight-hour law." Do you suppose that, when you have taught the public how little you care for law when it interferes with your convenience, you will find it an easy matter to enforce law against others when it interferes with theirs?

But here I wish, with perfect candor, to answer a question which does not seem to me to be adequately answered by the average " Evangelical Christian " in his arguments on this subject. Our German friend will ask whether it is not possible to make a distinction between the prohibition of labor, and the prohibition of recreation and orderly and innocent amusement. And *my* answer to him is (whatever yours may be), "Yes, it is possible, though it may be difficult ; and, whenever as orderly citizens you choose to move in this direction for amendments of the law, we are ready to discuss your proposals with simple reference to the greatest good of the greatest number." It is useless for us to say that public amusements, however quiet and orderly, involve labor on some one's part. So does public worship. It is labor to blow a church-organ, as much as to blow a concert-hall organ. No legislation pretends to protect every one's Sunday rest. The general principle is modified by considerations of public convenience and expediency. There is nothing in the world, then, to hinder us from entering into the candid discussion of any proposed amendment intended to relax the rigor of the law concerning amusements while still guarding, as far as possible, the provisions of the law concerning labor. Some of you will object, perhaps, that in our duties as citizens we are bound to be governed by the divine teachings, and that legislation ought to be conformed to the word of God. Agreed. But then, nothing is so clearly revealed in the word of God, whether in Old Testament or in New, if men would but see it, as this, — that the divine rule of public legislation is the rule of expediency, and not the rule of absolute right and wrong. The divine example of public legislation is to give "laws that are not good," when such laws are, on the whole, the best that the case admits. Legislation is never more contrary to the word of God, than when it is rigorously conformed to the word of God without regard to expediency, local and temporary. I repeat it, then : there is nothing in our convictions of religious duty to hinder us

from candidly discussing any measure that may be consid
ered to be for the good of society, and looking towards a
relaxation of the Sunday law respecting amusements, while
maintaining it in vigor respecting labor. Possibly this
might be accomplished by carefully amending the law.
But one thing is perfectly sure : *it can't be done by breaking the law.* You cannot break this statute half across,
and leave the other half sound. Some of these fine days,
as business grows brisk, you will get back from your
Sunday excursion or beer-garden, and find a notice that
next Sunday, owing to pressure of business, the factory
will run, or the shop will be open, and that you are wanted
for a day's work. And if you think that then you will be
able to plead, for your rest and your liberty, the very statute that you have defiantly broken for your amusement,
you will have ample time and opportunity to find out your
mistake.

Here, after all, we face this subject in its gravest aspect.
For I say it with all respect to this assembly, yet not
expecting you to agree with me, — expecting rather that
some of you will be shocked when you hear it said, — that
the sanctity of the sabbath is not so serious a matter as
the sanctity of human law and government ; that the damage and peril to society, the church, the state, and the
affront to the authority of God, in the habitual public
defiance of the Sunday-laws, consist less in the violation
of the commandment than they do in the violation of the
statute. The divine authority less distinctly binds us to
the commandment than it binds us to the statute. There
are, amongst us, citizens of many different religions, and
citizens of no religion at all ; and, even among Christian
citizens, there are the widest conscientious variations as
to the binding force of the Fourth Commandment on the
individual and the state ; and still further variations as to
the nature of the duties which that commandment enjoins,

if it is binding. You may lament these variations; you
may hold them blameworthy; but you cannot deny the
fact that they exist; and it will have a very wholesome
effect on our dealings with the matter, to look this inexorable fact distinctly in the face, and to bear habitually in
mind, that the traditionary notions of sabbatical duty to
which we are accustomed are the notions only of a very
small party in the Christian Church. But here is a point
on which the divine will is unmistakable, — a point on
which there is no room for variation among Christians, or
among good citizens, to wit : that the laws of man are to
be obeyed as under God's authority, and for God's sake.
The peril of the present time is not half so much that we
are becoming a nation of sabbath-breakers, as that we are
becoming — as a well-known writer has recently said —
"a nation of law-breakers." The question whether the
Sunday-laws shall be amended, or even repealed, and the
common rest-day of rich and poor be left unprotected
from the rapacity of commercial and industrial competition, is a question which, grave and portentous as it is, it
is nevertheless possible to contemplate with equanimity.
Whenever this question comes up, we are bound to meet
our fellow-citizens with patient argument, and abide the
arbitrament of the ballot-box. Under our form of government, if the majority, on such a point, will be fools,
there is no way but to let them learn their folly by the
consequences. But to this other question, whether law,
while it is law, shall be enforced and obeyed, there is but
one answer compatible with the dignity or life of the
state.

The argument which I have now set forth approves the
Sunday-laws of any state only so far as those laws confine
themselves, with simplicity and good faith, first, to maintaining the day of rest from labor as a universal privilege,

and, secondly, to taking the necessary precautions lest the
privilege be abused to the detriment of public order and
morals. For any thing beyond this, these laws must find
their defence — if there is any rational defence to be found
— in some other line of reasoning. But there can be no
higher act of wisdom on the part of those who desire to
see the universal repose and quiet order of the New-England sabbath-day revived and perpetuated, than, of their
own accord, to see to it that our Sunday-laws are cleared
of every thing which they ought not to contain. The
early legislation of New England on this subject was
undoubtedly directed, in some particulars, to the enforcement of a *religious* observance of the day. This was
consistent with the State-Church, or rather the Church-
State, notions of that time: it is utterly irreconcilable with
our own principles. I do not know that any vestige of it
remains. Judging from the digest of the Sunday laws
of New England, lately published by my friend Walter
Learned,[1] our statute-books are clear of any remainder of
it. If not, they ought to be.

Further, we are suffering, both in the community and in
private consciences, the re-action from overstrained statements concerning sabbatical duty. There is a canon of
Sunday observance, written, not in the Scriptures of
either Testament, but in the Westminster Catechism and
the traditions of the elders, commanding that "the entire time" that can be spared from works of necessity or
mercy shall be "spent in acts of worship, public or private." I do not speak of this as a rule that is seriously
professed by any of us. On the contrary, we have, one
and all, abandoned it as a rule of our own action, and we
keep it, if at all, only for torturing tender consciences, and
for judging our neighbors by. But it would not be altogether strange if the spirit of it might be found lurking

[1] In Good Company, No. II.

here and there in some neglected corner of the statute-
book.   If so, it is of high importance to the success of
our cause, that it be exorcised.

Further still, it is not an unheard-of thing for earnest
and zealous labors in behalf of a good cause to become
infected with that other spirit, which has been alleged to
have Boston for its metropolis, but which has its spheres
of lively activity in many a place beside, — the spirit of
"malignant philanthropy."   It is this spirit that is slan-
derously imputed to the English Puritans, who interfered
with bear-baiting, it is said, less out of pity to the bear
than out of spite at the enjoyment of the bystanders.
How naturally it attaches itself to such matters as we have
in hand, might be illustrated by many instances ; but it is
enough to take a single one from Mr. Gilbert Hamerton.
He tells us of a certain neighborhood in Scotland, along
the shore of a loch which it was sometimes necessary to
cross on Sunday.   The local code of ethics permitted the
crossing in such cases, but on condition that it should be
made with a row-boat, not with a sail-boat.   The row-boat
involved, indeed, more labor ; but the sail-boat might involve *enjoyment*, and this was a thing to be prevented at
any sacrifice !   If our Sunday-laws are to be preserved and
enforced, it must be made unmistakably plain that the
object both of the law and of its enforcement is *not* to prevent enjoyment, but to secure the universal privilege of
rest from labor without detriment to the good order and
morals of society.   No reasonable person will deny that it
is competent for the same law which interferes to liberate
men from labor, to interfere to protect society from the
disorderly abuse of this liberty.   The question of the
manner and degree of either interference is an open question to be decided by considerations of expediency.

We cannot, fellow-citizens, keep it too distinctly in mind
that this part of the sabbath-question, the matter of Sun-

day-laws, is a matter of government and police, — a political matter; and I know of no way of carrying political measures, in a republic, but to have votes enough. There is, indeed, a certain class of reformatory politicians who have a mystical idea of carrying elections without votes, — to whom there is no scripture in all the Bible so precious as that of the thinning-out of Gideon's army. These are men of faith, who believe that a few warm-hearted, earnest citizens, that will march fearlessly and vigorously up to the polls, and jam their tickets into the ballot-box with sufficient energy, can easily outvote ten times their number. It is well for us to leave this sort of imbecility to the school of professional reformers to whom it belongs, and coolly to take the measure of the difficulties of the situation, — for it has difficulties. The measures that are to be carried and enforced, let us remember, will not be carried by the votes exclusively of Evangelical Christians of orthodox doctrinal views, — that is, not without a very extraordinary revival in the mean time. It is well that we should ask ourselves whose the other votes are to be. It is well, for every reason, that we should put ourselves on ground so solid, so broad, so unselfish and unpartisan, so clearly right, that no reasonable man can object to it as unreasonable; that we should refuse to allow this great social interest to be complicated with other questions; in short, that we should *narrow the issue,* and *widen the basis of co-operation.*

THE SABBATH AND OUR FOREIGN POPULATION.

BY REV. REUEN THOMAS OF BROOKLINE.

ONE of the most perplexing and discouraging elements in this sabbath-rest theme is the existence among us of a very large and constantly increasing foreign population, — a population that has grown up in countries whence the sabbath has almost entirely departed. In this term "foreign population," it is not necessary to include Englishmen or Scotchmen, or North-of-Ireland Irishmen. I fear, however, that all other Irishmen will be found acting and voting with the foreign population proper on this question of sabbath rest; for the political and ecclesiastical sympathies of the South and West of Ireland have always been with the type of religion found in the South and West of Europe. New England, Old England, Scotland, Wales, and the Protestant cantons of Switzerland, together with Norway and Sweden, are substantially at one in their sabbath ideas. We may add, also, the colonial dependencies of Old England, — consisting of the Protestant parts of Canada, New Zealand, and Australia. Outside the territory represented by these names, the views held of the sabbath institution are either very indefinite, or very definitely hostile to what we consider to be the Biblical views. Every one knows that a Parisian Sunday is a day of gayety for the rich, a day of toil for the poor; and that which is true of Paris is substantially true of the whole of France. Now, as we have not here in the United States a numerically large French population, it may not seem to be of very great moment to us to take special note of what Sunday is in France. That, however, is a very

narrow view of the case. What American, travelling in
Europe, does not go to Paris? Is it possible for our
young men and women to visit that gay and brilliant city,
or to stay there for a season for educational purposes,
without receiving impressions altogether alien from those
sabbath ideas which belong to the strictly Protestant nations of Christendom? We know that young men and
women are naturally averse to that wholesome restraint
which not only in religion, but in every thing, is essential to
culture. Would it not be pleasanter for us to have something like that which is found on the Continent of Europe,
— to deck ourselves in all the gay livery of a Parisian
pleasure-seeker, rather than to wear the hodden gray of a
New-England Puritan? And not the young people alone,
but their fathers and mothers, are in danger of allowing
themselves to be persuaded that there is something reasonable in this, — that a more diversified Sunday is essential, specially for the young people. Now, it is no secret
that there is no country in the world where children have
so much influence over their parents as in this. I presume on the principle of development it is assumed that
the young of the rising generation must necessarily be
wiser and better than the old of the generation that is
passing away. Anyway, the fact remains, that that which
the children strongly desire, their parents are strongly
inclined to grant; and "how to train up a parent in the
way he should go," is the assiduous care of the younger
members of too many of our households. The effect on
the minds of many of our young people, of going to Europe,
is not seldom to create the impression that our methods of
spending sabbath-time are not founded on convictions, but
on mere prejudices arising from the older days when our
New-England people were removed far off from the rest of
the civilized world. Is it not that the growing want of
reverence for the sabbath as a divine institute is, among

the moneyed classes of society, no little attributable to impressions received in that gay and gilded Paris, and in other less ornate but not less irreligious European cities? But surely, to religious Americans, Paris ought to be a warning, not an example. In the memoir of the Rev. Robert McCheyne we meet with this passage: "Alas! poor Paris knows no sabbath : all the shops are open, and all the inhabitants are on the wing in search of pleasures, —pleasures that perish in the using. I thought of Babylon and Sodom as I passed through the crowd. I cannot tell how I longed for the peace of the Scottish sabbath. There is a place in Paris called the *Champs Elysées*, or plains of heaven, a beautiful place, with trees and gardens. We have to cross it in passing to the Protestant Church. It is the chief scene of their sabbath desecration, and an awful scene it is. Oh! thought I, if *this* is the heaven a Parisian loves, he will never enjoy the pure heaven that is above." If we cross into Belgium, we find that the Sunday wears pretty much the same aspect as in France. I have seen the workmen working there till four o'clock in the afternoon, and working at any thing and every thing. The evening is more of a holiday for them than most other days ; but, generally speaking, the women and children go to church, while the men toil on Sunday as on Monday. In the country-districts, the women are in the fields with the men, — toiling at hard labor every day of every week, snatching an hour at early morn or at noon for an attendance at church.

In Switzerland, and specially in the Protestant cantons, we have the most pleasing illustrations of sabbath consecration of time to be found anywhere in Europe. There is no city where a New-Englander might spend a Sunday with less to trouble his spirit than in Geneva. Calvin's influence remains there still.

M. Alexander Lombard, a retired banker of Geneva, is

the president of an international sabbath-observance society which is doing excellent service in Europe towards
calling back the minds of men to the loss they have sustained in desecrating the sabbath idea. Quite recently a
congress has been held, attended by delegates from all
parts of Europe. In a previous congress, in 1876, at
which four hundred and forty brethren, delegates from
all European countries, were present, the following simple but all-sufficient resolution was adopted : "The principle of an international confederation for the revival in
Europe of reverence for and observance of the Lord's
Day upon the basis of Holy Scripture, as printed on the
papers of the congress, is accepted." The texts of Scripture quoted, and on which the confederation was based,
are these three, — giving a broad, simple, yet adequate
base on which to build up right conduct on this question : —

"God blessed the seventh day, and sanctified it," that
defining the *weekly* recurrence of the sabbath.

"Remember that thou keep *holy* the sabbath day,"
that defining the spirit in which the day should be celebrated.

"The sabbath was made for *man*," that defining the
area over which the blessing extended : wherever there
is *a man*, there is a sabbath necessity.

May that confederation increase in influence until
Europe shall once again enjoy her sabbaths !

But what of Germany in regard to this question ?
Probably her population, thronging the cities of the ex-
pansive and fertile West, will exercise here an influence
for good or evil in many things, the magnitude of which is
hardly yet perceived even by the men of keenest vision.
The vote of our German population will, I fear, be ad-
verse to any thing like a perpetuation of the old New-
England ideas of the sabbath. We have only to visit

Cincinnati, Milwaukee, Chicago, and other cities, to see in what direction things are moving. On Sunday, Cincinnati is little else than a huge beer-garden rapidly on its way to become a huge bear-garden.

I was in Chicago in July, occupying the pulpit of the Second Presbyterian Church for three Sundays. The First Presbyterian Church is within a few hundred yards. Other influential churches are in that immediate neighborhood. But the whole of them together are not strong enough to prevent the opening of a huge beer-hall and garden close to their very doors. This, be it remarked, in what is considered the most respectable part of the city, where some of the wealthiest Chicago merchants live. This beer hall and garden is open every day of the week, but it seems to be particularly open on Sundays. On the Sunday in July to which I refer, it seemed to have a patronage far in excess of the most popular churches. And "if these things be done in the green tree, what shall be done in the dry?" If they be done in the very teeth of the most influential religious men of a city, — what will they do in those populous parts where the poorer men and women congregate, and from whence too often churches emigrate?

Germany is great in many things, — great in military power, great in the ability of plodding perseverance, great in theories for the regeneration and re-organization of society on bases of such a general involvement that the idle man shall be as well-to-do as the industrious man; and the fool shall be no worse off than the wise man; and the man of no character shall not be allowed to be oppressed by the man of reputation. She is great in philosophies and in criticisms, the most critical nation on earth, nothing if not critical. The most *divided* nation on the Continent of Europe, she has always been great at theories of unity; the most oppressed by military despotisms, she

has always been fruitful of theories of freedom for mankind. But though Germany has been, in her northern
parts at any rate, strongly Protestant, yet her Protestantism has never had full liberty to be thoroughly Biblical.
She has produced one Luther — but never two. The effort seems to have cost her almost all her religious vitality.
Now, there are many people who think that Germany is
a universal teacher, — that in every thing she is mentally
first. There is some truth in this, but much untruth.
She has produced many great philosophers, some great
poets, and a host of great critics. In the matter of the
criticism of the letter of Scripture, and criticism of every
thing else, she stands without a peer. Destructiveness
rather than constructiveness, analysis rather than syn-
thesis, seems to be the predominant tendency of the German scholastic mind. I doubt whether it can be fairly
averred that Germany has produced many really great
theologians, such as can compare with those belonging to
England, Scotland, and the United States. The sermons
which have been published in Germany, and in England
as coming from Germany, are remarkably poor. They are
altogether destitute of that living, throbbing vitality which
belongs to the sermons of the three countries already
named. More than any other country Germany seems to
me an illustration of the warning given in St. Paul's words,
"The letter *killeth.*" But what has Germany to teach
New England in either politics or theology? Really nothing. Since Luther's time she seems to have been singu-
larly destitute of what in Scripture is called "vision," —
vision as distinct from that intelligence which comes of
mental culture. "Where there is no *vision,* the people
perish." In the religious realm of things, Germany is
much more of a warning than an example. In an article
which appeared in the "London Times" newspaper of
Jan. 4, 1877, Dr. Peterman, a very eminent German, says,

" In England, Sunday is kept as a day for God and man, and above all for the workman. Oh that our poor misguided socialists would come to a place like London, in order to see how honestly, industriously, punctually, vigorously, and orderly, work is carried on there throughout the week ! then on Sunday comes the rest."

Now, I might quote from the experiences which all travellers have had of German, French, and Italian Sundays, as testimony to this one all-inclusive fact : that practically the sabbath has gone from those countries, and that their people grow up without any idea or thought of the necessity to godliness of the separation and elevation of every seventh day. There is really very little to choose between Germany, France, and Italy, in regard to the matter of sabbath observance. When emigrants from these countries come hither, they necessarily bring their anti-sabbatism with them. They swell that great army whose influence is in direct negation of all that belongs to the religious institutions of New England. It is a serious thing for the Christian institutions of this country, that they have to meet and conquer, or be conquered by, these men and women nurtured in ideas and under examples so foreign to the ideas and examples of the old citizenship of America. It they are allowed quietly to introduce and get established their anti-sabbath customs, on the simple ground of being foreigners, it will not be long before every theatre in America will reap its largest harvests on Sunday nights. We are moving in that direction so rapidly as to be almost within the circle of probability that, ere many winters have passed, not even Boston will be able to hold her own against the foreigner. For myself, foreigner though I be, so far as place of birth and past life is concerned, yet I feel humiliated, not to say indignant, when I see with what ease the descendants of those old sturdy men who, as Macaulay says, were among the most remarkable that England ever produced, will let go those pure ideas and purity-generating institutions on which their ancestors set so high a value that they deemed any sacrifice for their defence small. I can easily forgive a Frenchman, an Italian, a German, if, when he becomes an American citizen, he is found on the inhuman and undivine side of religious questions. When, in many Continental cities, for every forty persons who go to church on Sundays there are a thousand who go to the Sunday-theatre, what can you expect? A very large proportion of the people who come here from the Continent of Europe have had no religious training. German rationalism and French Voltairism have done their work. But New England has not been desolated by the one, nor devastated by the other. If the sons and daughters of New England are no better specimens of religious men and women than are those whose religious birthright has been sold for some paltry mess of rationalistic pottage, — then, I say, shame upon them! Allowing that in the generations past there was too much of rigidity and severity in the working-out of the sabbath-idea, yet I ask you to take ten thousand specimens of the men and women of New England, who were nurtured under that severity and rigidity, and ten thousand specimens of Frenchmen or Germans, to whom Sunday has been any thing but a sabbath, and judge by the results on manhood and womanhood as to which extreme (if we are obliged to adopt either) is most harmful. Even the *physical* results are noteworthy. Dr. Guthrie, writing of England and Scotland, says, "It is certain that the foreigner is a much less efficient workman than our laborers : as an English company lately found, who were engaged in constructing a railway in France, and found it cheaper to carry English navvies across the Channel, and pay them five shillings a day, than to employ Frenchmen at half the wages." But the *mental* and *moral* difference, between sabbath-observing nations and sabbath non-observing nations is even more striking. There is no such general education among the French and German common people as is found in New England. The masses in both countries are utterly neglected. And as to *morals* we will, for brevity, take one kind of evidence alone, which will suffice. It is not an agreeable kind of evidence, but that we cannot help. We will take six cities, and on inquiry we find that a few years since the percentage of illegitimate births in a single year in London was 4 per cent; in Paris, 34 per cent; in Brussels, 34 per cent; in Monaco, 49 per cent; in Vienna, 54 per cent; in Rome, 72 per cent.[1]

As to the *social* results, — the results to the good order of society, its peace and quietude, — Count Montalembert, one of the most eminent French statesmen, once wrote, " Men are surprised sometimes by the ease with which the immense city of London is kept in order by a garrison of three small battalions and two squadrons ; while to control the capital of France, which is half the size, forty thousand troops of the line and sixty thousand national guards are necessary. But the stranger who arrives in London on a Sunday morning, when he sees every thing of commerce suspended in that gigantic capital in obedience to God ; when in the centre of that colossal business he finds silence and repose scarcely interrupted by the bells which call to prayer, and by the immense crowds

---

[1] The *Examiner* (London) of October, 1868, gives the following statistics, the latest moral statistics obtainable : —

City.	Births.	
	Legitimate.	Illegitimate.
London	75,097	3,203
Paris	19,921	9,707
Brussels	3,448	1,833
Monaco	1,854	1,762
Vienna.	8,821	10,360
Rome	1,215	3,160

on their way to church, — then his astonishment ceases. He understands that there is *another* curb for a Christian people besides that made by bayonets, and that, where the law of God is fulfilled with such a solemn submissiveness, God himself, if I dare use the words, charges himself with the police arrangements."

Now, when foreigners themselves cannot withhold expressions such as these as they see the difference between society in sabbath-keeping countries and society in countries where the sabbath light is extinguished, — does it not indicate to us in what direction our duty and interest lie ? Not in trying to find some position of compromise between the Biblical ideas and that anti-sabbatic position occupied by Germany, France, and other European nationalities ; but in working into its most benevolent expression the Bible principle, so that, while the sabbath rest loses none of its sanctity, it yet shall become more and more *desirable* until the whole people shall be found mentally and heartily converted to the true sabbatic principle and practice. We need not fear that the old rigidity will return ; but we had better have *that and* a sabbath, than be without it and have no sabbath. We need not fear that the Puritan sabbath will be back upon us. We do not want the tree : we want the fruit. And yet, if we are to have the fruit, we shall hardly be likely to get it by cutting down the tree. But, as all the finest and sweetest fruits in our gardens have come from care and culture of once sour fruits, so the brightest, purest, sweetest sabbath that ever dawned on toiling men will come, I verily believe, not from Germany, not from Italy, not from France, but from the steady care for and culture of that old Puritan sabbath, that once (according to the reports of those who had no experience of it) was sour. On this sabbath-theme (I do not like to call it a question) the New-Englander has a mission to the man of the Old World.

Let New England stand resolute and determined in the
old ideas, — modernized it may be, expanded, ripened, but
in substance the same as those of the fathers, — *let her
hold to the Book, the Day, the Church, the School:* her
moral and intellectual supremacy in the land will remain.   Her numerical supremacy has gone.   That kind of
supremacy is at best very inferior.   Englishmen, numerically, are but one-fiftieth of the British Empire, and yet
they have the supremacy.   And so the time may come
when the population of New England shall be but one-
fiftieth of the population of these United States, and yet
it may still be the *head* of the body ; but *never* by adopting German ideas in regard to the sabbath or the Bible,
or other kindred themes.   Always and ever, the *purest*
ideas are not only the best, but the strongest.   These
brethren from foreign lands need to be shown that physically, mentally, and spiritually, a man is more a man, even
for this world, by having a sabbath.   And is it not the
great levelling day of the week, — but a day of levelling up,
— when the master is no longer master, the servant no
longer servant, the toiler no longer driven by stern necessity ; each and every man on that day *his own, his family's, and God's?*   The pure *manhood* of man never shines
so purely as when the sabbath comes, and for twenty-four
hours dissolves the inter-relations of life established by
commerce, and says to the man, To-day you are simply
a man among men — free to worship God.

  I presume that our friends who want museums, picture-
galleries, and other such places, open on Sunday, think
that thus Sunday can be made a little less objectionable to
the foreigner.   I have no doubt as to their *meaning* well
by these expedients, urged, as we sometimes hear, to keep
the drinking-men out of the saloons.   Personally, I have
made too many observations and inquiries, seen and heard
too much on the Continent of Europe and in England,

to believe even for the space of a second, that seeing Egyptian mummies, and stuffed monkeys, or even very fine works of art, in art-galleries, will ever do any thing in that direction. In England we have been successful so far in keeping all our public institutions closed on the Sunday, — with one exception. There is a famous library in the town of Birmingham which was opened a few years since. I was curious to know what class of readers frequented it, and what class of books was taken out on Sunday. I was informed that the most inferior books in the library were invariably called for on Sundays. Our brethren, who believe that some indefinite good is to come to somebody from keeping public, state, and national museums open on Sunday, have only to visit the countries where none of them are shut, have only to observe the kind of pictures which are most popular with the Sunday visitors, to have their faith shaken, and the ardor of their zeal cooled. My firmly-rooted belief is that it is not in the spirit of weak compromise on this, or any question, that strength lies. Our influence over the foreign population will not be in proportion to our likeness to them, but in the ratio of our elevation above them. The great reason why America is more attractive to them than France or Germany or Italy is, that she is different from all; and the difference is a difference of *elevation.* So it must be on this sabbath question. We must have a holier, a purer, a more beneficent sabbath, than Germany or France has, if we would have a brighter and cheerier sabbath. We don't want mere gayety. Gayety belongs to nations that are frivolous because at heart they are sad. However many your jets of gas, you can never multiply them into sunlight. We want the real thing, — the cheeriness which comes from a heart and conscience at rest; the bloom which indicates health; not paint. This part of the great theme, "the sabbath and our foreign popula-

tion," is not the least important branch by any means
when we remember how numerous that foreign population
is.   I suppose that every third man you meet in America
is a foreigner.   It would only be tedious to go into statisti-
cal details.   But as figures do not, and can not, lie or exag-
gerate (except at political elections), it may help us to see
the importance of this part of this variously-related theme,
if we take this State of Massachusetts and the State of
New York, and ask what is the proportion between native
and foreign.   The census of 1870 for New-York State
gives the native population at 3,244,406; foreign born,
1,138,353; having foreign father and mother, 2,043,112.
In Massachusetts the total native population, 1,104,032;
foreign born, 353,319; having foreign father and mother,
600,000.   It is difficult to estimate just what proportion of
these of foreign parentage are naturally inclined to uphold
the sabbath as a divine institution; who are with us, and
not against us.   I presume that not more than one-third.
How are we to regard the other two-thirds?   Not as enemies — that be far from us ! — *but as people who need instruction in order to conversion.*   For it needs no discussion, that either the sabbath idea must conquer them, or
they it.   Is New England religiously strong enough and
ardent enough to make her influence felt on this subject
all over this continent?   She has an advantage over any
other part of the land in regard to moral and religious
reforms.   Her *record* is her advantage.   She knows, and
we all know, that to secularize the Lord's Day is an object
that men are driving at (as Dr. Guthrie once put it) under
cover of regard to the interests of the poor.   Care for the
poor ! a wretched pretence on the part of many who make
it, and a delusion in all who believe it.   We have to make
it evident, that, let a breach be once made, and work, as on
the Continent, will rush in at the back of play ; and that,
in the end, seven days' labor will bring no higher wages

than are now earned by six ; that it is not in those Popish
or Protestant countries where this day is given up to
business or pleasure, but here and in England, in the two
countries where it stops the wheels of labor, closes theatres, and opens churches, that workmen can earn the
largest wages, enjoy the greatest freedom, and dwell in the
happiest homes ; that, in every country where it is honored, the sabbath is the palladium of liberty and the ark
of religion ; that a nation trained through its devout observance to the knowledge of God and practice of piety
will neither aspire to be tyrants, nor submit to be slaves.

CORPORATIONS AND THE SABBATH.

BY REV. WILLARD F. MALLALIEU, D.D., OF CHELSEA.

IN every effort put forth by the real friends of morality and religion to conserve the best interests of society, it is of the first importance that they should properly estimate the actual condition of affairs.

The antediluvian sinners are all dead. Not one of the wicked Egyptians of the time of the exodus has troubled the earth for a long time. The persecutors of the apostles and the murderers of Christ have all passed away. They may serve as examples, in some sort, and their fate may warn others of the danger of sin; but, practically, we have not much to do with them. Our difficulties are peculiar to the times in which we live, and our sinners are associated with us in the most intimate relations of life.

It is perfectly obvious that the civilization of the last half of the nineteenth century is altogether different from that of any preceding epoch. The world itself seems to have grown smaller year by year, and unremitting explorations and multiplied discoveries have removed the darkness which for centuries had enshrouded a large proportion of the earth. The human race, during the lifetime of men not far past the meridian, has made more rapid advances, and achieved greater victories in the conflict of mind with matter, than in the previous twenty centuries. All the world, and especially all Christendom, is in a condition of mental excitement. The tides of commerce ebb and flow with ceaseless energy. Vast bodies of men in inexplicable migrations are passing from continent to

continent. There is scarcely a stone of the old foundations upon which society has rested, that is not rudely or
maliciously assailed. Mount Sinai and the Rock of Ages
are not secure from attack. Even the Almighty is eliminated from the universe in the thought of vain men, puffed
up with much or little science.

Amid such developments as these, and others not less
momentous and threatening, the holy sabbath, God's day,
confronts a wicked, restless world.

Like every other law of the Decalogue, the Fourth Commandment is adapted to the needs of all men, and it is of
universal and perpetual obligation. It never has been
abrogated, and never will be as long as man dwells on the
face of the earth. The obligation to keep holy the sabbath rests simply and solely upon the plain, absolute command of God, that command being designed to promote
man's highest physical, mental, and spiritual welfare.

This law, being binding upon individuals, is also binding
upon all aggregations of individuals : hence it is binding
upon corporations.

It is a feature, and a very pronounced feature, of modern
civilization, that a large proportion of the actively-employed
capital is held by corporations, or organized companies.
The facts of our own country apply equally to other civilized countries. The vast wealth concentrated in our railroads and other means of intercommunication is owned
and controlled by corporations. The same is true of most
of our extensive and rapidly increasing manufactories.
Even many of the vast farms of the West are owned and
operated by corporations.

One of the notorious peculiarities of all corporations is
the almost universal assumption that the individuals com-
posing them have no personal responsibility for the good
or evil which may result from corporate action.

Corporations may grind the face of the poor, and defraud

the laborer, and do as many outrageous things as they deem profitable ; and yet all the individual corporators will wash their hands of any responsibility.

The laws of God and man may be violated with equal recklessness by corporations ; and all the time those professing to be moral and upright, if not Christian, will complacently pocket the profits of law-breaking.

As a matter of fact, the most of our corporations do not openly and habitually violate the sabbath. Our shops and factories of all kinds remain closed on the sabbath. If any work be done, it is the work of repairing, which is done by a very few, and without noise or disturbance of any kind. In most cases, even these repairs could be done on week-days or nights, and hence are unnecessary and in violation of the law of God.

The great sabbath-breaking corporations of the country are those controlling the railroads and steamboats.

Boston and Massachusetts may serve as an example of the manner in which the sabbath is desecrated all over the country.

Twenty-five years ago such a thing as a Sunday steamboat-excursion was unknown ; but now, all through the summer months, the harbor of Boston is alive with excursions. The last summer was worse in this regard than any that has preceded it, and the next threatens to be worse than this.

The churches are shut, or only open a half-day ; ministers are away, the saints are scattered or asleep, and the Devil holds high carnival. Press and pulpit are alike silent on the open and shameless violation of the laws of God and men ; and some go so far in their mawkish sympathy as mildly to apologize for all this wickedness. So much for the religious press and the pulpit. The secular press is utterly silent, or approves of the sabbath desecration.

But the railroads centring in Boston are worse, if possible, than the steamboats. Twenty-five years ago the running of a train of cars for any purpose was a thing to be remarked; but now there is not an exception to the desecration of the sabbath by any road. Not only are passenger-trains run on Sunday, but also freight, and these, in some instances, connecting with steamboats, as is notably the case with some of the lines running to New York.

This deplorable condition of affairs is growing worse and worse from year to year; and from present indications these great corporations will in the future as thoroughly ignore the existence of the sabbath as though there were none.

Along the same line of operations we see that the horse-railroads, especially in the summer-time, make the sabbath their harvest-day. Then it is that they are thronged by pleasure-seekers and Sunday visitors, who are thoroughly careless of the sabbath. These roads are run, not as a matter of necessity or mercy, but simply and solely for the money that is to be made.

These corporations, controlling the steamboats, steam-railroads, and horse-railroads, are the great, shameless, audacious, defiant leaders in the sin of public sabbath-breaking.

The evil consequences of this sabbath violation are threefold : —

I. First, there is involved the necessity of the employment of vast numbers of men to carry on the work that must be performed. Tens of thousands of men are employed by these corporations every sabbath; and it is almost an impossible thing for any man habitually to violate the law of God in the desecration of the sabbath, and still maintain a high standard of morality. The universal experience and observation of many years in this connection establish the fact that the character of workmen will deteriorate in morals in proportion as they neglect the sabbath. The men themselves may, or may not, be conscious — probably they are not — of the effect produced; but still it is none the less certain and destructive. And they seem to be equally unconscious of the fact that the tendency of late years has been to keep the wages of laboring-men down to the very lowest point of comfortable support; and in many cases they have been reduced so low that only with the utmost exertion could the necessaries of life be obtained, especially where growing families have been dependent. The result has been, that by working six days in a week, and three hundred and thirteen days in a year, honest, hard-working men have just been able to take care of themselves and their families. Now, the inevitable consequences of the sabbath-breaking so recklessly engaged in by these corporations will be, first, the destruction of the morals of the workmen ; and, secondly, the establishment of such conditions of labor that it will take three hundred and sixty-five days' toil to secure the same comforts of life as are now procured by the labor of three hundred and thirteen days. Hence *the sabbath-breaking corporations are the worst enemies of the working-man;* and this, equally in regard to his social, moral, and religious interests. And it should be added, with special emphasis, that any system or institution which debases thus the working-men affects in like manner their families. Nor can it be doubted that the security of our national future and the continuance of our present form of government, to say nothing of the success of the Christian Church, depend very largely upon the social, moral, and religious status of our working-men. Hence, in just so far as the corporations degrade the character of working-men by their conscienceless sabbath desecration, they are the enemies of the Republic.

II. Again, the great transportation corporations under

consideration constitute one of the greatest educational forces of modern society ; and it must be acknowledged, that, so far as they are related to the observance of the sabbath, their educational influence is all in the wrong direction.

In the olden time, when good people, and the community almost without exception, laid aside their usual employments at the close of the week, and carefully abstained from all labor on the sabbath ; when a quiet hush settled down on home and street, on shop and farm, every child conscious at all of what was taking place around him could but feel that he was brought into the presence of the divine command which produced these results, and almost into the presence of the divine Being who had given the command. This influence was felt not only by the children, but also by the youth, and, in fact, by all classes of people. From the very necessities of the case the minds of the people were called away from worldly and secular concerns, and all were compelled to feel that there were moral and religious obligations resting upon them which had been imposed by the Ruler of the universe. The quiet of the sabbath, and the cessation of all servile and unnecessary labor on that day, were moral forces for the conservation of the best interests of society which were of immeasurable consequence.

How different the conditions under which the people of this country are placed to-day ! In a thousand towns and cities may be heard the scream of the locomotive, and the rush of the railroad-train. Steamboat-excursions, and other means of Sunday pleasure-travel, are abundantly supplied. The ordinary time-tables, and flaming handbills conspicuously displayed, announce the business of the sabbath with the same particularity as that of ordinary week-days. The newspapers advertise Sunday excursions with as much regularity as they do the services of the sanctuary; and they give, in many instances, fuller notices of Sunday excursions and frolics than they do of the sermons.

The boy living on the hillside farm in the most rural town through which the railroad runs, looking upon the sabbath-trains that pass, whether freight or passenger, will, unless there be some mighty counteracting moral force, gradually and imperceptibly fall into the way of thinking that the sabbath has no special sacredness; and the end, in many cases, will be, that he becomes thoroughly indifferent to the claims of God which demand that he should keep holy the sabbath day. Let this same youth, thus perverted from the right and good way, become the father of a family, and, if his wife be like himself, his children will in all probability grow up in practical heathenism.

Now, the same influences are operating upon unnumbered thousands not only in our large cities and centres of population, but to a greater or less extent all over the country.

The Pilgrim Fathers left Holland, the land that had protected them and given them a home and shelter, and dared the perils of the sea and the wilderness, because they would not bring up their children in the godless society which surrounded them; but our children and youth are, in some respects, surrounded by as deplorable influences as those of Holland. If things go on as they have done for the last twenty-five years, there seems to be great danger that we shall become a nation of sabbath-breakers, and, as always happens in such cases, an immoral and irreligious nation, and, consequently, a nation upon which will rest the frown and curse of Almighty God.

III. The third evil consequence which follows in the train of corporation sabbath-breaking is the terrible waste which is necessarily involved.

If any thing has been established, it has been that men and animals can do more work in a year, working six days in a week, than they can in working seven ; and there is almost equally good evidence to believe that material such as wood, and especially iron and steel, will last longer when used only six days out of seven, than when used continuously all the days in every week, month in and month out.

If this be so, and if economy of force in the production and transportation of the means of living, and the necessaries of civilization, be an object, then surely these Heaven-defying corporations would do well to conform to the manifest laws of nature, which are in absolute harmony with the revealed laws of God, and allow both men and material one day's rest in every seven.

Concerning the magnitude and destructiveness of the evils of corporation sabbath-breaking, there can be no room for doubt. But, then, the question of pressing, practical importance in this connection is this : What are the duties of Christian men in regard to these corporations ?

First of all, it is incumbent that ministers of the gospel, and all good men, and especially the religious press, should denounce the sabbath-breaking of these guilty corporations. There must be a purpose and an emphasis in this denunciation, which will assure the transgressors that the moral and religious sense of the people so long and grievously outraged has at last found a voice and tongue.

As Whittier says, —

> "We need preachers like Woolman, or like those who bore
> The faith of Wesley to this Western shore;
> And deemed no convert genuine till he broke
> Alike his servant's and the Devil's yoke."

Somebody must cry out against this enormous sin which leads as directly to bald, blank atheism, as any sin ever committed against God or man. When we comprehend the evils which threaten, and are even now falling upon us with crushing power, we shall be dumb no longer. Above all, we shall not lend our countenance to the sin by further silence, nor by the acceptance of the utterly weak and worthless excuses and apologies which are made for the open and flagrant violation of the laws of the State and of the Almighty Ruler of the Universe.

But it is not enough that words of earnest condemnation should be spoken : the practice must conform to the precept.

> " Say well and do well, both end with a letter :
> Say well is good, but do well is better."

The vast bulk of Sunday travel, Sunday visits, Sunday excursions, has no possible justification or excuse. If regard were had to the law of God, if the moral sense were what it ought to be, if the conscience were rightly instructed, and faithfully performed its office, and if heed were given to its admonitions, ninety-nine and nine-tenths per cent of all Sunday patronage could be withdrawn from these terrible sabbath-breaking corporations.

Christian people must have a conscience in regard to this matter, or the sabbath which has been a mighty tower of defence against the hosts of sin will be swept away, and the resistless enemy will come in like a flood, and overwhelm us in one common desolation.

The evil example of an hour may neutralize the preaching of a life-time. Christians must stand clear in this matter, or their testimony against the sin will be of no avail.

One other point of practical importance demands our earnest consideration. Somebody owns the stock of these godless and soulless corporations. A very large percentage of it is undoubtedly owned by Christian men and women. In some cases the ownership has come by inheritance; in others money has been invested in the stock, in hope of profitable returns. It is altogether probable that some of these stocks are owned by Christian ministers. If the stocks pay a dividend, these men and women and ministers find their way to the offices of the corporations, and receive their share of the profits, and quietly go their several ways. No matter if the bodies and souls of men have been destroyed, the morals of the community debased, many congregations of Christian worshippers disturbed, the best security of our national perpetuity removed, and the wrath of a justly-offended God moved towards the people; still these professing saints accept the profits, and, if they are large, rejoice and buy more stock, and so sink deeper and deeper in this complicity with the terrible sin.

It is doubtful if there can be found on record a single instance, though there may be some, in which a Christian man has refused these profits, or sold his stock to clear himself, or has even uttered a manly protest against the continued and excuseless violation of the sabbath by the corporation of which he is a stockholder. It is a question whether there is conscience, or virtue, or religion, or simple, honest God-fearing, enough among the Christian stockholders of these corporations, to lead one of them to speak a word or cast a vote in opposition to the iniquity so recklessly practised.

When Christians themselves observe with more strictness the commands of God in regard to the sabbath, may we hope for some change for the better in the now deplorable condition of affairs. No ray of light dawns upon us from any other source. Oh that God would send us help out of the sanctuary! and that from this hour may be dated the beginning of a glorious reformation in the interest of a devout, consistent, and sanctified observance of the sabbath.

THE SABBATH AND RAILROADS AND STEAMBOATS.

BY HON. WILLIAM E. DODGE OF NEW YORK.

WE are called to confront a most gigantic obstacle to the maintenance of the sabbath of our fathers, — one of which they never had any knowledge. But who can for a moment doubt what would have been their action, had they been called on to confer on any set of men the chartered right to construct and operate railroads? We may be sure they would have made it a condition, that they should not be run on the sabbath.

It is within the lifetime of some present, that the first lines of steamboats and railroads were established; and they have grown so rapidly that they now extend from the Atlantic to the Pacific, and from the coasts to the far West in every direction; and steamers have taken the place of our sailing-vessels, and are running on all the navigable rivers and along our shores, and have brought all Europe within a few-days' journey.

As our railroads are the more important, I shall give special attention to them; for, while steamboats are principally owned and managed by individuals, our railroads exist by virtue of chartered rights, and are controlled by stockholders.

Railroads have wrought wonders in the rapid development and general prosperity of our country during the last half-century. They have become the great highway for the millions; have vastly increased travel; brought the distant parts of the country together; given to traffic and commerce a new impulse; equalized values of the soil and manufactory; made a journey of thousands of miles but as a pleasure-trip; and, with the aid of the telegraph, have enabled merchants while residing thousands of miles away to sell and buy in our principal coast cities, and even fix a date of delivery. They are building up vast centres of traffic along these lines; have added untold millions of wealth to the country, and are increasing at a most rapid rate; and, in a few years, will have united our entire country with iron bands. They have become every day more and more an absolute necessity.

With *thousands of millions* invested, hundreds of thousands of our citizens employed in connection with their direct management, and furnishing the necessary machinery and material, and with the vast number of stockholders and the entire travelling community, their moral influence is beyond calculation.

But if railroads, with all these wonderful advantages, cannot be conducted without changing the habits and customs of our people, and trampling on the right of the community to a quiet day for rest and worship, and training up the thousands in their employ to desecrate the sabbath, and rushing by our cities and towns and quiet villages, screaming as they go, *No sabbath! No sabbath!* — then they will become a real curse rather than a blessing. Consider the vast sums invested; the great competition of the principal trunk-lines; the constantly increasing demands for rapid passenger-trains, and the press of freight to the seaboard, becoming every year larger, particularly that bound for Europe, much of it sold for shipment by special steamers, and intended so to arrive as to be in time for trans-shipment at once, or with the least possible delay or expense; parties perhaps in Chicago, Milwaukee, St. Louis, or Cincinnati, — these having been made ports of entry and shipping direct to all parts of the world, — telegraphing the superintendent of the road, "We have shipped to-day twenty five cars of wheat, or perhaps ten cars of live-stock, which are to be delivered to such a steamer on such a day; and we shall depend on your giving us rapid transit and prompt delivery." Now, this superintendent feels his responsibility, and by this continual press and excitement, which the system of railroads and telegraphs almost of necessity creates, has come to lose all thoughts of the sabbath, or perhaps has tried to convince his conscience that these long lines of inland transportation are like ocean travel, — not expected to stop on the sabbath.

These difficulties are constantly increasing; so that whereas, a few years ago, the running of freight-trains on the sabbath was the exception, now, on many of our trunk-lines leading from the West, there are more on the sabbath than on other days, as the passenger-trains are generally less, and they use the sabbath to make up lost time, and hurry on the freight to the seaboard. The constant extension of lines West and North, tributary to these trunk-lines, only increases the evil; and, unless some prompt measure can be adopted soon, the matter of sabbath desecration by our railroads will be past prevention.

In regard to passenger-traffic, there is very great difficulty in drawing the line between entire rest and the running of such trains as the general public would demand for long or through travel, trains for the carrying of the mail, and, near our cities, milk-trains. If our railroad-managers could be made to feel their obligations to God, to the morals of the country, and their duty to their employés, so as on these long lines of travel to run only a single mail-train each way on the sabbath, it would of itself go far to honor God's day of rest.

The fact is, the railroad interest has become the all-powerful, overshadowing interest of the country, and every year is adding to its influence. Railroads will double in the next twenty years; and what is done must be done promptly, or their power will be beyond control. The question of the day, for every man who loves his country and believes in the importance and value of the Christian sabbath, as we in America have cherished and honored it, — I say, the great question is, Shall this vast railroad interest be so conducted as to prove a *blessing* to the land ? *or shall it defy and trample on all we hold dear, and become one of the principal instruments in changing our American sabbath into the Continental holiday,* or, as it is fast growing, a day like all the others of the week ?

I have no doubt that it is in the power of the intelligent lovers of the sabbath, in connection with the stockholders in these roads, to bring about a change which shall stop the transit of freight-trains, and reduce the passenger-traffic to such an extent that the influence shall tell on the side of sabbath observance. The fact of such difference between that and the other days will show clearly that there is *one* day of rest.

The great question before us is the popular one, "What are you going to do about it?" Let this come home to every Christian and true lover of his country, — Have I any thing to do about it, or any responsibility in connection with it ? The amount of money invested by New-England men in railroads at home and in the West may be estimated by hundreds of millions ; a sum so vast that, if it could be once known, would show the influence that New England has in this matter. I have not a doubt that if the Christian men of this country, when about to invest in the stock or securities of our railroads, would ask, "Does that road run on Sunday?" and, if so, refuse to put money into such roads, it would go far to settle this question. Those who build railroads are *shrewd men ;* and their interest would induce them so to conduct them that the good men of our country would wish to hold their securities.

Stockholders appear to act as if they had no responsibility in the matter. Their only question is, "Is the stock good?" "Does it pay regular dividends?" If so, no matter how they get the money; that is their lookout. I can go to church; and if the train does run past, drowning the voice of the preacher, I am fully compensated by the reflection that they are thus making sure my dividends. Don't be too sure. The poor, overworked engineers, conductors, and brakemen may soon lose their interest, become discouraged, careless, or incapable of that prompt action necessary at the moment of danger; and an accident may occur which will send many into eternity, and the loss to your company be so great as to prevent your dividend.

I remember a case in point. I had, as a teacher in my Sunday school, a man who for many years ran the morning express on the New-York and New-Haven road. One winter morning, as he came into school, he said to me, "Mr. Dodge, I suppose I have lost my position on the road." I said, "What has happened?" for I knew he was in all respects a first-class man, receiving the very highest wages, and had never met with any serious accident. Said he, "The superintendent sent for me early this morning, to get out my engine to open the road, as there had fallen a deep snow during the night. I sent word that on any other day I was ready to do any extra work; but I could not come on the sabbath. Before I had finished my breakfast, peremptory orders came for me to come at once, and get out my engine. I replied that I was just going to my sabbath school, and could not come; and I presume I shall get my discharge to-morrow." I said, "Go early in the morning to the superintendent, and say that, although you are only engaged to run the express-train, yet at any time, day or night, if any thing special should happen, you would be ready to do what you could for the company;

but cannot work on Sunday. And, if you are dismissed, I will secure you a first-rate position on a road in which I am interested, that never runs on Sunday." The next sabbath he told me that he began to speak to the superintendent, but he stopped him, and said, "I respect your position; and you shall never be called on for Sunday work again."

A few months after, there occurred to that express-train the awful accident at Norwalk Bridge, which cost so many valuable lives, and over two hundred and fifty thousand dollars to the company. I at once supposed my good teacher had "gone to his home," and made my way to the office of the company, to find instead that he had been permitted to leave for a few days on important business, and the train had been put in charge of a former engineer of the road, who had just returned from California.

"Oh!" said the superintendent, "no such accident could have happened if Smith had been on the engine."

By the determination of the managers to use the sabbath as any other day, they must either drive all good, sabbath-loving men from their roads, or so demoralize them that they may soon come to feel, that, if there is no binding force in the Fourth Commandment, there is none in the Eighth. Stockholders will find that they have a deep pecuniary interest in so conducting their roads that honest, faithful Christian men can be employed, and that they have a right to claim, in return for their faithful work, the one day's rest which God and nature demand.

Look at that poor, jaded engineer, who has run his engine over his prescribed route for seven days, with no opportunity for rest, or for visiting his family, or for changing his soiled clothes. He comes to his engine on Monday with no heart in his work; feels discouraged, degraded, and like a slave, who is working for those who have no sympathy with him; and he works because he must.

Some of you may never have stood on the railroad-engine, may never have watched the eye and the mind of the man who holds the brake, running thirty miles an hour, danger all around, knowing that he has a train of immortal beings. That man has his mind, his thought, exercised intently six days in a week. He is entitled to rest. Take the man whose family, whose children, hardly know him; who goes week after week toiling and toiling, covered with dirt and smoke, and has no time to dress, and meet his little family. You go on a Monday morning to see a poor, haggard-looking engineer, all dirty, kept up all day Sunday, and all night, and all worn out perhaps. He steps upon the engine. If you are a railroad man, you feel intense anxiety all the time. Now contrast this man with the one who runs his engine on a sabbath-keeping road, and who, as he works during the week, is looking forward to a quiet day of rest with his family. He goes to his work with a cheerful and contented feeling; takes pride in his connection with a company that sympathizes with its employés; believes that God understood the needs of man when he provided one day in seven as a day of rest; takes pride in having his engine always clean and in good order; and, when Saturday night comes, he goes to his home to meet a happy wife, and the welcome of his children; and on the Monday steps on board his engine, refreshed by the rest, and, with his clean clothes, feels he is a man, and ready in any crisis to act with a cool, clear head, watching the interests of the company as if they were his own, and able to do, and do well, in six days, what the other man is compelled to do in seven. He is worth vastly more to the company than if made to work seven days. What our railroads need is to secure respectable, honest men, who will have an interest in the success of the company. This they cannot have if they demand seven days work.

If Christian stockholders would unite in an earnest,

determined demand that their agents would confine their
sabbath work to the least possible mail-trains, and that no
freight-trains or work in shops or on the road should be
done on the sabbath, the thing could to a large extent be
done ; yet I do not lose sight of the fact that the most
powerful of the trunk-lines are controlled by a few men
whose ambition is unbounded, and who appear to look
only at their own, without regard to the claims of others,
or to the influence they exert on the morals of the country ; and, holding the terminus, they influence, almost of
necessity, all the lines connected with them ; and, because
they disregard the claims of the sabbath, they are gradually compelling the competing lines, who might desire to
lessen their Sunday service, to follow their example. And
as these great corporations grow stronger and stronger,
reaching farther into the interior every year, their sabbath-
desecrating influence is continually widening and extending. Many of our great Western cities are struggling to
hold the American sabbath against the demands of a large
foreign element in favor of a Continental sabbath. This
renders the sabbath desecrations by the railroads doubly
dangerous.

The question returns, What can be done ? There can
be no doubt that a very large number of roads are virtually
sabbath-keeping. "Where there is a will there is a way ; "
and there is abundant evidence that all the transportation
now passing, or that may be hereafter carried, can be done
in six days, if there were a readiness to arrange for it, and
that the companies would all be the better and more valuable for it.

Their "Monthly Journal" for July publishes the following petition of four hundred and fifty engineers, employed
on the New-York Central and Hudson-River Railways.
Its arguments and appeals well deserve the attention
not only of all who are in any way responsible for

Sunday railway traffic, but of the Christian people of this land : —

PETITION TO ABOLISH SUNDAY TRAINS ON THE N. Y. C. & H. R. R.R.

To WILLIAM H. VANDERBILT, *Vice-President:*

SIR, — The undersigned, locomotive-engineers in your employ, respectfully represent that the custom of running freight-trains on the sabbath on your line of road has increased, from the occasional moving of one or two trains on Sundays, during some great press of business, until it has in fact become a regular practice, and a great hardship upon your engineers. We have borne this grievance patiently, hoping every succeeding year that it would decrease. We are willing to submit to any reasonable privations, mental or physical, to assist the officers of your company to operate the road to achieve a financial triumph ; but, after a long and weary service, we do not see any signs of relief, and we are forced to come to you with our trouble, and most respectfully ask you to relieve us from Sunday labor, so far as it is in your power to do so.

Our objections to Sunday labor are : —

First, This never-ending toil ruins our health, and prematurely makes us feel worn out, like old men; and we are sensible of our inability to perform our duty as well when we work to an excess.

Second, That the customs of all civilized countries, as well as all laws human and divine, recognize Sunday as a day for rest and recuperation ; and, notwithstanding intervals of rest might be arranged for us upon other days than Sunday, we feel that by so doing we would be forced to exclude ourselves from all church, family, and social privileges that other citizens enjoy.

Third, Nearly all the undersigned have children that they desire to have educated in every thing that will tend to make them good men and women; and we cannot help but see that our example in ignoring the sabbath day has a very demoralizing influence upon them.

Fourth, Because we believe the best interests of the company we serve, as well as ours, will be promoted thereby, and because we believe locomotive-engineers should occupy as high social and religious positions as men in any other calling.

We know the question will be considered, How can this Sunday work be avoided, with the immense and constantly increasing traffic?

We have watched this matter for the past twenty years; we have seen it grow from its infancy until it has arrived at its now gigantic proportions, from one train on the sabbath until we now have about thirty each way; and we do not hesitate in saying that we can do as much work in six days, with the seventh for rest, as is now done.

It is a fact, observable by all connected with the immediate running of freight-trains, that on Monday freight is comparatively light; Tuesday it strengthens a little, and keeps increasing until Saturday; and Sundays are the heaviest of the week.

The objection may be offered, that, if your lines stop, the receiving-points from other roads will be blocked up. In reply, we would most respectfully suggest, that, when the main lines do not run, the tributaries would only be too glad to follow the good example.

The question might also arise, If traffic is suspended twenty-four hours, will not the company lose one-seventh of its profits? In answer, we will pledge our experience, health, and strength, that, at the end of the year, our employers will not lose one cent, but, on the contrary, will be the gainers financially. Our reasons are these: At present the duties of your locomotive-engineers are incessant, day after day, night succeeding night, Sunday and all, rain or shine, with all the fearful inclemencies of a rigorous winter to contend with. The great strain of both mental and physical faculties constantly employed has a tendency in time to impair the requisites so necessary to make a good engineer.

Troubled in mind, jaded and worn out in body, the engineer cannot give his duties the attention they should have in order to best advance his employers' interests. We venture to say, not on this broad continent, in any branch of business or traffic, can be found any class in the same position as railroad-men. They are severed from associations that all hold most dear, debarred from the opportunity of worship, — that tribute that man owes to his GOD, — witnessing all those pleasures accorded to others, which are the only oasis in the deserts of this life, and with no prospect of relief. We ask you to aid us.

Give us the sabbath for rest after our week of laborious duties; and we pledge you, that with a system invigorated by a season of repose, by a brain eased and cleared by hours of relaxation, we can go to work with more energy, more mental and physical force, and can and will accomplish more work, and do it better if possible, in six days, than we can now do in seven. We can give you ten days in six, if you require it, if we can only look forward to a certain period of rest.

In conclusion, we hope and trust, that, in conjunction with other gentlemen of the trunk-lines leading to the seaboard, you will be able to accomplish something that will ameliorate our condition.

In closing, we desire to say to the respected and honored gentleman, the president of this road, ripe in years, with a career unparalleled in the history of any country as a successful financial and business manager, we hope and trust that the abolition of freight-traffic on the sabbath, with the innumerable favors and privileges it would entail on his employés, would be an event in his life that would give the greatest pleasure, and from thousands of tongues would ascend an invocation to Divine Providence to spare for many years the author of this inestimable boon, — the cessation of Sunday labor.

M. RICKARD, Secretary.

The petition, it is stated, was presented by a large committee, who received a courteous hearing, but no assurance of present relief.

There are roads doing a large through business that run no trains on the sabbath. The Delaware, Lackawanna, and Western Railroad Company, with its leased connections, extending from Lake Ontario to New York City, — three hundred miles — runs no passenger or freight trains on the sabbath, except an early mail and milk train on the Morris and Essex Division.

This company was formed in my office thirty years ago, and has maintained its respect for the sabbath to this day. I make the following extract from the report of the sabbath committee : —

"The practicability of dispensing with much labor on Sunday commonly regarded as necessary is shown by such facts as the following. Within a few years past, several railways have changed the gauge of their tracks, and in most instances it has been done on Sunday under the plea of necessity. The Delaware, Lackawanna, and Western road, which runs no trains on Sunday, had occasion to change its gauge for three hundred miles. It having been reported that this had been done on Sunday, the president of the road addressed the following note to the paper making the statement : —

DELAWARE, LACKAWANNA, AND WESTERN RAILROAD COMPANY,
NEW YORK, May 31, 1876.

The gauge of this company's railroad was altered on Saturday, not Sunday last, as stated in error in your journal of Monday morning. Please make the correction, as we believe in the observance (by rest from labor, at least) of the Christian as well as the 'American sabbath,' and that railroad management should be exemplary in the proper obligations to the community.   Yours truly,
SAMUEL SLOAN, *President.*

"The report of Mr. Halstead, the superintendent, shows in detail how the change was made without Sunday work of any kind, without an accident to person or property, and with but trifling interruption of the regular traffic.

"A change of gauge was also made last year on the Houston and Texas Central Railway, for three hundred and sixty miles, under the presidency of Mr. William E. Dodge, and with Mr. J. Durand as superintendent, without any Sunday work, and with as little interruption of traffic as in other instances where the work was done on Sunday."

Our great cities are suffering from the demands of the foreign population that the sabbath shall be a day of recreation for themselves and families ; and in some of our cities the Continental sabbath begins to appear. The railroads and steamboats are ready to meet this desire ; and now thousands crowd every conveyance that will carry them out into the country for a holiday ; and our new lines of elevated roads in New York, while a great convenience on week-days, are becoming a great nuisance on the sabbath, and are run for no other reason than to make money.

Trains are rushing up and down our avenues as if determined to wipe out every vestige of the Christian sabbath ; and yet the men who started and now control these elevated roads are men who profess to value the sabbath and the house of God. Very recently they have put up large placards, advertising with great prominence that trains will run on the sabbath regularly, from half-past seven in the morning until half-past seven in the evening, from the Battery to Harlem.

A few years since, the sabbath committee addressed a communication to a large number of railroads, asking to know if they ran trains on Sunday, and, if so, how many, and their experience as to its being, on the whole, profitable or otherwise, and their views as to the necessity of running trains, and particularly common and freight trains.

They received replies from a very large number, sixty-five reporting that they did no work on Sunday; others, that they only ran mail or milk trains; others, that they did as little as possible; and many expressing anxiety to stop all work on the sabbath for the sake of their men. *The general excuse of many was that the running of the trunk-lines and competing roads made it necessary, though they would prefer to rest on the sabbath.* The impression, on the whole was favorable, and encouraged efforts to secure a general suspension of all freight-trains, and reduction of passenger-trains.

The rapid growth of the railroads, and their danger if not checked, should arouse to effort every lover of the sabbath. What we do, we must do at once. In all our principal cities, influences are at work to undermine and secularize our American sabbath. Let there be one earnest, united effort of God's people; let the clergy ring out the danger from the pulpits; the religious, and, as far as possible, the secular press, enlighten the people as to the necessity and value of a day of rest for the working-man. Above all, let there be constant, earnest prayer for a general revival of religion all over the land, that the Lord of the sabbath would open the eyes of the nation to a true sense of its necessity.

And now I want to say [throwing aside his manuscript] that I came up here with the idea that, as Christians, we were awake to the fact that we were just on the eve of losing our sabbath. I know that you, perhaps, in New England, in your quiet villages, do not understand it as

we do in the cities, — as our Western cities do, with
these railroads rushing through the towns and villages
everywhere, and with their shops at work on Sunday, and
with every thing indicating that this gigantic power of
railroads is to be increased. For it is but in its infancy
to-day; and when it shall be fifty years older than it is
now, unless something is done to check this evil to-day by
the Christian people of this country, it will be altogether
too late. There will be three times the number of miles
of railroad in twenty years from now that there are to-day,
and there is a monstrous responsibility connected with it.
It is not only the railroad interest, but there is a constant
letting-down of the sabbath day even by Christians
throughout the country. We must look the difficulties
right in the face, just as they are, and ask what we can
do, and ought to do, as Christians. What we want to
do, friends, is to fasten on the sabbath, if we love it, if
we cherish it, if we want our children and children's children to enjoy what we have enjoyed. God has spared my
life for more than threescore years and ten ; and I look
back to the quiet village in Connecticut where I was
brought up, and I cherish the New-England sabbath, and
I hope my children and children's children will know
something of its value.

But, if we would do any thing, let us be about it ; and,
above all things, let Christian men who are interested in
these railroads ask themselves the question whether they
can properly be partners in concerns that are deliberately
breaking down the sabbath. What an effect would be
produced among our Western railroad-men if it were
known that the New-England Christian men and the
New-England men who were not professed Christians,
but who loved New-England's quiet that had grown out
of the sabbath, would ask as the first question, when
they were called upon to invest in a Western railroad, "Is

your road going to run on Sunday?" and, if the answer
was in the affirmative, then they would say, "I don't want
the stock"! Would that Christian men in New England
would ask themselves the question on their knees, before
God, whether they could conscientiously hold stock in
railroads that were paying them dividends earned by
breaking down the sabbath! I think that many of them,
as they offered a prayer to God for the sabbath, would
find their mouths stopped before God when they remembered that they were partners in these gigantic companies
that were rushing through the land, and destroying every
vestige of the sabbath.

And now, one thing more. God lives, *God lives*, and
God hears prayer. If you look back over the long history
of the New-England Church, you will find that God has
been the hearer and the answerer of prayer. But what
we want now is one of those old-fashioned New-England
revivals throughout the length and breadth not only of
New England, but of the land ; and if Christian men and
women will only act like Christian men and women, and
hold no communion with the works of darkness, and refuse
to be associated with an institution that will dishonor **the
sabbath, we will see a great change for the better.**

THE LORD'S DAY AND THE MERCHANT.

BY RUSSELL STURGIS, JR., ESQ., OF BOSTON.

WHEN called to take the place of another in the presentation of the subject, "The Merchant and the Sabbath," it was not because I felt peculiarly fitted in any respect for the work, but, being urged to it by the committee, I gladly consented because of my deep interest in whatever tends to increase among all men the appreciation of a day which the Creator himself set apart to be an unqualified and universal blessing to all mankind.

"The sabbath was made for man," said the Lord himself; and if anywhere, or among any class, it fails to be a blessing, the fault lies not with God, but with men.

The "sabbath" of this convention is not the seventh, but the first day of the week, more appropriately called the Lord's Day. The great mass of the Church of Christ still makes the distinction, considering that sabbath means Saturday, and designating the first day as Sunday, or the Lord's Day. In Spain and Italy the only name for Saturday is *sabbatta*. There is, I think, some importance in the designation of this day. I suppose there are those to whom the word "sabbath" is endeared by many blessed associations ; but, on the other hand, this designation of the Lord's Day carries with it, to many, associations of a very different character, which make the day one of obligation rather than of privilege.

The difference between the words "the sabbath" and the "Lord's Day" is to many, in kind if not in degree, very like that between the law and the gospel. As the word "sabbath" is used to-day among Gentiles, it means

simply the day of rest: the Lord's Day is the day of
Jesus the Christ. The sabbath is the "shalt not" day, —
the day which condemned the picker of sticks to death,
and consigned to severe punishment every one who in-
fringed its laws. The Lord's Day is full of the blessings
of the resurrection, — the subsequent meetings of our Lord
and his disciples, the weekly collection for the poor, the
meetings of the disciples for common prayer and praise,
and the celebration of the blessed Supper. The "sabbath" was the day of obligation ; the Lord's Day, the day
of privilege. In dwelling upon the day as one of privilege,
I do not at all ignore its obligations. They are very great,
and every individual is personally responsible for his manner of spending this most blessed and holy day. Especial
blessings are promised in the Word to them that honor
the day, and its disregard is frequently classed among
Israel's heinous sins. True it is that few, if any, believe
that the restrictions of the Jewish sabbath apply to the
Lord's Day ; but we may positively assert that the blessing and the curse still attach to it as much as ever. The
greatest good to body and soul result from its honored
observance ; while, whatever may be the physical influence
upon him who disregards it, certainly he must be shut off
from communion with Him whose day it is.

The Lord's house on the Lord's Day is certainly the
place where the greatest good is likely to result to the
soul, and every possible inducement should be held out
to bring men there. It is the privilege of every man to
come to God's house, to meet Him and be under the influence of his Spirit. Our language to the unbeliever should
be, "You cannot afford to neglect this day, or be absent
from the place where God's people meet. By going elsewhere, and giving yourself up to simple relaxation and
self-pleasing, you make it almost impossible for God to
reach you, since by the former you remove yourself from

the ordinary influence of his Spirit, and by the latter dis-
sipate any extraordinary means which might influence
you. You *may* be reached by the infinite grace of God;
but remember that we have been told of but one Saul of
Tarsus. Do not deliberately rob yourself of heaven, and
bring ruin upon your soul." Such reasoning is readily
understood by all. I deprecate the way in which some
well-meaning persons approach the unbeliever on this subject. I believe that much harm has been done, and prejudice and ill-will created, by taxing him with the sin of
sabbath-breaking, when, in the nature of the case, he can
see no sin in it. As well argue with a dead man, as to
try and convince the spiritually dead of this sin. I speak
here from personal experience. When a young man in
business in China, I frequently spent all day Sunday in
shooting, nor do I remember having had any conscientious scruples concerning it: so I believe that when the
careless man is told that he is committing a great sin
in boating, driving, or shooting on the Lord's Day, it is
simply inconceivable to him. His conscience does not
trouble him; and he is either quite untouched, or else an-
gered, by the accusation of others. The latter result, however, is hopeful, since it indicates that he is not quite at
ease in the matter, and his conscience is not quite silent.
The simply moral man, because he has no spiritual life,
sees and can see no harm in spending the day of rest as
he may please. Perhaps he realizes that he needs the rest
and relaxation of one day in seven, and so thinks it wrong
to pursue his usual avocation and thus overtax and injure
himself. While, therefore, he lays aside his usual work,
he yet sees no reason for attending the services of the
church, or keeping the day holy. He rests and recreates
himself as he pleases.

No argument is to-day needed to prove that it is dis-
astrous to man to work continuously. The failure of **the**

ten days' experiment of the French Revolution demonstrates the wisdom of one day of rest in seven ; the madhouse and the grave-yard attest the ruin that follows continuous work. This is so well understood now, that there are few advocates for making the Lord's Day a working-day. It is certainly also true, that to spend the day in dissipation and intemperance will unfit any man for his weekly work ; but it does not by any means follow that mere physical rest and enjoyment of the day will not fully prepare the mere worldly man for his regular work. No argument can be drawn from the use of the day simply in amusement, to prove its physical harm. The mere earthly man uses the day as he pleases, is refreshed for his week's work, lives as long as others, and is as well. As to his sin in thus using the day, the sin of sins is the non-acceptance of Jesus as Saviour and Lord ; and until a man has done this the breaking of the Lord's Day is little if any aggravation of his guilt. Thus far we have been considering the purely worldly man. He takes advantage of the benefits to his mind and body of the Lord's Day, but ignores Him who gave him the day. It is to him a day of blessed opportunities, if he will but use them ; but, though he cares for his body and mind, he utterly ignores his soul and its requirements. Caring for the less, he completely neglects the infinitely greater. In fact, so little is the life of the flesh, in comparison to that of the spirit, that the highest possible development of the former is to the latter as death to life. So the Word of God describes it. He who attains to spiritual life is said to be born again. Without it man is said to be "dead while he lives,"—dead, too, "in trespasses and sins." This life is said to be "from among the dead." "Ye will not come to me, that ye might have life," said Jesus. "He that hath the Son hath life, and he that hath not the Son of God hath not life." A man, then, without spiritual life, is, in the eyes of God, without life. The man who is spiritually dead feels no true need of the Lord's Day, and gets along very well with the world's rest and play-day, just as he gets along without prayer, the reading of the Word, or any meditation upon God.

We have now said all we have to say concerning the relation of the worldling to the Lord's Day; and it all applies equally to men of every profession or occupation. We come now to the Christian, and his relation to his Lord and Master's day. He has been born again, born from above, and has a new life in him, — a life which proceeds from God, and depends entirely upon God ; a spiritual life which must be sustained by spiritual food. To the Christian the reading of the Word is extremely important, prayer an absolute necessity, since, without communion with God, he would be, in the simile of the Lord himself, a branch cut off to wither.

The needs of most Christians keep them busily occupied during six days of the week, and make the public services and private devotions of the Lord's Day of the greatest importance to them for growth in the knowledge of God, and power over sin. This need, however, is very different in different classes. For the clergyman, the Lord's Day is the busiest and most taxing, so that many give Saturday or Monday to rest and relaxation. Thus their physical and mental side is refreshed, while the very character of their whole work tends to keep in fullest exercise their spiritual life.

The Christian physician can rarely secure for himself the full benefit of the public services of the day : still, as he goes from place to place in his daily visits, he has much time for meditation, and his opportunities for spiritual work at the bedside of the sick and dying are second only to those of the clergyman.

To the Christian lawyer in large practice, the Lord's

Day is a greater blessing. The strain upon him is very great and continuous throughout the week-day, his faculties being often taxed to their fullest ability. Still his cases vary very much, so that his brain gets some relief even while it works. Then, too, his interest, however intense in any case, lasts only while it is in progress, nor does the result affect him personally; so that, when he has done what he can, he simply dismisses the subject, and clears his mind for the next case.

But, of all classes in the community who live by brain-work, the merchant is he who finds the greatest difficulty in laying aside the thought and care of his occupation.

It is intense, continuous, absorbing, anxious. Each separate venture has a direct effect upon the welfare of himself and family. Unlike the lawyer, the result is personal in every case; one day full of hope in the prospect of a successful venture, on the next alarmed at a probable loss. No venture is closed with the day or the week: a continuous interest runs through the whole year.

There is nothing necessarily elevating in an occupation which has for its direct object the making of money. On the contrary, the trials and temptations of the calling are peculiar and very great. We frequently hear of business honor as though it were something different from personal honor. There are men who would be very careful of what they said or did in other relations of life, who seem to have a different standard for business-transactions. The old adage, "All is fair in love and war," is accepted as the standard for commercial transactions; and under the name of sharpness, or even the softer name of smartness, statements are made, and bargains struck, which would not bear strict scrutiny. It was said to me a few days ago, of a man who stands high in the church, that you could not depend on what he said, but, if he put his name to paper, you might depend upon that: in other words, his bond was

good, but not his word.   Pre-eminently does the Christian
merchant need all the safeguards of religion to protect
him from evil.

But, great as are the dangers which beset the merchant,
it no more follows that he should cheat than that the lawyer should lie.   There is no proper calling that the Christian may not follow with perfect honor ; and, whatever his
calling, he should in it be pre-eminent for every virtue.
There are glorious living examples of merchants whose
business is as much consecrated to God as the study of the
clergyman, and whose lives are as completely devoted to
his service.   Such a man is George Williams of London,
the founder of the Young Men's Christian Association,
whose whole life has been one continuous work for the
Master ; and Samuel Morley, M.P., of London, who, doing
an enormous business, and employing a great number of
men, is himself head of a Christian Association among
them, attends their meetings, and encourages them to aid
him in conducting a mission school and chapel in the
neighborhood of his warehouse.   It is said of a Christian
merchant in a neighboring city, that every young man
who has come into his employ has been converted to God,
one of them saying to him, "I cannot be each day with
you without seeing that you love Jesus ; and I want also
to love him."   Do not such instances make the Christian
who employs numbers realize his great power for good,
and therefore the great responsibility that rests upon him ?
and he that employs but few, that he may bring each one
of them by his personal love to Christ ?   But there are
other reasons why the Christian merchant needs every
spiritual help.

He is "a city set upon a hill," and is watched carefully
and critically ; and he must avoid even the appearance of
evil.

Then, every Christian is exposed, as is no other man, to

the especial attacks of Satan.   St. Paul says, "We wrestle not with flesh and blood, but with wicked spirits in high places."   However careless our great enemy may be with reference to those who have not become Christians, and have no drawings Christward, he is very much in earnest to prevent any man coming to Christ, and equally earnest to overthrow him when a Christian, and so separate him from God, or at least prevent his good influence upon others.   Is it not an indication of this, that so many Christian men have become defaulters?   The slightest departure from honesty is quickly seen by the Christian's great adversary, and every means is used to tempt him lower and lower, till he falls.   Should it be a matter of surprise to us, that, when the Christian merchant begins to tamper with sin, his danger is much greater than that of the worldling?   It is positive gain to Satan, that the ungodly man should be successful in his business, and honored by the world.   How often is the ungodly moral man pointed out as an evidence that a man does not need religion to be a good man! and, sad to say, a comparison is sometimes made between him and the Christian, not at all to the advantage of the latter.   So also is it gain to Satan, that the Christian should become a stumbling-block to others, either by becoming wedded to money, or else dishonest, and so enable him and his followers to exult in his fall.   Truly the Christian merchant needs every spiritual help he can get.   The Apostle Paul's words come to him with peculiar fitness, — "Put on the whole armor of God, that ye may be able to stand against the wiles of the Devil."

The Christian merchant needs great knowledge of the promises of God, which are to be found only in the Word; and much prayer and communing with God, to enable him to appropriate and rest in those promises.   To him the Lord's Day should come in the fulness of blessing.   Whatever it may be to others, to him it is all-important. He is so much in the world on six days that he should live in heaven on the seventh. The Christian merchant should transact his business in *partnership* with God; and his Divine Partner will keep him from all tricks of the trade. There are those of whom this is true, and upon such an one it will not be needful to urge the blessedness of the Lord's Day. It will be the oasis to which his thoughts will travel in advance. While he works with the gladness and quietness which is given by the continuous sense of God's presence, he will yet haste to escape from his cash-book and ledger to the joys of the Lord's Day. His letters will remain in the post-office from Saturday till Monday; and no Sunday newspaper will enter his house to turn his thoughts business-ward, and interfere with the communion of his home and of his God. There is no such symbol of heaven as the Christian home on the Lord's Day. Blessed indeed is that home where every tender earthly tie is strengthened and purified, because Christ has come into the heart, and enlarged its capacity. The man of the world, much as he may love his home, knows but little of the wealth of the capacity of loving with which Jesus enriches his children. Blessed Christian home, where this wealth of love dwells in every heart, each to each, and all to Him! The gate is not ajar there, but open wide.

But, besides the responsibilities of the Christian mer-chant to himself and family, he has those which belong to him in his public capacity. Of these some have been already mentioned.

First, That he should be an example, in all his business-dealings, of the highest possible honor. No shadow of doubt should rest upon his reputation.

Second, His personal influence should be used upon his employés to lead them to his Master. This influence of an employer is very great.

Third, He should have nothing whatever to do with his business on the Lord's Day. His letters and the Sunday newspaper must be let alone. He will find it difficult enough, even then, to keep business out of his thoughts. In fact, the expulsive power of the love of Christ alone can do it. This love must be cultivated by loving communion.

Fourth, He should use all his influence to put safeguards about the Lord's Day. Times are much changed with us ; and everywhere throughout the land the effort is being made to lessen its restrictions, and open new places of amusement.

The man of the world is quite consistent with himself when he advocates the open public library, the Sunday museum, and the Sunday concert ; but the Christian, to be equally consistent with his conviction that the day is given especially as a religious blessing, — must set himself against every thing that tends to draw men away from the public and private worship of God. He must protest against, and resist, every encroachment upon the sanctity of the Lord's Day.

Let me here say a few words with regard to the merchant's connection with Sunday in its *external* aspect, in which I shall consider the day not so much as promotive of the salvation and spiritual well-being of himself and his fellow-men, as in the general effect upon the physical, moral, and social condition of citizens and communities. Merchants are observant ; and they have not failed to notice and to testify to the effects, in mercantile affairs, of regarding and disregarding the Lord's Day.

The following cases which I quote are entirely from a little book, entitled "Church and State," and written by the Rev. W. C. Wood, the secretary of this convention : —

"A merchant, who for twenty years did a vast amount of business, said, ' Had it not been for the sabbath, I have no doubt I should have been a maniac long ago.' This was mentioned in a company of merchants, when one of them remarked, ' That is exactly the case of Mr. ——. He used to say that the sabbath was the best day in the week to plan successful voyages. He has been in the insane-asylum for years, and will probably die there.'

" An old gentleman in Boston said, ' Men do not gain any thing by working on the sabbath. I can recollect men who, when I was a boy, used to load their vessels down on Long Wharf, and keep men at work from morning to night on the sabbath day; but they have come to nothing, their children have come to nothing. Depend upon it, men do not gain any thing in the end by working on the sabbath.'

" Amos Lawrence, his son tells us, wrote to the agent of a manufactory in which he was largely interested : ' We must make a good thing out of this establishment, unless you ruin us by working on Sundays. Nothing but works of necessity should be done in holy time; and I am a firm believer in the doctrine that a blessing will more surely follow those exertions which are made with reference to our religious obligations, than those made without such reference. The more you can impress your people with a sense of religious obligation, the better they will serve you.'

" In 1829 the merchant-princes of Boston, New York, and other cities, were among the foremost in urging the petitions against Sunday mails and mail-trains. Among the names appear those of Thomas H. Perkins, Robert G. Shaw, Peter C. Brooks, Samuel Appleton, Edward Tuckerman, Israel Thorndike, Amos and Abbott Lawrence, John Tappan, and William Ropes. Twenty-five years ago, London presented a memorial to the government against Sunday mails. This memorial is headed by Baring Brothers & Co., and is as follows : —

DECLARATION.

" ' We, the undersigned, being strongly impressed with a belief that there exists no greater necessity to justify the transaction of the ordinary business of receiving and delivering letters on Sunday in any of the post-offices of the United Kingdom, than in those of the metropolis, do hereby earnestly request her Majesty's government to take into immediate consideration the expediency and propriety of causing the same to be discontinued by ordering the post-offices in the country to be altogether closed on that day. This belief is founded on the following facts : —

" ' 1. That the metropolis, containing a population of twenty-two hundred thousand, has never experienced any necessity for the opening of the metropolitan post-offices on Sunday.

"'2. That the great acceleration which has recently taken place in the postal communications throughout the Empire must necessarily diminish to a very great extent any inconvenience which it might otherwise be supposed would arise from closing the provincial post-offices on Sunday. And, believing that the effectual preservation of the seventh day of rest from their ordinary labor is a principle of vital importance to the physical and social well-being of society, whilst the due observance of the Lord's Day is a duty of solemn obligation upon all classes of the community, we agree to take such measures as may appear best calculated to press the foregoing considerations on the attention of the government and the legislature.'

" Similar declarations were signed by other leading mercantile firms, the principal surgeons and solicitors, and the aldermen of London."

Our own merchants have spoken in the past : let those of the present day realize their own great opportunity and responsibility in this matter, and do all that they can to secure the blessings of the Lord's Day by the cessation of all Sunday work of whatsoever kind. When we consider the large number of merchants in our great cities, their character for intelligence, capacity, and enterprise, the vast amount of property which they represent, the immense power which this wealth yields, can we gauge too highly their immense responsibility ?

The managers of the great trunk-lines assure us they will gladly stop their Sunday trains, *for they do not pay*, if merchants do not force them by such orders as the following : A merchant telegraphs, " I forward forty cases, which will reach you on Saturday night. Deliver them in such a place on Monday morning." It is evident where much of this blame of Sunday railroading belongs. If our merchants were to take the stand which they should in the matter of Sunday freights, mails, and mail-delivery, the evil would cease at once, and God, who made his day to be a blessing, would richly bless them and their business.

Where we may, we must legislate. Where we may not, we must at least, as we do here in this convention, let the voice of the Church in this Commonwealth be clearly heard in behalf of a sanctified Lord's Day.

THE SABBATH THE POOR MAN'S BENEFACTOR.

BY REV. EDWIN B. WEBB, D.D., OF BOSTON.

As the vast majority of the human race are, and always have been, and probably always will be, poor, this topic is one of no ordinary interest. However theoretical or speculative other topics, this is altogether practical, real, and present, commending itself to the great mass of mankind.

I. *And, first of all, the sabbath is the poor man's benefactor because it brings him needed rest.* . . . It has been demonstrated too often to need repetition here, that all men — all the world's great weary toiling masses — must have a weekly as well as a daily rest.

But the hardest work done in this world is not the work of the hands. The mind is most to be considered. And in regard to the mind the testimony of physicians is this : "From neglecting proper intervals of rest, the vascular excitement of the brain, which always accompanies activity of mind, has never time to subside ; and a restless irritability of temper and disposition comes on, attended with sleeplessness and anxiety, for which no external cause can be assigned." "If this fatigue and over-excited condition of the brain be not speedily arrested, it soon terminates, according to the constitution or circumstances of the individual case, in derangement, palsy, apoplexy, fever, suicide, or permanent weakness." Do those men who work the year round without a rest, and boast that their best work is done on the sabbath, know what the peril of this work is ? — "derangement, palsy, apoplexy, fever, suicide, imbecility ! "

Such is the testimony of the highest medical authority concerning the absolute necessity for rest, — rest weekly as well as rest daily. And the authority, the institution, the Lawgiver, that provides this needed rest, is a benefactor. The sabbath, set apart and established and made sacred by the Creator's repeated commands, — the sabbath urged upon man by the constitutional necessities of his nature, as well as by the weight of infinite authority, — furnishes this needed rest ; and therefore the sabbath is the benefactor of mankind, and especially the poor man's benefactor.

The poor man's benefactor especially. For the rich man may rest when he chooses, may have many holidays ; but the poor man, compelled by the necessities of his position to labor six days in the week, must welcome the sabbath as his special boon and blessing. And how rich the benefaction ! The love of a Father for his children is in the appointment of this day ; the wisdom and skill of the Good Physician are in the appointment of this day ; the wisdom and good-will of the best human government are in it ; mercy and the means of redemption are in it ; the reflection and resemblance of heaven's sweet rest and joy are in it. Welcome ! — let all tongues join in saying — welcome the beneficent rest of the sabbath !

Only let the conviction be distinctly and indelibly engraven upon all minds, that the sabbath, to give this essential and universal rest, must be accepted as of universal obligation. Instituted at the birth of the race, before men were divided into nations ; having its reasons in necessities peculiar to none, but common to all ; designed for the benefit of mankind, — the sabbath must be received and kept by all, in order that it may be enjoyed by any. This is a consideration that must not be overlooked, and cannot well be overstated. And, that it may be kept and enjoyed by all, the day must be accepted as an appointment of

God, and not merely as a necessity learned from human experience ; as a command of God, and not as an optional good ; as binding the conscience, and not merely as a better means to health and prosperity. The nature of the obligation to keep the sabbath is such that the appointment of the day merely as a civil law can hardly be maintained. The higher ground of divine authority being ample and indestructible, it is better — as it is indispensable — to rest the appointment of the sabbath on that. For such are the complications of society, such the immediate interests of individuals, such the greed of selfishness, such the reckless eagerness of passion and pleasure, that, unless recognized as of divine authority, the keeping of the sabbath becomes a matter of individual interest or taste, or judgment or prejudice. Suppose the divine authority to be withdrawn, or ignored, or denied, by the majority : then, notwithstanding the constitutional necessity for rest, the keeping of the day becomes optional. Become optional, work and play are sure to be chosen by some. And if one city opens its concerts and theatres on the sabbath, then all cities will open concerts and theatres. If one furnishing-store opens "for accommodation," all furnishing-stores must open ; and the army of clerks and porters must plod on seven days a week, the year round — "seven days a week for six days' wages !" If one factory rings its bell to summon the weary workers on sabbath morning as on other days, all factories must, in time, do the same thing. If one company run horse-cars on the sabbath to the forest beer-garden, all rival companies must run ; and all conductors and drivers must work, or lose their places. All gravitate towards the same level.

It is the sabbath, therefore, as established and maintained by the divine authority, of universal obligation, securing to all perpetual renewal of strength, vigor, and freshness, which is God's benefaction and blessing upon the poor.

II. *Secondly, the sabbath is the poor man's benefactor because it furnishes him with the means of mental enrichment and elevation.*

Every thing depends upon the mind. Leave the mind barren and puerile, and nothing goes well : make the mind strong and rich, and every thing goes well. The poor man's promotion in life does not come of indolence or error, but of mind, developed and disciplined. There must be the plant in the head before the increase in the hand. Many benevolent efforts are made, many co-operative societies formed, for the poor man's benefit. These must be commended as in many ways helpful. But, for the most part, they are superficial and delusive. They attempt to make the fruit good without first making the tree good.

The poor may be divided roughly into two classes, — the vandal poor and the virtuous poor. Both have a benefactor in the Christian sabbath ; the one class in the means of mental revolution and advancement, the other in the means of mental nourishment and growth.

A family which has never known the sabbath has coarse tastes, low affinities, and minds barren of thoughts of God and immortality. Put them into a house, five years ago the home of the refined in the court end of the town, and how long before all traces of its former elegance are obliterated ? There is vandalism in the mind ; and the sabbath furnishes just the means, the best, the most efficient, the divinely-appointed means, of eradicating it, and at the same time of supplying new thoughts and new themes and a new life. It is good to give a poor man a house and grounds, but vastly better to give him mind and purpose to earn and maintain a house and grounds. You may toss a sick eagle into the air; but give him health, and he will himself ride above the clouds, and look the sun in the face. The rich man may give every day to study and culture. The poor man can give only his sabbaths. His sabbaths, accepted and used according to God's design, furnish him with the needed intellectual revolution, refinement, and wealth. Vandalism cannot live in one who accepts and uses the sabbath aright.

The sabbath is also the benefactor of the virtuous poor. Its frequent, regular recurrence, like a celestial visitor, tells of higher spheres and loftier spirits, and has a mighty power to sustain and nourish noble principles and holy aspirations, and presents the motives which buoy a man up above the cold, ingulfing waters of poverty. Look into our New-England parishes : what numbers of young men come forth from the homes of the virtuous poor to become leading merchants, bankers, professors, lawyers, ministers, and missionaries! As Dr. Spring says, "Many a sleeping genius, reposing within the curtains of its own unconscious powers, has been awakened to hope and action by the instructions of the sanctuary. It were a curious but not unprofitable inquiry to institute, how many well-educated men, in Christian lands, have received the first impulse and suggestion in their lofty career from the instructions of the sabbath." And why not? The growing of an oak from an acorn, in moisture and sunshine, is not more natural than the development of mind in the religious keeping of the sabbath.

The mind enlarges towards the proportions of the themes which it dwells upon. And what themes the sabbath presents for contemplation and study!—the majesty and manifold perfections of the Creator ; the principles, rewards, and penalties of the divine government ; the relations of this life, checkered with smiles and tears, and rent with antagonisms, to the life unseen and everlasting ; the dark consciousness of sin, and the hope inspired by the remedy of the gospel, — ah! what themes! themes to arouse every latent energy of thought ; truths by which the soul is seized in a grasp from which it cannot fly, and with which it wrestles, and grows strong while wrestling. Nothing develops, quickens, enlarges, and enriches the human mind, like the subjects of thought that the sabbath brings with it. And, as the poor man is limited to this as his only rest and opportunity, so, in this respect, in giving a day for mental development and vigor in the contemplation of the most divine and enlivening themes, the sabbath is the poor man's benefactor.

III. *The sabbath is the poor man's benefactor because it gives him moral invigoration and elevation.*

All history and all experience testify that such are man's inward susceptibilities and lusts, and outward temptations, that, unrestrained, he gravitates to the earth, and becomes earthy. In the wilderness, in the mines, on the sea, he needs the society that is fashioned and vitalized by the law of the sabbath to keep him up. Crowd the sabbath out of our homes, and all vices will come in ; one like a thief, to steal your jewels ; another, like a plague, to destroy bloom and beauty ; another, like famine, to consume your substance ; another, like a mocking fiend, to sneer at piety and defy the Almighty. Exclude the sabbath, and over the cemetery's gate will be written, " Death is an eternal sleep ; " the churches will become theatres and arenas where the blood of gladiators and wild beasts will flow for the entertainment of the people.

Moral principle is the foundation of all family life, good neighborhood, and just government. But, just as your best fruit-trees degenerate, so the moral principle runs down. Every individual, every community, needs the regular, frequent, and powerful appliances of a moral education. The conscience must be invigorated, and the sources of the whole moral nature must be constantly renewed. The sabbath, spent as God designed it should be, just meets this necessity. Other men might possibly com-

pensate for the loss of it by devoting some portion of the
week to the study of ethics and religion; but the poor
man has no other adequate time for the education of
his moral nature. The most perfect system of ethics —
by confession of the infidel even — is taught every sabbath day in our churches. The moral teaching of the
ancient philosophers is a muddy pool, compared with the
pure fountain of the gospel. And the Christian sabbath
is for the unfolding and applying of this perfect morality.

Moreover, the sabbath presents the conditions most
favorable in all respects, for impressing, arousing, and
enthroning the moral sense. These moral instructions
come regularly at a time of rest; they are given on a
day that has twined around it, for most men, tender and
sacred associations; they are given in a reverent assembly
made up of families, and friends, and neighbors; and they
are given with clearness and with frequency. As a vigorous and comprehensive writer said, many years ago, "In
order to give public conscience a quick, discerning eye,
and to pour upon it the only steady and unerring light,
that of divine truth, the fixed and eternal distinctions between moral and religious right and wrong are clearly and
strongly defined; and not only in the case of those which
are broad and palpable, but also in the case of those which
are minute and delicate, so that men, if they will, may
walk with safety through even those regions of action
where the separating grounds between right and wrong
are most narrow and difficult."

And still further, this morality, so essential to the individual character, and to the continued prosperity of every
country, is taught rationally; the boundless evils of wrong-
doing are portrayed in lurid light, and the benefits of right-
doing affectionately spread out; and, besides all this, the
teachings of the sabbath are presented as under the eye of
a holy, heart-searching God, and sanctioned, as no other

teachings are, by the unutterable solemnities and retribu-
tions of a coming judgment-day.

It seems safe to say, therefore, that as the means of enlightening, invigorating, and confirming the moral nature,
the sabbath is the poor man's benefactor. God's wisdom
and beneficence are in the appointment of the day : God's
blessings are upon the keeping of it. Mental and moral
superiority is the inheritance of the people who remember
the sabbath day to keep it holy. They shall ride upon the
high places of the earth.

IV. *Again, the sabbath is the poor man's benefactor because it brings before him the pattern of a right and perfect
life.*   .   .   .   .

The sabbath, by bringing before us the Lord of the
sabbath, the quickening central thought and theme of
the Christian sanctuary, gives to the poor man what all the
treasures of wealth, and of art, and of learning, and of
experience cannot give him, — the true ideal, aim, and
end of life.

V. *The sabbath is the poor man's benefactor because it
brings before him the true principles and relations of right
living ; in other words, the true idea of human society.*

This proposition implies, as all that goes before implies,
that the sabbath is a day for religious instruction and worship. If the routine of ordinary work be sponged from
the day, and the sabbath be left a blank, — a day of idleness, — then is it a curse, and not a blessing. If the sabbath is that the pleasure-seeker may multiply his pleasures,
and the good liver prolong his dinners, then I am dumb.
Or, if the sabbath is that the Frenchman may dance his
bears, or the great showman manœuvre his circus, and
excursionists throng the cars and boats and beaches, then
I am no advocate of a sabbath : the day is a lowering, and
not an uplifting, of society. Better a night of labor than

of debauchery; better the work-day than such a sabbath. The beneficent sabbath is that which is given to religious instruction and worship. This is the day which, with its rest and elevation, its acknowledgment of duties and relations, brings the true principles and pattern of human society. The kingdom of heaven, as introduced by the Lord of the sabbath, is the ideal of the perfect social condition. "Thy will be done on earth as it is in heaven," is the goal of all true aim and right progress. "Love thy neighbor as thyself," is the divine specific for the highest, happiest, human society.

That poor men, the world over, are dissatisfied, restless, and ready for something, — they know not what, — there is too much evidence. The German army did not burn Paris; but a band of her own citizens, organized, and aspiring to be the government, saturated the palaces and public buildings with petroleum-oil, and fired them for inevitable destruction. Their object was to destroy every trace and memorial of previous government, to equalize all classes in the community, distribute property, and organize society anew! But what is the new society to be? After what pattern, and on what principles, is it to be organized?

Only two years ago, — in the summer of 1877, — the workmen, fed out of the earnings of our great railways, seized the property, tore up the rails, burned the cars, freight-houses, and stations, and crippled the engines. The men intrusted with the safety and success of the roads, acting the part of traitors and robbers, assumed to make right and exercise control over the courts and the commonwealth. Well, suppose these men triumph, and divide the property. Then what? Of course, revolutionize all forms of law and justice. Then what? Organize society anew. But on what basis? after what rules and pattern? Grant that something is wrong in the present condition of society; grant that this restless, violent, imperious feeling of communistic organizations is provoked by sore and protracted grievances: are destruction, arson, and murder going to secure any thing better? The world over, he that sows the wind must reap the whirlwind!

The same spirit of destruction and terror, and frenzy to control, is seen in other countries, smothered and kept down for the present, but ready apparently to break forth any hour. How Russia grapples with the burning, remorseless Nihilism of her unhappy millions! Germany, too, has her half-concealed orders, whose presence and purpose are flashed from the pistol that was loaded in secret for Chancellor Bismarck or Emperor William. In every country are secret organizations, trades-unions, societies, that, Samson-like, blindly grasp at the columns and heave at the foundations of the structure whose fall inevitably involves their own ruin. Our mines, too, have their Molly Maguires, and our cities their operatives who refuse to work except for the price their agent may dictate, and declare it death for others to take their places. The Pacific coast, with its working-men's combinations, and factions, and revenges, shows us what uncertain ground may be beneath our feet. But what is the aim of all these restless, revolutionary measures? What would these poor men come at? How many of them have any idea of the first simple principles of social prosperity and happiness, which the history of communities and nations indorses as right, and safe, and good? Suppose capital is despotic: is labor, combined and concentrated, a despotism less cruel and arbitrary? Does opposing wrong with wrong afford that satisfaction and repose which are the conditions of prosperity, and that security which is essential to the enjoyment of one's labor? Society has wants unsatisfied; but feeding men as paupers, or forcing them into places for which they have no qualification, will not fill the land with plenty. Society is afflicted with manifold evils, divided by conflicting, selfish interests, torn with suspicion, jealousy, and discord. Peace and prosperity are not to come of brute force and blind sortie. By what means are these evils and troubles to be avoided or overcome? By what means, individual or combined, is the true, happy ideal to be obtained? This is the question to be answered by the restless, imperious, revolutionary spirit that is showing itself in Nihilism, Communism, Socialism, and Unionism.

Who has the answer? Where shall they go for it? To the Christian sabbath and the Christian sanctuary. Jesus has taught poor men the prayer to be offered, — the prayer that springs from depths that all our philosophy is too shallow to fathom, and rises to heights and memories known only to Him, — "Thy kingdom come ; thy will be done on earth as it is in heaven." And one great part of the sabbath service is to show men how this will is done in heaven, and how it may be done on earth, that thus the face of earth may reflect the happiness of heaven. Jesus has left us the germs and elemental forces that must enter into every settled, happy, human society. The kingdom which he came to establish is charged with vital powers which are to turn the world upside down : and the sabbath is essential to the development and spreading of these seminal, spiritual forces. The telegraphic instrument makes available the hidden electrical forces of nature for the service of mankind. The sabbath is to the transcendent forces of Christianity what that instrument is to the hidden forces of the material world, — the means of making available on human society all the gracious and vitalizing powers of the kingdom of heaven. It surpasses all other means of benefiting the human race. It is the divinely-appointed instrument of communication.

Consult experience and history. What is the great

enemy of human society? Mutual hostility. But the new society which the Lord of the sabbath places before us is a society organized in love. What is the fiery ambition of men, wasting and imbittering life? To rise above and subdue each other. But the Lord of the sabbath says, "Whosoever will be great among you shall be your minister; and whosoever of you will be the chiefest, shall be servant of all." Men overreach each other, but the Lord of the sabbath says, "Exact no more than is appointed you." Men make false representations, and unite in arrogant combinations, and force each other to give more and take less than is due; but the Lord of the sabbath says, "Do violence to no man; and be content with your wages."

Vice, too, — dishonesty, duplicity, idleness, intemperance, lewdness, — is the enemy of society. These impoverish the rich, enfeeble the strong, and eat out every noble element of manhood. But against these vices the Lord of the sabbath repeatedly utters his condemnation, backed by infinite authority and sanction of law.

Some people imagine we have the means of arresting all these evils, and of attaining a perfect society, in open libraries and art-galleries, colleges and schools. But Liddon, in a Bampton Lecture, says, "When Greek thought was keenest, and Greek art most triumphantly creative, . . . Greek society was penetrated through and through by an invisible enemy, more fatal in its ravages to thought, to art, to freedom, than the sword of any Persian or Macedonian foe." All the wonderful art and oratory of Greece could not give them the society which they craved, nor even preserve what they had. Nor will schools of art and education give to the rising nations of to-day the society they crave. They must come to the Lord of the sabbath.

Others think that society is to be perfected, relieved

of its evils, enriched with virtues, by the organization of lodges and guilds, and charitable associations. But the brightest ray of excellence in any one of these is only the reflection of a common ray in the perfect society which the Lord of the sabbath has introduced. Oppressed, worn out with toil, disheartened, the poor man may find a little sympathy and cheer in these organizations. But the instinct of the soul unsatisfied reaches out after something better. The ear still longs for the true sound : the eye wanders around the horizon for the divine model, for that society in which all animosities, evils, and vices are suppressed, and all virtues and graces and affections nurtured ; a society organized in love and not in hate, in mutual helpfulness, not in rivalry ; a society operated in the spirit of benevolence, not in the spirit of selfishness ; a society where every one is aiming to minister unto others, and not demanding to be ministered unto : this is the divine pattern, the pattern towards which the sabbath urges and contributes as does no other institution. Jesus is the perfect pattern for the individual ; and his kingdom, as he introduced it, the model of a perfect, happy, human society. Whatever is needful to stimulate industry, and satisfy aspiration, is here. Whatever is needful to preserve the good, and still evolve the better, is here. Just in proportion as a community is leavened with the divine leaven of sabbath teaching, fashioned after that pattern of society which the sabbath, kept holy to the end of it, tends to create, is it happy, peaceful, and prosperous. And the sabbath is the day for the poor man to study this perfect model, while, with his neighbors and fellow-Christians, he goes up to pray, " Thy kingdom come ; thy will be done on earth as in heaven," and learns to love his neighbor as himself.

And the urgent work for the Church as regards poor men, the world over, in things temporal as well as spiritual, is to give them the Christian sabbath, and the words of wisdom and love spoken by the Lord of the sabbath.

> "Blessings abound where'er he reigns :
> The prisoner leaps to loose his chains;
> The weary find eternal rest,
> And all the sons of want are blest."

ADDRESSES.

THE SUBJECTS, WITH ONE OR TWO EXCEPTIONS, WERE OF THE
SPEAKERS' OWN CHOOSING. THE ADDRESSES ARE GIVEN
ONLY IN THEIR SUBSTANCE.

THE SABBATH NOT GONE, AND NOT GOING.

BY REV. A. H. PLUMB.

MR. PRESIDENT, — If this Sabbath Convention appear
like a council of war, it is a council of the victorious leaders of a conquering King. It ought to be the keynote
of this meeting, it ought to be the courageous thought
of all Christians, that *the Lord's Day is not gone, and the
Lord's Day is not going.*

One good reason for cherishing that thought is that we
still have *the mighty power of Christian example in keeping
the sabbath holy to the Lord.*

Seven thousand who have not bowed the knee to Baal?
Millions upon millions, everywhere, who hail the return of
the sabbath with joy, and keep it a holy day.

In a recent tour through the West, I visited regions
with which I was familiar a score of years ago; and even
a casual observation revealed a cheering growth of certain
forms of aggressive Christian work. I saw an enlarged
and increasingly intelligent attention paid to sabbath-
school instruction, to young men's Christian associations,
and to various departments of Christian work in which
women are engaged.

384

I remarked with great interest, that, in places where the Bible and the sabbath were formerly in considerable disrepute among leading men, now many enterprising and successful men of business, bankers, merchants, and others, are active in sabbath schools : they go to the institute at Chautauqua, and talk about it in their circles of influence.

A few days since in a distant city I followed reverently to his grave an honored friend, sixty years a member of one church, sixty years an occupant of one pew. There he brought his youthful bride ; there in later years their children, one after another, gave themselves to Christ ; there some of them have been given in marriage ; and there in that pew almost every sabbath all the while sat that man, his head becoming silvered with age ; and at last it was the devout men of that church carried him to his burial. Three thousand sabbaths he lifted up his testimony for the sanctity of the day. Such an example of steadfastness is an inspiration.

Far away in the North-west I met a gentleman of wealth and culture, a graduate of an Eastern college, residing on the borders of a wilderness on account of his large landed interests near ; and, as often as the sabbath returns, he and his accomplished wife gather with their neighbors, a dozen or a score, some of them in the rudest attire, in a rough little schoolhouse in the bushes, and there, opening the Bible with song and prayer, they seek with all the solemnity and earnestness in their power to worship God. It is the habit of their lives. Just so they did when Sunday came in Philadelphia, in Paris, wherever they have lived. Such example, men reverence : they cannot help it.

What is culture worth, what are all the blessings of a high civilization worth, if they do not first of all inspire in a man some sense of obligation to God ? — a sense that will lead him, wherever the sabbath finds him, to lift up the banner of allegiance to God, to go to church, and to go not so much for what he is to get, as for what he is to give, — tribute to God. "Let my prayer be set forth before thee as incense, and the lifting-up of my hands as the evening sacrifice."

Friends, are we not almost tired to death of the listless, lifeless, vapid spirit of much of our modern culture? Everywhere around us we have young men and women, called the fairest products of our civilization, easy-going, cultivated, full of æsthetic knowledge, very amiable and pleasant companions, but with no grasp of spiritual truth: they hold no great spiritual verities; and as a consequence there are no surges of spiritual life agitating their breasts, no system or principle in ordering their conduct with reference to the divine authority, no regularity in Christian worship; a great deal of capacity to sneer at the infelicities of the old-fashioned worship of the Puritans, but no capacity to understand or appreciate the simplest obligations of a creature to its Maker.

Of this sort of culture we have a right to be tired. There is no inspiration in it. It is a relief to turn from it to men of another class, to men who have some "pulp and brawn" in their moral nature, to men of symmetrical development; and there are multitudes of them all over the land to-day, who are recognizing their obligation to God, and rejoicing in the institution of the sabbath. They are happy that it calls them, as often as it returns, into relations of confidence and sympathy with their Saviour and their King. To them the sabbath is dear. When it comes to them, they cry, —

> " Sweet day, thine hours too soon will cease;
> But, while they gently roll,
> Breathe, heavenly Spirit, source of peace,
> A sabbath to my soul."

And that example is contagious and inspiring : it will prevail. "The Lord's day therefore is not gone, is not going."

I argue this, again, from *the providential dealings of God.* They are on the side of the sabbath.

When crime increases with frightful rapidity; when a race of tramps is hard to handle; when communism will not down, with all our incantations of popular suffrage and free schools and a free press, — men say, "What shall we do? where shall we look for some power to lay this dreadful spirit we have conjured up, but cannot manage, that grinds us with taxes, and threatens all we hold dear?"

Good friends, you need a little moral principle in the community; and you are finding out you cannot have it, when you blot out religious sanctions, by robbing the world of its sabbath, and by nailing up the doors of the sanctuary of God. God is writing these lessons in letters of fire and blood; and they are easy to read, and plain to understand.

Even our liberal friends, so called, are taking alarm.

· A few sabbaths ago, Rev. Robert Collyer, in assuming the charge of the Church of the Messiah in New York, took for his opening sermon the text, "I was glad when they said unto me, 'Let us go into the house of the Lord.'" That was the very word too, he announced, that he left as his parting charge with the Church of the Unity in Chicago.

"A wise and gracious friend" there, he said, remarked to him after church, "'I wish you had preached that sermon twenty years ago, instead of the one I remember you did preach, in which you told us we might worship God better perhaps in the woods or meadows, or in our own homes, sometimes, than in the sanctuary.'" "I remember saying to myself," said this gracious friend of the preacher, "We do not need such exhortation. We are ready enough to stay at home, or wander about the world. Our minister has no idea how glad we are to hear such

doctrine." The minister himself confesses, "I had no idea
how easy it was for the men and women of our free
thought and free ways to drift from the service of the
sanctuary." He quotes those who say, "There is no need
for me to go into the house of the Lord. I have outgrown all that, and am now my own temple and my own
priest." He asks, "What do you really do in the woods,
and on the waters, and in your own homes, and what does
it all come to?" "The drift" of it all, he says, is "to slay
faith, and to touch with paralysis the nerve of any grand
endeavor." "Few and far between," he thinks, are those
who can withstand its baleful power; "while, with multitudes whom no man can number, this own temple and
own priest business is merely seeming, and the dumb
things that run and fly worship God more truly than they
do." He adds, "There is one God of such things, and his
name is the one they got from their godfathers and god-
mothers; one supreme service, and you spell it with four
letters, s-e-l-f; one grand purpose here, and that is to look
after the first person singular; and one thing to which
they look forward when they get to the end, and that is a
leap in the dark."

Mr. Collyer quotes the remark of Rev. Dr. Bellows,
which has been going the rounds of the papers, "I never
knew one man, or woman, who steadily neglected the
house of prayer, and the worship of God on the Lord's
Day, who habitually neglected it, and had a theory by
which it was neglected, who did not come to grief, and
bring others to grief."

Herbert Spencer, after doing his best to destroy religious faith, seems alarmed lest he leave the world without
any authority in morals, and comes hurriedly up, therefore, just now, with a new book on ethics, anticipating its
order in the series of his volumes, he says, because of the
urgent need. The need is urgent, in so far as his per-

nicious influence has prevailed ; but his new book is a mere straw to restrain the flood of immorality which his denial of the authority of a personal God has let loose to ravage the earth.

Professor Goldwin Smith says, in "The Atlantic Monthly," "If religious faith has gone," — as he strangely thinks it has, because in certain narrow circles abroad it has disappeared, — "then morality has gone too ; for, in the past, without religious sanctions men have never been able to live under a government of law." You may add to that, that without the religious sanctions of the Bible, without God's positive institutions of the sabbath and the sanctuary, men have never been able to live under a free government.

Our people go travelling in Europe, and come back in love with foreign customs, and want to bring them in on us here. They say, "People get along very well over there without the sabbath." But they do not have universal suffrage over there. The free institutions we live under are born of the New Testament, and they depend on the power of that book to make them a success. Just as soon, and in so far, as you lessen the power of the Lord Jesus Christ in the land by taking away the sabbath and the sanctuary, and those functions of the ministry and the church which are indispensable to the prevalence of the Christian religion, you lessen every moral restraint, — you imperil every thing in society that you and I value, and without which we would not consent to live in the land at all.

The old argument, that Robert Hall states in his sermon on modern infidelity, never has been answered. "In vain," he says, "may the infidel expatiate to a vicious person on the advantages of a virtuous life. He will reply, 'My tastes are of a different sort. There are other gratifications I value more. Every man must choose his own pleasures ;' and the argument is at an end."

Washington, you remember, says, " Reason and experience both forbid us to expect that national morality can prevail in exclusion of religious principles. In vain would that man claim the tribute of patriotism, who should labor to subvert these great pillars of human happiness, these firmest props of the duties of men and citizens." That man does labor to subvert these essential supports of society, who attacks or neglects the holy day of God.

Once more : The Lord's Day is not gone, and is not going, for *all power is given unto Christ.*

I have not been so encouraged and uplifted in a long while, in regard to the anxieties which oppress the Christian heart, as in perusing the sermon of President Magoun, before the American Board at Syracuse, the other day, on the words of our Lord, " All power is given unto me."

Oh, friends ! could God give us a glimpse of that day when the power of the Lord Jesus shall prevail, when men of standing and of power, whose pernicious examples have been quoted in the past, shall come out as his loyal representatives, honoring his name, we should rejoice in anticipation of the happy hour.

When Gen. Grant was in France two years ago, Marshal McMahon invited him to attend the public races on a sabbath afternoon, and the American ex-President declined — thanks be to God !

The American idea of the sabbath is a priceless inheritance. Why should we pluck from our brow the fair diadem which God has given to us as a Christian nation, and cast it under our feet, in order that we may put on the badge of shame which the effete nationalities of the old world wear ?

God in his mercy has honored this nation in its past observance of the sabbath ; and his power is still displayed here in developing men of influence and of public worth, who honor and reverence his holy day.

And yet, all the while, many of God's own children are made to tremble for the future of the sabbath, because so many men of public station and influence disregard it.

Here was Mr. Sumner. We have had our great men, — men who have done noble service, whose names will always live in grateful recollection. But, because a man has rendered eminent public service in certain ways, is every thing he does a public service? If he has his public diplomatic dinners regularly on the sabbath day, are we therefore to think the holy day of God can be trampled under foot by any man at will? Who is Charles Sumner, and what is his example worth, as a guide to men who can read God's word, and can see the course of his providence, and, above all, can hear the approaching footsteps of the King of kings, coming to reign over all the earth? Under the advancing power of Christ are coming, in place of some of our great men to whom we too readily bow, men of more eloquence, of more culture, of more breadth of view, greater statesmen, greater men in literature, men of larger grasp in all the high ranges of thought, and greater because of their loyalty to Christ, because of the uplifting force of his grace on all their powers ; and these men will hallow his holy day. I seem to hear the tread of those advancing hosts of the mighty men of God. I see them springing into life all along the future, near and far ; rising up to bless the world, and to pay homage to Christ, " King of kings, and Lord of lords." Thanks be to him that his promise has gone forth, that "the greatness of the kingdom under the whole heaven shall be given unto the people of the saints of the Most High, and all dominions shall serve and obey him ! "

A friend, in prayer-meeting the other evening, said, that, at the Profile House at the White Mountains this summer, they had their sabbath-evening worship in the parlors ; and once a group, standing around the office, were

noticing the people pass in to worship God, when one of
the group sneeringly said, "That will do for those who
don't know any better."—"I don't know any better,"
said a fine-looking man, walking in. Who does know any
better? Is it a mark of broad culture, of wise comprehen-
sion, for a man to think he knows better than to reverence God, and keep his holy day? In the great future
that is coming, the strong, stalwart men will look back,
and despise not only those men of eminence in our day
who failed to honor the sabbath, but will despise still more
the weak people of God, who were carried away by their
bad example, who thought all power of guidance was
given to the little great men, or the one-sided great men,
of their times, and forgot the boundless power of Him
whose name is above every name.

At his call, one day, "sweet sabbath morn" shall come
to all the earth. It shall find the populations of the globe
assembled in their sanctuaries, worshipping in the name
of Christ; and from "high tower and lowly dwelling" one
universal hymn of praise and thanksgiving shall go up, in
acknowledgment of his power to save.

"THE CUNARD LINE'S SABBATH POLICY."

BY REV. LEWIS B. BATES, OF EAST BOSTON.

It is my good fortune to live in the Island Ward, where
steamers come from over the sea, and where they take
their departure, and, during the two or three years past,
freighted as never before; and I am happy to say, sir, that
the Cunard line is managed, so far as we can see, according to our faith in the sabbath. It is owned in England

chiefly, and managed chiefly by Englishmen. They arrive on Saturday sometimes with an expensive cargo, but sabbath morning all is quiet on board of their steamers, in their docks, and in their warehouses. Such is their management universally. If they arrive sabbath morning, the passengers go on shore; but all work is suspended on the sabbath. The other lines, I am sorry to say, have not pursued this course; and yet it is strange, in their judgment, that they have made no quicker passages, they have been no more successful in carrying freight or passengers, than this line that has respected the sabbath day.

At certain seasons of the year, in the Island Ward, you might have witnessed strange scenes. A certain railroad, owned in part by the State, has done as much perhaps to break the sabbath as the steamers, if not more. Long freight-trains have been thundering by, the bell and the whistle sounding incessantly; and the people along the track never would know it was the sabbath from their surroundings. But, after the call for this Convention was issued last spring, these large steamers, some of them, would arrive Saturday afternoon, and commence to unload. Sunday morning all hands would be there ready to discharge, and a fine-looking man in blue would walk on board, and hand a document to the officer in command; and he would read it, and say, "All business must be suspended;" and it was suspended. It is very convenient for a certain railroad in this city to land within a mile or less of the wharf a thousand cattle Saturday night, and then — as a matter of mercy — load them Sunday, and send them away Sunday night. And a certain gentleman who has considerable to do in the freight department, and especially in the management of cattle, said that there was one ship that the officer in blue could not stop. A few weeks ago this ship arrived, — the largest ship afloat that carries cargoes, the largest ship aside from "The Great Eastern" that does float, — and on sabbath morning all preparations were being made for her discharge. Two gentlemen in blue walked on board, — one, I suppose, to keep up the courage of the other, — and passed a paper to the officer. There were about a hundred men all ready, with coats off and sleeves rolled up, to commence to discharge. But the officer in command said, "You must suspend : this is sabbath in America, as sure as you are alive;" and the work was suspended, and the great ship lay there all day quietly, and the hard-working men went home, and some of them went to church, for I saw them in the evening; and at the close of the meeting they said, "Who did this?" Well, I could not tell them, for I didn't know. I don't know now ; I don't know whether it was the mayor of the city, or the chief of police, or the governor of the Common-wealth : all I know is, it was done — thank God! I think the impulse that caused it was the call for this Conven-tion. The good people in office began to think there was really something going to be done.

I hope, sir, that this good work will continue, and I think, from the spirit of this Convention, that it will. I believe to-day, sir, that Christian ministers and Christian members of the church hold this matter in their hands in this old Commonwealth of Massachusetts. We may have quiet and peace in this old State to-day if we will. I think, such is our moral power, that these excursions which have been referred to may all be quieted. Such is our moral power, a power that shall go out from the minis-try and the church and the better class of citizens of this Commonwealth, that we may say to this steamboat-propri-etor and to these railroad-stockholders, "You are chartered to run six days in the week, and not on the seventh;" and they shall feel this, and feeling it they shall yield to the claims of God.

God bless this Convention!

WHAT IS SABBATH-KEEPING?

BY REV. WILLIAM BARROWS, D.D., OF READING.

RULES for Sabbath-keeping are formed from one's theory concerning the Sabbath.   There are four theories : —

I. *The Natural Sabbath,* whose basis is in the physical and mental constitution, which needs rest and recuperation.   No moral element is implied in it, and no uniformity of laws or of observance is possible.

II. *The Judaic Sabbath,* the theory of which makes it begin and end with Judaism.

III. *The Ecclesiastical Sabbath;* which is, that Christianity did not inherit the Sabbath from Old-Testament ministrations, nor did Christ or his apostles intend to establish or transmit such an institution ; but among the early Church fathers sprung up a kind of Sabbath, out of the necessities of the case and times.   The first day of the week became, on the example of the Apostles, a festal sacred day, commemorative of the resurrection, and finally a day for Christian worship and teaching.

IV. *The New-England Sabbath.*   Men educated under it, and seeing its fruits, wherever New-England influences have gone, have assumed its basis variously, and defended it more or less logically, always earnestly.

They find it instituted in creation, put in statute for mankind at Sinai, and inherited and imposed, as the other nine commandments, by Christianity.   They assign to it a physical, mental, and moral basis, demanded by our laws of being, with physical, mental, and moral health in view. Rewards and penalties are attached to its observance, and these are involuntary and inevitable.   But it is held to be permanently a moral institution, having place among the ordinary moralities. A glow and ardor for its perpetuity and defence come up grandly out of its history ; and the dissecting-knife of logic, cleaving joints and muscles asunder to discover the sources of its life and force, may not add to its power over the community. It is an institution wrapped up in its spirit rather than in its letter.

The Protestant Church is divided over these four theories ; and devoutest men, bishops, ecclesiastical antiquaries, scholars, and every-day Christians, are advocates of each. Yet all unite in saying, "Remember the Sabbath day." To perpetuate the day and its glorious fruits, our wisdom and strength lie in the union of sentiment, without insisting on a union of reasons.

As to definitions, rules, and regulations on Sabbath-keeping, only general statements can be made with harmony, in the present status of the subject.

1. *A schedule for Sabbath-keeping can be neither very inclusive nor very exclusive.* Principles and spirit must be expected to rule, rather than laws.

2. *Physical rest should be provided for by a cessation of ordinary business.* Yet our argument for the Sabbath must not lean very hard on this point. Doubtless, as a whole, a grand pause should be made in worldly activities, as there was of creative activities when "God rested from all his work."

3. *Intellectual labor, as a business, should be suspended.* Nature calls for this. Mentally, as well as physically, the working-man is a seven-day clock, and needs the winding-up.

4. *The ulterior aim and end of Sabbath-keeping must be regarded as moral and spiritual.* So far as God makes its end manifest, at creation, or Sinai, or in the outgrowths of the Christian dispensation, this is it : the spiritual part of man, the immortal side, demands this

day. For reflection and instruction on the better part of one's being, for attention to the higher and nobler social relations of life, and for intimations and for preparations concerning the momentous hereafter, the Sabbath is made for man. There are other obligations and rights and issues connected with the day, but the spiritual is prior, fundamental, and supreme.

THE SABBATH AND THE CHILDREN.

BY REV. ASA BULLARD, OF CAMBRIDGE.

THE words of our Saviour are, "The sabbath was made for man." That, of course, includes the children. There is no system of religion, but that of the Bible, that makes the good of the young a specific and prominent object.

I think the sabbath can be made, and should be made, the "day of all the week the best." It should be a day ever welcome to the children. There should be no such unpleasant restrictions and restraints, no such exacting requirements, as will make the thought of an eternal sabbath in heaven unwelcome to the child. That was a sad state of things that made a little boy dread the thought of going to heaven, where his grandfather had gone, because "Grandfather will always be saying 'Tut, tut!' to me, whatever I do;" and that was a sad state of things when a little girl said she did not want to honor her father and mother, because the Bible said her days would be *long;* and her sabbaths now, with all the requirements made of her, and the restrictions imposed upon her, were so long that it almost wearied the poor child's life out of her. I have no doubt that in Puritan times, and perhaps at the present day, there are many families in which there are restrictions and requirements very unwise, and very unhappy in their influence upon the minds of the young. Yet, I repeat it, I believe the sabbath may be made a welcome day, — a day that the children will delight to have return ; such a day that they will be prepared to enter into its services, and find it one of the most delightful of the week.

What children need, in order to make them contented and happy, is employment. Every one knows that a hammer and a nail, a knife and a few pieces of wood, will make a boy contented, day in and day out, rain or shine ; and that a needle and thread, and a few pieces of cloth to make patchwork and to dress her dolls, will make a little girl contented and happy, day in and day out.

But would you give such things to children on the sabbath ? Well, no, not exactly ; but I would put into their hands those things that would occupy their attention, that would gratify them, and that would be associated with the sabbath as a holy day. I may say in regard to my own practice, a large number of Scripture illustrated cards were purchased, and a large number of blocks with religious engravings were put into their hands, only to be used on the sabbath day, never to be seen except on that day. The consequence was, the sabbath always came to them as a day of delight, giving them employment and much instruction. There is no end, at the present day, of those beautiful cards, dissected maps, and all kinds of similar things to interest the young. Games — Scripture games — too. "Games," you say, "for the sabbath day !" Well, that is rather an unfortunate word. However, these "games " lead the children to study the Bible ; and for hours they will be interested in learning a great deal of Scripture and all those things which relate to Scripture objects, scenes, events, and characters. I know that many children have a very shrewd way of doing a great many things with these games, — if you please to call them so, — as older people do on the sabbath day. A great many people think it is right for them to read all they find in a religious news-paper, — about politics and every thing, — because it is in a religious paper. Now, many of these boys and girls will show their shrewdness in this way : —

Two little boys were using their Scripture blocks, mak-ing all kinds of objects, erecting their little houses ; and by and by the elder one said to the younger, "You must not build houses on the sabbath day."

"But *you* are building a house."

"Well," said he, "I am going to put a steeple on mine, and it is right for me to make a meeting-house on the sab-bath."

Then again they were playing keeping store, when the elder said, "It is not proper to keep store on the sabbath day."

"But *you* are keeping store."

"Oh, I am keeping an apothecary-shop."

I would make one more suggestion. Teach children from early childhood to attend public worship. We have come upon a time when children have done with their habits of going to church on the sabbath : they attend the sabbath school, and then they go home, and spend their time in the ways I have mentioned, or in sleeping or play-ing or walking. Now, I would not, for the life of me, lose the association of going to church with our father and mother, and our large, old-fashioned Puritan family of ten children. What an inspiration for a minister to look over a congregation, and see households present, father and mother and four or five children !

They say the children cannot understand the preach-ing : they understand a great deal more than we think they do. A little girl in Cambridge went to church one day when the minister preached on the passage: "Thou hast left thy first love." Monday morning, father and mother got into some sort of a dispute — I don't know whether it amounted to what is now called an unpleasantness, or not; but it was so much of a dispute, that, after the father had left the house, the little girl said, "Mother, you must not forget what the minister said yesterday, about leaving your first love." A great many children are receiving instruction on the sabbath day, which they will call up in after-life.

Now, if there was no other thing that I could say here or anywhere else, I would say to all fathers and mothers: Take your children with you to the sanctuary. There is nobody and nothing in this world that has a right to stand between parents and children; and then after that there is nothing that has any right to stand between the minister and the children, — no sabbath school or any thing else. I would not hesitate to say to any father or mother or child: If you cannot go but to one service, go to church, whatever becomes of the sabbath school.

But can it be that the children cannot go to the sabbath school and one service at least on the sabbath day? Take them to the church, and the minister will be interested in them. They say the minister won't preach to them: why should he preach if they are not there? Let him see the pews filled up with the children, and I venture to say that either in his prayer, or in something, he will so direct the service that the children will remember his instruction. We are training up a whole generation of non-church-goers; and if these children and youth are trained up now not to attend church, when they get to an older age they will not be seen in the church. May God help us to revive the old plan of households going to the house of God on the sabbath day!

SUNDAY OBSERVANCE IN NEW YORK AND IN EUROPE.

BY REV. W. W. ATTERBURY, SECRETARY OF THE NEW YORK SABBATH COMMITTEE.

I HAVE been asked to say a word in respect to the practical question, What has been done in New York City, within the past few years, towards the enforcement of the Sunday law? A little more than twenty years ago, attention was called to the increasing Sunday desecration, and the alarming amount of disorder and crime connected with it. Some previous efforts at Sunday reform had been injudiciously managed, and had resulted in evil rather than good. The government of the city at that time was in the hands of a party who pandered to the prejudices of the lowest class of the people. Large numbers of immigrants of the lower classes were pouring into the city, — the better classes going to the West, — whose influence was to turn Sunday into a noisy holiday. Numerous low-class theatres were opened on Sunday night, offering attractions of free admittance to females and a very low charge for young men, with such plays as you might expect in such places, and with the selling of liquor in the auditorium. Military and society funerals, target excursions, and other processions were accustomed to parade the streets with bands of music. Liquor-shops plied their traffic without restraint, and the noisy cries of newsboys were heard throughout the city. In this state of things it was thought that something should be done; and so a large number of gentlemen came together, and concluded to organize an association for the purpose of suppressing this evil, if possible. They selected about twenty gentlemen, — laymen, men well known in the community, representing the different walks of business life as well as different religious interests, — to act as the hand and the voice of the Christian constituency who agreed to stand behind them, to supply the means, and to sustain them in every way in which they needed to be sustained. This committee went to work, in the first place, to investigate the facts in the case, and then deliberately took up one evil after another, and sought to suppress the evil.

For instance, there was the nuisance of newsboys vociferously crying their papers from one end of the city to the other, right in front of our churches and homes. Nobody seemed to think the evil could be suppressed. The committee went to work, and through the papers called attention to the matter; and by and by people began to feel that this was an evil that should be stopped, — that there was no reason why the quiet of Sunday should be disturbed by this noisy outcry. Nothing was said against the selling of the papers, but it was against the noisy selling of them. After a little while, public sentiment having been properly aroused, the police went to work, and put the thing down, and it has staid down ever since. Sometimes it springs up for a little time; but, on proper complaint to the police, the evil is easily suppressed, and we are substantially free from this annoyance.

Then they went to work at the Sunday theatres. It was found that the old Sunday law would not meet the evil, so a special law was prepared and enacted at Albany. This law was enforced: certain parties litigated it, and the question was carried up to a higher court, where the law was sustained, and it has been enforced ever since. We do not have any theatres open in New York on Sunday even-

ing, and have not had for fifteen or sixteen years, except
as occasionally the law is broken, when the proper punishment is inflicted. This theatre-law does not forbid concerts ; it was found impracticable to get the law through
with that word in it : so the word was left out, and in
many of our theatrical buildings there are concerts in the
evening ; but they are not in costume and accompanied
with all the stage arrangements : they are simply concerts,
and are not allowed to step beyond that. Theatrical and
similar performances are prohibited.

Then attention was turned to the enforcement of the
liquor-law on Sunday. This has always been found the
most difficult thing to deal with in our great city. We
have always had law on the subject, but it has been difficult to enforce the law. However, during three years,
from 1867 to 1870, it is an important historical fact which
no subsequent failures can obliterate, we had a liquor-law
that was enforced in New York. Before that time a law
prohibited the selling of liquor with pains and penalties ;
but it was not enforced, and the licenses from liquor-
shops in the city of New York for years before had
averaged only some twelve to fifteen thousand dollars a
year. In 1866 a law was passed, called the Metropolitan
Excise Law, that was enforced for three years, and it was
made the interest of the better class of liquor-dealers to
see that every man paid his license, and that the law was
enforced. The result of it was that for three years we
had revenue from licenses in the city of New York of *one
million dollars* a year. The arrests for disorder and
drunkenness, which had always been twenty-five per cent
more on Sunday than on Tuesday, — as an average week-
day, — at once decreased, and became *forty per cent less*
on Sunday than on Tuesday. That law continued in
force until the *régime* of Mr. Tweed, when it was repealed
and the city put under the State law ; and, although we

have had a semblance of the enforcement of the law ever since, it is only partially enforced. But the outward, glaring display of the traffic is restricted; and, if there is any disturbance or nuisance in any particular instance of the traffic, it can be suppressed even under the present imperfect administration of the law.

Then we had another evil to contend with, — the Sunday processions. It was a violation of the laws of good neighborhood for bands of music to pass right up and down before our churches and homes, creating a disturbance. It was not simply that they played for funerals, but on their return they would play lively airs, and were followed by a noisy rabble of idle men and boys. The police were powerless to resist the evil. But by and by there came that trouble in New York, when there was a fight over the Orange parade on a week-day; and this, with some other difficulties of a similar sort, made people feel that it was quite time to put restraint on processions in our streets. The Sabbath Committee had been waiting for this opportunity, and they said, Now is our time. They secured the enactment of a law which put processions on weekdays under the control of the police, and which prohibited all processions with music on Sunday in New York, except in the case of *bonâ-fide* military funerals while escorting the body. That law has been enforced impartially ever since; and all classes, except a few who always want to have their own way and hate all Sunday restraints, agree as to the excellence of the law.

Various other sources of Sunday disturbance have engaged from time to time the attention of the committee. Often these have been abated by private remonstrance, without appeal to the officers of the law. Meanwhile vigilant attention has been paid to the course of legislation at Albany, so that any unfavorable measures may be met with timely resistance.

Some of the principles upon which the committee have always sought to work may be noted. One of these principles is to make the distinction clear between the civil sabbath and the religious sabbath. From the start the Sabbath Committee emphasized this point, — that you cannot make men religious by law, and that you must avoid seeming to enforce the religious observance of the day by the authority of the secular law.

Another principle of the Sabbath Committee has always been this, — to avoid entangling alliances. Keep the Sunday issue distinct from every other. Do not mix it up with the temperance question, or with the question of the Bible in the public schools. Let the issue stand by itself, so that you may get the very largest number of persons to co-operate with you. Here is a question where men who differ on other subjects may stand together. The Protestant and the Roman Catholic, the Lutheran and the strictest Puritan, have alike an interest in maintaining our Sunday law ; they will all stand with us in endeavoring to secure that to which every good citizen has a right, — rest on the sabbath day, and enjoyment of its quiet.

Then, again, the committee have aimed never to undertake an issue until the people were prepared for it, until there was good reason to believe that the object could be reached. It has been felt that it is never wise to run one's head against a wall ; but, if a thing be obviously impracticable, it is better to let it alone until, in the good providence of God, the way be opened to accomplish it. The Sabbath Committee have always recognized the controlling power of public sentiment ; and they would never take a step until they had gone to work deliberately, week after week, and sometimes month after month, before taking the step, to prepare the way by enlightening and arousing public sentiment. Much use has been made of the press. The documents of the committee have been widely circulated, and by these as well as by public addresses, sermons, &c., much has been done to móuld public opinion.

Furthermore, the committee have sought to work as far as possible through the constituted authorities, and have avoided giving to their own agency needless prominence.

On such principles as these, — taking one step at a time, advancing wisely, patiently, discreetly, and yet with courage, — the Sabbath Committee have done a quiet but most important work. When you remember that there are, in the city of New York, five hundred thousand foreigners, sixty thousand or more Jews who do not keep the first day of the week, and a transient population of travellers, sailors, &c., estimated at thirty thousand, it is encouraging that the sabbath is as well observed as it is.

For a few years past, there has been a growing interest in the question of Sunday observance, on the Continent of Europe. In Germany many of the prominent pastors have felt the vital need of a more religious observance of the day, and are actively engaged in promoting it; and the supreme church council of Prussia, and several of the provincial synods, have earnestly taken up the matter. The Reformed Church assemblies of Bohemia and Hungary have recently called attention to the same subject. In the Roman Catholic Church, in France and to some extent in Belgium and elsewhere, there exists a similar movement; and a religious association formed for this purpose a few years ago received the special benediction of Pope Pius IX. The lately deceased bishops Dupanloup, of Orleans, and Bataillé, of Amiens, advocated the cause with great earnestness and ability.

Societies have been formed in nearly every country of Europe for promoting the secular and civil as well as the religious observance of Sunday. The Social-Democrats of

Germany, at their Gotha Conference in 1877, affirmed as one of their principles, the suspension of work on Sunday to be assured by the State. The subject has been brought up in the German Imperial Parliament. In Switzerland, where the lead has been taken in these movements, some important ameliorations have been made by the government in the Sunday employment of officials.

In 1876 an International Confederation was formed, with headquarters at Geneva, for the purpose of combining and encouraging national and local efforts in favor of the observance of Sunday, which, while resting on the basis of the divine obligation of the Lord's Day, welcomes the co-operation of all who will aid in promoting its practical ends. The confederation has received assurance of the approval and sympathy of the Emperor of Germany, the Duke of Baden, and many others prominent both in Church and State. It held an important congress at Bern, in September, 1879, attended by upwards of three hundred delegates, representing nearly every nation on the Continent, as well as Great Britain and the United States.

REWARDS OF SABBATH-KEEPING.

BY HON. WILLIAM E. DODGE OF NEW YORK.

SOME forty years ago I was bound to New Orleans on a hasty and important mercantile trip. I had been riding three days, day and night, in the stage. The stage was full, and on Saturday, as we approached evening, I said to my fellow-travellers, "What a blessed thing that we have the sabbath to-morrow!"—"Well," said one, "wouldn't it be! but I am so situated that I must go on. I wish I could rest; but I can't." I found from the driver that at about eight o'clock in the evening we should reach La Grange, Ga. I said, "Let me out there." When we arrived, I took my valise, and went into the hotel. It was a very small hotel; but I slept soundly. The sabbath morning was beautiful. At the breakfast-table there were none but the landlord and three children. I asked the children, "Have you a sabbath school?" — "Oh, yes, sir! we are hurrying to get through to go." — "Will you let me go with you?" — "Yes, sir; certainly." They led the way, and crossed a beautiful little park to an academy in a grove, where I found, to my astonishment, a large sabbath school. The children went in, and I sat down by the door, an entire stranger. I was superintendent of a sabbath school in New York. The superintendent, seeing me, came and said, "Stranger, there is a Bible-class of young men from the academy; their teacher is sick to-day. Will you teach them?" There were eight or ten fine-looking young men, and I had a pleasant time with them. The superintendent came and said to me, "Stranger, where do you come from?" — "I am from New York." — "Now look here," said he, "we have just started a sabbath school here, a union school. We are Baptists, Methodists, and Presbyterians. We never had a sabbath school here until now. Now won't you talk to the teachers and scholars?" So, in my plain way, I undertook to talk to the children. Then the school was dismissed, and we went towards the church, where I heard an excellent plain sermon. There were three or four churches on the green; and, as I came out, quite to my astonishment and pleasure, one of my customers — forgotten that I had a customer in La Grange — came up to me, and said, "Why, Mr. Dodge, where did you come from?" and he introduced me to three or four gentlemen, and one gentleman said, "Now don't go back to that hotel: come and take dinner

with me." While we were eating dinner, in came three
gentlemen, among them the principal of the large academy,—a brother of the Rev. Dr. Beman of Troy,—and they
said, "We want you to talk to the people in the church
this afternoon. We will give up the services in the other
churches, and attend this." The church was as large as
this, and in front were about sixty of the young men from
Mr. Beman's academy, and then the children of the school
filled up nearly the rest of the centre; and the galleries and sides were crowded full. I spoke to them for half
an hour. In the evening, they said they had just started
a teachers' meeting, and they wished me to come to the
teachers' meeting. I went, and we had a good talk together. I went home, and slept well, and rose on a delightful morning. I had to run the risk of the stage being
full. Well, when I came out to go, there were some
twenty or thirty of the citizens of La Grange to bid me
good-by. I had come a perfect stranger, but they were
waiting to see me off. The stage came, and I got my
seat; and on I went travelling that day and night. Next
morning we reached a little railroad built out from Montgomery, Ala., where we were to take the steamer for
Mobile. As I got on the train I was anxious, and said
to the conductor, "Is there any boat down the river
to-day?"—"Two went down yesterday," he said: "there
won't be another until Thursday."—"Well," I said to
myself, "it has always turned out well when I have tried
to spend the sabbath right." We arrived in Montgomery.
As the train stopped, a man sung out, "Any passengers
for the boat? It is just off." The best of the two boats
had waited to take in a hundred bales of cotton, and they
concluded to await the train. In ten minutes we were
going down the river. The next day we overtook the
other boat at a wooding-place, and there were my friends
who had rode with me in the stage, and could not stop

over Sunday, waiting there on board that boat ; and, our boat being the faster, we got into Mobile one day ahead.

A few years after that, before the days of steamships, I was on my way to Liverpool in one of the largest ships that ever sailed out of New York. We had a twenty-four days' passage to the mouth of the Channel, and there we rested : there was not wind enough to carry us farther. There came out from old Kinsale a pilot-boat ; there was just a little breath of air sufficient to move the little boat with its large sails. I was anxious to stop at Cork, to see Father Mathew ; and quite a number of us made an arrangement to get on the pilot-boat, and go on to old Kinsale, and thence through the country. Well, soon after we left the ship, we found there wasn't wind enough for the boat, even ; and, just as we got under the head of Kinsale, the tide began to run out swiftly, — for it rises there thirty feet, — and we had to lie under the head of Kinsale all night, a terrible night too. Next day was the sabbath. The sun rose beautiful, and about seven we ran in with the tide to the little village of Kinsale. We were all tired ; many of our friends had been sick during the night, and it so happened that each one of them had a most pressing excuse to go on. Some of them had never travelled on the sabbath at all, but they were so situated that they must go on ; and particularly one lady who had come out in charge of two girls ten or twelve years of age, and she was very anxious indeed to keep on travelling. A gentleman and his wife from New York, Mrs. Dodge and myself, were all that remained. We had nice rooms in a little bit of a hotel, where we changed our clothing, and washed ourselves, and got breakfast. We went to a beautiful little church, and had a delightful service. After service, the young preacher, seeing us there as strangers, made us welcome ; and we attended service again in the afternoon. On Monday morning, as the coach came up, we found this young clergyman was to be our companion to Cork; and he said, "Now get up on top of the stage: I know all the country, and will show you every thing." We had a beautiful ride of two days and two nights. But the second day, about ten o'clock, we stopped at one of the principal stage-villages, and there on the platform stood every one of our poor passengers that had come along with us. There they stood; and that poor woman with her two little children. They had travelled day and night, and they had got tired, and waited for this stage to come along; but there wasn't a seat in the stage, and we left them there all forlorn!

"In the keeping of His commandments there is great reward."

THE SABBATH IN FOREIGN MISSIONS.

BY REV. N. G. CLARK, D.D., OF BOSTON, SECRETARY OF THE AMERICAN BOARD OF COMMISSIONERS FOR FOREIGN MISSIONS.

WE should have very little hope of success in the missionary enterprise, without the Christian sabbath. It is needed for the proper education of those who are brought out from the darkness of ignorance and superstition into the knowledge of the truth. Errors of every sort must be cleared away. Traditions ingrained into the very life of the people can only be eradicated by the most patient instruction, and new principles of life introduced. Hence, everywhere, as a missionary principle, the strict observance of the sabbath is carefully taught.

Some very striking examples of fidelity to sabbath observance, and the happy results which have followed, may be cited from mission-fields. Some years ago the Queen of Madagascar was informed by representatives of two European powers that they would do themselves the honor to call upon her on the following sabbath. The queen acknowledged the intended courtesy, and politely informed those gentlemen — representatives of Christian governments — that she observed the sabbath, and could not receive them on that day, but on the day following. It was quite in keeping with such a character, that, instead of preserving the forms of royal state in her intercourse with her people, she was found by Dr. Mullens, on his visit to Madagascar, in attendance upon a public-school exhibition, distributing prizes to the best scholars. In explanation of her course, she remarked, " I love God, and I love Jesus Christ, and therefore I care for the education of my people." The remarkable success which has attended missionary effort in that island finds one of its explanations in these incidents. Of hardly less significance is sabbath observance in our own New England. Amid the rush of many interests, absorbing our time and thought, we need the quiet of the sabbath to deepen and broaden our religious life, as much, perhaps, in New England as in Madagascar.

RIGHT SABBATH LAWS A NECESSITY.

BY REV. O. P. GIFFORD OF BOSTON.

" Law is the embodiment of the moral sense of a community on any subject." And our duty to our fellows demands that our moral sense on this Sunday matter be embodied in law. Law cannot give life ; but it can guard life, and give it a chance to develop. Fences about trees will not hasten growth, but will keep the cattle off.

The Sunday sentiment should be crystallized into Sunday laws, that shall protect men against their own ignorance, the avarice of individuals, and the greed of corporations.

Law cannot force men to worship; but it can provide rest, and the privilege of worship. Law cannot say what men shall do; but it may say what they shall *not* do. It cannot force them into churches and Sunday schools; but it can shut them out of beer-gardens and horse-races, and keep them from harbor-excursions.

Law can and ought to guard conductors and drivers, so that they can rest Sunday without risking their places on the horse-cars. It ought to limit the running of horse-cars to certain hours, and diminish rather than multiply cars on Sunday, and, so far as possible, prohibit the running of horse-cars at all on Sunday.

Law ought to prohibit all excursions down the harbor Sundays; ought to shut all the dram and tobacco shops, and three-fourths of the drug-shops, and all that retail liquor for other than medicinal purposes upon prescription.

Law ought to prohibit the sale of Sunday newspapers: first, because they are a source of profits to the publishers, and in common with all business should cease Sunday; second, because the reading of them lowers the tone of public morals by interfering with rest of the brain, and filling the mind with unhealthful mental food; third, because the sale of them is educating a class of boys to be Sunday-breakers, and thus fitting them to be poor citizens by and by.

The laws that shut the doors of trade in dry goods, groceries, &c., and allow excursions, and traffic in liquors, tobacco, and newspapers, discriminate in favor of the less useful and more harmful, restrict necessaries, and legalize luxuries. The moral sentiment of the citizens ought to be embodied in laws that shall express in the State the principles that govern the private life of Christians so successfully, in order that vice may be restrained, good order maintained, and the rising generations educated to perpetuate the institutions so dear to every American heart.

But we want our convictions crystallized into laws, not only for the defence of the present, but still more for the education of the rising generation. The boys in our homes and schools to-day will be men to-morrow; and what kind of men, depends largely on their education in the State by the laws on the statute-books.

Henry Clay once said in the United-States Senate, "What the law declares to be property, *is* property;" and the declarations of the State in the form of law educate boys to perpetuate the idea in those declarations. The tide along the shore sets its own limit by the sand it shapes into bars; and so the public sentiment of one generation shapes and determines that of the next by the laws it leaves. Laws are the pilled rods that determine character.' Face the rising generation with righteous laws, and the future is secure.

OUR INCREASING MATERIAL PROSPERITY DEMANDS THE SABBATH.

REMARKS BY HON. EDWARD S. TOBEY OF BOSTON.

Two instances have recently come within my own knowledge illustrating the fact that the best men of all denominations are more divided on the subject of the proper observance of the sabbath than on almost any other.

I know an intelligent deacon of one of our oldest churches, who, as well as other members of Orthodox churches, I have heard justify excursions down the harbor on the sabbath. On the other side, a very prominent member of a Unitarian church was one of a party with whom I went down the harbor on a week-day excursion not long ago. As we walked together around Fort Warren, and looked down on the passing steamers, he voluntarily spoke of harbor-excursions on the sabbath. I confess that I was greatly astonished and gratified to find him in perfect accord with myself on that subject. He condemned sabbath excursions in unmeasured terms, with evidence and striking facts to support his opinions as to persons whose first downward step was thus taken.

This convention, and the movement leading to it, comes most opportunely. It was always needed, but never so much as at this particular juncture. The community have been steadily, for the last twenty-five years, drifting unconsciously into the European idea of keeping the sabbath, which some are pleased to call "liberal." Such an increase in immigration as may make it doubly difficult to stem the tide of erroneous public opinion and action in regard to the sabbath has already commenced. A great re-action has taken place in business affairs from the terrible depression we have been through, — a re-action even more rapid than some have anticipated; and our country is on the eve, undoubtedly, of great material prosperity. It therefore requires extraordinary effort to bring the spiritual condition of the people to bear it, and to prevent its naturally demoralizing effect.

Within three days I have conversed with an eminent gentleman from England, familiar with public affairs; and he expressed great apprehension at the present condition of affairs on the Continent of Europe. The elements of disturbance are very active there, and the industrial classes are in a distressed state. That gentleman, a member of Parliament, read a letter in public, recently, from his constituency, in which they alleged that they were starving in England. Such a state of things on the other side of the ocean, in connection with the prosperous state on this side, is sure to stimulate an immigration beyond any thing seen for the last ten years. Therefore it is now especially needful and opportune to disseminate right opinions regarding the sabbath, and to counteract the tendencies which must inevitably come from such a class of population to desecrate it.

The question is, how most effectively to do it. This organization has taken one of the first steps towards it. Let me say that unless we can impress our public teachers, whom we gladly reverence as the ministers of the gospel, with the idea that the church itself must be taught on this subject, that its spiritual condition must be so elevated by teachings on this theme that it will be ready to accept true views, we cannot hope to influence or move the great mass of the community, who have no conscience on the subject. Legislation has been alluded to as one of the methods to guard the sacredness of the sabbath. It suggests the question, Who are to be our legislators? The men who have passed middle life are rapidly passing off the stage. The laws are soon to be made by your sabbath-school scholars. Now they are within the reach of the preacher and the sabbath-school teacher; and if, with the Bible in hand, — and there is more in the Bible on this subject than most people are aware of, — the conscience of the people can be educated, they may safely be trusted to make laws and execute them. But even church-members must be so instructed that they will quite understand and decide whether it is right or wrong to ride for pleasure, for example, on the sabbath, or to go to the post-office, and receive their letters, or put their ships to sea, and indulge in various other practices on the sabbath which, without reflection, seem to them rather harmless, but which are wholly opposed to the *spirit* of Bible instruction on this subject.

I knew a young merchant in this city who thought he might properly drive on Sunday afternoons. He was a conscientious young man, and could not understand why he could not pursue his thoughts and contemplations as well in his carriage as in the house. He tried it. When he returned, a single observation brought that young man to realize his duty with regard to keeping the sabbath. The poor hostler said, when the young man came to the stable, "There is no sabbath for a poor fellow like me." The thought came into the young merchant's mind, "Then I have obliged this man to stand here all day, if perchance I should fancy to ride out for pleasure, that he might serve me, and thereby surrender his sabbath. If it is right for me, it is right for every other man who can command a horse, to do the same thing. This is all wrong: I will never do it again." And he never did.

Again, I recollect another instance in regard to this same young merchant, who then attended an Orthodox church. A good deacon, mild and gentle in his manners, remarked to him, "Don't you think it is rather a poor plan to go from the church directly into the reading-room, and take your letters, and turn your mind so suddenly from subjects peculiar to the sabbath?" Well, he began to think, and at once concluded that it was not right. That young merchant never went again for his letters.

It was the custom then for merchants to put their ships to sea on Sunday; and this same good deacon made a quiet observation, in the form of a question very carefully put, to the young merchant, whether he didn't think it was rather a poor plan to spend the forenoon of the sabbath getting his ships off to sea. The young man was again convinced, and admitted it to be wrong. He never after that sent a ship to sea on the sabbath. These three incidents illustrate what an influence may be exerted in a quiet way by a faithful Christian monitor.

At the seashore, villages have been greatly demoralized by the example and influence of people from the cities, who come there to spend the summer months, and who disregard the sabbath by driving for pleasure and by absence from church. They are church-members, too, many of them.

It is a trite remark, "that the sabbath is the bulwark of free institutions;" but it cannot be repeated too often, especially to those who are coming forward to take the responsibilities of legislation and of guiding our political institutions. This country cannot permanently retain its nationality without a religious observance of the sabbath. No nation can ever maintain a popular form of government unless there is enough of religious principle in the masses to sustain the sabbath and prevent its desecration. Without this our country will descend gradually, as papal countries have, from one form of wickedness to another, until the people can perhaps endure the bull-fight as they do in Spain, and cock-fighting as they do in Mexico on the sabbath. With the foreign population swarming upon us, this must be the inevitable result, unless the Church of 'Christ raises its banner and influence to resist the tide of false ideas on sabbath observance which are rapidly becoming popular.

CO–OPERATION OF FRIENDS OF THE SABBATH.

BY REV. YATES HICKEY OF PHILADELPHIA, SECRETARY INTERNATIONAL
SABBATH ASSOCIATION.

I WANT to give words of encouragement. I have been
among the commercial men of this country a great deal.
I have been in concerted action with managers of railroads
for ten years past in putting infamous literature and the
abominable connected evils off the thoroughfares of this
country. Now, as to the sabbath, among those men who
are denounced as men who care not for the desecration of
the sabbath, there are scores who are just "biting a file"
on that subject; and I believe *there is a rising of moral
sentiment in commercial circles through the increased attention forced upon business men and railroad-managers by the
financial discipline through which we have been passing
these years.*

What are the facts? While these railroad-managers
find it difficult to agree with each other in relation to their
freights, and many things in which their interests clash,
in the abolition of Sunday trains they would, I believe,
honestly and earnestly welcome pressure to bring them
together in efforts to stop running Sunday trains. One
man said, "We should save one-fourth of our expenses
by stopping our Sunday trains." The first vice-president
of the Pennsylvania road said to me, "We want every
wheel stopped on Sunday for financial reasons." An
officer on the Baltimore and Ohio Railroad stated that
every dollar taken in on the middle division of that road
for Sunday traffic cost the company two dollars and a
half. The greatest obstacle to sabbath observance to-

day is the thoughtless habits of Christian people themselves.

Railroad-men know this. Col. Scott knows this; Mr. Vanderbilt knows it; Mr. Jewett knows it; Mr. Garratt knows it. I have been to these men personally, and they have said not one word of discouragement; but, "If only the people will stop demanding of us Sunday traffic, we will gladly see that no wheel shall be turned on Sunday." So we are going to petition Congress to instruct the Postmaster-General to stop making Sunday contracts for carrying the mails, and that would stop hundreds of trains. Then we shall ask the Postmaster-General to discontinue collection and distribution of mail on Sunday; and I think, *if the great city of London can get along without mail-distribution on Sunday, any other place can!*

No local railroad-train runs Sunday in Canada. No canal-work is done: no mail-work in Ontario, Sunday; and they are working for that result in Quebec. They would have no through traffic on their great thoroughfares, but for competition with American lines. When, in one place, some of the people started some local trains, the community came down on those trains, and they had to stop them because it would not pay; the people would not let them pay.

My word in closing is, *The necessity for concert of action, union of effort, and organization to this end, in all parts of our country.* Now, as to knowing where we stand, and what answers to give: I was asked by as high a railroad-official as there is in this country, "What kind of a law are you going to bring on us?" supposing, perhaps, we were coming with a kind of claw-hammer law; but I replied, "The divine law." I had written on one side of a sheet the Commandment, "Remember the sabbath day to keep it holy;" on the other side, God's comment on it; and, as that comment is the only speech I usually make, I repeated it to him : " If thou turn away thy foot from the sabbath, from doing thy pleasure on my holy day, I will cause thee to ride upon the high places of the earth, and feed thee with the heritage of Jacob thy father ; for the mouth of the Lord hath spoken it." Then said I, " Colonel, I think *there are dividends in it.*" Said he, " That is what the stockholders want."

HORSE-CARS AND THE SABBATH.

BY M. FIELD FOWLER, ESQ., OF BOSTON.

THERE has been much said about steamboats and railroads, but little about Sunday horse-cars. You may ask why I am invited to speak on this question. I was one of the original corporators — you might say the projector — of the Metropolitan Railroad in Boston. We applied to the Legislature in 1853 for a charter, and in the same session of the Legislature the people of Cambridge also petitioned for a charter for a road into Boston ; and, to show the change in public sentiment in twenty-six years, the charter of the Cambridge road was opposed by the people there, unless they would insert a clause that the road should not run on Sundays. When the Metropolitan road was first put in operation, we did not run Sundays : we did not suppose the people would tolerate it. We went on some months running week-days. Finally some of the church-going people, good Christians I presume, came to us, and wanted us to run a few cars to accommodate them in going to church. That was the entering-wedge. We put on a few cars to please them, and they were crowded. Of course we could not keep the public from them, and the clamor was for more cars. A distinguished merchant of Boston, who resided at the South End, said to me, "My wife and I waited half an hour last Sunday for a horse-car. You should run more cars." Soon after I met another merchant who said, "Mr. Fowler, if you run your horse-cars Sunday, it is sacrilege, and I go in for taking up your tracks." If we had heeded his opinion, I think we would have been much better off; but the majority favored Sunday horse-cars, and we wanted to please the public; and they ran them in New York, and why shouldn't we in Boston? The result was, we ran our cars Sundays almost as we did on week-days.

This thing went on. Soon I saw some of the evils growing out of this business. In the first place, we had much trouble with our conductors in keeping them honest. It is impossible to get honest men, and keep them so, and make them work on Sundays. You employ them to violate the Fourth Commandment, and expect them to respect the Eighth: you find human nature is such that both conductors and drivers suffer. Drivers become reckless, are not careful; their faculties become blunted, and more accidents result. The managers employed detectives. I remember a young man came to one of the directors, and wanted to know why he was discharged. "Because we think more money goes into your pockets, than comes out." He confessed it; and the reason he gave was, that his driver said, if he would not divide with him, he would put him over the road so that he wouldn't get half as many passengers. In every way it was demoralizing.

Furthermore, as to the horses, what is the result? You work horses every day, year in and year out. Talk about cruelty to animals: why, it is like putting a horse on a treadmill, and keeping him going until he almost drops. The result is, you use up horses in a very short time. Of course some work them harder than others; but I believe

two or three years is considered about the average length
of usefulness of a horse on New York roads, and three or
four here, perhaps. The harder you work them, the more
you have to feed them. The president of one of the horse-
railroads in New York told me he made an experiment, and
decided the thing to his satisfaction. He found, that, on
every thousand horses, it cost them a thousand dollars a
day more to feed them than if they had Sunday to rest in.
People do not understand this. I often hear it said, "You
must have more horses, so as to let them rest." Now,
suppose you employ six hundred horses, and work them
six days in the week. Buy a hundred more, and they
will make up one-seventh. See how that would work.
Suppose your horses, like Balaam's ass, could speak. You
go into your stable Monday, and say, "All those horses
that rested yesterday, we want to work to-day." You find
one hundred that have lain still quite ready, the other six
hundred say, "We have been working seven days." All
you can do is to let another hundred rest, and so the next
day you still have five hundred that have had no rest for
eight days. I am convinced by investigation that the running of horse-cars on Sunday involves the employment of
certainly twenty-five per cent if not more of horses than if
you rest them on that day. Take the omnibuses: they
don't run Sundays. Mr. Hathorne tried it one year, and
he said if kept up it would ruin him. New York omnibuses do not run Sundays; there is no profit in it. The
Philadelphia horse-cars did not run for ten years after they
were started; and I have investigated the subject, and I
have found invariably that those horses that work only six
days in the week earn six hundred and seventy dollars a
year, while the Metropolitan horses, working seven days
in the week, earn only about six hundred and two dollars
a year; and the horses of Philadelphia save all the expenses of conductors and drivers on Sunday.

Mr. Hathorne told me, I think, that his horses in six days will travel from one hundred and twenty to one hundred and thirty miles, while horses worked seven days a week, like the Metropolitan and others, travel only about one hundred miles. You cannot get so much work out of them as when you give them one day to recuperate. What is the average life of a horse? Perhaps few can answer. In 1856 I was at the stables of the Metropolitan road, and the superintendent said to me, "There's a fine horse some gentleman ought to own. It is a pity to put her on the horse-cars, she is so young." — "How old is she?" — "Four years old : she is a nice traveller." I purchased her, and kept her for twenty-two years : she died two years ago from an accident, I think. So she lived to be twenty-six years old. I have heard of horses thirty years old, but you don't find them on the horse-cars.

We know the arguments in favor of horse-cars on Sunday. They say they take people to church, and that is considered a valid argument. Well, perhaps it is, and you might argue that to build churches on Sunday was a good work. But I contend there is no necessity nor exigency to-day that there was not before horse-railroads were established. They bring people in from the suburbs to churches like Trinity and Park Street that do not need their support ; and these out-of-town churches languish for want of these very people who should stay at home. People say — I go to St. Paul's — "How are we to go to St. Paul's Church if you take off the horse-cars?" I say, "If the horse-cars didn't run on Sunday we would have a church as good as St. Paul's in our own neighborhood; but if you must go to St. Paul's I would furnish you a car and horses on condition that you employ your own driver, and pay him ; and I would not charge you a cent. The car might carry you down and back on Sunday." But you say, "You work your horses, then, on Sunday." Suppose we grant the use of twenty horse-cars on Sunday, — that would take forty horses. Those forty horses could lie still next day: forty horses out of two thousand is a trifle.

Now, some say the Fourth Commandment was made for the Jews only, and applied to them only. Well, it says, "Nor thy cattle, nor thy stranger that is within thy gates," — the cattle are put before the stranger even. Now, do you suppose the Almighty intended only the Jews' cattle should rest on Sunday? Didn't he intend the Gentile cattle as well, and all other cattle?

There is one thing you are pretty unanimous in, that running steam-railroads Sunday is an evil. Well, I want to put this to you: Take ten horse-cars, ten conductors, ten drivers, and during the day it takes a hundred horses, and run them fifty miles up and down the streets of Boston; or hitch those horse-cars, and make a train, put on one engineer, one stoker, and one conductor, and take them fifty miles out into the country: which is the lesser evil? The steam-railroad: it saves the horses, and takes comparatively few to run the train. Our friend Mr. Dodge, of New York, said he was sorry that the elevated railroads run Sunday in New York. So am I; but, if they will or must have cars on Sunday in New York, the elevated railroads are the lesser evil, because one dummy on the elevated railroads will do as much work in a day as ten horse-cars, ten drivers, ten conductors, and a hundred horses.

I believe honestly, that, if the horse-railroads here should stop running Sunday, their expenses could be reduced from twenty-five to thirty-three per cent, and they could carry passengers at four and five cents instead of five and six as now, and make just as much money. They tax the people who ride on week-days to support the Sunday travel.

Now, is it right to run Sunday horse-cars? You must

answer for yourselves. But I am amazed to think Episcopalians—and I am one of them—go to church Sunday after Sunday, and in response to the Fourth Commandment say, "Lord, have mercy upon us, and incline our hearts to keep this law," and then go out, and get into a Sunday horse-car.

I have given you the result of my twenty-five years experience and study in connection with horse-railroads,—I am not connected with any of them now, I am thankful,—and I am very glad to see this subject of a sabbath convention taken up in such earnest. Years ago, as soon as the scales fell from my eyes, I went to work in Boston to get up a sabbath committee. We had several meetings: the venerable William Ropes took great interest in it; but it was during the war, and the public mind was too much occupied; and the thing died out. But I am glad to see this movement, and I hope it will go on; and if we all go to work honestly and faithfully, and pray God to help us, some of us will live to see the observance of the sabbath throughout the land.

THE OLD PATHS OF OBEDIENCE TO GOD'S LAWS.

BY REV. S. F. UPHAM, D.D., OF BOSTON.

IF any thing permanent comes out of this convention, there will be a getting-back to the old paths.

I very much like to hear that the law of the sabbath is based in man's necessities; yet I do most fully believe the chief reason why every man and woman who claims to be a Christian should keep the sabbath day is because God has ordained it. There must be a going-back to the old, never-to-be-obsolete book, the Bible ; and because in that book God has said, " Remember the sabbath day to keep it holy," we must keep it holy. I do not subscribe at all to the doctrine that the Fourth Commandment is abrogated. The Fourth Commandment is doubly binding on you and me, because the rest of God our Maker is conjoined with the resurrection of God our Saviour. We must even present this thought to the people, that Sunday is the Christian sabbath ; and that any man who takes down the shutters of his store Sunday morning takes down the curses of God Almighty ; and to run a train of cars on the Lord's Day is to invite a Wollaston disaster.

Now, these are old-fashioned truths, and they smack a little of Puritanism. I wish it would rain Puritanism for a month ! It is high time we got through sneering at the zeal and constancy and faith of our New England fathers. I remember well in my boyhood the Puritan Sunday, and I say it was not to me a dull day, but a day of delight. I was made to go to the house of prayer ; I was made to hear two good square sermons on the Lord's Day : and I am all the better for it.

The pulpit is somewhat responsible for the present state of things. The church ought to be like modern hotels on the European plan, where they have meals at all hours ; in other words, the church of God ought to be open for services all through the Lord's Day. Somebody said here to-day, that no man could preach more than one decent sermon a day.

The fact to be made emphatic is, *God has a law.* There are people in New England, who have got beyond that idea, — a moral kind of people who contend that there is no law that is binding upon them : they are cultured people, they are ; they have been through some of the schools, and they know how to eat with a fork ! and the idea that there is any kind of a law binding upon them, why, it is ridiculous! Now, then, God has a law, a law holy, just, and good, and as eternal as the throne of God; and his law is, that we shall remember the sabbath day to keep it holy.

I knew a man in Chicopee, who had a godly wife, a member of the church; and he was a livery-stable-keeper. His wife used to say to him, "Now, my husband, it is absolutely wicked for you to let horses on Sunday." She didn't say any thing about the financial question at all: she simply said it was wicked. She said that over and over to him, and he would parry the blows. At last, one New Year's morning, it happened to be Sunday, he did not go to the stable as usual; and she said, "What is the matter?"—"Oh, nothing!" he said: "only I made up my mind this morning, that I will try to act on what you have been saying to me. You have told me all these years that it is wicked to let horses on the Lord's Day, because it is the sabbath. Now I am going to try this year: if I fail, I fail; but no horse shall go out of my stable through all the year, on Sunday. Now," said he,—for he told me this story himself,—"I kept God's law as my wife would have me keep it; and the result was, that was the very best year financially I had ever had." *It pays to keep God's law!*

HISTORICAL SKETCH.

BY REV. WILL C. WOOD OF SCITUATE.

THE Massachusetts Sabbath Conventions had their inception in the Evangelical Ministers' Association of Boston and vicinity, familiarly called the "Alliance."

In January, 1879, the Alliance adopted a resolution presented by the secretary, Rev. Will C. Wood, to hold these conventions.

The committee appointed were, Rev. Andrew McKeown, D.D., *Chairman*, Rev. Alexander McKenzie, D.D., Rev. William W. Newton, Rev. Cyrus Cunningham, Rev. Albert H. Currier, Rev. Franklin Johnson, D.D., Rev. J. C. Foster, D.D., Rev. Daniel Steele, D.D., Rev. Heman Lincoln, D.D., Rev. Will C. Wood, *Secretary*. The subcommittee were Rev. Dr. McKeown, Rev. A. H. Currier, Rev. Dr. Foster, Rev. Will C. Wood. They were intrusted with the entire arrangements for the convention, and the revision and publication of this volume.

They early put themselves into communication with the pastors of Springfield, who heartily entered into the plan, and appointed an efficient committee, — Rev. Messrs. W. T. Eustis, Washington Gladden, A. K. Potter, John C. Brooks, L. H. Cone, and Joseph Scott.

Besides the eminent writers secured, many distinguished persons were invited, who could not attend, among them Gen. Hawley, whose noble word is worth a hundred speeches: "BEFORE GOD, I AM AFRAID TO OPEN THE CENTENNIAL GATES ON THE SABBATH."

A "Statement of Principles," drawn up by Rev. W. W. Atterbury, Secretary New York Sabbath Committee, was sent out in letters-missive, as the basis of the convention.

STATEMENT OF PRINCIPLES.

The convention is called on the following basis, and will consider only questions directly relevant thereto. The statement appended will be read at the opening of the convention, and will be voted upon at the close of the second day's morning session : —

First. — We hold the Sabbath, or weekly rest-day, as founded by the Creator in the constitution of man, as embodied in the fourth commandment of the Decalogue, as recognized and confirmed by our Lord Jesus Christ, and as re-appearing with new spiritual significance in the Lord's Day of the Christian Church.

We aim to promote among Christians the sense of its divine authority, and the more conscientious observance of it against the influences which now prevail to secularize it.

Second. — While the State can not and should not enforce or inter-fere with the *religious* observance of the Sabbath, yet the weekly rest-day exists also as a *civil institution*, maintained by law and cus-tom from the beginning of our history, and vitally related to the well-being of individuals and of society, and to the stability of our free institutions.

We aim to promote among our fellow-citizens of all classes such a true understanding of its value to themselves, to their families, and to the State, as will lead them to resist whatever tends to deprive them of it, and to sustain the just laws which protect their right to it.

We, therefore, as representatives of the evangelical churches of Massachusetts, affirm the foregoing principles, and pledge ourselves more faithfully to teach and observe the religious Sabbath, and more watchfully and strenuously to maintain against all encroachments the civil Sabbath, as a principal cause of the intelligence, freedom, secur-ity, and happiness of our beloved Commonwealth.

The Springfield Convention comprised the evangelical churches west of Worcester County. Its sessions were Oct. 15 and 16, in State-street Baptist Church. "The Springfield Republican" of Oct. 16 and 17 gives ample reports. The convention was "notable in the number and reputation of the clergymen present." "The audience in the evening packed the church." "The strangers present were hospitably entertained by the State-street Baptist people." Rev. President J. H. Seelye, D.D., of Amherst College, made an extemporaneous opening address, and papers were read successively by Rev. Messrs. Atterbury, Thomas, Bacon, Gordon, Peck, Smyth, King, and Love. The Springfield committee considered their meeting a grand success.

The Eastern convention met at Boston the next week, Oct. 21 and 22. Eleven hundred letters were sent; but many churches were unrepresented. Hon. James White was president; the vice-presidents were Rev. Edwin B. Webb, D.D., Rev. W. W. Newton, Rev. William R. Clark, D.D., Rev. C. B. Crane, D.D., Rev. W. M. Baker, D.D., Deacon Ezra Farnsworth, Hon. E. S. Tobey, Rev. E. K. Alden, D.D., Rev. N. G. Clark, D.D., Rev. Joseph Cummings, D.D., Rev. Lewis B. Bates, Rev. Raymond H. Seeley, D.D., Rev. J. W. Wellman, D.D., Rev. S. E. Herrick, D.D., Deacon G. W. Chipman, Hon. J. Warren Merrill, Rev. W. S. Studley, D.D.; *Secretaries*, Rev. Will C. Wood, Rev. W. J. Batt, Rev. A. E. Manning, Rev. D. Henry Taylor; Treasurer, Rev. D. W. Waldron.

Mount-Vernon and Somerset Churches were generously opened to the conventions. The people of Boston furnished ample entertainment to delegates.

The opening prayer was by Rev. Dr. Blagden. The sessions occupied two days and evenings. The "Statement of Principles" was adopted unanimously, as it had been at 'Springfield, by rising vote.

On motion of Rev. Dr. McKeown, it was then resolved, —

" That a committee of thirteen be appointed as the State Standing Committee on Sabbath Observance, whose duty it shall be to procure the appointment of a similar committee in each town of the Commonwealth, which, together with the central committee, shall constitute a Sabbath League, to take such measures from time to time as shall seem to them necessary and feasible for the better maintenance of the Lord's Day."

That committee now stands thus: Hon. James White, *Chairman;* Rev. Dr. McKeown, Hon. E. H. Dunn, Russell Sturgis, Esq., M. Field Fowler, Esq., Rev. William Graham, D.D., Rev. O. P. Gifford, Rev. A. H. Plumb, Deacon O. M. Wentworth, Hon. Rufus S. Frost, John F. Colby, Esq., and Will C. Wood, *Secretary.*

As a basis of operation and co-operation, they awaited the discussion in January, 1880, before the "Evangelical Ministers' Association," on "What is just, wise, and humane to insist upon, at present, in the execution of our Sunday laws?" The points presented, by a committee of which Judge E. H. Bennett of Boston University was chairman, were unanimously indorsed by the Association, by a standing vote of some three hundred ministers present. March 1, 1880, they issued a "circular" containing in full the Massachusetts Sunday law, with

SIX POINTS: BASIS OF OPERATION AND CO-OPERATION.

I.   Under General Statutes, chap. 84, sects. 1 and 2, the absolute legal right of every employee of corporation or individual to the rest of the entire Lord's Day. We desire to call the attention of employees throughout the State to their legal right to a Sabbath free from call, order, or command of employer, corporate or individual, and free from liability to discharge, or diminution of wages for non-performance of Sunday work.

We call the attention of railroads, manufactories, and other corporations to the fact that in demanding Sunday labor they infringe law, oppress labor, and demand and expect what they have no legal right to require, — work when the law secures rest to men in their employ.

II.   Under chap. 84, sect. 2, the stopping of all Sunday passenger-trains, except from considerations of necessity and charity.

Under chap. 84, sect. 2, the stopping all excursion-trains whatever.

Under chap. 84, sect. 2, the stopping of all freight-trains whatever within the limits of the Commonwealth, in whatsoever place they may happen to be at sunrise of the Lord's Day.

Under chap. 84, sect. 1, the stopping of all work in railroad-shops.

Under chap. 84, sect. 1, the stopping of all railroad-work in making repairs, building bridges, &c., on Sunday.

III. Under chap. 84, sect. 1, the stopping of the Sunday issue of papers, magazines, &c.

Under chap. 84, sect. 1, the stopping of the sale by publishers, newsboys, store-keepers, or carriers, of papers, magazines, &c.

IV. Under chap. 84, sect. 1, the stopping of all sales of merchandise on the Lord's Day, including wares, fruits, confectionery, cigars, tobacco, and intoxicating liquors; excepting for necessity and charity, medicines, and, until nine o'clock A.M., milk, bread, and other cooked eatables.

V. Under chap. 84, sect. 4, the stopping of all Sunday-evening entertainments, except "concerts of sacred music."

VI. Under chap. 84, sect. 1, the stopping of all games of ball, or other sports, in streets of the town or fields of the country.

It is, perhaps, too early to express an opinion of the conventions, and this volume, their fruitage; but we think we are not wrong in gratefully recognizing their general superiority, like

"the tree of life,
High eminent, blooming ambrosial fruit of vegetable gold."

From the outset, our New England fathers regarded the Sabbath as a fountain of life. This century has witnessed great united efforts to keep that well unchoked and undefiled.

The first Sabbath Convention we are aware of was the Middlesex County Convention, Sept. 5, 1814, at Burlington, Mass., and Concord, Oct. 26. Thirteen towns were represented. Rev. Justin Edwards, D.D., of Andover, was prominent. An "Address" was published. In 1801 an "Address" had been published from Northampton by the Northern Association, of Hampshire County, to their churches.

In May, 1828, in New-York City, three hundred delegates met, representing fourteen States and Territories. Those present, these three days, declared they "never witnessed an occasion of such interest." The design was to form a general Sabbath Union ; and an auxiliary convention met in Boston, May 30.

A great Sabbath movement culminating about this time was the Sunday mail agitation. In 1810 a law passed requiring Sunday delivery, which was made more exacting in 1825. But in 1829, 467 petitions were presented to Congress, deprecating Sunday mails. Among the petitioners we find Josiah Quincy, Thomas L. Winthrop, Samuel T. Armstrong, Isaac Parker (Chief Justice), John C. Warren, M.D., Robert G. Shaw, Abbott Lawrence.

In May, 1830, Senator Frelinghuysen presented the subject to the United-States Senate in a form in which we trust it may yet be agitated successfully : —

"*Resolved*, That the Committee on Post-Offices and Post-Roads be instructed to report a bill, repealing so much of the act on the regulation of post-offices as requires the delivery of letters, packets, and papers on the Sabbath ; and, further, to prohibit the transportation of the mail on that day."

In Great Britain a nobler policy prevails. The "International Sabbath Association Reporter," 1880, of Philadelphia, states : —

"1. London has no Sunday delivery or collection. 2. Edinburgh, Glasgow, Belfast, and 114 other towns have no carrier delivery. 3. 3,000 rural postmen rest. 4. 1,781 post-offices are closed on the Lord's Day. And the work of closing out all postal work in Great Britain is steadily progressing." "I did not," adds Mr. Hickey, "watch the London Post-Office the whole of any one Sabbath ; but I saw no mail work whatever transacted, except the depositing of mail-matter by the people in the street boxes, and I was assured repeatedly that there was none. So much for personal knowledge. The wholly reliable authorities I give are as follows : One document of the London Society for Lord's Day Observance, called 'Sunday

Postal Work,' 1878, from which the above facts are given; 'The Postman's Friend,' which seems to be later, and gives 4,000 instead of 3,000 who rest, and Belfast and 120 towns instead of 114, with no Sabbath delivery, showing a fine *growth* in observance. '*Every district may for itself cause Sunday deliveries to cease;*' and 'every individual may decline to receive letters on Monday.' Local petition thus helps the work. The same authority says, 'In London no letters are delivered from the post-office on the Lord's Day, nor collected; and a few years since, when a proposal was made that there should be a delivery, it was met with such opposition from merchants, solicitors, general traders, and from every class in society, that it was abandoned.'"

In 1840 met a "Bethel and Sabbath Convention" in Cincinnati.

In 1842, July 20 and 21, a convention of great interest assembled at Rochester, N.Y. Three hundred delegates were present. Their pamphlet of ninety-four pages contains letters from Seward, Frelinghuysen, and Chancellor Walworth. Mr. Seward wrote, "I need not assure you that every day's observation and experience confirm the opinion that the ordinances which require the observance of one day in seven, and the Christian faith which hallows it are our chief security for civil and religious liberty, for temporal blessings and spiritual hopes."

The year 1844 was prolific of conventions, in many states. Dr. Edwards was a prime mover. He was Secretary American and Foreign Sabbath Union, established in 1843. Jan. 10 and 11, the Baltimore Sabbath Society had a meeting addressed by Hon. Willard Hall. They called a National Convention, which met at Baltimore, Nov. 27 and 28. John Quincy Adams presided; and he remarked, "So far as propagating opinions in favor of the sacred observance of the Sabbath, I feel it to be my duty to give all the faculties of my soul to that subject." Dr. Edwards was present: Chief Justice Hornblower, Walworth, Frelinghuysen, sent letters. The pamphlet of eighty-two pages contains an Address to Railroad Directors, — quoted from the New-York Sabbath Convention, — also to canal commissioners, and to the public.

The same year, earlier, May 30 and 31, met a State Convention at Harrisburg, Va., in the Legislative Chamber. Dr. Edwards was present.

Aug. 28 and 29 assembled the New-York State Sabbath Convention at Saratoga Springs. President Eliphalet Nott, D.D., was chairman ; Dr. Edwards was present.

In 1846, Feb. 10 and 11, a Sabbath Convention was held in Frankfort, Ky. Rev. Drs. Edwards, and Scudder of India, were there.

Two years later, in 1848, March 23 and 24, an Anti-Sabbath Convention met in Boston at the Melodeon. The call was from Garrison, the Jacksons, Parker, and others. Men of other opinions spoke. They opposed Sabbath laws, yet their address says, "A day of rest from bodily toil, both for man and beast, is *not only desirable, but indispensable.* They need more, and *must have more instead of less rest.*" A meeting of the Free Religious Association in 1877 produced four addresses, "How shall we keep Sunday?"

In 1857, commenced a really great organization, permanent in power and usefulness, the "New-York Sabbath Committee," which has restrained Sabbath desecration in New-York City, pursued investigations on both sides of the Atlantic, and published valuable documents. For twenty-two years they have continued their "unobtrusive but persevering labors."

A similar society, the "Maryland Sabbath Association," was organized in 1867. Its twelfth report shows a grand work in the face of opposition.

A younger organization (1878), the "International Sabbath Association" of Philadelphia, has the motto, "Organization, Co-operation, Devotion, and Continuance."

In 1863, Aug. 11, 12, and 13, a National Convention met at Saratoga Springs. Nearly all the loyal States were represented. Norman White, Esq., Hon. G. H. Stuart, and Hon. William E. Dodge made addresses. Valuable papers were presented: by Dr. Schaff, "The Anglo-American Sabbath;" by Willard Parker, M.D., "The Sabbath in its Physiological Relations to Man;" by Rev. H. B. Smith, D.D., "The Philosophy of the Sabbath;" and by Rev. President Mark Hopkins, D.D., "The Sabbath and Free Institutions."

Then follows our Massachusetts Convention, which, we are confident, has made a profound and powerful impression. We fondly believe that it stands massive and lofty as a Pharos. The crest of light on this edifice is this volume, which, we hope, is destined to take rank as a superlative contribution to Sabbath literature.

Two composite volumes extant have value. In 1862 the New-York Sabbath Committee published discourses, delivered on successive Sabbath evenings, by Rev. Drs. Rice, Hague, Ganse, Adams, and Vinton. In 1850, in Edinburgh, a composite volume was prepared by Wardlaw, James, Bickersteth, and others, presenting more than twenty Sabbath themes. Dr. Chalmers was to treat "The Sabbath and Workingmen," but his decease prevented. "The Influence of the Sabbath on the Piety of Individuals" was illustrated by the lives of Hale, Edwards, Howard, Wilberforce, and Chalmers.

Such were these conventions whose outcome is this volume. Thankful for guidance, mindful of conspicuous providences which remarkably aided, we would reverently inscribe, as Smeaton at the base of Eddystone, "Except the Lord build the house, they labor in vain that build it." May it shine, to the glory of God and his Sabbath, a luminous landmark in the century which, for weal or woe, stretches out before America!

INDEX.